VEIL

BOOKS BY JONATHAN JANZ

STANDALONE NOVELS

House of Skin

The Darkest Lullaby

Savage Species

Dust Devils

The Nightmare Girl

Wolf Land

The Siren and the Specter

The Dark Game

Marla

The Dismembered

Veil

THE CHILDREN OF THE DARK SERIES

Children of the Dark

Children of the Dark 2: The Night Flyers

THE RAVEN SERIES

The Raven

The Raven 2: Blood Country

THE SORROWS SERIES

The Sorrows

Castle of Sorrows

VEIL

JONATHAN JANZ

Published in 2025 by Blackstone Publishing
Cover and book design by Bookfly Design

Printed in the United States of America

First edition: 2025
ISBN 979-8-8747-1692-9
Fiction / Horror

Version 1

Blackstone Publishing
31 Mistletoe Rd.
Ashland, OR 97520

www.BlackstonePublishing.com

To Monica, Jack, Juliet, and Evana,
I love you four, and I'm so thankful you're in my life..

Break on through to the other side.

—The Doors, 1967

PART ONE
TORN

1

I hold the front door open, but my fifteen-year-old doesn't even glance at me as he brushes past. I tell myself tonight will be good for us. It has to be. Sam goes back to his mother's in a couple days, and our week so far has been about as fun as a catheter insertion.

At least the night sky is clear. It's nearing the end of May, and the precious few months of nonshitty Indiana weather are just beginning. I step out onto the porch behind him and draw in a luxuriant breath. "You believe school's over?"

Sam doesn't answer, just crosses the yard, and I have to hurry to catch him, my bum leg slowing me down. We move side by side up the road, but I might as well not be there.

"I bought ribs," I tell him. "We can grill out tomorrow when your friends are here."

"Can't go to the park after curfew though," he answers.

Dammit.

I want to tell him a thousand things, that even in normal times—which these are decidedly not—I can't just give him permission to break the law. The Hollow closes at sundown, so if I let him and his buddies venture there after dark and their parents catch wind, I'll be the negligent father who lets the kids run wild.

What's next, John? Gonna buy 'em beer?

If my son and his crew would simply sneak out, the way my friends and I did at that age, all would be well. But Sam is honest, and he has to ask permission. No virtue breeds as much trouble as honesty.

"Drew's dad lets us have fun," Sam says.

I consider a subject change—an upcoming movie or even a fucking knock-knock joke—but I know he won't be deterred. So I say, as nonconfrontationally as I can, "You'll still have a good time. There's the fire pit, the trampoline—"

"Too old for the trampoline."

"You could play basketball—"

"Until eleven."

I sigh. "Our neighbors have to work in the morning. You have any idea how loud a basketball is on concrete?"

Sam mutters something under his breath, and we're at that tipping point where I should let it go, but I hear myself demanding, "What did you say?"

"You're nicer to the neighbors than you are to me."

I clench my jaw. Sam's a sweet kid most of the time—when he gets his way—and my own dad and stepfather were such shitbags that I want to be better. So to most of Sam's requests, I say yes, but he requests things *all the time*, and it can't always be yes, and now I'm fuming because this isn't how it's supposed to go. We're supposed to enjoy a night walk to Insomnia Cookies; instead, we're fighting and I can't control my own anger, much less his.

"You're so nice to your students," he goes on. "Everyone thinks you're this great guy…"

I steel myself.

"…but you're not like that at home. Why do you always

have to be the responsible parent? Why can't you be fun for once? Mom is."

Outstanding, I think. *The Mom Card.*

I tell myself: *Turn down the temperature, don't engage*, but this is bullshit. For the billionth time, I wish my son could see who I really am, instead of some grumpy old bastard.

Or maybe you really are a grumpy old bastard?

"And now he gives me the silent treatment," Sam says. "Fantastic."

I draw in a shuddering breath. "I don't want to fight with you."

"Then let us have fun."

That word again: *fun*. According to Sam, I'm The Thief of Fun, The Stealer of Joy, The Mangler of Hopes and Dreams. Are other kids like this? I don't know. Sam's our first, so I've got nothing to judge by. All I know is that other dads act like they never have problems. They puff out their chests and proclaim, *"I just show my kids who's boss."*

"Look," I begin, "I know the past year has been tough on you."

"Don't," he says and looks away.

A hollow feeling gusts through me, and in its wake comes the guilt.

He has *been worse since you and Iris separated. You can't blame him for circumstances you created.*

"There've been three disappearances," I say, but Sam is ready for this.

"They weren't even kids, Dad."

"The seventeen-year-old was."

"And she probably just ran off! The other two were old, so don't pretend there's some child predator on the loose. People go missing all the time."

I want to argue that the other two missing people aren't old—they're twenty-eight and thirty-four for Christ's sake—but a worm of disquiet is insinuating its way into my guts. I don't like the energy tonight, and not just between me and Sam. It's like the shadows of the historical homes looming over us are denser than normal, fiendish creatures eager to slurp us up and digest our bones. But if I turn back now, Sam will use it against me. We round the corner, Sam enumerating all the reasons why the disappearances are nothing to fret about, that three in the same day are simply a coincidence.

"You need to follow your own advice," Sam tells me. "What do you always say to us in class?"

I shake my head and try to ignore the dull throb at the base of my skull.

"Be a scientist, Dad. Think about *why* we're always arguing. It's not complicated."

"You're right," I say. "It isn't. Whatever you get, you want more."

He makes a scoffing sound, and I recall how pleasant it was to have Sam as a student this year. No matter how poorly we were getting along outside school, as teacher and student, we were fine. Because school was uncomplicated. There, Sam trusted me, or pretended to. There, he believed I was competent.

As a dad, he considers me an abject failure.

"You might not believe this," I say, "but I care about you. I want you to be safe."

"This is the safest town in the world. Can't you just loosen up?"

Yes, I think. *I do need to loosen up. But not about this—there's no way I'm giving you permission to run around the woods at night after three people have disappeared—but in general, yes. I need to loosen up. Your mother tells me the same thing.*

Sam is stalking forward, moving too fast for me. He's ordinarily sensitive to my limp, but not tonight. I grit my teeth and push my bad leg harder, needles of pain piercing me from sole to knee.

"Did you see the Cubs score?" I venture. But I sound out of breath. Old.

He shakes his head at the obviousness of my gambit, and God, I hate this. Why does it always have to be so strained, so stilted? I glance at his profile and observe the strong jaw, the flawless nose, and simultaneously admire the handsome man he's becoming and lament the little boy who once loved to spend time with me.

We reach the edge of campus, Insomnia only two blocks away. I want to believe, once we get our cookies, that everything will be fine. But I know they won't make this better. My son is too hardheaded, and I guess I am, too.

I can't let this slide into stony silence without telling Sam how I feel. After staying at his mother's last week, he seemed reluctant to return to me, a reluctance that's been growing with insidious persistence since Iris and I separated.

You're losing him, a voice whispers.

There's an office building on the right, a parking lot beyond, Insomnia on the other side of that. Time's running out.

I stop. "Hey, Sam?"

He pauses at the far edge of the office building but doesn't turn. "What?"

I swallow. "Whatever I do . . . I don't do it to control you. I do it because I love you."

His shoulders sag, and he puts his hands on his hips. "I know you love me. I just wish you remembered what it was like to be young."

With that, he rounds the corner and enters the parking lot.

A thickness in my throat, I follow him, and when I limp around the corner, he's not there.

It's possible he's just run ahead or merely hiding, but I know in my gut that he's gone.

Just gone.

2

I scour the area for several minutes before hobbling to the police station. *He's fine*, I keep telling myself. *He's just wandering around campus*.

But I don't believe that. And with several disappearances already, I know I should report it as soon as possible.

I do. Then I use the lobby phone to call my wife. Soon after, Iris rushes into the station, her long brown hair slightly disheveled. "Emma's at the Morgans'," she says. "Tell me what happened. Tell me everything."

I recount the incident, noticing as I do the way her eyes narrow. My story doesn't add up, her expression declares. She eases down beside me, but an invisible wall crystallizes between us. In her mind, I've gone from an overcautious high school science teacher to the irresponsible failure who endangered her son in the middle of a citywide crisis. Of course, we don't know it's a crisis until Officer Harris, a kind-eyed, goateed man who looks perpetually embarrassed, tells us there's been another disappearance this evening.

"*Five* disappearances?" Iris asks.

A sigh from Harris, like this is his fault. "Actually, your boy makes six. Another happened last night but wasn't reported until today."

We stare at him. Words are impossible. Six disappearances in a single day in a city with a population under fifty thousand?

"Did your son say anything about running away?" he asks.

I open my mouth, but Iris answers, "He and my husband were arguing."

Thanks for that, I think.

Harris shifts his kind eyes to me. "What did he say before you lost him?"

"He said, 'I wish you remembered what it was like to be young.'"

"You'd put your foot down about something."

I tell him about Sam's request to play in the Hollow, striving to keep it clinical, but I can't help but feel a little vindication as I recount the argument. *See?* I want to shout. *I'm not a shitty father! I was trying to keep him safe!*

Harris nods. "I'm glad you—"

He breaks off as cell phones chirrup, his and Iris's. I hear others through the windows. Not mine, though, because I left it at home. I wanted to be in the moment with Sam.

"Amber Alert," Iris says.

"Shadeland," Harris confirms, referring to a sleepy little hamlet twenty minutes away. "Hang tight a minute. I've got to check on something."

When Harris is gone, I ask Iris, "How are you holding up?"

"Our son is missing," she answers. "How do you think I'm holding up?"

She's frayed, distraught. I get it. But I'm still taken aback at the unvarnished accusation in her voice. We stew in morose silence until Harris hurries through the door, his frown setting off new alarms.

"Twelve-year-old girl," Harris explains, settling down with a sheaf of papers. "Last seen playing in her yard." A deep sigh. "Nationwide, there've been an abnormal number of disappearances the past few days. The average is around two thousand three hundred people—"

"Per *day*?" Iris asks.

He nods. "—but most of those people are found. Yesterday alone there were more than six thousand, and the majority of those are still missing."

Iris and I exchange a glance.

"I don't have the first damn clue why," he says. "I don't think anybody does."

Into our bewildered silence, Harris continues, "Couple nights ago, there were missing persons reported in thirty states. Nothing peculiar there. Lots of them were runaways. But others were harder to explain. Couples on their way home from dinner. Downtown Louisville, a guy jogs ahead to start the car, his girlfriend's on her phone texting. She reaches the car, only he's not there. He's not anywhere."

We listen in appalled silence.

"Last night, nearly every state reported disappearances, but it wasn't till today that folks began to notice the similarities."

"Similarities?" I ask.

Harris shakes his head. "People are just . . . vanishing. All at night."

I look at Iris, and despite the distance between us, a distance that's broadened considerably in the last few minutes, I know we're thinking the same thing: *Emma*.

Iris heads for the door. I tell Harris to call us any time,

twenty-four seven. He says something meant to be reassuring, but I miss most of it because I'm hustling after my wife.

There's a real possibility she'll leave me at the station.

—

We pick up our daughter and head to my house. Emma scarcely speaks, but when I hug her, she clings to me, and that's something. My thirteen-year-old isn't as demonstrative as she used to be, but I guess few teenagers are. Still, holding my daughter fills a need in me I didn't realize I possess.

I climb the stairs to my room, the one Iris and I once shared. The one we'd still be sharing if she hadn't filed for a separation instead of going to counseling with me.

When I enter, Iris is sitting on the edge of the bed, some piece of clothing clutched in her fingers. Moving closer, I see it's one of Sam's baseball jerseys. It's scarlet and gray, our school colors. When Iris looks up at me, shiny eyed, I realize my vision is blurring. I've been holding it in. Playacting the strong man. The stalwart presence. But I'm neither of those things, not even a good father. If I were, we'd still have both our kids.

She tucks a loose strand of hair behind her ears and gazes up at me, and though I want so badly to embrace her, I hesitate. The moment passes, and she heads into the bathroom.

I sit down on the bed and check my phone, but there are no messages, no texts. Sam is gone, could very well stay gone.

I hear a pill bottle rattle, the Xanax Iris reserves for Really Bad Nights. I know she's about to head downstairs to the guest room, but I don't want her to. Having her here reminds me of the happy years we spent together, years I'd give anything to relive.

When she comes back in, she says, "Can I ask a really stupid question?"

I lean back on my elbows.

"Promise you won't get mad?" she asks.

I promise, but I'm suddenly guarded. I don't like that about myself, but it doesn't take much for those walls to go up.

Iris eases down beside me. "What if Sam just ran away?"

When Harris asked this question, I was amazed I hadn't considered the possibility. I'd also experienced a quickening of hope. If Sam *had* run away, this might all be over soon. He would come to his senses and return, and even though we had issues to work out, our son would be with us. We'd be together. And in the end, that was all that mattered.

But coming from Iris, the question stings.

You've alienated our son to such a degree that fleeing into the night is preferable to getting cookies with you.

"You promised you wouldn't get mad," she reminds me.

I take a steadying breath. "It's possible he ran off. He's got friends at Purdue."

And he does. Though just completing his freshman year in high school, Sam's a hell of a baseball player, and through camps, he's gotten to know kids at the neighboring university. A tantalizing ember of hope glows in my mind, and I want to protect it, want to believe Sam's at one of their dorms now, sprawled on a couch watching TV.

"All kids run away," Iris says. "I did. When I was seven, I told my parents I was leaving. I went out to my dad's workshop and hid for hours. I even packed a bag. I forgot food though, so when I got hungry, I came back."

She's told me the story before, but this time it provides comfort. *This is normal,* her tone implies. *This is part of growing up. Sam got mad; he's blowing off steam. Now agree with me before I lose my mind.*

"It's possible," I say.

She gives my hand a squeeze. "When he comes back, we'll be firm with him, that he can't ever do anything like this again. The timing was awful. The disappearances and all..."

And the hope in her face dims. We both know it's bullshit. If we truly believed Sam had spent the night with someone, we'd have called them by now. We feel the truth in our bones. Whatever happened is something else. Something worse. We finish getting ready for bed, and I can tell by her torpid movements that the Xanax is kicking in. Good. She deserves a respite.

She leaves for the guest room. I try to read a book but can't focus. Can't do anything but fight the urge to go outside and look for Sam. I power off my e-reader, roll onto my side, and face the spot Iris once occupied. It takes a few minutes for my eyes to adjust to the gloom. Iris is so light-sensitive that she taped over the tiny lights on the TV and the charging ports, and I've never bothered to remove the tape.

There is light slanting under the curtains, and it's by this somber glow that I peer at her vacant pillow. I imagine Iris's face. The tears on her cheeks. I did this to her. To our family. As they sometimes do in the small hours of the night, my thoughts spiral into those malign, skulking places in my head, to the stygian hell where I can no longer hide from unacknowledged truths.

You kept her at arm's length.

You refused to be vulnerable.

I close my eyes, accepting the torment.

You blamed her for holding back, but you've always *held back. She got tired of being open with you, so she followed your lead, and you both ended up embowered in your castles, alone and afraid. And now this earthquake comes, and both your castles fall.*

I'm weeping, but the voice won't stop.

But you, John... you created these ruins. They're yours. You own them just like you own what happened to Sam tonight.

I squeeze my eyes shut and hate myself until sleep takes me. And when it does, my dreams are nightmare reels where everyone I love is taken, where this house becomes my castle. My prison.

My ruin.

3

The next morning, it's everywhere. I want to shield Emma, but Iris keeps the television blasting out dire news. A CBS anchor calls them *vanishings*, while MSNBC refers to them as *disappearances*. Iris finally settles on CNN, whose chyron reads "Night-mare."

I sit beside Emma on the couch and put my arm around her. She leans into me, and a slow tear trickles down her cheek. Her dark brown hair is just like her mother's.

"Hey, honey?" I say to Iris, though it's difficult to make myself heard above the reporters and whooshing graphics. "Can we give the TV a rest?"

Iris doesn't answer. I notice the way her hands tremble and the dark circles under her eyes. She watches the screen so raptly I wonder if she heard me at all. When a story about a disappearance at a high school softball game in Oregon begins, I kiss Emma on the head and say, "Let's get some fresh air, huh? Take a walk together?"

She looks up at me. "Like you and Sam?"

My mouth goes dry. *Jesus.*

The TV continues to boom. "...and just prior to the fourth inning, Dale Jackson told his wife he needed to use the restroom. He was seen approaching these portable units." The reporter flourishes a hand at some port-a-pots. "And he hasn't been heard from since."

Emma shudders. Her knees are drawn up, her pink pajama shorts and *Purple Rain* T-shirt the same ensemble she wore to bed. Her eyes never leave the screen. I glance over at Iris, see the tears crawling down her cheeks, and I've never felt so helpless.

"The story of the Jacksons has been repeated all over the country, and though federal authorities have declined comment, it seems likely there's a connection."

"Where is Sam?" Emma asks. "He can't just be gone."

Our eyes remain riveted on the screen, and we're adrift in an overloud sea of portentous news, my son one of at least fifteen thousand inexplicable disappearances across the country.

Fifteen thousand.

A national night-mare.

The news worsens as the day drags on. More disappearances last night than initially believed. Rural areas slow to report.

I'm losing my mind. I can't endure the television, and I can't leave the house. Can't open the bookshop because I can't deal with people today. I call everyone who might have a clue where Sam is. His friends. Girls he likes. His Purdue acquaintances. And all the time, my phone feels like a live grenade in my hand. Any moment I might get the call: *Mr. Calhoun? I'm sorry to inform you we found your boy...*

Every molecule of the house bears remnants of Sam. Chipped drywall all over the basement. Water spots on the ceiling from when he overfilled the tub. Dings in the garage door from baseballs and basketballs. And every imperfection I encounter makes me miss him more. *Where are you, my beautiful, exasperating boy? The kitchen wasn't destroyed this morning from your midnight snack. The bathroom rug wasn't soaked from your shower. The house is too goddamn orderly.*

Iris has set up camp in the family room, the news a never-ending cavalcade of dire anecdotes, her ringtone blaring every half hour. Before today I liked Journey, but now the opening notes of "Don't Stop Believin'" jangle my nerves like a maniacal chorus of kazoos. I leave the room before I hear her inevitable declaration of "No news yet" or "They're pinging his phone but can't find it."

It's possible Sam's phone ran out of battery, but its last recorded position was the exact part of campus where he disappeared last night. What are the odds his phone would go dead at that exact moment? I imagine grim abduction scenarios, a masked man overpowering him and dragging him into the back of an SUV, but there are too many stories like ours for this to be plausible. People are simply vanishing, and my son is one of them.

I find Emma at the kitchen island and ease down beside her. "How are you holding up?"

She stares at her folded hands. "Scared."

"Me too." I force a smile. "But your brother's a resilient kid. We'll find him."

"I'm so sick of people."

"What do you mean?"

She scoots her phone away. "Everybody. They're saying the dumbest things."

"Like what?"

She swipes away a tear. "That Sam was taken by the

government. Or it's one of those alien abduction things where they beam you into their ship and… It's so stupid. Did you see *anything?*"

Had anyone else used that tone, I'd be pissed. I'm going on maybe forty minutes of sleep, no food, and the very real possibility I'll never see my son again. *Oh, and our last interaction was an argument. Can't forget that.* But with Emma, I don't get defensive. I tell her how it went down.

"And then?" Emma asks.

"He walked around the corner."

"How was he walking?"

No one has asked me this yet—not Iris, not the cops I spoke to last night.

"Not slowly," I say. "Slightly hurried. Like he wanted to get away from me."

"It's not your fault," she says, and the words are so unexpected that I have to turn away to hide my tears. She plucks a pair of napkins from the wooden holder and hands them to me. I clean myself up and murmur, "Thanks."

"So he walks away kinda quickly," she prompts. "Then what?"

"I followed him around the building."

"Did you hear anything?"

"There weren't any voices."

An impatient headshake. "I don't mean voices. I mean were there any *sounds?*"

Emma's tone compels me to go back, to relive the moment from which I've been trying to flee. I take a deep breath, exhale, and stare at the stainless-steel refrigerator, which is smudged with fingerprints—the small ones Emma's, the larger ones Sam's. I'm walking with my son, and he's losing patience. It's quiet since Purdue let out weeks ago. Just the faraway drone of car motors.

"Anything?" she prompts.

I'm no longer at the island with her. I'm striding after Sam. I'm in that three-second interval in which my life is about to change, and I'm accelerating slightly, limping past the squat brick office building, and I hear something.

"There was a sound," I tell her.

"Describe it."

I close my eyes. Sam is speaking his last words to me. Then...

"Just before he turned away, the sound kicked on. A low, insectile buzzing. A buzz-hum."

"What was it?"

I open my eyes and shrug. "A cooling unit? There's one behind Insomnia, I think."

She searches my face. "Do you think it's a clue?"

Despite the circumstances, I have to smile. For as long as I've known her, Emma has taken cruddy situations and found silver linings. I wish I could be like my daughter.

"You hungry?" I ask.

"I'll make myself eggs."

"I can do it," I say, starting to get up.

"Dad," she says and gives me a flat stare.

I sit. We both know her cooking is better than mine.

4

Antsy as hell, I cast about for a diversion and settle on the flowers. As I step onto the patio, I pass the windchimes my son bought Iris for Christmas, and a memory of that day knocks my breath out. Sam grew obsessed with raking people's yards last fall, and as Sam's obsessions usually do, this one consumed the entire family. Because he's only fifteen, we had to drive him to all the jobs and either wait around or drive back to pick him up when he was done. He scheduled four or five lawns per week, which kept us running until Thanksgiving and often found him raking past suppertime.

"What do you need all this money for?" I remember asking him.

He answered that he'd be driving soon and that was expensive, but it wasn't until Christmas Day that we understood the true reason he'd been working so hard.

He wanted to buy his family presents.

A person can be many people. That's Sam. He can be self-centered. But he can also be the sweetest, most generous soul alive, and that Christmas he gave Emma and Iris and me hundreds of dollars' worth of gifts. And as he watched us open them with a contented smile on his face, I saw the husband he one day might become. The father.

Wiping my eyes, I twist on the spigot and lever on the sprayer attachment. I start with the window boxes, then graduate to the flowerpots. I inhale the perfume of the lilac bush as I brush past it, but my nose is too clogged from crying to enjoy it much. I'm halfway through the marigolds when I hear a voice behind me say, "Sorry about your boy."

I turn and see who it is.

Dean Dawson. Of Dawson & Sons Law Firm. He lives three blocks over. Three states over would still be too close.

I don't speak as Dean sidles up to me, his voice almost sympathetic and all the more grotesque for the off-key warmth. "Is there any way I can help?"

"Just waiting to hear from the police."

"I'm sure there's nothing you could've done," Dean says.

I move to the next flowerpot, this one bursting with impatiens, their petals pink and vibrant, the leaves a deep, lustrous green. I douse them with the spray nozzle and wait for Dean to leave.

"They think it might be forty thousand," he says. "They're getting reports from Europe, China. Even some of the African countries where there's nothing but sand."

There's a marshy heat in my throat, like my Adam's apple is swelling.

Dean side-eyes me. "You haven't been watching the news?"

"I'm a little preoccupied."

He nods, but a disapproving scowl draws his brows together, the lines over the bridge of his nose deepening. What does my wife call them? Elevens.

"Of course," Dean says, "the solution's simple."

"How's that?"

A sarcastic grin. "Don't go out at night. All the disappearances happen after sundown. No matter what country it is, the victims get taken in the dark."

Victims. Goddammit...

I study his face, the black eyebrows, the salt-and-pepper hair. Dean was an athlete when he was younger, an *exceptional* athlete, he often boasts, and for a man in his late fifties, he's in respectable shape. I realize I've been spraying the same pot for half a minute; several pink petals have been torn from their stems and now float in a moat of muddy water.

I move to the next pot. "What else has the news been saying?"

Dean shrugs and visors his eyes. "Stuff like this brings out the crackpots. One guy, somewhere in Spain, he claims to have seen his daughter taken."

I look up. "Did he say by what?"

"Says she got dragged from their backyard. He ran after her, but before he could reach her, she was lifted off the ground and... pulled through, I guess."

"Pulled through *what*?"

"Into nothingness," Dean says. He chuckles and I consider spraying him in the face. "Like I said, it's nonsense. I just hope..." He shakes his head.

I lever off the sprayer. "Say it."

"I hope we don't go into lockdown. The stock market's already tanking. Last time we had a crisis, the country got itself trapped in a cycle of handouts and fearmongering."

Easy to talk like that when you inherit the family business, I'm on the verge of saying, but Iris is striding across the lawn, a hand clutching her peridot necklace, which was a Christmas gift from Sam. She doesn't acknowledge Dean's presence.

Dean stifles a yawn. "Maybe the folks at the university will figure something out. Lots of good scientific minds there."

Iris takes my arm. "John is a biology teacher. A damn good one."

Dean glances at me. "High school, right?"

"What's your point?" Iris demands.

Dean raises his palms. "I'm not insulting Johnny. But I'm a *Purdue* guy. You understand."

I resist an urge to break his nose.

Dean peers up at the facade of my old house. "Yeah, last night was the worst of it. Things'll get back to normal soon."

Iris glowers at him. "That's a really thoughtless thing to say. Our son is missing."

"Hey, I'm not downplaying your situation. I hope it all works out."

Iris threads her fingers through mine. "Come on. I made coffee."

As we move toward the house, I hear Dean call, "If there's anything I can do, say the word."

"How about you go fuck yourself?" Iris answers, and I feel closer to her than I have in ages.

—

But the nightmare doesn't desist. It intensifies.

The waiting. The silence.

It's a blessing Iris has muted the television, but it's still on, and when I pass through the room, I can't not look at it, can't unsee the headlines.

MULTIPLE DISAPPEARANCES IN SOUTHERN MAINE.

FAMILY MISSING IN VENEZUELA.

OFFICIALS BAFFLED.

NATIONAL GUARD MOBILIZED.

Mobilized *where*? I wonder. And for what? How do you neutralize a threat if you don't know what it is? How do you prevent harm when you have no idea where it will occur?

No word on Sam, no calls from anyone.

Except Iris's parents. They don't ask to talk to me, and it feels like an unmasking.

We were polite to you all these years, John, but you're not family. You're not blood. You lost our grandchild, and we won't participate in the charade any longer.

This could be my imagination, but I don't think so. Iris's half of the conversation is too ominous: "Yeah, Mom... that's what I asked him. He says he didn't see anything. Sam just disappeared... I know... I know..."

I head upstairs to check on Emma. She's in bed, her furry cow-spotted blanket tented over her, her laptop glowing from within. I ease down onto the bed. She hasn't eaten since breakfast, and she hasn't spoken to us in hours. I slide the blanket down, exposing half her face.

"What can I get you to eat?" I ask.

She's silent a moment. Then, "I miss Sam."

I take her hand. "I'm gonna go run an errand—"

Her eyes widen. "You can't go out there."

"It's not dark yet," I say, although I'm still dubious about the whole *they-only-come-out-at-night* thing. There *is* no "they." There's only a phenomenon that science will soon solve. Maybe there's a virus going around that causes erratic behavior. Maybe it's some online trend my son got mixed up in. People don't just disappear. If I'm not able to find Sam, the police sure as hell will.

There are surveillance cameras everywhere. Witnesses. Someone saw my boy. Someone knows where he went.

I assure Emma I'll be home before dusk, then head downstairs to tell my wife what I have planned. Iris looks at me, really looks at me, for the first time since this began, and in her eyes, I read relief: *You're finally doing something. Good.*

Whether she feels this way or not, I leave the house under a pall of self-loathing. *If you'd taken action earlier*, my conscience declares, *Sam would be home by now. You haven't even looked around.*

I'll look around, I think.

You haven't gone back to the police station.

I'll go back to the police station.

A better man would have fixed this by now. But fixing things isn't your specialty, is it?

I clench the wheel so tightly I hear the vinyl creak. Motoring toward Northwestern Avenue, all I remember are Iris's words about her dad, my father-in-law, a good man, but to hear Iris tell it, a cross between Captain America and Eli Whitney.

When I was little, I used to love watching my dad fix things.

Translation: You can't fix things.

I'm grinding my teeth so violently I nearly forget to turn onto Stadium Avenue. I veer across two lanes of traffic, but there aren't many cars out, people no doubt glued to their devices watching the apocalypse play out in real time.

"This is not the apocalypse," I mutter, then make the mistake of turning on the radio. I catch seven words—". . . and if these people are never found..."—before popping the dial hard enough to sting my palm. I roll into the station and discover cars packed into the lot and several messily slanted in the grass. I kill the engine, circle the building, and am met with a sight that takes my breath away. At least two dozen people are waiting outside, most staring at their phones, some speaking into them. A trio of men is having a heated discussion, a couple women similarly engaged. But most disconcerting of all are the silent ones, the folks just brooding on the steps or slumped against the redbrick facade, forearms on knees. No one takes notice of me until I reach for the door.

"They won't let you in," a man says.

He's leaning against the brick, his shaggy black hair and curly beard tinged with orange from the early evening sun. He's got tattoos on his forearms, one a werewolf, the other some words in what might be Korean. I test the door and discover that he's right.

"They locked us out," the man explains. "Said we were being belligerent. I'm Jae-Hyun. I go by Jae."

"John," I tell him. I look around. "Are all these..."

"People who've lost someone," Jae confirms. He's a burly guy in his late thirties, his white T-shirt an XXL at least, and there's a reddish stain on the belly I hope is from food.

"You have a wife?" he asks me.

"Wife and daughter." I swallow. "And a son."

He nods. "My girlfriend, she went outside. When I went to check on her, she was gone."

"I'm sorry," I tell him.

He doesn't acknowledge this, and he doesn't ask me my story. I'm grateful.

"Wanna hear something bad?" he asks. "See that lady over there?"

The woman is in her late twenties, her black hair full of multicolored clips. The arms poking out of her faded vermilion tank top are willowy, and she's slumped on the station steps, her head between her knees.

"She lost her daughter," Jae says. "They were at the park when it happened."

I look at him, not getting it.

His eyes widen. "It was *early evening*. Still light outside. Her girl was on this little bridge thingy. You know, connecting the parts of the playset?"

I nod.

"She only lost sight of her for a second, and then..."

And all at once, I remember why I haven't conducted a half-ass manhunt for my son. It's because I have a daughter at home. And a wife. And even if I can't fix things, I can be with them. I can keep them safe.

"Thanks," I say and hurry down the steps.

I'm jogging by the time I reach the parking lot.

5

Night falls.

I know I should tell Iris about the girl abducted at the park, but two things stop me. First, I don't want to scare her any more than she already is.

Hey, honey. You know the worldwide phenomenon that took our firstborn from us? Yeah, it's worse than we thought. Not even dusk is safe now. Yep, we're really screwed!

Second, and I know how horrible this sounds, I'm afraid, if I tell her about the girl at the park, she'll assume I'm justifying my failure.

See? I'm not the only negligent parent in the area. I might call this woman up and form a support group.

Iris makes tortellini that no one but me eats. This isn't abnormal. Emma usually forgoes her mother's cooking for a snack tray of yogurt, fruit, and turkey slices. We call it her toddler tray, but what the hell. She's eating, right?

After scarfing as much pasta as I can, I unload the dishwasher and reload it. Remarkable how the mundanities of life continue during a crisis. Still gotta eat, still gotta clean up. When

I'm done, I find Iris in the guest room and immediately know something's wrong. I mean, wrong beyond the fact that our son is missing and the world appears to be falling apart. She isn't on her phone, and she doesn't have her laptop. She's not even working a sudoku, her go-to strategy when she's trying to decompress. She's cross-legged on the bed, nibbling on a thumbnail.

"Need some alone time?" I ask, standing in the doorway.

A distracted shake of the head.

I sit beside her. "Did something happen?"

"I spoke to my parents."

Son of a bitch, I think. I know what she's going to say even before she says it.

"Dad thinks we should come stay with them," she declares.

I keep my tone level. "South Bend is two hours away."

"I'll leave in the morning with Emma. I'm sure they'd be okay with you coming, too."

I know my smile is pure acid, but I can't suppress it. "That's generous of them."

Iris gives me a flat look.

I raise a hand in truce. "Sorry. But Sam is *here*. Why would you go to a different part of the state?"

"Dad says it's safe there. Mom's got the garden . . ."

"We're not in survival mode, Iris. We're fine—"

"It happened *blocks* from here. Whatever's happening, our area is one of the most dangerous zones. Dad says we're in a pocket where things are worse."

"I don't give a shit what your dad says."

She shoves off the bed and flings open the door, which bangs against the brass stop. I follow her through the kitchen, a voice crying, *De-escalate!*

Emma isn't in the family room, thank God, because it's here Iris pauses to collect her laptop and the folders she uses for her realty work. *She's actually going to leave*, I think. It's like those movies when a space hatch opens and everything gets sucked into the void, the hero clinging for life while steel boxes and other detritus carom past. Only instead of space garbage, it's my life, my family.

I hang my head. "I'm sorry."

Iris hesitates. I realize that what I say in the next fifteen seconds will determine whether or not our family is separated. Separated more than we already are.

"Whatever we do," I tell her, "we should do as a family."

"We're not a family anymore, John."

I look away so she won't see the hurt on my face.

I feel her hand on my shoulder. "I'm sorry. You know I'll always care about you."

I find it impossible to answer.

"But both of us don't need to be here," she continues. "You stay in case Sam shows up. If there's no news, you can join us in a few days."

"Listen," I say, and I know *Listen* is a mistake because her hand falls from my shoulder. "This is the worst thing that's ever happened to us. What we need, what Emma needs, is normalcy—"

"*Normalcy?*" Iris answers, and I think, *Strike two*. "People are being dragged away!"

I pull back a little. "What do you mean 'dragged away'?"

She's looking at me in wonderment. "You haven't been online, have you?"

"There was a woman at the police station," I begin. "She and her kid were at the park—"

Iris is shaking her head.

"—and her kid was taken. Right there, in a public place, *before dark*."

She shakes her head. "No one's saying that on the news. It's all at night. The security footage of the clown—"

"The clown?" I ask and utter a breathless laugh. I can't help it.

Iris rips her phone from her pocket, jabs it, and holds it out for me to watch.

It's a video, no sound, of a city street, the camera mounted above the intersection. The clown's at the bottom right waiting for the okay to cross, some sort of bag slung over his shoulder, a pair of enormous shoes clutched at his side. He must be wearing sneakers, though it's too grainy for me to tell.

I start to shake my head, but Iris says, "Watch."

The clown stands there several moments, and when the crossing light changes, he begins to move. He takes two strides and falls flat on his face, his floppy shoes tumbling away. He's prone on the ground for a moment, his body stiff with surprise. Then he's yanked backward, out of view.

I stare at the vacant intersection, unable to process what I've seen. Iris slides the play bar back ten seconds, and when it happens again, I can distinguish several things clearly. The clown's sneakers are fully in the frame before he's hauled backward. Even though something drags him away, nothing seems to touch him. I reach out, move the cursor to the moment his body jerks, and this time I catch it: the way the fabric of his fluffy pantaloons sinks at the base of his calf. Like something seized him by the leg.

And for the first time, I truly consider the question:

What could do this? What could make itself invisible, seize a full-grown man, and drag him away?

I feel a pulse in my temple, then murmur, "Where is this?"

"Indianapolis," she answers, as if this proves her point. Indy is an hour south of us. Evidently South Bend clowns are at less risk than Indianapolis clowns.

She continues collecting her things. Maybe if I wait a couple hours and broach the subject again before bed, she'll be more amenable to staying. Maybe by tomorrow morning we'll have news of Sam. Maybe...

The family room seems to dissolve before me. We're on our night walk, and Sam is telling me he wishes I remembered what it was like to be young. He's rounding the corner, but instead of being in my body this time and seeing it through my eyes, I'm watching Sam on a grainy security camera, and he's halfway across the parking lot. He jerks, his body jarring from the force of whatever's seized him, and he's yanked hard, hurtling through the air, toward the shadowy space behind Insomnia Cookies. I hobble into the grainy footage, too slow and decrepit to save my son, and stare stupidly at the empty parking lot.

I don't realize I'm crying until Iris touches my face. She enfolds me in her arms, and we're sobbing together, and for the first time since our imperfect life went to hell, I feel connected to her. I can't let her leave, can't let her take our daughter. Iris and I grasp each other and sink to the floor. She's sobbing and so am I, the heat searing me from scalp to stomach. My tears sting, but I welcome the pain, welcome anything other than the hollowness. How can Sam be gone? How could I have failed this spectacularly?

Iris clings to me, and I need that on an elemental level. Need to pretend she needs me, too. We cry together on the floor, and I haven't felt this close to her in years.

"I'm sorry," I tell her. "I'm so sorry."

She rests her head in the crook of my neck. "You didn't do anything wrong. I'm sorry for acting so angry." Her voice dwindles to a thick whisper. "I just miss him."

I cry with her.

6

When I wake up, my wife and daughter are gone.

Heart slamming, I thunder down the stairs and tell myself there's no way Iris has taken off, not after last night. I'm about to check Emma's room when I discover the note on the island scrawled in my wife's loopy handwriting.

> Went to store. Be back soon.
>
> Love you,
>
> Iris

I exhale. *Thank God.* I put a hand on my chest and wait for the panic to subside. I'm making waffles for Emma when I remember to check my phone. There's a voicemail from only a couple of minutes ago. Muffled static, then the voice clarifies. My father-in-law's gruff baritone.

". . . and I know you're probably mad at her, but this is really the safest place. We'll keep her and Emma safe, and if you come to your senses, you're welcome to join us. We've got the generator, plenty of canned goods . . ."

I stare at the phone as my father-in-law's voice buzzes on.

"No," I breathe.

I stumble through the house to the mudroom and slide on the first shoes I encounter—my son's baseball cleats. I'm wearing sweatpants; my T-shirt is inside out, but I don't care. My wife and daughter are rolling away from me, and every second increases the distance, and when I scramble around the Highlander and manage to wrestle open the door, I catch sight of the sign mounted on the garage wall: THE BEST PLACE TO BE IS TOGETHER.

What a joke. We haven't been together in a year.

I utter a helpless whimper and think of Emma. I have to get her back.

I've got to catch Iris.

I emerge from the neighborhood into denser-than-normal traffic. I detour through residential streets to avoid Salisbury, the main drag in this part of town, but even the alternate route is bustling. I count four dads loading suitcases into the backs of vans or SUVs, a mom wrestling with a rooftop container so crammed with junk that it refuses to close. A blue Camaro damn near plows into me backing out of its driveway, so I gun the Highlander and veer into the oncoming lane. I catch sight of an older woman leading her Jack Russell terrier down the sidewalk and shaking her head at the chaos.

I call Iris, but it goes to voicemail. I call Emma—no answer. Has Iris confiscated her phone? I return to Salisbury and realize I haven't outwitted anyone; the gridlock here is worse, and it takes a full dozen cars before someone admits me into traffic. Two minutes later, I'm on Sagamore Parkway, which I'll take to the Hoosier Heartland, the highway my wife and daughter are on. They can't be far ahead. I'm crawling along Sagamore when I discover the pandemonium at Payless grocery store. Cars wrap the parking lot in a gleaming death grip, the heat of their engines and the overwarm morning sun shimmering the air. Patrons jog their carts through the lot. No one can get in or out. No sign of law enforcement, but there are plenty of raised voices and fulminating disputes over parking spots.

The gas station is no better, the digital price on the sign ticking six cents higher while I crawl past. Two motorists spray gasoline into faded red containers. A stocky man in a St. Louis Cardinals T-shirt rips a gas can from another man's hands, this guy scrawny and decked out in a navy-and-white Hawaiian shirt. As the scrawny man protests, the Cardinals fan chucks the gas container aside and wrenches the pump out of the scrawny man's hand.

Ten minutes later, I rumble onto the Hoosier Heartland Highway, where I start eating up some road. I swerve into the left lane—I have a feeling I'll be living in the passing lane for the foreseeable future—when a horn blast hurls ice water over my neck. I glance in the rearview and behold a white Dodge Ram so close he might as well be sitting in my backseat. I check the speedometer and see I'm doing seventy in a sixty, but traffic is so dense I'm disinclined to push it harder. Rear-ending someone won't improve the situation. Every half mile I encounter stranded cars with accordioned bumpers or smoke-belching hoods. I hold my breath each time, hoping it's not Iris and Emma. Sure, a fender bender would make things simpler—*Let's just head home in the Highlander and forget this ever happened*—but I sure as hell don't want them getting hurt.

The pickup driver lays on his horn again for a full five seconds, and I resist an urge to fly the middle finger. There's a cherry-red Charger to my right, and the driver, a white-haired man in Oakley shades, is accelerating as I accelerate, refusing to let me in. Behind me, the pickup blasts his horn, and I'm on the verge of losing it. I'm doing eighty-five, but I'm finally surging ahead of the Charger, and when I coast into the right lane, the white pickup zooms by, honking like someone's just gotten married.

I scan for Iris's white Sienna. I ease off the gas to peer around a Walmart semitruck, and in retribution the cherry-red Charger behind me gives me an aggravated blat. I try Iris's cell, but it goes to voicemail again. I consider calling her folks, but I'm too pissed at them. Whether they helped orchestrate this splintering of our family or merely sanctioned it, I want to scream in their faces that their daughter is forty-eight now, and her allegiance should be to her children and husband, not her parents.

You're estranged, a voice reminds me. *There's no allegiance to you anymore.*

Traffic ticks down another notch, and the dread begins to seep in, the devil-cruel voice declaring, *You've lost two more, Johnny. First your son, now Iris and Emma. Gone. All gone.*

I start to change lanes, but I glance over my shoulder in time to see a beige RV trundle out of my blind spot, its elderly driver fixing me with a stern look, his black shades so large they resemble VR glasses. My heart is thumping, and there's a patina of sweat on my chest. I tell myself to get it together.

I wait until the phalanx of vehicles caterpillars by, then swing into the gap and growl ahead of the Walmart truck. I remain in the left lane, hell-bent on eating up ground. I suppress a bright flare of anger at my wife, but I remind myself that she's going through hell, too. Son missing, world short-circuiting. The stress is beginning to overtake me, so I'm almost relieved when I see that traffic is stalled ahead.

I frown at a spot, maybe a hundred yards distant, where the highway trends left and enters a stretch of forest. Drawing closer, I see where the leaves admit the sunlight, dappling the bumper-to-bumper vehicles in an apricot glow. Deeper in, the trees have a massive spread—bur oaks, hackberries, and bitternuts—that steeps most of the highway in shadow. I creep closer, the hardly moving traffic snarls incongruous in this sleepy patch of countryside. I reach the fringe of forest, and traffic stops. The driver of the white pickup, the serial honker, climbs out and hitches up his belt, no doubt *To Get to the Bottom of This*. Others follow suit, including the RV octogenarian with the blocky VR glasses and a fiftyish woman with MYRA and LEE bedazzled with fuchsia stones on the butt cheeks of her jeans.

"See anything?" she calls to Honker, whose broad chest and ample belly tax a black Kawasaki T-shirt to the breaking point.

Honker hitches up his belt. "Has to be a crash. Most of these dickheads don't know how to drive."

The pair, as well as other motorists, are wandering forward, and I wonder, *What happens when traffic moves?*

To my right, the forest is deeply shaded, a pine grove so dense it seems impenetrable. To my left, the emerald-green canopy of leaves should be teeming with birds and woodland creatures, but at the moment it seems oddly motionless. I lean out my window, and it's then that I hear something I first assume is my overactive imagination. It's a deep buzzing hum, nearly subaudible, and I tell myself it's just the traffic, all these cars and vans and semis congregated together.

I reach for the handle, then sit there thunderstruck, my airway closing. Where the highway bends into the forest, there's a white Toyota Sienna.

Iris and Emma.

I swallow. Should I get out and go to them? If I do, traffic could move and leave me behind. Or is this my only chance? If I don't go, will I regret it forever?

I slam the door on this thought because it's alarmist, the same muddled logic that got us into this in the first place. Sam will be back soon. *All* the missing people will be back. There will be a logical explanation, a *scientific* explanation. Not aliens, not the rapture.

I'll walk up to Iris and smile at her through the window, and she'll smile back at me and know she made a mistake. I'll give Emma the biggest bear hug of her life and maybe even toss her up in the air the way I used to.

We'll be together.

With a sob of joy already trembling in my throat, I climb out of the Highlander. The idling engines render the air balmy, the humidity pushing it to maybe ninety degrees. My shoes clop as I make my way down the center line. I study the necklace of cars ahead, and my good spirits fade. As far as I can tell, Iris and Emma are still in the van, but below the growl of the engines, I hear it, the buzzing thrum I heard the night of my son's disappearance.

I walk faster.

I can't articulate the dread, can't do anything but notice the way people are climbing out of their cars. As I pass a pair of onlookers, a teenage boy and a sixtyish woman, I catch a snatch of conversation.

"...idea what the problem is?" the woman asks.

"My app says there's an accident a mile up the highway," the boy answers.

"Must be a bad one," she remarks, and I lose the rest because I'm limping faster. I catch sight of Myra Lee, who's chatting with a young mother, a toddler on her hip, the little boy red-eyed and cranky. I'm only ten vehicles behind the van now, and I know it'll be awkward, painful even, but it's going to work because it has to. We belong together. My family belongs together.

Something moves in the woods. Probably some guy taking a leak or maybe letting his kids scamper around the forest to keep them entertained. Eight cars from my wife and daughter, the buzzing thrum grows louder. I see the old man with the VR glasses gesticulating at someone in a Mini Cooper, hear their raised voices.

"It's none of your business what other people do," VR Glasses proclaims.

The man in the Mini Cooper's got a goatee, black hair shaved nearly bald on the sides, what's on top stylishly shaggy. He's twentysomething and garbed in a maroon-and-gold Cleveland Cavaliers jersey.

"I'm not telling you what to do," Cavs Fan says. "I'm trying to keep people safe."

"People can think for themselves," VR Glasses shoots back. The old man's gray eyebrows are so bushy they poke out over the top of his glasses.

The Cavs Fan's passenger leans across him. "Dude, haven't you been paying attention? It's happening during the day now."

"You need to get back to your vehicle," Cavs Fan insists, but I scarcely hear this or the old man's rebuttal. Because the words are echoing in my head: *It's happening during the day now.*

I lick my lips and hear a choking sob, and when I swivel my head, I spot a woman in her thirties crashing through the underbrush. She's weeping. Both Honker and Myra Lee take off at a jog toward her, and when she stumbles into Honker's arms, she gibbers, "It took her, it took her."

"Took who, dear?" Myra Lee asks.

"My daughter!" the woman wails. *"It took my Anneliese!"*

I think of Emma, and when I look up, I discover my wife

standing outside the van, gawping at the woman from the woods. The sight of Iris blots out everything. I start that way, moving in a foggy half run, and I'm four cars away when a blood-curdling shriek pierces the day. It comes from ahead, where the road bends in earnest, and when I zero in on the commotion, my mind can't make sense of it. There are two people—a woman in her late twenties and her prematurely balding husband—on their stomachs on the grass between the road and the woods, their hands grasping each other. But the husband is sliding backward toward the forest and dragging his wife with him.

"Holy shit!" someone yells.

"Did you see that?" another shouts.

A tall woman in a red sundress backpedals from the struggling couple, a hand clamped over her mouth. Just as she passes from my field of vision, I see it, the balding man getting dragged into the forest, though I can't tell what's dragging him. His wife gets towed along for several yards before losing hold. She pushes to her feet, takes a couple steps to pursue her husband, screams, and turns to flee, and that's when she's jerked backward into the trees, her arms and legs thrust out from the propulsion.

Everyone begins to scream.

I whirl, see my wife slamming the van door, and take off toward her, but she's shoving it into gear and cutting the wheel. She bumps the car in front of her, a Jeep Cherokee, and I hear yelling. Iris reverses, almost in position to split off from her lane, and as her van lurches forward, I reach them. I limp alongside, pounding on Iris's window, and she gapes at me like she doesn't know me. I hear Emma berate her, and Iris's trance seems to break. She rolls down the window and shouts, "Get in!"

I scrabble for the handle, and one moment the back door is opening and the next it's blasted away, a semi crashing into it and bulldozing it forward. I stumble back. The vehicles grind ahead, and then the van detaches from the semi, its tail end mashed but the vehicle still functional.

I hear a cry and watch a figure sliding toward the massed shadows, the woman in the red sundress, her hands outstretched in mute appeal. The next moment, she's swallowed up by the undergrowth. Gone.

Some survival mechanism kicks in. I sprint for the Highlander. I stumble, flirt with a fall, but catch myself and curse my gimpy leg. Cars and SUVs peel away from the gridlock and weave onto the grassy shoulders. But the shoulders are bottlenecking too, so more people veer off.

My leg throbbing, I dig for the Highlander. I'm acutely aware of my age, my scant lung capacity. All over the highway, doors are slamming. I catch sight of Myra Lee's bedazzled butt jiggling toward an enormous black SUV, and then a wail redirects my gaze toward the forest, where I spot a teenaged boy, his mouth hinged wide and his bony body scraping through the green-black screen of bushes.

"Oh my God," Myra Lee drawls. She rushes forward to help the boy, freezes, her eyes widening, and gets plowed by a pickup truck. She bounces into the brush, her body shattered.

Just when I think I'll get dragged away or run over, I reach the Highlander. I jerk it into gear and almost get T-boned by a Prius jostling its way down the rumble-stripped shoulder. I veer over as well and roll along behind the Prius, but I can't wait any longer and stomp on the gas to shoot by.

Ahead I see a white pickup truck—Honker?—cut through traffic, careen down the grassy embankment, then swerve uphill and clip another car. The pickup overturns, rolls, and the vehicles around it collide like billiard balls. Smoke billows, traffic utterly snarled. There's a narrow gap at the base of the hill between the overturned pickup and the woods, and I aim for the gap, jouncing down the decline and hoping to God the Highlander doesn't flip. A Honda Element has the same idea I do. It seesaws down the ridge, and I brake in time for it to slip past, straight toward the trees. The Element slams into an oak stump, the driver's head bashing the windshield and leaving a messy stamp of blood. As I surge past it, I see the spiderwebbed glass, the driver slouched in his seat, his forehead glistening and his mouth open in unconscious surprise.

The van, I tell myself. *You have to reach Iris and Emma.*

I'm nearly to the gap between the overturned pickup and the forest, and despite the chaos, I see Honker crawling out of his shattered window directly into my path. I contemplate chancing it, threading the needle between his broken body and the trees, but when it becomes obvious there is no gap, that the only way through is *over* him, I consider doing it anyway. He's obviously dying, and I don't have time to play Good Samaritan, but then my foot is easing off the accelerator, and I skid to a halt before the man, who's crawling on his elbows, his face and hands bloody and quivering.

Numbly, I get out. Honker's hands no longer resemble hands, and his face is scarcely recognizable through all the blood and glass. He actually grins at me. "I fucked up," he says. One of his incisors is embedded in his bottom lip.

I grasp him around the waist. Though he's a bulky guy, I wrestle him toward the Highlander, but he lets loose with a croupy cough, and a splat of blood stipples his shirt, and he goes limp in my arms.

Numb, I stride around to my door and see an SUV barreling toward my back end. I'm gonna get rammed, same as Iris did, so I thrust the Highlander into gear, gun it over the bloodstained grass, and somehow outrun the SUV. Then I'm jolting over uneven ground, baring my teeth and leaning toward the windshield. I'm doing a neck-jarring twenty-five when I spot the plume of black smoke around the curve. The woods are darker here, the sun only slipping through in apologetic blips, and if the scene behind me was mayhem, ahead is a fiery hellscape, cars blazing, semis overturned, voices shrieking in anguish. A woman is on her knees with her head thrown back, her broken-hearted wail somehow worse than all the rest. The path forward is completely blocked. The only way to go is backward, and soon that'll be cut off. Terror leaches the moisture from my mouth.

A capsized tractor trailer bars my way. I stop and spot something pale through the wavering black smoke. I climb out, already dreading what I'll find. I want the smudge of white to be the van, but I don't want it to be. *I can protect you,* I think. *I can keep you safe.*

I venture closer, shielding my face from the flames. Distantly, I hear someone moaning, maybe the semitruck driver, and then I'm through the smoke, and I spot Emma, who's standing beside the tree line, a slender rivulet of blood trickling from her hairline to her jaw.

Twenty feet away. Only twenty feet.

I start toward her, and she points an index finger into the woods. "They took Mom," she says.

No. I lurch toward Emma, expecting at any moment for her to get taken too. Then I have her in my arms. My baby girl.

I wheel about and scream Iris's name, but there's no sign of her. I hear the soul-crushing hum all around us, like a million cicadas, and Iris is nowhere. She's gone.

I take Emma by the hand, and with tears in my eyes, I lead her toward the Highlander.

7

Emma has the presence of mind to withhold her questions, to let me navigate this nightmare world of smoke and death. I can hardly see the road through my tears. We're motoring away from the wreckage when she says, "I didn't know we were leaving you. Mom told me we were just grabbing some clothes from her house."

I grasp her hand. That's all I'm capable of.

It takes ninety minutes to go fifteen miles, the horrific scene in the forest one of many. Near a minuscule town called Buck Creek, we find another pileup. There are no woods here, just open fields, but I don't trust the Highlander to churn us through the soft soil and decide to backtrack, try our luck on country roads. And though we encounter a few wrecks, we eventually reach West Lafayette.

We roll into our garage. When we amble into the house, Emma collapses onto the couch. I go around locking doors and checking windows before joining her, and when I do, she's got the TV on, and it's worse than I thought.

The chyron reads: THOUSANDS MORE TAKEN. I note

the alteration in wording—people are no longer merely missing, they're taken. I wet a washcloth and tend to the laceration at Emma's hairline. Not deep enough for stitches. I can't imagine going to a hospital now anyway. She massages her neck, and this brings to mind how the semi crashed into the van, how whiplashed she must be. She offers a brave smile. "It's fine, Dad. It only hurts a little."

I rest a hand on her forearm and gulp down tears.

On television, one expert posits the number of worldwide missing is over two hundred thousand. I wonder how one can be an expert on this sort of thing, but that's what each guest is introduced as: "Expert on Quantum Physics," "Founder of the Johns Hopkins Institute of Meteorology and Expert in Natural Phenomena," and finally "Brian Scheller, Pentagon Whistleblower." Scheller tells an NBC reporter that the phenomenon is "indisputably alien in nature, and the attacks will redouble until the military neutralizes the threat."

"How," the reporter demands, "will the military neutralize the threat?"

Scheller, a ruddy-skinned man with a round face, folds his hands. "That depends on the nature of the threat."

I mute the TV. Emma sits shell-shocked. "We're safe," I tell her. She shakes her head, and when her composure crumbles, I draw her into an embrace. She sobs against me.

After a while, she asks, "Have the police called?"

I realize I haven't checked my phone since the nightmare on the highway. I fish it out, see that no one has called. I think about calling Iris's parents but decide I can't have that conversation now, so I busy myself with lunch. Emma joins me, and soon we're slouched over the kitchen island. Emma crunches a Triscuit, but she's watching me closely. "*Are* we safe here?"

I know it's a pivotal moment, not because she needs

reassurance, but because our future interactions might hinge on my answer. If I lie now, I'll have to keep on lying.

I opt for the truth. "I don't know."

"Do we still have Grandpa's gun?"

I frown at her. Grandpa was actually her great-grandpa, the man who helped raise me. He passed away two years ago, and among his possessions he left me a Ruger pistol he purchased in 1954. I know the year because the bill of sale is still in the box, along with the polishing rag and bullets. Where I'm careless about many things, Grandpa was fastidious, his experiences in the Great Depression and the military conditioning him to take care of things and to never, ever waste.

I try a smile. "Why would we need a gun?"

She doesn't answer, but the moment the words leave my mouth, I remember Myra Lee and her bedazzled butt getting walloped by the pickup truck, the wholesale pandemonium that gripped the highway.

We migrate to the family room, where we watch news reports pouring in from all over. There are plenty of videos, but none of them disclose more than what we witnessed in the forest. The very absence of a detectable culprit is what renders the videos so chilling. On the highway, there'd been the encompassing trees, the dense brambles. You could tell yourself the victims were taken deeper into the woods, even if you knew that wasn't true. But in several of the videos, people disappear into thin air.

The one that chronicles this phenomenon most disturbingly, an eighteen-second clip that's been reposted over twenty million times, is of a family get-together in Alabama and a couple boys, brothers probably, the younger about five, the older seven. Adults slouched in lawn chairs guffaw and egg the younger boy on as he snatches a Nerf football from his brother's grasp and takes off running. There's a noodle sprinkler tossing water in all directions, and the older boy keeps slipping in the grass as he attempts to chase the younger one down. He's closing in when the little boy, still sprinting, glances over his shoulder and then... disappears. There are no buildings or trees in the background, just grass and a cornfield in the distance. One moment the five-year-old is running and laughing; the next the little boy is gone. Whoever records it has the presence of mind to keep filming, and as the adults spring to their feet, someone can be heard asking, "Can you hear that?"

It's this section of the video my daughter and I keep replaying on our phones. The noise is identical to what we heard on the highway, that deep, dreadful thrum that's half cicada, half cement mixer. The video ends with the surviving boy staring at the camera with naked fear.

Watching this, I wonder, *Where did it take the boy?*

And the most important question: *What is doing this?*

It's not until two that afternoon that I think of reporting what happened to Iris, but when I call the city police, then the county sheriff's office, I can't get through. I try 911, and when that goes unanswered, I realize how profoundly the world has changed—not just for our family but for everyone. It's midafternoon when the emergency broadcast system kicks on, the blue screen and discordant intro jangling my overtaxed nerves. In a voice that sounds like a robot filtered through a defective microphone, we're told, THIS IS A MESSAGE FROM THE EMERGENCY BROADCAST SYSTEM. EVERYONE SHOULD STAY IN THEIR HOMES. IF YOU ARE NOT INDOORS, YOU SHOULD SEEK SHELTER IMMEDIATELY.

Emma looks at me. "Well, no shit," she says.

—

I double-check the window locks and doors, then head to the garage to scrounge whatever I can to fortify the house. There isn't much. I've got a few stray boards but not enough to reinforce even a tenth of our windows. And if I can only cover a few of them, what's the point? I crawl under the house and rummage through the storage area, but it's as I suspected: Other than snow sleds and Christmas ornaments, there's nothing down here that will make us any safer. Dispirited, I head back inside. I draw the family room blinds, but in the front of the house there aren't blinds, just sheer curtains, and the dining room picture window that fronts the street doesn't even have curtains. We're woefully exposed.

I instruct Emma not to linger near windows, to pay attention so she'll notice if something is amiss. I don't need to remind her not to go outside. At seven that evening, I try the police again and get an automated message directing me to some website. I scribble down the URL, open my laptop, and type it in.

It's a form for reporting missing persons. Name, age, date of birth, physical description, social security number. It occurs to me I don't have the SS numbers for any of my loved ones, and it feels like an indictment. Iris would have those memorized.

I rummage through our personal documents and finally get Iris entered. Sam too. When I'm done, I make the mistake of opening social media, where the usual series of dumpster fires has become a conflagration:

"We gonna keep pretending the alien overlords haven't come for us?"

"This is why the 2nd Amendment matters, militias will keep us safer than the government will."

One post simply reads, "Repent."

It's the next one that puts me over the edge: "WAKE UP PEOPLE ITS A HOAX!!!!"

My feed is haunted by disappearance videos and photos of missing loved ones. I snap the laptop shut, grind my palms into my eyes, and consider the possibility I'm losing my mind. I'm sitting like that when my phone rings. My mother-in-law.

I answer it. "Yes?"

"Oh, thank God," Patricia breathes. "I was so worried you'd all been taken—"

"Iris was. I brought Emma home, but Iris is gone." Despite her shocked gasp, I can't help adding, "They were on their way to you."

Patricia's voice is frantic: "You don't know that. She's probably in a hotel somewhere—"

"Emma saw it."

Instant venom. "You held them up! They would have made it to—"

"*Bullshit*," I growl, and she falls silent. I'm squeezing the cell so hard, the screen might crack, but this is the first emotion I've experienced beyond sorrow and disbelief, and I'm going to ride it. "When people get married, they become a family. You two refused to cut the cord, and Iris is gone because of it."

Breathless sobs from the other end, and I don't feel a damn bit sorry. Iris never would have gone if her parents hadn't encouraged it.

"Put Max on," I demand.

A shuddering breath. "He's on the couch. He was hurt in the accident."

"Accident?"

"We were supposed to meet Iris halfway. But before we got there, the traffic was stalled. Someone broadsided us. We drove to the hospital but..." A gulp. "You should have seen it, John. Parking lot full, cars lined up on the service roads. The ambulances couldn't get out. Max told me to take him home, that we'd deal with it... but his leg... it's not good."

For a moment, I forget to despise her. "Did you see anything?"

"People were smashing into each other. No one cared how they were driving. I've never seen anything like it. A man on the road, he'd been run over. His legs were crushed..."

I massage my brow. "I don't mean the people, Patricia. Did you see anything else? Did you see anyone dragged away?"

Silence from the other end. Patricia isn't unintelligent, but unless information jives with her lifetime of Bible study, she can't process it.

Her voice is scarcely more than a whisper. "I thought I saw something. When we were trying to get out of that horrendous traffic, Max was pulling a U-turn. We heard this sound... like demons in some macabre chorus..."

I hold my breath.

"We were halfway through the U-turn... he had to do it slowly because there was a fence post and Max didn't want to ram it... but when we were starting to curve, the air in front of us, it... *wavered.*"

"What do you mean?"

"It shimmered, but not the way heat does. You know, over an asphalt road in summer? Max must've seen it too. He lost control of the wheel and crashed into the fence post. He backed up and got us moving, but it was only a minute or two later that the stupid kid in the pickup truck ran an intersection and sideswiped us. Fractured Max's leg. Our engine was smoking, but he was able to drive us home. His leg is so bad, John..."

I drum my fingers on the couch. I've got to get upstairs to make sure Emma's okay, and my reserve of sympathy for the people who betrayed me has just about run out. "Put Max on the phone."

"I don't think he's up to it."

"You said it was his leg."

Her voice sharpens. "Don't blame him. He won't be happy with how this turned out."

"That supposed to make things better?"

A weary exhalation. "Is Emma safe?"

"She's with me," I answer.

A long pause. In a small voice, she says, "Goodbye," and hangs up.

I sit glaring at the phone. The groan of a floorboard from overhead jars me back to reality. I head upstairs and find Emma's door open. Typically it's shut and locked, the faint notes of some eighties song drifting through. She's not sprawled on her bed but rather in the far corner of the room, a low-ceilinged area that feels like the cabin of a ship. She's lounging on the makeshift daybed Iris created for her, a cushion-and-pillow combination Emma never uses except to store piles of laundry. There's a book open on her lap, but I can't see what it is.

"I talked to your grandma and grandpa."

She raises her eyes. "Are they okay?"

"Max got banged up on the road, but they're fine."

I only feel a slight twinge of guilt at the rosy picture I've painted. Perhaps Emma senses my deceit, but she lets it go.

"What're you reading?"

"Photo album," she says, and I'm unsure whether I can handle this or not. But she's scooting over, and I join her. The album is open to a picture of me as a kindergartner. I'm wearing a Superman cape and pretending to zoom around the house.

Emma grins at me. "You've always loved Superman, huh?"

I nod, and Emma flips the page, and I'm confronted with a picture my wife took when our kids were little. Em and Sam are four and six, respectively. Emma was emotionally volatile when she was little, and while the majority of our pictures depict a cherub-faced sweetheart, there are several—all of them family favorites—of her pitching a fit. In this one, Sam is sitting next to me, his legs dangling from our playset. Emma's in my arms, but she's shoving against my chest, face pointed skyward, caterwauling and streaming tears. The image is so ridiculous I start laughing and so does Emma. She flips through more pictures, many of Sam and Iris, and when we come to another all-timer, this one on a beach on the Gulf of Mexico, we break into heaving gales of laughter. The picture shows a four-year-old Sam attempting to hold hands with a two-year-old Emma but instead having to support her as she sinks to her knees, bawling, her eyes squeezed shut in a primal toddler breakdown.

The pictures get us through the evening.

—

But the night is worse. The night is hell.

Emma and I absorb as much as we can from TV news, and when we can't take that anymore, we go online, side by side on our laptops in the family room. It's unbearable, conflicting numbers and hyperbole and the end of the world. Only a few facts are clear:

Everyone must stay indoors.

No one should travel unless absolutely necessary.

Highways are especially hazardous.

Em asks if we can watch *Rio*, an animated movie about birds mating to propagate an endangered species, but not only does the story remind me of my wife and son, I find myself imposing social commentary on the film that was never intended: *We're like those birds*, I decide. *Soon there'll be none of us left, and all because no one was careful. They never should have ventured to Rio. If they'd stayed at home, none of this would have happened.*

Neither of us laughs during the movie, and our eyes drift frequently to the windows. Though the blinds help the family room feel less like a fishbowl, the open floor plan still allows sight lines to the living room and dining room windows.

What's out there? I wonder. *What the hell is doing this?*

Every time Emma gets up, I hold my breath. I hear her puttering around in the kitchen—opening the fridge, closing drawers—but sound isn't enough. I need to *see* her. Not just because she's all I have left but because I love her, goddammit, and I want her to live forever. Iris and Sam aren't dead, but they're gone, and I have to keep this wonderful girl safe.

When she comes back, she's grinning.

"What?" I ask.

"You breathe loud," she explains. She sits beside me, careful not to spill her bowl of Cinnamon Toast Crunch. She always pours too much milk.

"I breathe loud?"

"I'm glad you do," she answers through a mouthful of cereal. "I always know you're there."

We finish the movie, start the sequel, but our hearts aren't in it. As we head upstairs, she asks, "Can I stay with you tonight?"

We chew melatonin gummies since we're the family insomniacs, and I take my antianxiety meds. I figure the circumstances warrant a double dose. When Em asks me if I have anything to help her doze off, I hand her a liquid capsule of an over-the-counter sleep aid. But Emma doesn't sleep. Neither of us does. It's one thirty in the morning when she murmurs, "Dad?"

I reach for her. "You okay?"

"Do you think it's aliens?"

"I don't know," I answer, and though I understand her need

for reassurance, it feels good to say those words. Too many people don't say them, speaking instead in tones of certitude—the pundits on the news channels, people on social media, and editorial writers for mainstream and crackpot conspiracy sites alike. They think what we want is definitiveness, they think it makes them authoritative. What it creates is a sea of clashing voices that inundates us and sucks us under.

"You think we'll see them again?" she asks.

"Yes," I answer.

Em faces me in the near darkness. "How long will our supplies last?"

It's the first I've thought of food as *supplies*, but like usual, Emma is a step ahead of me. I calculate what's in our refrigerator, our cabinets, our pantry.

"A few weeks? If we don't pig out every night while we watch TV."

Emma gives me a distraught look. "Will TV still work? Will the internet?"

I nod, thankful to be on scientific footing. "There are over a hundred and fifty thousand cell towers in the US alone. It would take a massive, coordinated onslaught to bring down all of them."

Emma nods.

"The satellites," I tell her, "will continue their orbits. Most will beam their signals for a decade or more. I don't think we have to worry about losing the internet."

"What if the power goes out?"

"I doubt it will. America still relies on fossil fuels. The power plants pretty much run themselves."

She closes her eyes.

I lie there and hold Emma's hand, the only noises outside a whippoorwill chant and the screech of a great horned owl. It's deep in the witching hour when she finally falls asleep. I drift away soon after but am awakened by an elbow in the ribs—Em performing a nighttime martial arts routine. I work the blanket under her. The barrier effectively mummifies her limbs, though she might still Houdini her way out of it. With my daughter cocooned, I open my Kindle and read. It's raining outside, but the ceaseless murmur and grumble of thunder do nothing to soothe me. It's after four when I nod off again, and neither of us awakes until ten the next morning.

8

The morning brings more dire news. The media has graduated from the shock and awe of vanishings to almost unwatchable dissections of the videos: "And you can see right here," the expert tells us, "where the woman's feet begin to disappear."

Oh hell, I think.

Yet Emma and I plant ourselves before the TV and torture ourselves with these postmortems.

"The astounding thing," the expert continues, "is how the body continues its disappearance at that *exact spot* on the campus green."

"So to you," the reporter says, "this video is not a hoax."

The expert, a guy in his sixties whose frizzy brown hair looks inexpertly dyed, says, "It's indisputably authentic."

"What about the others?" the reporter asks.

"The most astonishing aspect of this event," Frizzy answers, his tone far too enthusiastic, "is the sheer breadth of video evidence. *Hundreds* of recordings, with more coming in every hour, and while we haven't had time to study them all, the vast majority seem to be genuine."

I imagine my wife's fingers furrowing the dirt as she's dragged away, and I want to scream. *Where did you go, Iris? Just where in the hell did they take you?*

The doorbell rings, and I nearly leap out of my skin. Emma and I stare at each other; then, we break for the door. I know it's not Sam, not Iris, but the doorbell hasn't chimed in days, and the familiar sound sends vague rockets of hope spiraling up inside me. I fumble with the lock, wrest the door open, and my spirits plummet.

Dean Dawson.

There's a pudgy man with him, Chris Burkhardt. The Burkhardts live a couple blocks over in a renovated Tudor, no doubt paid for with Chris's family money. I have no idea what he does for a living. Most of the time he seems to be returning from the Purdue golf course. Even now he looks dressed for it—a red Top Flite ball cap, baby-blue polo, and beige shorts that showcase milk-white shins.

I open the glass storm door just a crack. "Yes?"

Dean smiles nervously. "You mind letting us in, Johnny? It's not exactly a picnic being out here."

I suppose he has a point. Estimates now suggest three hundred thousand taken worldwide.

I let them in. In the foyer, Dean's expression morphs into what's probably meant to be sympathy, yet his grimace suggests intense physical pain, as if he's passing a gallstone.

"We were sorry to hear about your wife," Dean says. "What happened?"

I'm not going to relive yesterday with anyone, least of all Dean or Chris, who's peering over my shoulder like he's eager for a tour of my house or maybe a crack at the refrigerator.

"What can I do for you?" I ask.

Dean clears his throat. He's clutching a clipboard with a

ballpoint pen attached by a string. He hands it to me. "Some of us in the neighborhood are attempting to get organized. It won't take but a minute."

Something about that word, *organized*, sets off an alarm in my brain. When I look at the spreadsheet, I feel a chill.

"Why do you need to know how much food we have?"

"We're on lockdown, Johnny. We hope it doesn't last long, but if it does, we need to be prepared."

I scan the sheet. "Weapons? Special skills? Is this for real?"

He gives me a patient smile. "You might not experience much tucked away in your classroom, but I've seen some things. I know how malicious people can be."

"You're an estate lawyer, Dean. Not a combat veteran."

He glowers at me. "Are you going to fill that out or not?"

"I'm not."

He snatches back the clipboard. "You know, you're the first person not to comply."

The word *comply* triggers more mental alarms.

Chris takes a step forward. "We know you've been through a shock, John. It's got to be hard to lose your wife and son."

I fight an urge to punch him in the teeth. Then a thought occurs to me. "How did you know about Iris?"

"The database," Dean answers. "All the missing are listed there."

He turns to go, but Chris lingers a moment. He lowers his voice. "Dean's right. We really do need to get organized. We stick together, we'll make it through this stronger than before." He gives my shoulder a chummy squeeze and follows Dean out.

I stare after them.

"I'm glad you didn't do it," Emma says from behind me.

"Yeah?"

"It's a power grab. Someone like Dean, it's his fantasy. He's been hoping for this his whole life."

"Maybe you're right."

"I am," she says. "Lock the door. I'm gonna make us nachos."

—

Several days pass in an agony of waiting. It becomes apparent that the second wave of disappearances—the one that claimed my wife—has ended. As near as anyone can tell, they began, worldwide, at 9:30 a.m. Eastern Standard Time and ended three hours later. That would mean Iris was taken near the beginning of the three-hour window, which tells me nothing helpful. In fact, Nothing Helpful might as well be our slogan. When we look online, we find Nothing Helpful. When we attempt to contact the authorities, we can't get through. I contemplate driving to the bookshop to make sure it hasn't been looted, but as Emma points out, that would be a senseless risk. A truth begins to sink in, one I need to remember. For all the time I spend brooding over my missing son and wife, I'm all Emma has. She's lost her mother and her brother, and if something happens to me, she'll be alone. It's this thought that galvanizes me to climb the pull-down ladder in the garage, venture to the far corner of the attic, and unearth my grandfather's Ruger from its hiding place.

Back when we found the Ruger among Grandpa's effects, my first thought was to sell it. The ones listed on eBay ran for a couple hundred bucks, and I figured, why not make some money? Then I spoke to my cop friend Troy, and he told me the kind of private sale I was contemplating was precisely how problems could start. Who'd be purchasing the gun? Could I be sure it was aboveboard and legal? On Troy's advice, we agreed to take the gun to the police station and let them deal with it. But I never got around to it. I kept telling myself I'd dispose of the damn thing but never did; instead, I kept it hidden in a corner of the attic where our kids never ventured. I stored the ammunition in a separate hiding place, but still the gun would occur to me in the middle of the night. Images of Sam and his friends finding it…

When I reenter the family room, Emma looks up from her phone and sees the Ruger in my hand. "Is that Grandpa's?"

"Yeah."

"How does it work?"

I shrug.

She cocks her head. "YouTube?"

I nod. "YouTube."

We watch a few videos about Rugers that look like ours. I wonder what will happen when the internet ceases working or the power grid fails, and it occurs to me we should watch more videos about survival. So we do. By the end of the day, Emma and I aren't expert preppers, but we're not as clueless as we were before, and I consider that a win.

We settle into a routine. Go to bed late since we're both night owls, wake up around nine. I no longer shave. I do shower, brush my teeth, and eat breakfast. We've run out of waffles, but we still have frozen pancakes. After that, we spend some time alone. We come together for lunch and catch up on the news. By midafternoon, we're both in need of something lighthearted, so we revisit old sitcoms. After that, we work out, me with weights, Emma with yoga videos. I lift for nearly an hour and hop on the treadmill, where I hobble through my requisite mile. The running leaves me drained, and my shirt sticks to my chest, but the lifting feels good. I'm benching three hundred pounds, and for a man on the wrong side of fifty, I judge this respectable. We wolf down supper and start a horror movie around eight o'clock. The June weather is beguiling, and we both long to step outside. But common sense and the government mandate make leaving the house both perilous and illegal. The only vehicles we see are police cars, delivery trucks, and the occasional rebellious citizen.

At first, Emma follows my directions and keeps to the centers of rooms. But increasingly, she wanders closer to the windows and starts peeling back the blinds to peer out. I realize this might be good for her. The kid has to be going stir-crazy, and if she can't venture outdoors, seeing the trees and blue sky might improve her mental health.

We're a few weeks into lockdown when a woman stops at our house in a silver Subaru Outback with CITY OF WEST LAFAYETTE stenciled on the door. Emma's upstairs at the moment, so I watch through the window as the woman parks in our driveway. A moment later, my cell rings.

"Is this you, Miss City Worker?" I ask.

Her voice is impassive. "John Calhoun?"

I sober fast, realizing this might have something to do with my missing family members. "Speaking."

"I need to ask you a couple questions," she says in a bored voice. "Do you have any pressing medical concerns or important prescriptions that need filled?"

I have enough antianxiety pills to last the summer. Our only other medications belong to Sam and Iris. I realize Emma is the only unmedicated member of our family.

"Mr. Calhoun?"

"We're okay," I tell her.

I watch her type on an iPad.

"I also need to know how much food you have."

This sounds too much like Dean Dawson. "Why do you need to know that?"

A sigh. "We're coordinating with the local grocery stores. Your date will be based on need. It's just you and your daughter, correct?"

I consider this a cold thing to say, but I tell her yes, it's just me and Emma at the moment.

"Do you have enough to eat?"

I tell her we're getting low.

"How many days can you go without a trip to the grocery store, Mr. Calhoun?"

Now would be a good time to lie. Most people would. Even if their coffers were stocked, many would claim to be out of everything. But I reflect on all the elderly people, families who really need food, who don't have a dozen cans of soup and half as many boxes of Rice-A-Roni in the pantry.

"We're fine for another week," I say.

"Okay. Today is the twenty-third. This card is for the thirtieth." She leans over and drops it out the passenger window onto my driveway. "Present it at the Aldi on Sagamore Parkway between three and five o'clock that afternoon."

She ends the call. She's backing out of the drive when I redial her number. She frowns as she answers, "Yes?"

"I forgot to thank you."

She exhales, and I realize what I've mistaken for callousness is actually terror. "You're welcome."

I'm not sure why I keep talking, but I ask, "Is the job scary?"

"Sure it is. But the government considers me an essential worker."

"Thanks for helping us. Please stay safe."

A small smile. "Take care, Mr. Calhoun." With that, she shifts the Outback into gear and rolls onto the road.

I cross to the storm door and stand looking through the glass for a minute or so. Then, taking care not to make much racket, I go through, ease the door shut behind me, and trot down the sidewalk toward the driveway. A squirrel chatters at me from our oak tree, but I'm too nervous to spare it a glance. As I near the place where the Outback was parked, I become aware of birdsong. There's a sweet gum tree that spreads over our driveway, and as I pluck the appointment card from the concrete, I hear an amiable cry from overhead. I straighten and peer into the boughs and make out a pair of hermit thrushes. I have no idea whether they're together or not, but they seem to be conversing, or flirting, one trilling out its flutelike song, the other whistling its answers coquettishly.

Somehow, the walk back to my front door isn't as nerve-racking.

I go upstairs to tell Emma about the city woman, but I hear her giggling through the door, probably FaceTiming with a friend or a boy. Either way, it's a good thing. I head to the living room couch, open my laptop, and watch vanishing videos.

—

Two hours later, I snap the laptop shut and skulk into the kitchen for a snack. I'm there when I hear the rumble of a motor. I enter the dining room and peer into the overcast day. The motor's growl magnifies until it rolls down the hill, a sea-green beater almost as old as I am. When the car nears my house, it slows to a crawl, and I distinguish three people inside. I can't make out the driver, but the guy in the backseat wears a baseball cap. The dude riding shotgun looks familiar, and it isn't until the beater passes that I make the connection.

Jae-Hyun. The burly guy whose girlfriend was abducted.

I watch after them until the beater disappears, then head upstairs, where I fall down a rabbit hole of abduction videos.

Before I realize how much time has passed, darkness has fallen. After a moment's debate, I crack open the window to admit the night air. I wonder how many people are disobeying the lock-down order, how many are straying onto their lawns tonight and gazing up at the star-shot skies.

I think of Sam and how we used to take night walks to the graveyard nearby. Back then, he was into *The Lord of the Rings*, so I'd fashion a Frodo cape for him, equip him with a plastic sword, and we'd rush down the cemetery paths pretending we were being pursued by Ringwraiths. I'd play the other members of the Fellowship, affecting godawful accents for each. I made him the hero of our adventures, vanquishing our foes with Sting. Our night walks never ended with arguments. Just a closeness more powerful than any magic.

I can't lose Emma. I'll do anything to keep her safe. Anything. My fingers are on the windowsill when a distant crack rings out. A gunshot.

My hands tremble as I close the window. Maybe someone shot an intruder. Or maybe the intruder was the one that fired. The thought compels me downstairs to check the doors and windows. I consider the Ruger, stored in a kitchen cabinet high enough that even I, with my six-four frame, have to stand on tiptoes to reach.

I debate, then fetch the gun and carry it upstairs.

PART TWO
TETHERED

9

Tethering they call it. A rope will work but they recommend a heavy-duty extension cord. The cord they use on TV, the expert demonstrating for the grinning news anchor, is bright orange like the ones I have in the garage. They say to trim the cord to thirty or forty feet in length, double-knot the ends around your waist and the waist of your loved one, and practice moving through the house together. This, the expert explains, will permit pairs of people to venture out safely for supplies.

"And what happens if your loved one is seized?" the anchor asks.

"It becomes a tug-of-war."

"What if you lose?"

The expert chuckles grimly. "Then at least you'll disappear together."

"Dick," I mutter.

Emma looks at me. "Wanna practice?"

I fetch the extension cord from the garage, a hundred-footer. I measure it out and use my snips to make the cut. Even a pedestrian action like this hurts my heart because my son is mechanically inclined, and he used these snips way more than I did. Before I get gloomy, I rejoin my daughter in the family room, and we set about tying the knots. I'm no Eagle Scout, so it takes a lot of fumbling and laughing. I take the sheared end of the cord because it's scratchy. Emma's end contains the socket, which makes for a better knot. After I've cinched her end without corseting her waist too tightly, I begin to backpedal. There's a clear shot from the family room in the rear of the house to the living room in the front. Emma's in the family room, and I'm in the living room, and when I turn and look at her and give the taut cord a shake, we smile at each other.

I feel my smile fade.

"I think we're ready for Aldi," she says.

Are we? I refrain from asking.

Two days from now, we'll be leaving the house for the first time since that hideous morning on the highway. I'm a paranoid father at the best of times, so striding into the parking lot with the only person I have left, my too-good-for-this-world girl, feels reckless and stupid. But our food won't last forever.

I'm untying us when my phone rings. When I answer, I hear a shuddering exhalation, and my first thought is *Iris*. Then the voice speaks, and I realize it's Iris's mother.

"John?" she asks.

"Hey, Patricia," I answer. "How are you two getting along?"

A long silence and I know it's bad. The only question is how bad.

"It's Max's leg. A neighbor set it for us. But yesterday Max caught a fever. And last night..."

I notice Emma's frightened stare and decide I should've taken the call in another room. Too late now.

"Where's Max now?"

"On the couch."

"Can you put him on?"

"I..." She falters. "I'm not sure he'll want to..."

...talk to the man whose life he destroyed? I almost finish.

But his voice comes on. Still sturdy, still deep. "Hey, John."

I look at Emma and remember this is her grandpa. "What are your symptoms, Max?"

"Why, you gonna look them up and play Dr. Google?"

Maybe I will, I think. *Asshole.*

"How high is your fever?"

"One-oh-four."

Shit. "Any other symptoms?"

"It hurts like hell. Every time I move, it feels like someone's taking a sledgehammer to my leg."

Emma leans closer. "Ask him if there's swelling."

I ask him.

"My knee looks like someone pumped it full of pus," he answers. "My thigh's purple and yellow, but that might just be the bruising."

"Max, you need to get to a hospital."

"You think it's that bad?"

Emma nods vigorously, and I say, "I do. I think it's infected."

He blows out a weary breath. "I wondered about that. Patricia told me we needed to go this morning, but I said let's wait and see. I'm more concerned about her insulin. We're running out."

"They'll have that at the hospital too. You should go as soon as we get off the phone."

"Okay," he says, his voice uncharacteristically subdued. "Heard anything about Iris or Sam?"

"Nothing yet."

I wait for the apology I know won't come, and a moment later, my mother-in-law is back on the line. "Thank you, John. Please give our love to Emma."

We hang up.

"Will Grandpa be okay?" Emma asks.

"I hope so."

"Grandma's a terrible driver."

I smile. When Max and Patricia immigrated to America, one of Patricia's brothers taught her how to drive using both feet. Whether this was done as a prank, I'll never know. But the one time I rode in a car with her was like a catastrophically turbulent air flight.

"Can humans be invisible?" Emma asks.

I glance at her. "No."

"Why not?"

"We see things when light bounces off them and reaches our eyes. The material we're comprised of interacts with light, and light is everywhere."

She frowns. "If we can't become invisible… how can those things do it?"

Those things. I realize this is the first time we've addressed this specific topic.

"Their technology must be more advanced than ours."

"But how would that work?"

I consider. I've been mulling this over a good deal and realize I'm excited on some level to articulate it. "There are several possibilities. They might have engineered a cloaking device."

"An invisibility cape?"

"Sure. Only less clunky. For them to perform complex operations like kidnapping people, they must have full range of motion, flexibility…"

"But you don't think that's it, do you?"

I regard her a moment longer. Then I push to my feet. "Come on."

We head to the basement, where I find the books I need. The first is on marine life. We sit cross-legged on the floor, and after riffling the pages, I come to the picture I'm looking for.

Emma's eyes widen. "What's that?"

"A butterfly fish. Sometimes called a sea angel. It's achieved almost perfect invisibility."

We study the picture, deep blue ocean showing through the butterfly fish's body, its only conspicuous feature a cylinder of bioluminescent organs.

"Is it a defense mechanism?" she asks.

"Partially. It also helps them hunt."

Emma shivers, and I regret my wording. I flip to the next page. "Here's another."

"'Glasswing butterfly,'" Emma reads. She studies the delicate-looking insect, whose wings are nearly invisible. Only a burnt-orange framework is discernible around the transparent sections. "It's pretty, but you can see a lot of it," Emma concludes. "So... do you have a theory about the creatures?"

"I have a few. I'm not ruling out a cloaking apparatus, but there are several problems with that. While beings capable of interdimensional travel might possess the technology to construct such..."

"Suits?"

I nod. "They'd have to manufacture so many of them. It's not impossible, but it doesn't seem like the most efficient method."

"So...?"

I nod at the book. "If animals have achieved near-perfect invisibility, who's to say life-forms on other planets haven't taken it a step further?"

"Spill it, Dad."

"Okay, if you boil it all down, there are two possibilities. One, they've evolved in such a way that light interacts differently with their bodies. Or two, they're comprised of substances invisible to the human eye. That are part of the invisible spectrum."

Emma cocks an eyebrow. "Invisible spectrum?"

"Infrared or ultraviolet light," I explain. "We see wavelengths. The light we see is part of the visible spectrum. But some wavelengths are too short—ultraviolet—or too long—infrared—for us to see. Human eyes can only detect what's between those extremes."

"The creatures are made of invisible stuff?"

"They could be." I scoot around to lie on my stomach in front of the book, and Emma does the same.

She tilts her head at me. "You look different with a beard."

"Cool different?" I ask.

"I haven't decided."

Smiling, I flip to another picture, this one of a roach-shaped creature swimming in a pitch-black sea.

"What's that?" Emma asks.

"Cystisoma. It's a type of amphipod." At her look, I explain, "Amphipods are marine crustaceans." I tap the picture. "Cystisomas are extraordinary creatures. Their shells are coated with microscopic nubs that cancel out nearly all light reflection."

Emma nods. "They change the way that light interacts with them."

I give her forearm a squeeze. "Exactly."

But as she peers at the picture, her smile fades.

"What?" I ask.

"If these things have shells. I mean, if they're like cystisomas, does that mean we'll never be able to see them? They can just keep doing this until there's no one left?"

I bite my lip. "Why don't we grab some food?" I get up and

proffer my hand. As we head up the stairs, I notice she's tucked the book under her arm.

—

Middle of the night, can't sleep. Story of my life. But instead of worrying about the mortgage or the kids growing older, one of my kids is actually gone. My wife too. Missing. Abducted.

I sit up and feel lost in the darkness, and before I know it, I'm out of bed and to the hallway, down the stairs to Sam's room, where I hit the light switch.

The room is empty. Of course.

The overhead light is a ruthless taunt, like I'm onstage being handed the Shittiest Father Award. I look at Sam's bed and can almost imagine the rumpled covers and twisted pillows are my son, my firstborn child.

It's pitiful, but I whisper, "Where are you?"

When the room remains silent, I repeat the words but am met with nothing but the suboctave hum of the vent. It's chilly down here on the main floor, and the cold air elicits a smile. Before Iris moved out, she and Sam always tangled over the temperature. Sam loves it cold, but he turns the thermostat so far down, it takes half the day to heat the house back up. The Air Conditioner Wars, I used to call them.

Until Iris moved out. Since then, I've let Sam do whatever he wants with the thermostat since we tangle about damn near everything else.

My God, Sam. Where are you?

I meander over to his bulletin board. His baseball pictures, mostly, and a few from Cubs games we attended. In one, he's only three years old, and seeing him there holding up a baseball and beaming, I break down.

Where are you, Sam? Just where the hell did you go?

I stand there sobbing for I don't know how long, and then I make my way over to his bed. I sit, and for no reason at all, I say, "There's something I need to tell you." I grasp the satiny coolness of his comforter. "You know how my mom divorced my dad when I was four? My biological father wasn't ready for fatherhood. He was just a kid. He was pretty screwed up, and he did a pretty awful job. And I still missed him like crazy when he left, and later on, I hated him. God, I hated him. Then he died, and I don't even know how to feel about it. But he's gone and that's that."

I'm breathing better than I have since this nightmare began, so I draw the pillow closer. Pretend Sam's lying on it. Lying on it and listening to me the way he did when he was little and didn't think I was a loser.

"When my mom remarried... Well, you know about that too. How I hated my stepfather, how demeaning he was, how relentlessly condescending. How he firebombed my self-esteem, which was fragile in the first place. And all that time I spent hating both my biological dad and my stepfather, I was thinking I'd never treat my kids the way they treated me. I'd be the father I would've wanted."

I close my eyes and feel a torrid heat building in my throat. "I knew what *not* to do, Sam. I knew not to be an abusive drunk or a miserly turd, but I never, no matter what I tried, figured out what *to* do. And I can't just blame that on the fact that there was no one there to teach me. Because someone's got to learn, right? We can't just keep heaping our mistakes on the people who raised us. I should've been smarter. Should've been better. More patient, more proactive. I should have..." I break off and press a palm to my forehead. "And that's the unholy truth of it, Sam. I *still* don't know. Even if you were here now." I caress the pillow and catch a whiff of my son's scent. "Even if we were together right now, I wouldn't know how to be your dad. I'm sorry. I'm so sorry for not being better. I love you, Sammy. Please come back to me."

I breathe deeply, but the scent is gone. I get up and turn off the light and make my way upstairs to Emma, where I lie beside her and cry myself to sleep.

—

The day of our grocery trip arrives. I wake up early but can't concentrate on anything. When I join Emma at the island, she's bouncing among several open tabs on her laptop. One is for the grocery store. Another is the State of Indiana website.

"They don't tell you what to do," Emma says. "They say it's up to the individual stores."

"Punting the problem," I say, shaking some dry-roasted peanuts into a bowl.

Emma gestures at the screen. "I mean, there are all these protocols in place on the Aldi website, but there's nothing about how they're going to enforce them."

I smile grimly and wait for her to draw the conclusion.

She frowns. "Are they expecting the workers to do it?"

I crunch some peanuts.

"What bullshit," she says. A couple weeks ago, I would've reprimanded her, but given all we've been through, I let it slide.

"Do you mind eating together?" I ask.

"What do you mean?"

"You'll be fourteen at the end of the summer. Sometimes teenagers don't want—"

"*Dad,*" she says and gives me a flat look. "It's fine."

I chuckle softly.

"Besides," she says, "it's nice eating lunch with someone for a change."

"School just ended," I point out. "You ate with your friends every day."

She doesn't answer.

I stare at her. "Didn't you?"

A shrug. "Girls are mean sometimes. You remember volleyball season?"

I feel an internal tightening. Volleyball was a pain in the ass. Emma had been placed on the B-team, and many of the A-team kids had treated her like a subhuman species.

Emma says, "The A-team sat together, and there wasn't room for me at the table."

"So you sat by yourself?"

A nod.

I stare at her. "Volleyball was in the fall."

She lowers her eyes.

"You ate by yourself all *year*?"

Her lips tremble.

"Oh hell," I say and lay a hand on her back. "Why didn't you tell me?"

A rueful laugh. "I wasn't exactly proud of it."

"Your teammates were dumbasses. There's no one I'd rather eat lunch with."

A wan smile. "Thanks, Dad."

We lapse into silence, Emma surfing websites, me munching peanuts and swilling water and imagining how nice it will be to have coffee again.

She opens a document and says, "They say to bring cash, in case there're problems with the card readers."

This strikes me as ominous. Our internet has been spotty for the past couple days. What *does* happen if technology stops working? If we can't communicate and we can't leave our houses...

"No more than two cans of any item, and no more than twenty cans total," Emma says.

"We should make a list."

"Gotcha covered," she says and clicks on another document.

She's organized the items into three columns: YES, MAYBE, and HOPEFULLY.

I lean forward. "You put dill pickles in the Yes column?"

"They're in a *jar*, Dad. They don't count against our twenty."

I scan the list. "Move black beans from maybe to yes."

"You don't eat black beans."

"No," I say, "but you do."

She grins and moves the item, and I resist the urge to kiss the top of her head. She always groans when I do that, so I try to limit myself. The last thing I want is to drive her batty by being too affectionate.

"Have you seen the celebrations?" she asks, clicking on the *USA Today* website. REVELERS OBSERVE NATIONAL FREEDOM DAY, the headline reads. The article includes pictures from Miami, Nashville, Boise. All of them feature large crowds. Fireworks. Boat parades.

Right on cue, we hear a firework crump and sizzle outside.

"'In defiance of the White House's stay-at-home order,'" Emma reads, "'tens of thousands nationwide are participating in National Freedom Day. Colton Blaylock, owner of a pool maintenance company in Gainesville, says, "We see it every time there's some media-generated hysteria. People lose their minds and forget what made this country great in the first place: individual liberty."'"

She eyes the screen glumly. "Looks like we picked a bad day for our grocery run."

"Or," I answer, "whatever is doing this will be too busy attacking all the partiers to notice us."

She whaps me on the arm. "*Dad.*"

"What?" I ask, toting my glass over to the sink. "I'd rather some dipshit on a jet ski gets taken than you."

She shakes her head and smiles. I kiss her on the head. Incredibly, she doesn't even groan. I feel good as I head upstairs to retrieve my laptop. For most of the day, I feel good. I feel good right up until late that afternoon, when the nightmare descends on our town.

10

We're so excited to grocery shop, we're shaking. We tether in the garage, then realize how awkward it will be getting into the Highlander that way. We decide she'll climb over the center console since she's more flexible. Once inside our vehicle, we look at each other.

"Ready for this?" I ask.

"No."

"Just think of dill pickles."

"I keep thinking of Mom. And Sam."

My hand was on the key, ready to fire the ignition for the first time since that terrible day, but now I take Emma's hand, which is cool to the touch. "I won't let anything happen to you. I swear."

"What if something happens to you?"

"I'll grab on to something."

"What if it doesn't matter? You've seen what those things can do. How strong they are. If they drag you away—"

"I won't let that happen."

"It's not up to you!"

I'm taken aback. I can't recall Emma ever shouting at me.

Tears shimmer over her bottom lids. "I know you love me, I know you'll do your best, but this isn't in your control, Dad. It isn't in anyone's. If one of them grabs me, or you, there's nothing we can do."

"We can fight."

"How do you fight something you can't see? Even if you used the gun, where would you shoot?"

"Honey, these grocery trips have been going on for over a week."

"But those people on the news," she says. "National Freedom Day? It's like they're tempting fate. Daring whatever it is to attack again."

I shake my head before the undertow of fear can pull me down. "We have to go. If not today, we'd have to go very soon. We have to eat." I reach into my pocket and produce the document she printed. "We've got our list. We'll be efficient. We'll get everything, and soon we'll be home again. I promise you, nothing will happen."

"You can't promise that."

"I'll keep you right beside me. If anything grabs you, it's gonna have to take me too."

Bright fear shows in her eyes.

"But nothing's gonna grab you," I say.

With my hollow promises spent, I press the garage door button and back into the sunless midafternoon. I'm nearly to the end of our driveway when something taps on my window. I gasp and look up.

Dean Dawson.

Heart slamming, I roll down my window.

"Finally crawling out of the cave?" Dean asks. He's attired in a periwinkle polo and white shorts a size too small. Some sort of gun is holstered on his hip.

"Grocery store," I say.

His eyes flit to the console, where our appointment reminder rests atop my wallet.

"Oh boy," he says, "I see you've got your sheep card."

Emma leans over to ask, "You don't have one?"

A gloating grin. "Been twice already. No one's going to tell me when I can go to the store."

"How?" she asks.

"Walked right in. I just told them I forgot my card." His grin broadens. "Got enough food to last 'til fall."

I glance at the clock. "Our appointment's at three. We really need to—"

"It's a good thing running into you," Dean interrupts. "Now, when we take stock of your provisions, it'll be up-to-date. In fact, you could just bring them to my outbuilding." When I only stare at him, he adds, "The Boiler Barn?"

Dean owns one of the largest houses in the neighborhood, situated on a double lot, the other side of which contains a two-story black outbuilding with BOILER BARN stenciled in gold. Years ago, Dean played tennis for Purdue, and he wants everyone to know it.

"What does your barn have to do with my groceries?" I ask.

Dean gives his shoes an embarrassed smile. "Many families are choosing to store their goods there for safekeeping."

"Safekeeping."

"You heard the gunshot the other night?"

I compress my lips. I haven't told Emma about it. I feel her bemused stare on me as he explains, "Home invasion down on Meridian Street. Husband killed, wife assaulted. Everything they owned—food, twelve-gauge, even their clunky old Buick—gone. The Boiler Barn has a security system, same as Casa Dawson. Somebody tries to break in, they get a horde of cops." He taps the holstered gun. "If they survive that long."

"How does your wife feel about your system?"

He averts his eyes, and I think, *Bingo.*

"She went to stay with her family," he explains. "You know, her parents are getting on in years."

You mean she left you, I think. *Probably got tired of your bullying. And I suspect she's damned glad to be rid of you.*

I glance up our hill. "I really need to get going."

"We'll be over tomorrow."

"That won't be necessary."

"Don't be difficult, Johnny. Do what's best for your daughter."

"I think I know that better than you do."

He steps back from the Highlander, his gaze several notches cooler. "Clearly you don't. Why isolate yourselves when everyone else is showing solidarity?"

"You're telling me everyone in the neighborhood agreed to this?"

He gives a shrug. "Most everyone. Once things deteriorate, the holdouts will come crawling back."

I slide into gear, roll my window up, and bump out of the drive. Through my window, I hear Dean call, "Think about it, Johnny," and I resist an urge to fly the middle finger. But I remind myself of my mission—*Get groceries. Keep Emma safe.*

Rolling through the neighborhood, it's uncanny how rundown the houses look, how overgrown the lawns have become, how shot through with weeds. In an ordinary summer, most of these yards would be tended by lawn care services. Only peons like the Calhouns mow their own grass and pluck their own dandelions.

We reach Grant Street (no cars), then merge onto Salisbury, where we encounter a post office vehicle (we've only gotten mail twice since this started, all bills), a city utility truck, someone from Duke Energy, and a random Jeep with the top down and half a dozen college-age kids in tank tops. As Emma and I pause at the stoplight, I hear melodyless music thumping from the Jeep, a poor match with the otherwise funereal silence of the streets.

"Freedom Day," Emma murmurs, and I imagine this crew in a lake somewhere, knee-deep in water, chugging cheap beer and daring whatever's lurking out there to do its best. After the light turns green, we glide past houses that appear even more dilapidated. The owner of a little ranch with bloodred wooden siding has displayed a white sheet that reads, "We will NOT be told what to do by the deep state. DON'T TREAD ON ME." Two houses down, we behold a message on foam board: "John 3:16." What draws my attention, however, is a two-story home set off the road, where someone has nosed an Audi right up against the front door and not only boarded up all their windows but affixed plywood panels over much of the facade. Though I doubt very much that plywood will repel whatever we're facing, I understand the owner's fear. Just because we haven't heard of anyone being taken from their home doesn't mean it can't happen.

We reach Sagamore Parkway, and though the traffic here remains light, there are more cars than I anticipated. The Payless parking lot is half-full, the cars crowding the doors, several vehicles lining the sidewalk out front. Fresh Thyme, a grocery store specializing in fresh produce and overcharging its customers, is equally bustling, a cluster of sign-bearing individuals stationed before the entrance.

"What are they doing?" Emma asks. "None of them are tethered."

"I suspect that's the point."

"You've gotta be kidding me," Emma says. "Antitetherers?"

When we reach Aldi, we encounter a smaller but no less vocal contingent of protestors. Pulling in, I read their Sharpied signs:

"AMERICA is about FREEDOM."

"The nine most terrifying words in the English language are *I'm from the government, and I'm here to help.* —Ronald Reagan"

"Why choose to be SHEEPLE? Be PATRIOTS instead!"

"Park in a handicapped spot," Emma says. I frown, but she heads me off. "*Dad.* The fact that you limp doesn't make you any less of a person."

I halt in the parking lot, knowing she's right but still unwilling to enter one of the handicapped spots. Iris suggested it a few times when we were dating, but I always shut her down.

And why did you do that? a voice asks. *Because of your idiotic pride. As if applying for a disability plate would change anything. Everyone can see your limp. The closer you get Emma to the store, the safer she'll be.*

Against my will, I scan the storefront, but all the disability spaces are taken.

I give Emma a shrug and roll into a regular parking spot. "Remember the plan?"

She nods. "We focus on essentials first—milk, noodles, bread—before we head to the chip aisle."

"And after we check out?"

"I climb into the car while you unload the cart, which is awkward and makes no sense since it would go faster with me helping—"

"And when I'm done," I override her, "you climb out and return the cart with me."

She grunts. "I still can't believe you're going to return the cart."

"Would you rather have some poor kid working minimum wage running all over the lot retrieving carts?"

"Depends on who the kid is."

I chuckle. "Come on." I reach for the door.

"Wait," she says. "What'll we do about the protestors?"

"They're irrelevant."

"What if they get in my face?"

"You have my permission to clobber them."

"*Sweet.*"

We climb out, and as we approach, it becomes apparent that the protestors are hostile and aggressive, their ire focused on tethered people. A curly-haired woman of fifty bellows vitriol in people's faces. She appears to be the ringleader of the quintet, her shirt a giant American flag.

The clouds have blotted out the sun, giving the scene a doomsday aspect.

"Almost there," Emma says, and we grab our cart, bypass the chanting protestors ("Free-DOM! Free-DOM!"), and slip through the automatic doors.

We stop inside and stare. There are no fewer than four arguments in progress. Nearest to us, a pair of men, both affluent looking, is engaged in a dispute over broccoli. I'm confounded by this but move on to grab some vegetables. As always, Emma asks for items that aren't on the list, and as always, I tell her yes. The kid has been a trooper, and if she wants junk food, she can sure as hell have junk food.

When we're done with the fruits and vegetables, we discover the shortages we've been hearing about. Bread is scarce, and the only milk available is soy. "I don't mind soy," Emma says, restoring some of my positivity. We swing around to the next aisle, and my positive attitude takes another hit. Not only is there a dearth of canned goods, there's an argument taking place between a young woman in a black ball cap and a man in a dandelion-yellow T-shirt, the man totally defying the "Take No More Than Two" signs.

"...care about anyone else?" I hear her finish.

"You worry about you," he answers. "I've got mouths to feed."

"I've got three kids under the age of five," she says. "We've all got mouths to feed."

He sweeps another armful of cans into his cart. "Then do right by them."

He stalks away, and the young woman stares at me, slack-jawed.

"Jerk," Emma mutters.

"Unbelievable," the woman agrees.

Emma and I pick through what's left and move to the next aisle. The rest of our food hunt is uneventful, except for an unnerving moment when a tall woman elbows aside a shorter one to snatch the last package of chicken breasts from a refrigerated shelf. More than once, our electrical cord, which drags on the unswept floor, gets tangled up with other patrons. But for the most part, people are civil, and we're able to untangle before tempers flare.

Things don't get truly disturbing until we line up to check out. Emma and I are the seventh cart in line, and as we wait, I survey our haul. Though the pickings are slim—no fresh meat, a paucity of frozen goods—I decide we'll be set for a month. More, if we stretch it. I hope the world is in a better place by then, but it could just as easily be worse. The man in the yellow T-shirt seems to prove this when, two aisles over, he cuts into line.

"You can't do that," another guy says. He's slim, in his twenties, and his ears are pierced in that stretched, circular way that always reminds me of fidget spinners. He's tethered to a young woman in baggy blue sweatpants and a Bob Marley tank top. Their tethering cord, I note, is the same road-hazard orange that Emma and I have. Yellow T-Shirt gives a dismissive laugh and turns his back on the couple.

"Hey, dickless," the woman in the Bob Marley shirt says. "You need to go to the back of the line."

Yellow T-Shirt doesn't even turn. "Make me."

The guy with the ear hoops moves toward him, and when he latches onto Yellow T-Shirt's cart, Yellow T-Shirt whacks him in the mouth with an open hand. I jolt and Emma sucks in breath. The woman in the Bob Marley shirt lunges at Yellow T-Shirt, and he holds her off, laughing, as she rains punches that deflect off his shoulder. One blow sneaks through, catching him on the side of the mouth, and he snarls at the man with ear hoops, "Get this bitch off me before I knock her teeth out."

"—can take whatever I want!" a voice shouts, and we all turn to another register, where a woman in a paisley lavender jumpsuit is wrestling her cart away from a clerk.

"*Ma'am*," the clerk says, "you have too many cans. And you're only supposed to take one package of toilet paper."

"My family *needs* these things," Jumpsuit shouts, "and you're not going to deprive us."

"Amen!" a man shouts.

"Quit being an asshole," someone says to Jumpsuit.

"Here," Yellow T-Shirt mutters and flings some crumpled bills on the conveyor belt, "keep the change."

He rams the cart in front of him, an elderly woman who barely steps out of the way before she's run over, and trundles his overladen cart toward the exit. The clerk, a boy of maybe eighteen, examines the bills and calls, "Sir... this isn't enough," but Yellow T-Shirt is gone.

"It's okay, honey," someone says, and I realize the young mother with three kids has placed a hand on my daughter's shoulder. Emma has paled at the ugliness around us, and I remember to do my job, to be a father instead of a mute rubbernecker.

"Thanks," I tell the young mother and draw Emma closer to me.

The young mom mops sweat from her brow and surveys the grumbling patrons. "The world's going berserk."

I look at Emma. "You okay?"

She gives me a smile. "Fun grocery trip, huh?"

I start to smile back, then pause.

"What?" Emma asks.

I say to the young mother. "Could you watch our cart for thirty seconds?"

"I'll try."

Emma's frowning at me. "Dad, what—"

"Come on," I say and hurry over to the nearest aisle, hang a left, Emma almost dragged along by the cord, and when she sees where I stop, her face lights up in the first genuine smile I've seen today. We each carry a large jar of dill pickles back to the cart.

It's another five minutes before we check out, but when we do, the card reader works, and the clerk thanks us for not being assholes. Deciding that would make a terrific sign—*Aldi Appreciates Non-Assholes*—I lead Emma through the automatic doors.

Where we're beset by the protestors. We're the only cart rolling through the lot at the moment, so three of the protestors hound us all the way to our vehicle.

"You're encouraging a system of oppression," one man scolds.

"What a shameful example for your daughter," a blonde woman laments.

I open the rear of the Highlander, and when Em begins unloading the cart with me, I tell her to stick to the plan.

"Screw the plan," she says. "I want to get out of here."

I don't like her being in the open like this, but I see her point. The clouds have grown shroud-like, and the humidity is so suffocating it's like breathing through gauze. There's an electrical buzz in the air, and I suspect we're in for a doozy of a storm. And of course, there are the protestors.

"What will you let them regulate next," a bespectacled man demands, "when you can go to the bathroom?"

I ignore the harassment and transfer more grocery sacks. One ruptures in my hands, and I'm just able to plop it into the trunk before cans tumble all over the lot. We finish loading, and as I slam the hatch, I catch sight of the bespectacled man's T-shirt: A PATRIOT DEFENDS HIS COUNTRY FROM HIS GOVERNMENT.

Emma takes one side of the cart and I take the other, and together we hurry it toward the corral along the front of the store. There, the most belligerent protester, the curly-haired ringleader with the stars-and-stripes T-shirt, spots us and makes a beeline for the corral. "And *you*," she says, "you bind your daughter and make her a slave. And why? Because of fear." We sidestep the woman's vitriol, but she moves with us, spittle flying from her mouth. "You're indoctrinating your child into fear. Grooming her! You're *shameful*!"

At this, her cronies give out a cheer. Emma side-eyes the woman with distaste.

"Fuck off!" someone calls, and I see it's the guy with the hoop earrings on his way to return his cart. His companion in the Bob Marley shirt is staring at her phone, her face taut. Whatever she's reading, it isn't good.

"*Aww*," the bespectacled man says, "more tetherers."

Em and I move to pass the ringleader, but she calls out, "Tetherers! The newest generation of morons!"

Roars of approbation from the protestors.

Emma's hustling single-file behind me, but everywhere I step, the ringleader is in my face with her odious grin and her frothing spit buds.

"What's next, Papa Sheep?" she croons. She's nearly a foot shorter than me, but her frenzied fanaticism makes her implacable. "You gonna barricade yourselves in your house and wait for the government to starve you to death?"

"Hey," the woman with the Bob Marley shirt says as her partner rams their cart into the corral. "There's something seriously wrong—oh, get out of my *face*!" she shouts. The bespectacled man has shoved his poster at her, and she smacks it, rips it in half. He gives her a shove. Hoop Earrings pushes the bespectacled man away, but the guy is back on the instant, brandishing the torn poster in the couple's faces.

"The strong will inherit the earth," the ringleader is shouting at me, her grin a triumphant rictus. "You will waste away in your homes while we rise and replace you with—"

She jerks into the air, and Emma and I stumble back, watching the ringleader fly higher, her eyes terror-huge and her hands groping toward us. She's fifty, sixty feet in the air, and then she disappears into the sky, and for a swollen moment, no one reacts.

The woman in the Bob Marley shirt starts gibbering, "That's what the alert says, they're attacking, they're pulling people up! *No!*"

But Hoop Earrings is rushing into the sky, his limbs flailing. Forty feet above us, he vanishes, too.

I seize Emma's hand and sprint for the Highlander.

"Wait—" the bespectacled man calls.

I turn in time to see him pinwheeling his arms, rising, and I don't wait for him to disappear because I've seen it twice already. A car zooms toward us, and Emma's reflexes are faster than mine. She skids, hauls back on my arm, and the black Mercedes barrels past, flubs a hairpin turn, and crashes into a cement-wrapped pole. We take off as the airbag deploys, the man inside batting at it like it's a rampaging silver blob, and I rip open my door. Emma clambers through, and I fumble for the keys, damn near drop them in the abyss between the seat and the console. I fire up the Highlander. Behind us, the protestors are scattering, their freedom-themed posters forgotten on the asphalt, and as I'm backing out, a shopping cart judders toward us, caroms off the rear bumper, and overturns. I can't run it over—what if I blow a tire?

I make a move to climb out, but Emma snags my arm. "No, Dad." A figure streaks across the windshield, another shopper bullwhipped into the air, and craning my neck, I realize it's the young mother with three children, and she disappears into the bleak gray sky. I floor it in reverse, grinding the fallen cart, and as soon as I shift into drive, I pound the accelerator. I hear the mangled cart tumbling after me. We somehow make it out of the parking lot, and I don't want any part of Sagamore Parkway. I ignore the red light, blast through the intersection, and when Crew Car Wash appears on our left, I spot some teenaged kid about my son's age haring toward us. I have time to think, *A car wash is an essential business?* then slow down to let him in. He's shambling at a diagonal and he doesn't see us, so I give the horn a beep, and he turns, actually smiles, and breaks for the Highlander. I slow down, and the kid's almost to us when our vehicle jolts, and he launches into the sky. Heart jittering, I spot him at the top of Emma's window just before he disappears, at least seventy-five feet in the air. Stomach roiling, I jam the accelerator. I hang a right, and zigzagging through neighborhoods, make it to our house safely. We don't see anyone else get taken.

Until we turn on the news.

11

"The video you are about to see is disturbing," the CNN voice-over says.

"Can't that be assumed by this point?" Emma remarks. We're side by side on the couch, her heels drumming on the rug, my thumbs tapping my knees.

The footage is of a National Freedom Day event at Dale Lake, Tennessee. What I first judge to be a large family gathering is revealed, as the camera zooms out, to be a sprawling community affair. Sun-drenched tubes and inflatables mingle with all manner of watercraft—fishing boats, speedboats, pontoons, even paddleboats. Country music drones on in the background as people guzzle beer cans, toast each other with longnecks, and whoop it up. On the decks of several pontoons, people are dancing and grinding against each other.

"This *is* disturbing," Em says.

Even though I anticipate what's coming, I'm not prepared when a little boy on an inflatable seahorse gets yanked into the air, the camera losing him for a second, then tilting up just in time to see his bare legs disappear into the cloudless sky.

"What the hell?" someone says, and then three people on rafts are jerked into the sky. We see one disappear only twenty feet above the water, another soaring to maybe two hundred feet before vanishing.

Chaos ensues—people knocking friends out of the way, others seizing whoever's nearby and positioning them as human shields—but what brings a hand to my mouth and causes me to sink back into the couch is the sight of people being jerked underwater. A teenage girl in a white one-piece. A hairy, sunburned man with a jiggly beer gut and aviator shades. A fortysomething dad in a baseball hat, slammed to the deck of a pontoon, his Solo cup of beer sloshing over his wife's face, who goes scudding off the side and is swallowed up by the water, the only proof he was ever there—his beer-soaked wife and the floating red cup.

The abduction of the kid on the seahorse shows again in excruciating slow motion as a voice-over explains, "No fewer than thirty celebrants were taken on Dale Lake alone. More are unaccounted for."

"We should get the groceries inside," I murmur.

Emma gets up slowly, her eyes never leaving the screen, which replays the dad getting hauled off the pontoon, his scrawny butt skimming along the artificial turf deck like some new and terrible aquatic sport.

As we gather up the grocery sacks in the garage, Em asks, "Should we board up our windows?"

I've been mulling this over. Hell, I've considered shifting our entire operation to the basement, where there's only a single daylight window.

"We don't have enough lumber," I say, tromping up the steps to the mud room. "The leftovers from the fence would cover a few windows, but that's only a start."

In May, I decided to extend our privacy fence an extra twenty feet, and after an exorbitant quote of nearly eight grand, I opted to tackle the job myself. Though it took me roughly ten times longer than an experienced carpenter, I completed the job, and it doesn't look half bad. It even garnered me a congratulatory text from my father-in-law, to whom Iris had sent pictures. Pitifully, the text made me swell with pride.

Emma and I make two more trips to the garage, then spend the next half hour putting groceries away and sampling from various cheeses and crackers. I know we should pace ourselves, particularly given this ghastly new series of incursions, but our distress is giving way to hunger, and I figure we deserve to indulge a little.

As the day wears on, we return to our phones and the TV. The news is catastrophic. In America alone, at least sixty thousand more people have been taken, with the count rising every minute. Old pros now, people have captured seemingly endless videos of abductions. Emma and I watch these tragedies with a mixture of fascination and dread, and though part of me condemns my judgment for allowing Emma to witness these horrors, the greater part understands that the world is deteriorating, and preparing her for it is better than pretending it's not happening. Unless I take away her phone, she's going to see the videos anyway, and I'd rather be there to help her process these grisly images than let her do so alone.

We snack. Not wanting to deplete our paltry supply of lunch meat, I bypass the salami and opt instead for celery. Emma attacks the dill pickles with abandon.

"What do you think hit the Highlander?" she asks as she chews.

"Probably the kid from the car wash," I answer.

"What if it was the thing?"

I stop chewing. "Thing?"

We move wordlessly to the garage, where we inspect the point of impact. The dent isn't severe, but it's visible. The black paint appears scored there.

Emma watches me. "What do you think?"

I frown. "Could you flip on the lights?"

She does. With the overhead lights glaring down at the black paint, the dent looks much worse. Uglier. I bring my face right up to it. The scoring is deep but capillary thin.

Emma rocks onto her toes to see better. "Could claws do that?"

I shake my head faintly. "Not claws. Whatever scraped us made dozens of tiny scratches. The creatures… their skin must be armored with something sharp."

Emma gives a little start. "Cystisoma."

I frown at her.

"The book you showed me," she rushes on. "The roach thingy!"

I turn back to the dent. Yes. Something with a coarse shell could have done this. But rather than feeling the thrill of scientific discovery, I'm consumed by a slow-moving fog of dread.

—

By moonrise, the news cycle has turned to analysis. ABC begins a segment called "CONNECTING THE WAVES: ARE FAMILIES BEING TARGETED?" which Emma and I watch with our breath held. Two minutes into the report, my phone rings, and when I disconnect it from the charging cord, I see it's my mother-in-law.

"Hey, Patricia," I say, and then the room around me, the blaring TV, the potato chip bag in my lap, my daughter's dread-laced eyes, all of it drains away, and I'm left with the nearly inaudible weeping of my mother-in-law. I stride from the room, not wanting Emma to hear whatever Patricia is about to share, and I think, *Iris. She's heard from Iris. Or Sam. Please let them be okay.*

"Patricia?" I say, stepping inside the guest room and closing the door behind me. "What is it?"

She utters a single word, her voice holding on that last sibilant consonant: "Max."

I consider locking the guest room door but don't. Outside, a peal of thunder shakes the neighborhood.

The hackles on my neck rising, I sit forward. "Is everything okay?"

Patricia says, "I went in to check on him a few minutes ago. He'd been sleeping so serenely. His leg looked bad, but I thought he might be getting better... his body fighting the infection..."

I wait.

"I was putting the soup on the nightstand when he began to twitch. And then he..." She breaks off. "And then he was flailing, knocking things off the nightstand, moaning and thrashing and oh *God*, John! Please tell me what to do!"

I tense as thunder rattles the windows. "Have you called the hospital?"

"Of course I have!" she shrieks. "No one answers! Nobody answers but you!"

And we're two hours away, I think. I tell myself she won't ask, but I'm still not surprised when she says, "Can you come, John? You and Emma?"

I try not to get angry. She's in her late seventies, she's all alone, and her husband appears to be dying. But if she thinks I'm taking my daughter out there on the highways when the entire planet is under attack, she's lost her mind.

Rain begins to pelt our windows. I glance up in time to see plump droplets smacking the glass.

I ask, "Have you tried your neighbors?"

No answer.

"Patricia?"

"I thought I heard a noise."

"What did it sound like?"

"Not like *them*. I've heard that on the news..."

"What did you hear?"

"These people, they live on the other side of the factory. You know the factory?"

I do. Many times during our visits to South Bend, our kids have played in the factory parking lot after business there closed for the day.

"Even before this whole thing started," she goes on, "there were rumors they were robbing houses. A couple nights ago, I heard someone trying to force the lock on our back door." A sob. "John, what if they break in?"

The thunderstorm is lashing our house now. I have to raise my voice to make myself heard.

"Your car is in the garage?"

"The Civic is too banged up. We barely made it home last time."

"What about the RV? Does it run?"

"Of course it runs," she says. "Max checked everything before all this started. We were—" I hear a boom on the other end, and she cuts off.

"Patricia?"

No answer.

I grip the phone harder. "Patricia?"

"*Shh*," she says.

I listen.

A crashing shatters the stillness.

"Oh no," she says in a choked voice.

"Patricia?"

Raised voices. Snickering. I hear Patricia pleading, telling someone to leave. I'm holding my breath, but goddammit, there's nothing I can do. Patricia screams. More laughter. Several male voices. I hear her grovel, wail, and then there's a thud, and I can't hear her anymore.

"Patricia?" I whisper.

The sharp crack of a gun.

Oh my God. Oh my God.

Another gunshot.

No.

I hear voices on the other end, businesslike. I hear all sorts of clanks and thumps, the murderers looting what they can. I sink down on the couch and end the call. With a shaking hand, I dial 911, but no one answers.

When I turn, I see Emma in the doorway. "Is Grandpa going to live?"

Oh my God, I think.

"What's wrong?" she asks. Lightning strobes over her frightened face.

I arrange my features into a look of hopeful concern. "Their neighbor," I say, "the one who set Grandpa's leg? He's—" Thunder drowns out my voice.

"Is Grandpa in bad shape?" she asks.

I lick my lips. "It sounds like it."

I watch her mental cogs turning. She says, "Grandma's tougher than she looks. She'll take care of him."

I don't contradict her.

She nods and goes out. I'm left watching after her as rain batters our house.

Now that we're holed up for what looks like a long time, we rededicate ourselves to learning all we can about what's happening. Sure, we've been learning all along, but our study has been reluctant, our minds dragged toward understanding as surely as the people who've been dragged away, so embracing the dire news reports feels like crossing some threshold. When Emma's not researching, she's drawing. The creatures, someone on C-SPAN posits, must be adaptable enough to travel on land, in the water, and through the air.

"We could've told them that," Emma says without looking up from her sketching.

"These beings must have immense strength," the expert continues. The graphic identifies him as Gregory Balfour, Yale professor of paleontology. He looks about seventy, his gray hair wispy enough to reveal a liver-spotted scalp. "They possess the muscularity to bear a three-hundred-pound man into the sky. Until today, we believed this to be a land phenomenon, but now we've adapted our model to accommodate these newly exhibited abilities."

The anchor looks into the camera and says, "Yes. Can we…?"

The screen cuts to an artist's rendition of Balfour's creature. It reminds me of a Quetzalcoatlus. I only remember what it's called because Emma used to be fascinated with the prehistoric, winged beast.

"This is quite a departure from your earlier iteration," the anchor says.

Balfour colors slightly. "It is. But what we've seen today has changed our thinking, and like nature, we must adapt."

I hear the *shoosh-shoosh* of Emma's shading pencil as she says, "Everything this guy draws looks like a dinosaur. What do they expect from a paleontologist?"

It's true. The sketches resemble what each expert wants

them to. Over the next few days, we see renderings that look like tigers, Bigfoot, the Roswell aliens. But now many of these depictions include wings.

Some don't believe the cause is sentient beings at all. A hydrologist from Oxford believes the culprit is a fluky meteorological phenomenon. An astrophysicist is convinced that some inventor has found a way to generate miniature, temporary black holes whose gravitational pull is inescapable. When asked why anyone would devise something so nightmarish, the specialist shrugs and suggests, "Toppling society. Sowing chaos. Creating a new world order."

Various religions claim we've entered the end times, the abducted people either saved or damned. I can't stomach this, can't believe someone as wonderful as Emma would be left behind, and I don't believe that Iris and Sam are being punished. These apocalyptic notions pick up adherents, yet it's Balfour's winged dinosaur theory that gains the most traction.

What no one can explain is why so many abducted people are related to one another.

It's these news segments and internet articles that trouble me the most. So many experts toss the word *targeted* around that it's difficult not to believe it. Worldwide, there have been over two million abductions. Americans account for roughly 260,000 of those, which is wildly disproportionate since our population is only about 4 percent of the world's. Among the Americans taken, it's estimated that 30 percent have had a relative abducted too. Some pundits dismiss this figure as irrelevant: "Just look at the videos. When there are attacks, family members tend to be together. It stands to reason they'd be taken too since most of us keep our family close."

But that doesn't account for cases like ours, where the abductions occurred at different times in different places.

Targeted. That dreadful refrain keeps sounding. *Your family has been targeted.*

It's two weeks after the horror show at Aldi when Emma plops down beside me, a *Finding Nemo* folder in her lap.

"Are you ready?" she asks.

I glance at the folder. "Where'd that come from?"

"You keep all our old stuff. Wanna see them or not?"

"Hit me."

She pulls out the first sheet, and I feel my stomach muscles clench.

"There are at least three species," she says as I stare at the drawing. The body reminds me of an arachnid, only there are six legs instead of eight. In the center of these hairy legs rests a face that's eerily humanoid. Hostile eyes. Hooked teeth. Nostrils wide-set and flaring. There's even hair on the creature's head. Black, stringy hair that dangles past the creature's pointed chin.

"Good Lord," I murmur.

"We don't know where they come from, but they have to be able to survive in our habitat," she explains. "At least in short bursts. It's possible they wear some sort of mask to breathe, but that's not as much fun to draw."

I examine the terrifying eyes. "This was fun?"

"Ready for the next one?"

"No."

She produces it, this one obviously suited to the water. The face is humanoid, but the body resembles a shark with arms.

"One way I agree with Balfour," Emma says, tapping the drawing with her eraser, "is that the creatures must have bone-crushing jaws."

I imagine the sharkish creature mauling my son, my wife, and have to stave off a spate of wooziness.

"And here," she says, revealing her final sketch, "is what attacked at the grocery store."

Some dim fatherly region in me glows at the way she's forsaken every other rendering to devise her own. Emma's beast has wings, but though they're bat-like, they're sheathed in a stony carapace. She's accomplished this by peppering the creature with thousands of tiny dots. But the face of the beast... that's where paternal pride gives way to dread, and it's all I can do not to turn away in revulsion. She's carried the bat theme into the beady eyes, the enlarged ears, the triangular nose. Even the ridged forehead reminds me of a bat.

"Creepy, huh?" she asks.

"Creepy," I agree.

"Which one do you like best?"

I raise my eyebrows.

She laughs. "Which one do you think is the scariest?"

"The third, I guess." I cross my arms. "But you really nailed all of them."

"I did?"

"You know," I say as she peruses her drawing, "you should—"

There's a scream outside. Emma stares at me, her artistic fervor gone. I rise from the couch and move into the living room. Peering through the windows into the greenish-hued day, I spot the woman who lives catty-corner from us, Mrs. Chen, staggering toward her ruby-red sedan, her husband following. As she fumbles in her purse, I hold my breath and hope she doesn't get hauled into the sky. Mr. Chen says something we can't hear, but he seems resigned to her departure.

"Think he hit her?" Em asks.

I mull it over as Mrs. Chen backs out of the driveway. "I'm guessing a lot of relationships are reaching their breaking point."

"Makes sense," she says. "You're driving me nuts."

I gape at her. She giggles silently.

"*Damn*," I say. "That's cold."

Emma grins. "That's why I'm here."

—

The weeks tick past, and we burrow deeper down our research rabbit hole. It rains frequently, but this makes no difference to us. The sea-green beater cruises past our house again, though I don't get a look at who's inside. One afternoon, we see angry black smoke rising from a few streets over, almost certainly a house fire. But there are no sirens, no sign of anyone at all, and when the sun rises the next day, the horizon is still smoldering.

I call the government hotlines every day, and no one knows anything. Of the legions who've been abducted, a grand total of zero has returned. After a while, no one answers the hotlines.

I've never felt so isolated. My parents have been dead for years, I don't have any close friends, and the ones I keep in touch with seem distant when I call them, like they're afraid whatever grotesque curse befell my family might be contagious. Emma asks about her grandparents, and I tell her I don't know. She never challenges this, but my sense of responsibility nags at me. How long can I allow the lie to persist?

We watch the news and study the internet. Both are growing spotty. I shudder to think what will happen if the power goes out when winter rolls around. It's only early August, and those lonely frigid days seem part of an impossible future, but our supplies are getting low, the fresh food from our late-June excursion long since spent.

New studies emerge, most of them maddeningly inconclusive. One reveals that no one over the age of sixty has been abducted, and the average age is a mere twenty-eight. That young people are at greater risk has become cause for rampant speculation. Do they want us for our healthy bodies?

That's what Gregory Balfour argues. Somehow he's become an expert not only on paleontology, but on all things vanishing related. Thankfully, he seems to know what the hell he's talking about, and he's one of the few experts that can be interviewed in person rather than remotely. The video calls the networks rely on have become increasingly laggy. Balfour, apparently, is living near the building from which C-SPAN is broadcast, which makes him a near-constant fixture. We're watching Balfour address the possibility of interstellar invaders when I receive a text from an unknown number.

> **Hey Johnny. It's Dean. You haven't responded to my emails and refuse to provide info. I'll be by in the next day or two to collect supplies. Hope you cooperate. Thnx.**

I feel my daughter watching me from the other side of the couch. "Dean and his people want our groceries," I explain.

"We're not going to do it, are we?"

"No," I say. "We're not."

But I don't relish Dean's impending visit. Not one little bit.

12

We're munching popcorn and attempting to watch a horror movie when Emma asks, "Why did Grandma commit suicide?"

I hit pause. "What made you think of that?"

"I always think about it."

I draw my knees up, and she does the same. "When my stepfather got sick..."

"Lou Gehrig's disease?"

I nod. "... my mom didn't know how to deal with it. He was only fifty-one, and he went downhill fast."

"How fast?"

"A year. By the end, she was doing everything for him. It was like he was already gone."

"How'd she die?"

"Why do you—"

"Just tell me."

I meet her big brown eyes. "She took too many pills. Almost a whole bottle."

She falls silent, chin on her fist.

"You okay?" I ask.

"It's sad we never got to meet them. Me and Sam."

I consider reminding her they didn't miss out on anything with my stepfather, but at the mention of Sam, my eyes begin to sting.

"Families belong together," Emma says, and I think of what my son said to me the night of his abduction, tossing my own mantra back at me: *Be a scientist, Dad.*

I feel my mouth drop open. Holy shit.

"Dad?" Emma asks. "What is it?"

"Get your drawings," I say, "and meet me in the basement."

When our school started offering online summer classes, I brought home materials so I could teach remotely. I'm struggling to tape a life-sized diagram of the human body to the basement wall when Emma hustles down the steps, *Finding Nemo* folder in hand. One side of the diagram exhibits all the major organs; on the other side are detailed renderings of the brain and heart.

"The first thing I need to say," I tell her over my shoulder, "is that we really know nothing about these creatures."

"We know they're abducting us," she counters. "We know they have powerful talons or fingers because we've seen the outlines of them whenever they snatch victims."

I add a swatch of masking tape to an upper corner of the diagram. "It's very little to go on. The aliens might be completely incomprehensible to us, their physiology like nothing we've ever imagined. They might not even have bodies in the traditional sense. Or families."

"You're stalling," she says.

I tear off another scrap of tape. "I'm just reminding you that

"Yes." I take a deep breath. "I believe the aliens have a brain disease. Why else fixate on the young?"

"Longer-lasting brains," Emma murmurs.

I nod. The thrum of discovery, of actually doing something, supercharges my body. "For humans, the brain is the final frontier of transplantation. We've never accomplished it, and it doesn't appear as though we'll figure it out anytime soon. But maybe they have."

"Balfour said they might be abducting people to reproduce. That could explain why they're all younger, right?"

I shake my head. "If you want to reproduce, you don't abduct family members. That's basic biology. The more diverse your gene pool is, the healthier the offspring will be. Plus, why abduct small children?" I move closer to the diagram. "They wouldn't want the entire brain. That would erase the identity of the recipient, supplant all familiarity between the aliens, all connections between family members. But harvesting specific parts of the brain and replacing dying cells with healthy ones? For example, the hippocampus, where episodic memories are stored—"

"Episodic?" Emma asks.

"Things that happened to you." I tap the diagram. "The cerebellum, which governs implicit memories." At Emma's look, I explain, "Muscle memory, basic biological functions . . . things that deteriorate at the end of life."

"Like what happened with your stepdad?"

My mouth goes dry. "Yes. Like that."

She hesitates. "Is it possible you're fixating on this theory because you've seen someone suffer from a brain disease?"

For a moment, I'm speechless. In truth, I hadn't considered the possibility.

She gives me a sad smile. "It's okay. Seeing that would've affected me too."

I clear my throat. "Right. There's also the prefrontal cortex, where short-term memory comes from. If they can take healthy tissue from these areas and replace the dying tissue in their family members..." I shake my head.

"What is it?" she asks.

I brace a hand on the wall. "There's a concept I keep coming back to, a force no one has been able to completely explain." I look at her. "You remember *Interstellar*?"

Her face lights up. It's one of our favorite movies. A wondering look comes into her eyes. "You're talking about love."

"I am. It's the most powerful force in the universe, yet no one really understands where it comes from. Maybe it exists in the mind. And if so, maybe the aliens have found a way to quantify love. To perform this procedure while preserving the parts of the brain where love resides."

"Maybe the aliens don't feel love."

"Maybe they don't. But from what we can tell, most of the advanced species on Earth, especially mammals, seem to feel love, or something like it." I run my fingers over the diagram. "What if they're blending our healthy brains, our consciousness, with their failing ones, but by matching relationships—husband-wife, sister-brother, father-daughter—they're able to restore their loved ones' minds without sacrificing their emotional bonds?"

I notice Emma fidgeting with her shirtsleeves.

"I know I'm making too many assumptions," I admit.

She shakes her head. "It isn't that. It's just... your theory makes things worse."

"How?"

"Could a person survive something like that? Having parts of your brain harvested?"

I lower my eyes and set the antenna aside. "Let's finish our movie, huh?"

She nods, but her expression is glum.

As I follow her up the stairs, I think, *Nice going, John. Next time, instead of being a scientist, be a dad.*

—

It's a quarter to nine the next morning when our doorbell rings. Without thinking too much about it—*Just act natural,* I tell myself—I abandon the pancake batter I'm whipping and move to the dining room, where I can peer through the picture window. I can't see Dean Dawson—he's screened from me by the outcropping house—but there are at least three others with him: Chris Burkhardt, Jeff Marino, and Buddy Scott. Marino's leaning into the lumberjack look, his bushy umber beard creeping down his neck and his already ursine frame growing fluffier from inactivity. Buddy Scott is his opposite, all bones and angles. It occurs to me I don't know Buddy's real name, and I really don't give a shit. Four people is too many. *One* is too many. But four? Just to persuade a father and his daughter to let you inventory their supplies?

They want to store *them*, I remind myself. *In the Boiler Barn.*

The doorbell rings again.

"Is it Dean?" Emma asks. Her face is tight, and I feel my tension tick up another notch. A kid who's been through so much already, the last thing she deserves is a band of dickweeds showing up uninvited and intimidating her father.

"Take over the pancakes for me, will you?" I say, and without waiting for a reply, I hustle up the stairs to retrieve the Ruger. I hope I won't have to use it, but this is too much. Guys like Dean talk about liberty, but what they're really talking about is *their* liberty.

I'm sweating by the time I open the interior door, gaze

through the storm door, and behold Dean in an *I-Mean-Business* outfit. Black shirt and black shorts that display a decent body for his age but not nearly as impressive as he believes it to be. I take stock of the others: all decked out in dark clothing.

All four carry guns.

Mine is tucked in the waist of my cargo shorts, in back because I'm afraid of shooting myself in the crotch. Also, I don't want to make this worse than it has to be. I know Emma's watching and what I do matters more because of that. We've lost so much already; I can't lose her respect.

"Hey, Johnny," Dean says through the glass. "Ready to get with the program?"

Burkhardt watches me evenly, Marino looks almost bored, but Buddy Scott, his jittery drinker's eyes skewer me, the pale-blue irises invaded by tendrils of bloodshot.

"We're doing fine," I tell them.

Dean's smirk never wavers. "You're not, Johnny. If you're not responsible enough to put your daughter's well-being above your pride, you need outside intervention."

"You're talking about raiding my house."

Dean winces. "God, really? We're your *neighbors*. Some of us even patronize your pitiful little shop."

Which is bullshit. Buddy once showed up asking for some obscure true-crime book I didn't carry and walked out grumbling. That's the sum total of their patronage.

Dean sighs. "So we're gonna do this the hard way, huh? Okay . . ." He reaches for the brass door handle, but I beat him there, straight-arm it open, the steel edge driving him back. The porch isn't large, so Dean has nowhere to go but off the three-foot drop. He lands badly, his foot jarring the mulch between the hosta plants, and he stumbles a few paces before he regains his balance and stands grimacing. "What the hell, Johnny?"

The other three have retreated to permit me room, so Marino and Buddy are ranged on the sidewalk, and only Chris Burkhardt remains on the porch beside me, looking shamefaced.

"C'mon, Johnny," Burkhardt says. "We're all friends here."

"Friends," I repeat.

"Well, sure," he says. "You see me driving through the neighborhood. I watch you and your son right there in the driveway, playing catch."

"My son was taken," I say. We're almost nose to nose. If I nudge him, he'll join Dean in the hostas.

Dean says, "You've been through something traumatic, none of us doubt that. But it's affected you. You're not thinking rationally."

"You want to take my food."

His face is incredulous. "The murder down on Meridian Street, Johnny. The wife assaulted—"

"So everyone needs the protection of the Country Club Mafia?"

Marino pushes out a fed-up grunt and mumbles something to Buddy.

"We've been patient with you," Dean says, "but our patience is just about gone."

Burkhardt's sweating. Not only is his face beaded, but his mauve T-shirt is pitted out. I nod at him. "You know what a farce this is, Chris. Call them off."

Burkhardt looks miserable. "Please, Johnny. You don't even have to use the barn. We just need to know what you've got in there."

"Why?"

"In case things get worse."

"Chris is right," Dean agrees.

I turn to Dean. "I've lost my wife and son. How can it get worse?"

Marino steps forward. "That's why you, more than anybody, should listen to reason."

I spot Emma in the dining room window. She looks scared enough to puke, and I wonder if there isn't something in what Dean is saying. *Am* I just being prideful? Am I putting Emma through more trauma just to satisfy my ego, to scratch out a Pyrrhic victory?

"Think of your daughter," Burkhardt says.

Dean creeps closer. "Just let us get an inventory and we'll forget this happened. We don't have to move the stuff today."

I look down at him.

No, I think.

No.

I bulldoze forward, my shoulder clipping Burkhardt. "*Oh shit,*" he mutters and nearly breaks his ankle dismounting the porch. Marino squares up to me, and I can't see Buddy Scott, but I tell myself, *Focus on Dean. He's the one who matters.* I step off the porch, and Dean retreats. I'm bigger than he is, and I can see he's never considered this fact. He casts a panicked look at the others, and I wonder if Buddy will draw his gun.

I stalk toward Dean. "Get off my property."

Dean's eyes flicker to the others. He tries a smile. "Johnny..."

I loom over him. "Get the fuck out of here."

When he doesn't answer, my hands shoot out, and he flails back several feet. He steadies himself. "You're really screwing this up, you know?"

"My daughter and I are making pancakes. Whatever you have, we don't need it."

Someone mutters something, the words unintelligible, and

I turn to find Marino restraining Buddy Scott. There's a gun in Buddy's hand.

"Let's just go," Burkhardt moans.

I reach back, my heart thundering, and remove the Ruger, and when Marino sees it, his expression changes, not to fear, but to comprehension. He's still grasping Buddy, but Marino's eyes tell me he's up for this, maybe even craves it.

Emma's watching us, her hands tented at her lips, and for the first time, I consider what might happen. If one of these men kills me, what will happen to her? I've never fired a gun, never even taken target practice. Jeff Marino and Buddy Scott are enthusiasts. The kind who've lusted their whole lives for a scenario like this.

"Let's go," Dean says in his courtroom voice. The others look at him, uncertain. But Burkhardt starts to move, and a few seconds later, the others follow.

"This was a big mistake, Johnny," Dean says. "You know how this will end."

I don't answer, just watch Dean's glitter-eyed gang skulk past.

"See you soon," Marino says.

The four of them trudge up Hillcrest Road. The only one who looks back is Buddy, his rheumy eyes dark with thwarted desire.

My limbs are trembly and sheened with sweat. From the doorway, Emma peers not at my face but at my hand.

I remember the gun. I go inside and I pause at my wife's Steinway. I'm feeling woozy and need to sit, but first I want this hunk of steel out of sight. I raise the piano bench, place the Ruger inside, then cover it with a songbook—*A Charlie Brown Christmas* by the Vince Guaraldi Trio.

"Dad."

I look at Emma.

"Pancakes?" she suggests.

I nod absently and close the piano bench. I don't like the Ruger there, but I want it nearby in case Dean and his entourage return.

When they return.

The day crawls by and we hardly speak. I hover near the front of the house without realizing I'm doing it, a dreadful gravity drawing me to the piano bench. I put a knee on it, as if I can keep it bottled up like some djinn. But by midafternoon, I realize Emma is uncharacteristically absent. I find her in her room. She's got earbuds in and tears in her eyes. I sit on the edge of her bed, and when I wrap my arms around her, she sobs into my chest and asks, "Are we going?"

"Going?"

"We can't stay, right? Those jerks will be back."

I'm aware of how far we are from the gun. What if Dean and his cronies break in and I can't get to it? Even if I can, what would I do against four of them? When they return, they might have heavier artillery.

"Maybe I should've let them in," I say, but the words are scarcely out of my mouth when Emma cuts in.

"Are you *crazy*? Where do you think it would've ended? If they take the food, that means we have to… what, go to Dean's every time we want to eat? Then they start assigning the women to cook it. And pretty soon… I saw them looking at me."

I'm gripped by dismal horror. *She's only a kid*, I think. *No one could possibly…*

But the more I consider Jeff Marino and the bored expression that only changed when he laid eyes on my gun… the more I think of Buddy Scott's psychotic stare…

I grasp her shoulders. "No one's going to hurt you."

"We have to go."

"Emma—"

"They're probably coming *right now*," she shouts. "We'll find a farmhouse—"

"We have less than a quarter tank of gas."

"—somewhere in the country."

"Emma..."

She pushes off the bed. "We have to *go*, Dad. It's stupid to stay here." She starts yanking clothes out of drawers.

"What makes you believe somewhere else is safer? There are Dean Dawsons all over. You think country people are automatically more reasonable?"

"There are fewer of them."

"Honey, you don't have as much experience—"

"Oh *please*," she snaps. "Please spare me the 'You're too young to understand' bullshit."

I can't help but recoil.

"You used that tone with Sam all the time." She wings a sweatshirt at the bed. "Acting like you were right because you're older, and look how that turned out."

It knocks the wind from my chest. "You want to be hurtful? Be hurtful. But here are the facts: We drive out to the hinterlands, we're exposing ourselves to whatever's doing this."

"You were outside the house today."

"We have no destination," I press on. "That's a pretty crucial detail, don't you think?"

"There are a thousand farmhouses."

"All stocked and ready for us, I'm sure. Just like going on vacation."

Her back is to me now, and I know I should stop, but I'm pissed.

"The chances of finding a barren house are close to zero. The best we could hope for is someone who'd take us in for a couple days."

"You don't know that."

"Would *you* want to take another family in? Give them our food? Share space with them twenty-four seven?"

No answer. She might be crying.

"And what if your mother and Sam come back—"

She turns and her eyes flash incredulously. "They're not coming back."

"I don't believe that."

"Because you can't stand to be wrong. You always have to have the last word."

"You're angry. I understand—"

"This isn't about me; it's about you. Haven't you noticed how Mom gave up arguing with you? It's because you always have to be right."

I gape at her. "You act like it's a bad thing, wanting them back."

"How many people have come back, Dad?" She steps closer. "Have you heard about a single person returning to their family?"

"Just because it hasn't happened doesn't mean—"

"We're all we've got," she says, her eyes brimming. "It's just you and me, and you're putting us in danger."

"Em..." I reach for her.

"No," she says and pulls away. "You want me to act like it's okay, but I won't. Not until you stop being so goddamn stubborn."

"Emma—"

"Just leave me alone," she says. "Please."

So final is her tone that I can only comply. I shut the door behind me and stand in the hall listening to her sobs.

13

We go to bed that night without reconciling. I've never been so miserable. Every word she spoke, every verbal dagger, is still embedded in me. Festering.

I'm out of anxiety pills. I've been telling myself I'll be fine without them, but increasingly I find my thoughts veering into those howling places where every mistake is replayed, where regret over the past and fear of the future reign.

I imagine my daughter alone at the lunch table. Shunned for an entire school year because her volleyball serve percentage was a trifle too low. What kind of a world punishes a kid for something so trivial? Even worse is the fact that Iris and I didn't even know about it, that Emma had to endure it alone, because we were evidently too busy with our jobs, too busy quibbling over money to save our family.

I roll onto my back and throw a forearm over my eyes, but the pain, bright and pink and mocking, fills my mind. I remember the conversation Iris and I had, the one where we decided to buy the bookshop.

But who am I kidding? *I* was the one who pushed for it. It

didn't matter that physical books were being replaced by audio and digital. For me, that was a reason to buy the shop. Like I could single-handedly save the print industry.

We were struggling financially, scarcely able to pay our mortgage. They tell you it's good to be the worst house in the best neighborhood, but what they don't tell you is that being the worst house in the best neighborhood is still really expensive. Iris's realtor commissions were slow, my teaching salary inadequate. We needed another source of income, and that's when I saw the For Sale sign in the campus bookstore window, then called O'Malley's Books. I went inside and talked to the owner, who I already knew from frequenting his shop. He didn't lie to me. Not exactly. But he did neglect to mention that the landlord was about to raise the rent.

It seemed like the perfect opportunity. I could work there during the summer months, and the rest of the year we'd employ college students the way O'Malley did. I'd be investing in my community, in my alma mater. Most importantly, it would help fund my children's college educations and give our family some breathing room.

But The Constant Reader Café didn't even break even. Our arguments about money intensified. Iris had never been frugal, and it killed me to even broach the topic of moving to a more modest house. That, I argued, was admitting defeat. Poetic justice, I guess, that she moved out and let me stay here.

I miss Iris. And not just because she was taken. I've missed her for the past year. It's been torture, though I've never admitted it. Not to her, not to Sam or Emma. And now it's too late. I once believed that every failed marriage was caused by infidelity. Hell, I used to say it. The moment I heard a couple was having problems, I'd joke, *Which one is cheating?* Now I know better. God, do I know better.

I don't believe Iris has seen anyone else since she moved out. I know I haven't. With teaching, and Sam and Emma, and the bookshop, I haven't had time. But even if I did have the opportunity to date, I can't see myself doing that. It's not that I don't have desires—it's just . . .

I still love my wife. And I'll probably never get the chance to tell her.

I close my eyes. From our backyard, some bird, a robin maybe, sings a lonesome nocturne. It makes me miss my family even more. I switch on my sound machine and try to distract myself with other, nonapocalyptic thoughts, yet all of them lead back to my family. I keep expecting Emma to make her way in, to stay with me the way she has since we lost her mother. But she doesn't, and it feels like I'm losing my last family member.

When I finally nod off, it's maybe two in the morning. In my dreams, I'm alone and wandering through an alien landscape. At some point in the small hours, I come awake and realize I'm not alone.

When I open my eyes, Em is hovering over me with her phone clutched to her chest.

"You okay?" I manage in a croaky voice.

"It's happening indoors now," she says.

I blink at her.

"They're in *houses*, Dad. They're taking people away, and the news is saying it's the end. The internet is failing, so it's hard to get a full story, but there are so many abductions, and they're all the same and . . . and . . ." I gather her into my arms and she's breaking down, and I realize she's already tied the orange cord around her waist, and instead of wanting me to hold her, she's looping the cord around me.

—

She's right about the internet. It's spotty as hell. It's just as well since the news has never been direr. Reports from all over the world confirm that the phenomenon is occurring inside buildings. Workers ripped from meatpacking plants. Doctors and nurses dragged screaming down hospital corridors. Parents taken from dinner tables.

Children snatched from their beds.

No one talks numbers anymore. It's beyond speculation. The news anchors have never looked so grim, the glitz and sizzle of the story gone. If they're infiltrating buildings, what good is a cord? There've been stories of tethered people being taken as pairs, one grabbed and the other jerked along for the ride.

Still . . . there've been enough anecdotes to give viewers some hope.

Two accounts from the Northeast—Maine and New Hampshire—both featuring welters of people grabbing a cord and engaging in a life-and-death tug-of-war. In one case, some construction workers were able to rescue their foreman, who escaped with a fractured leg and some contusions. In the other, two parents and a teenager saved a thirteen-year-old girl from abduction, though one of her feet was severed. The girl looked nothing like Emma, but her age bored into my brain and refused to be dislodged.

Another story from this morning: a woman in her mid-twenties whose fiancé was seized. She'd been standing next to him at a double vanity popping a pimple while he brushed his teeth, when he gasped, hit the floor, and skidded through the doorway. The jerk on their electrical cord had been so ferocious that the woman had been yanked off her feet and dragged too. She'd braced her bare feet on either side of the door, and just as it seemed her fiancé would be dragged into the nether, the invisible menace lost its hold. The man scrambled to his feet and stumbled into the bathroom, where they locked the door and huddled together in the bathtub until the danger passed. According to the man, who looked dazed rather than relieved, whatever had gripped him had been so powerful he was astonished his leg hadn't been ripped from his body. To substantiate this, he'd raised his foot for the camera, exhibiting three wine-dark bruises, each of them thicker than cucumbers.

Another story, this one a young father in Washington State saving his four-year-old boy. The father had been pushing his son on a backyard swing—why they were outside was a question the reporter was too merciful to ask—when the tethered boy reached the apogee of his arc... then proceeded into the air at a steep diagonal. The father was wrenched upward and just managed to hook his elbow around the swing chain. The cord tethering them was approximately twenty feet long, so when it went taut, there was a tremendous tug, one so powerful it broke the creature's hold. The child came tumbling down and landed on a boxwood bush. He was scratched up and his tibia had been fractured by the compression of the unseen creature's stranglehold, but he'd escaped severe injuries and sat happily on his dad's lap during the interview.

I imagine being like that dad, being Emma's protector. I realize I'm imagining myself protecting not only my daughter, but Iris and Sam as well, and I know I should cut that off, but it's so pleasing that I let the fantasy run on. I'm on the verge of crying, so I put a fist to my lips and listen to the TV report with Emma, even though the screen keeps freezing.

My musings circle back to the eternal question: Should we stay, or should we go? If they're snatching people from buildings, is one place better than another? Is the basement safer than the second floor? Is brick preferable to vinyl siding? The TV is still frozen on a reporter, her mouth half-open, her eyes in mid-blink. I look over at Emma and think, *What if it happens now? What do I grab on to?*

Where is safe?

As if to underscore this question, the TV jags into motion, and the next story warns that the video we're about to see is graphic and disturbing. I know I should turn it off, but I sit numbly as a dashcam shows an untethered policeman approaching a black SUV. Looking supremely uneasy, the cop bends down to peer into the car. After a moment, he stumbles backward, a forearm to his mouth. He's in the middle of the road when the driver's door opens and a woman steps out, her hands extended toward him. A cord trails behind her, and as she pursues the retching cop, an object tumbles out of the car behind her and is towed along by the tether. My mind doesn't make sense of what it's seeing, but as she shuffles on, dragging the object behind her, I realize it's a man's upper body, ripped in half just below the belt and bumping over the road like a mangled scarecrow.

Emma and I scoot closer together on the couch.

A couple days later, Emma asks, "So, why a bookstore?"

We're lying on the basement floor, a Lincoln Log fort between us. I'd bought two canisters for Sam when he was very young, but no one's used them since Emma was six. But with so much time on our hands, we've been resurrecting all sorts of childhood artifacts.

I add a log to the wall. "Books changed my life. When I was young, I didn't read because I didn't think I was smart enough."

She situates a blue window. "That's when you discovered Stephen King?"

"I was fourteen when I read him. For the first time, I felt capable. Clever even. Reading him improved my self-esteem."

"Why not become a librarian or teach English?"

I place a half log on the wall and wince when I almost topple the damn thing. "I was gonna major in English education, but my counselor at Purdue talked me into science instead. Said there were more of those jobs in the area."

Emma nods. "But why a bookstore?"

I glance at the stubby log in my palm. "Remember *The NeverEnding Story*?"

She smiles. "Sure. Atreyu. The Luck Dragon."

"Remember when the little boy hides in the bookstore and steals the book?"

She nods.

I nod. "That whole sequence . . . talking to the old bookdealer. Hiding in the school attic. The darkness, the storm . . . all of it. I wanted to create a store that made people feel that way."

She appears crestfallen.

"What?" I ask.

"I feel like we failed you. None of us are readers, not even Mom."

"Mom listens to audiobooks sometimes."

"Sam and I don't even do that," she says. "When we come to the shop, we only look at the coffee cups and the magnets."

"It's okay."

"It's important to you."

"Take it easy on yourself. You've got your whole life ahead of you."

A crooked grin. "What is it you always say?"

"There's no such thing as a nonreader. Just people who haven't found the right books."

"Hey, Dad? I shouldn't have yelled at you." I shake my head, but she overrides me. "I cussed at you. Sam didn't even do that, did he?"

"Actually, no."

"I'm sorry."

I don't want to ruin the moment by crying, but my eyes betray me. "Don't be sorry. You've been amazing."

"I was an asshole."

"You're the best friend I could ever ask for," I tell her. She reaches for me, and I kiss her head. "I love you, Em. I love you so much."

She tells me she loves me too, but amid the warmth, something sharp hews through me. I tense, acutely aware of this new emotion. And after a moment, I identify it:

Hatred. For the creatures. I hate them to the core of my soul. Humans are far from perfect, and perhaps we need a course correction. God knows we've made a mess of things.

But we don't deserve this. Culling. Extinction. Whatever the hell is happening, we don't deserve it.

And this incredible girl doesn't deserve *any* of it. She deserves laughter and joy, and I'm gonna get her through this. It's all I have left.

She's all I have left.

14

It's late afternoon, the time of day when we used to eat. But Emma and I rarely feel hungry this early anymore. It's a time of shadows and melancholy and wondering if this will ever end. I tell myself we should be grateful to have each other, but my mind wanders to the past, to the things I didn't do or should have done better. Or the future, which is even worse. What if this never ends? The human race gradually picked off, our safety ever dwindling, reduced finally to hideouts no larger than closets, makeshift cells from which we're too afraid to venture. What kind of life is that? What if, ten years from now, Emma and I are still in hiding? Will she never get to be a college student? Will she never get to meet someone, have kids, and mess them up the way Iris and I did? She deserves to, damn it. Deserves every good thing, every single thing she wants.

We're at the island, both of us with books. I realize I'm not reading but listening. The neighborhood has been quieter today, the only sounds the persistent knock of a woodpecker on some distant tree and the plaintive cry of a finch. As I sit here, the words on the page doubling because of insufficient light and my rapidly aging eyes, I realize I'm listening for Dean Dawson and his men. Someone like Dean, he's got to save face. He'll demand justice for the incident on the lawn. Maybe he'll strong-arm his way in here, have Jeff Marino or that freak show Buddy Scott hold me at gunpoint. Maybe Buddy will shoot me. The gleam in his eyes suggested he'd like to. I listen for their voices or the doorbell, but they don't come. What comes is a low-toned hum, a buzz not unlike that of an overstrained air conditioner.

My chest constricts. I set my book on the island. Emma is looking at me with wide eyes. She hears it too. Oh, Jesus.

I slide my chair back and nod at the cord around her waist. "Make sure it's tight."

Her hands tremble as she tests it. I rise from the chair and edge into the open space where the rooms converge: the kitchen behind me, the family room to my left, the living room to my right. The buzz-hum comes from the living room. The front of the house.

I reach back and Emma is there. Her warmth reassures me, and as I rotate my body to face the sound, I make sure she is squarely behind me. Our tether has plenty of slack, so I wind it around my arm, and Emma is shaking violently now. My movements are brisk but steady, a calm falling over me. Whatever this is, it's in front of us, and it has to go through me to get to her.

I won't let it.

The buzz-hum grows louder.

I wind the extension cord around my wrist and tell myself it'll have to rip my arm off to get my daughter. I brace my feet apart. If I'm hauled forward, there's the doorway ahead, and I can starfish my limbs to catch myself, to give us that jarring break that the woman in the bathroom used to save her fiancé, that the father in Washington utilized to save his little boy.

I bare my teeth. No one is taking Emma. No one.

The buzz grows louder, deeper. I fill my lungs, but my

breathing grows shallower. The sound, it's too much like the one I heard the night of Sam's abduction, that damnable chorus that filled the highway when I lost my wife. This can't be happening again, it can't. They've already taken so much from me—

Stop it! Concentrate!

I finish winding the cord around my forearm. I consider moving with Emma into the coffin-like half bath. I even start to sidle us in that direction. Then I glimpse a flash of crimson fabric through the window.

Someone on the sidewalk.

"Son of a bitch," I mutter.

The creatures and Dean's men have arrived at the same time.

The buzz-hum sounds like it's emanating from the front room, the source near the window, but it's difficult to tell, our open floor plan sending echoes in all directions. The Steinway and its bench aren't far from me.

Just go away, I think as a shadow flits over the window. *Just leave us alone.*

The doorbell clangs.

For a fleeting moment, I want whoever it is to break in, to saunter into whatever is creating the buzz-hum. I picture the assholes smashing the door in, Dean leading the way, Dean striding right into the creature's grasp, his face slack with shock, his body yanked into the ether and his men scattering when they realize what they've walked into. I'm picturing their shrieking retreat when something smashes through the front window and clunks to a stop next to the couch. It's a Wisconsin boulder, softball-size and pink with gray flecks. We use them to border our garden beds.

"*John Calhoun!*" Dean bellows. Like a lawman in some old Western. "*You and your daughter have one minute to come out!*"

A silence. Then, "Dad?"

Emma's voice is muffled because she's speaking into the back of my shirt. The fear in her voice and the trembling of her body enkindles in me a rage unlike any I've experienced. The buzz-hum—the *thing*—is in my home. Threatening us. And those jackwads are in my yard, God knows how many, threatening to storm our house. I don't muse about people being as bad as the creatures because I'm not feeling philosophical. Because this... this is primitive. Life wants what other life has. What's mine is mine—what's yours is negotiable. You either go with that, become one of the takers, or you cling to some scrap of goodness.

But if I box us inside the bathroom, Dean and his men will break in and, at the very least, loot our possessions. Most likely, they'll rip open the door and drag us out and whale on me and do God knows what to my daughter. I think of Jeff Marino and Buddy Scott, the stolid gleam in the former's eyes and the lunatic hunger in the latter's.

And they're not even the most dangerous part of this situation, not by a long shot. The invisible creatures are coming for us, and if they can get in here, they can pursue us anywhere. The bathroom, the basement, the Highlander if we make a break for it. This is the third incident with the creatures and our family. They're after us for a reason.

We can't hide. Can't flee.

The only answer is to fight.

I lower my eyes to the piano bench fifteen feet away.

A pounding on the door. "C'mon, John..."

Chris Burkhardt.

"...just let us in and it'll be over. You'll be able to access the Boiler Barn any time. After your detainment, it'll be like normal..."

Detainment? I think. *Are you kidding me?*

"Dad?" Emma whispers.

Another shape swoops at us, and I barely have time to register the boulder before it crashes through a windowpane and batters the hardwood floor with a concussive *thunk*. Jesus. The boulders have to weigh ten pounds. How the hell are they lobbing the things in?

Marino, I decide. The dude is dangerous and amoral, and I can't let him anywhere near my daughter.

"Get back, honey," I mutter.

"No," she promptly answers.

I grit my teeth. No time to explain. The last boulder landed five feet from me. The men out there have guns. The problem is, to get to the piano bench I've gotta get closer to the buzz-hum.

It's growing louder. More jagged. I can't believe I've fixated on the men outside when the real danger is in my house.

Go upstairs, a voice urges. *Go to the basement. Just get Emma away from the buzz.*

At any moment, something will come through the… what? The portal? The gateway? No one knows how it works, but one moment you're here, the next you're lost forever.

Not forever, I tell myself. But my conviction is weak. I can't cling to it.

"You're down to twenty seconds!" Dean bellows. "I'll fire a warning shot at zero. Then we're coming in."

"Family room," I tell Emma, waving her back, and this time, she listens to me. If Dean fires a gun, I don't want Emma anywhere near it.

The buzz-hum is crackling now, the hair on my forearms standing to attention. Deep in my gut, there's a slithery feeling. My heart thunders, a rapid tattoo throbbing in my temples. I'm sweating, creeping forward, the piano bench six feet away. I'll grab the gun, hustle back to Emma, and make my stand in the rear of the house. If the creature comes for us, I'll blast it. If Dean or anyone else breaks in, I'll shoot them too.

The buzz-hum amplifies. My fillings thrum in my molars. The electrical pulse in the air reminds me of a lightning storm about to unleash. Three feet away, I reach out. It occurs to me as my fingers near the piano bench that the creature might seize me, might haul me through the portal, and Emma would be dragged along behind me, screaming, helpless.

Better be quick.

I touch the lid, and a teeth-rattling crack rips the day, Dean's warning shot. For a split second, I'm frozen, my fingers on the bench. Then I hear Emma say, "Dad?"

I turn. Emma's standing in the rear of the family room, forty feet from me. Behind her, I can see the dreary daylight in the windows. There's no blood on her white T-shirt, nothing visibly wrong.

Except the way she's standing. Ramrod straight. As if… as if…

"We're coming in!" Dean shouts, but I scarcely hear him. I take a step toward Emma, unconsciously grasping the extension cord. I stride toward her and swiftly pay the cord through my sweaty hands, and for a moment, it's taut.

"*Dad?*" Emma whispers. I limp toward her. There are indentations on her arms, as if she's being gripped by invisible talons. And she's—*oh, Jesus Christ*—she's floating two feet off the floor.

Her eyes are welling with tears, and she's never looked so small or young, and I'm rushing toward her, and that's when the cord between us drops, severed, and I look up, reach for her, and she's yanked backward, her hands splayed toward me, the toe of a sneaker grazing my fingertips. I dive for her and crash against the wall.

But Emma is gone.

PART THREE
SEVERED

15

My mind can't process what happened. All I know is Emma's gone, and so is my life. There's a heavy thud. A face appears at the side door, the light blotted out by Jeff Marino's broad shoulders.

Tap tap tap.

I swivel my head to the back door, where Buddy Scott stands leering at me, the creepy fuck.

From the front of the house, the thudding comes again, and I think, *Battering ram?* Where the hell did they get one of those? Then, a crash brings my attention to the side door, where an aluminum bat has just obliterated the glass, Marino chopping down at the tempered window like a lumberjack splitting a cord. Another thud from the front of the house, then a crunching *BOOM*, and I know they've shattered the door.

I remember the piano bench.

I sprint that way, and Marino snatches at me, knocks me off stride, and I swerve toward the island, shove away from it, and stumble toward the living room. They're pouring through—Dean, Burkhardt, others—and though they don't know I'm going for the bench, they'll get to me before I reach it. I launch myself at Dean, shoulder-first, and I upend him, but hands are grabbing for me. I push to my feet, but someone falls on me. Fists batter my rib cage. I double over, am struck between the shoulder blades, and suddenly, I'm face down on the hardwood. I attempt to rise but a boot catches me in the kidney. Something bashes the side of my head, and the pain is secondary to the outrage of having them do this to me in my own home. Part of me welcomes this, this punishment. Expiation for my failure. Emma is irretrievable and none of this matters, the blood dripping from my head, the expletives and abuse. I'm borne toward the door, a pair of men hooking my armpits and others grasping my legs, and I see one of my neighbors holding the storm door open, smiling as though eager for a tip. Then I'm manhandled down the porch steps into the yard, where I'm dropped, the grass cool under my bloody palms.

"John Calhoun," Dean calls, "you have turned your back on your community. You've thought only of yourself and have only yourself to blame. You will be remanded to the detention center, and your daughter will be put to work."

The fact that Emma's been taken and this sadistic son of a bitch doesn't know it rallies my fighting spirit. I push to hands and knees and peer at him through a scrim of blood and down-hanging hair. He stands, arms akimbo, at the base of the porch and sneers, "All you have to do is apologize."

"Fuck you," I say. Blood drools from my lower lip.

He struts toward me. Behind him, goons flood out my front door with canvas storage bags stretched to bursting. Our food. Our possessions.

Dean says, "Everyone has gone along, Calhoun. Everyone." He spreads his arms to make his point, and I become aware of just how many people are out here. Two dozen at least. Mostly men but a few women scattered here and there.

"Here we are," Dean continues, "attempting to make sense of this terrible new normal. Trying to find order in the ruins. And you insist on clinging to self-interest."

I manage a few drunken strides before a knife-thrust of pain pierces the base of my skull and I'm down again. Dean does a little crow hop and boots me in the underjaw. The pain is immense, searing, and I'm on my back staring up at the oak boughs, the patches of slate-gray sky.

Emma, I think. *Emma*.

Dean crouches over me and whispers, "We need to make an example of you, Johnny. I'm sorry. It's the only way to win over the holdouts."

The insanity of the statement is blotted out by a *whooshing* sound, and when I turn, I see a flicker within the house and a wisp of white smoke through the shattered living room window.

"*No*," I murmur.

"Tell us where your daughter is so we can save her before the place turns into an inferno."

"Don't," I say and try to roll onto my stomach. But the pain is too intense, my body a glancing drumbeat.

"Last chance," Dean says.

"Don't burn my house," I manage, but Dean addresses someone else.

"She must've run for it. Track her down and bring her back."

My chest heaves. I push to my knees. "You'll pay," I tell him, but even to my ears I sound defeated. Slurry.

"Let it be known," Dean announces, "that Calhoun is threatening me." He starts pacing. "Just like the other day. In front of three witnesses, in front of his daughter. He pulled a *gun* on me. Didn't you, Johnny?"

There's fervent assent, Dean's congregation surrounding me, blighting my yard with their glazy-eyed zealotry.

"I treated you with civility," Dean continues, "with respect. And what did you give me in return? Threats. Promises of violence."

"Kill him!" someone shouts.

Dean pauses. "I'm just your appointed servant. I'll abide by the will of the group."

"Do it!" someone shouts.

"Kill the motherfucker," a woman says.

A figure breaks free from the throng. Chris Burkhardt. He murmurs something, but Dean hardly seems to notice. Dean's eyes glitter out at the crowd. "What will it be? Lock him up, or deal with him here?"

"Deal with him!" comes the immediate response. Someone protests, and a flurry of voices hushes that up, and below that, I hear a low hum. A buzz-hum?

But it isn't. Nothing would please me more than the invisible monsters taking Dean right now, taking Marino, taking all these ghouls. Taking me, for that matter. I have nothing anymore.

"So what will it be?" Dean asks as if he hasn't already received the answer, and I realize this is what he's wanted all along. This time there are no dissenting voices, no help from anyone. Burkhardt has evidently seen which way the winds are blowing and doesn't want to get swept away. Dean takes out his gun.

Executed on my front lawn, I think. Smoke vomits from the shattered windows, the living room licked by orange tongues of flame. The humming gets louder. Guttural now. Aggressive.

Dean calls, "All in favor, say aye."

The voices answer in unison.

Something in the house pops. A lightbulb maybe.

"Those opposed?" Dean asks.

Not a single voice speaks up.

"Then if everyone's in agreement, I'll carry out the unanimous will of the people."

Smoke engulfs us. Dean waves it away and coughs.

"Finish him," someone mutters.

"Too bad Buddy isn't here," Marino says.

"Well, find him," Dean answers.

"He's hunting for the daughter," Marino explains, and a vulgar ripple of laughter greets this. White smoke envelops us, crawls like a fog over the lawn, and through the ghostly haze, I see the gun float up until it rests against my temple.

"John Calhoun, you have given me no choice. Let this be a lesson to all who attempt to hurt the community, who attempt to impinge on our freedoms with their selfish tyranny."

The hum grows, but it's not the creatures. It's a car. The muffler is shit, and it's growling down the hill toward us, and all the fanatics turn, looking annoyed.

For a moment, the muzzle of Dean's gun remains against my temple. Then the car—the sea-green beater—materializes out of the smoky haze, jumps the curb, and marauds over the grass toward us. Mob members scatter, and the piece-of-shit car skids to a halt six feet from me and Dean. The gun finally goes away, and I hear him demand, "Who the hell are you?"

Doors fly open and two figures step out. My eyes are watering from the smoke, and Dean's voice is muffled, but I still make out, "...out of here! Just who do you think—" But a mountainous figure crashes into Dean and catapults him backward. Someone seizes me. I resist, assuming it's another mob member, but then I'm at the car, being shoved inside, and piling into the backseat with me is a younger guy with a bushy red beard and curly red hair under a Dodgers baseball cap. He's muttering something to the driver, a woman in her early twenties with a dark blonde ponytail.

She shouts something, and then she starts to drive. A burly figure lumbers through the cloud of smoke, lunges through the open passenger door, and we swerve around the oak tree and loop toward the road, the car jouncing over my yard toward a man I don't recognize, but the man has a gun, is aiming it at us, and the Dodgers fan shouts, "Look out, Miranda!" and instead of twisting the wheel, she heads straight for the gunman. The smoke isn't as dense where he's standing, one foot on the curb and one on the road, so I see his eyes swell to moons when he realizes he's about to be run down, and as he pivots to dive out of the way, the front of the car pops him in the left butt cheek and hurls him into the road.

The driver, Miranda apparently, cuts the wheel in an attempt to avoid the curb on the opposite side of the street. She bounces right over it, and for two or three seconds, we're hiccuping through my neighbor's yard. Then she wrestles the junkheap back toward the road, and I hear her laughing. The guy in the Dodgers cap is shaking his head. I glance at the big man in the front seat, the man who tackled Dean. He's got a goatee, bushy black hair, and I remember him outside the police station the day after Sam's abduction. Jae-Hyun is his name, but he goes by Jae.

Dodgers Cap says, "You're a crazy son of a bitch, Miranda," and when I catch her reflection in the rearview mirror, she tips me a wink.

I look at the Dodgers fan.

He shakes his head, face pale. "Stone cold crazy."

We hardly talk on the way out of the neighborhood. I can't think of anything except my daughter. Dodgers Cap turns out to be Tommy, and Tommy keeps twisting in his seat to see if we're being pursued. It doesn't seem we are, but what does it matter? Emma's gone. I should probably thank the people who saved me, but I can't muster the energy.

"Jae told us about you," Tommy says. "Guess it's good we came along when we did."

Miranda must see my frown because she drawls, "We check the database of folks who've had people taken. You're on it twice. Your son and your wife."

A pause.

"You had a daughter," Jae says gently. "Did those people…"

"She was taken. Right before they dragged me out."

Tommy's voice is tight. "From inside?"

I don't bother answering. We've taken a left toward campus, and I wonder fleetingly about my shop. Whether it's been looted. We roll down the hill, past Mackey Arena. The stoplights don't even blink red. Everything is dead.

"We've got a lot to talk about," Miranda says.

"Give him a moment," Jae tells her.

"Ain't got a moment," she answers. "Especially if one of them peckerheads back there follows us."

"If there's trouble, we deal with it," Tommy says.

Miranda turns a gum-chewing grin on him. "You mean Jae'll deal with it."

Tommy stares out the side window.

"Where are we going?" I ask.

"A safe place," Tommy answers.

"Nowhere's safe if they're taking people from inside," Miranda reminds him.

Tommy glares at her. "Dammit, Miranda!"

"No use sugar-coatin'."

Tommy flails his hands, and I notice the young man, who's maybe twenty-five, has got chiseled arms. "They haven't found us yet."

"She's right," I say. "The thing... it severed the cord. Right in my family room. It grabbed my daughter..." And before I realize it, I'm crying. "Please take me to my shop."

"Shop?" Tommy asks.

"The Constant Reader Café."

"That's yours?" Jae asks, brightening. "My girlfriend loves that place. She's the one with orange hair? Bunch of piercings?"

I remember her. She likes poetry, which sticks out to me since almost no one browses poetry, much less buys—only undergrads dabbling in the Romantics.

Miranda's eyes swing up to the mirror. "Jae's girl got taken early on."

Tommy shakes his head. "Jesus."

"They took both my parents," Miranda explains. "Tommy here, they took his twin brother."

"Could we please stop talking about it?" Tommy asks.

"Miranda had multiples," Jae says. "Even with all the abductions, the odds are against having multiple people from a family taken at different times. Miranda's dad was taken first, her mom later." Jae's eyes sweep me up and down. "Yours were taken at three different times."

"Guess you're the champ," Miranda says.

"Goddammit, Miranda!" Tommy shouts.

"She's right," I say.

They all look at me.

I stare straight ahead. "I win."

16

The Physics Building is a place I know well. My grandpa worked there as supervisor of the store where all the professors in the science department would go for supplies. Grandpa would keep inventory, help the profs get what they needed, and drink coffee with them when they felt like chatting. Not all of them did. Grandpa's was a nondegreed position, which made him a nonperson to some of them. But to others, as to me, he was a cheerful, good-hearted man who was more perceptive than just about anyone I've ever known. He died a couple years ago at ninety-five, and I still haven't gotten over it.

Miranda guides us past the Neil Armstrong Building and hooks a left at a service road. I remember as we pull up to the rear that this was where they'd deliver supplies for the store, remember Grandpa explaining it to me when I visited as a kid. And reflecting on his smile reminds me of my son, Samuel Lewis Calhoun, named for my grandfather, and my eyes are leaking again, and I think, *What am I doing here?*

"Take me to my shop," I say.

"Just come in for a few minutes," Jae says. "After that, we can go wherever you want."

Miranda creeps us closer to the massive rolling door and says, "Your turn, Tommy."

Tommy gapes at her. "I did it yesterday. Hell, you sat in the car while we got out and saved this guy."

"I was behind the wheel, dipshit. The Green Goblin isn't self-driving."

"The longer we sit here, the more dangerous it is," Tommy says. This close to him, I smell the kid's sweat. The brim of his hat is dark with it.

"So type in the code," Miranda says.

"It's not my turn," Tommy persists.

Jae heaves a sigh and opens his door. As he lumbers over to the keypad, I notice he hunches forward to present a lower profile. The door rattles up. Jae ducks under it. Miranda pulls in after him and stops the car. The door rumbles down, and we climb out. There are two other vehicles in the loading bay, a sleek black BMW and a white Toyota van a couple years newer than the one Iris drove.

The group leads me through a door, down a short hall, down some stairs, the basement illumined with a pinkish light. I'm surprised to note Miranda's only five one or so. It might be the pink fluorescents, but it seems there's a strawberry tint to her dirty-blonde hair. She's got a smattering of freckles on her cheeks and nose, and her eyes are a striking shade of hazel green. She's wearing a red-and-black flannel shirt over frayed jean shorts, the cuffs of the flannel rolled up past her elbows.

We reach a fork in the hallway, and Tommy leads us right. We move that way for a stretch, and at the next T, we go left.

Jae explains, "We've been moving everything to the basement."

"Tracey thinks it's safer there," Miranda says. "You know, since they've started coming indoors."

They, I think.

I imagine Emma ahead of me, the pink-lit corridor becoming my family room, the toes of Emma's shoes hovering in the air.

They.

The depressions on her arms, her skin white under the brutal press of the creature's talons.

They.

My fingertips skim her sneaker as she flies backward into nothingness.

If I had a gun right now, I'd shove it in my mouth.

"They move him yet?" Jae asks, and Tommy throws him a look I can't interpret. Fear? Embarrassment?

We pass a propped door into a lengthy room, maybe fifteen-by-forty, that reminds me of an industrial kitchen; only instead of sinks and stoves, rolling carts are scattered about, tables that don't quite align, desks on opposite sides of the room. There are corkboards, but nothing is pinned to them. I stand there taking it all in, and Jae goes ahead of us and almost crashes into another man sweeping through the inner door. This guy is tanned and wears a lavender polo shirt, his black hair parted on the right. The man clutches his chest and says, "Jesus, Jae, you scared the hell out of me."

"My bad," Jae says. "John Calhoun, this is Dr. Richard Kehler."

Kehler notices me. "Calhoun? One of the two-timers?"

"Three," Miranda says. "His daughter just got taken."

Kehler blinks. "I'm sorry."

"Tracey around?" Tommy asks.

Kehler nods over his shoulder. "In the lab." He finally takes in my physical state. "My God. What happened to you? Don't tell me you *fought* one of those things."

I don't respond.

Jae explains, "A mob of people. They set fire to his house."

I should say something, but I can't. Not only is my pain ratcheting up, hatchet strokes that make it difficult to remain upright, the grief is so raw that I don't want to be anywhere and certainly not in the center of this sterile space being scrutinized by strangers.

Kehler smiles bracingly. "Well, I'm glad we were able to rescue you."

Tommy backpedals from the group. "I gotta piss. Be back in a minute."

Miranda looks at Kehler. "You gonna show him Whitey?"

The man stiffens. "That will be up to Tracey."

"She still got your balls in a sling?" Miranda asks.

Kehler gives her a look, seems about to respond, then fetches a sigh. "Mr. Calhoun, perhaps we should show you where we're bunking."

The room plunges into darkness.

"Son of a bitch," Miranda says. "They finally did it. They knocked out the power."

Kehler's phone throws a wedge of light over us.

"Shouldn't the generator kick on?" Jae asks.

"Internet works," Miranda says, peering at her phone.

"For now," Kehler answers.

Lights flood back on.

"Thank God," Kehler says, pocketing his phone. "Have you told Mr. Calhoun what we're doing here?"

"He just got the shit beat out of him," Miranda explains.

"The monsters took his daughter," Jae says, and somehow the way he says it makes me feel like a human being again and not a hollowed-out husk.

Kehler winces. "Could we please not call them monsters?"

"Why not?" Miranda says. "Fuckers took my mama and daddy. You gotta be a monster to do that."

"Amen," Jae says.

Rapid footsteps sound from the other room. Tommy bursts in, chest heaving, and rests his hands on his knees. "Holy shit . . . I was in the bathroom when the lights went out . . . phone's almost dead." He shakes his head. "I started imagining what it'd be like to be trapped down here. All alone. Whole damn building's a maze. You could stumble around in the dark until you starve to death." He makes a face. "I pissed all over myself."

When we notice the stain on his cargo shorts, Jae and Miranda start to crack up.

He glares at them. "What the hell's so funny?"

Jae leads me to a low-ceilinged room. There are two mattresses stacked against the far wall, no box springs. Without pause, he ambles over there, balls up a baby-blue blanket, chucks it aside, and drags the top mattress off. Hauling it across the room, he says, "I'll give you as much space as I can, but it'll be tight." He lets the mattress flop, then scoots it against the unpainted trim board. He sees me eyeing the narrow mattress. "You'll only be here a few nights."

"I'm a bad sleeper," I tell him.

He lets out a mirthless chuckle and crosses to a door I first mistook for a closet but now see is a bathroom. "I think a custodian used to live down here."

I follow him to the bathroom and look around.

He nods. "Shower works fine. Toilet, sink." He sets to scrubbing his face, and I stand there musing about nothing except my daughter's expression when that thing took hold of her.

When Jae rinses off, I ask, "What do you mean I'll only be here a few nights?"

Water drips from his beard. "I better let Tracey explain that." He plucks a towel from beside the sink and wipes his face. "This is her show. Kehler's her second-in-command."

"She a doctor too?" I ask.

"Astrophysicist," he answers, then nods at me. "How about you get cleaned up? Your nose is leaking blood."

I glance at myself in the mirror and realize he's right. I look terrible. One side of my face is puffy, and there are contusions on my cheeks and forehead. My bottom lip is split and beginning to crust over. I spit into the basin, my saliva bright red.

Jae brushes past me, his broad shoulders barely squeezing through the door.

"There are hundreds of rooms in this building," I tell him. "I don't want to offend you, but I think I'll—"

"I'm not thrilled about it either," Jae interrupts. "But since it's happening indoors now, we're bunking together until the procedure."

"Procedure?"

"Tracey's the one who figured it out."

I lower my chin. "Figured *what* out?"

Jae slings the towel over his shoulder. "How to get our families back."

I shower off the blood and dirt. Every inch of me aches, but I have to know if what Jae said is true. If it turns out to be false hope, I might kill him.

By the time I'm out, Jae's got clothes for me. "They're Kehler's," he explains. "He's the closest to your build."

Kehler is a couple inches shorter than me and rail-thin, but though the red T-shirt and beige cargo shorts are snug, they're better than nothing.

Jae and I head back to join the others. Miranda and Tommy are circling each other in the middle of the long room, Tommy concentrating, Miranda grinning. But even though the two of them are sort of a spectacle, it's the figure in the far corner that seizes my attention. She's seated at a desk, angled away from me. She's got shoulder-length hair, her violet ensemble business casual with the exception of her sneakers, which once might have been white but are now a scuffed beige.

Giving Tommy and Miranda a wide berth, I move deeper into the room. The woman is poring over papers, wearing a frown and a pair of glasses that teeter on the tip of her nose.

"Try this one," I hear Miranda say, and I look up in time to see her lunge at Tommy, who stumbles back. She loops a punch that Tommy is just able to parry, then throws another at his groin, which he swats away with the side of his hand.

"Too low," he says, slightly out of breath. "That's illegal."

"Fuck legal," Miranda says and comes in with a sweeping kick at Tommy's knee. Tommy crumples sideways and rocks on the floor, cursing and writhing.

"*Jesus Christ*," he manages, eyes squinched shut. "You told me you wanted to learn how to box."

"You said you knew how," Miranda answers.

"I do," Tommy moans. "Best in my division."

"You were in the military?" I ask.

"Minor League Baseball. Me and a few teammates boxed in the offseason."

Jae grins. "Wanted to be ready in case the benches cleared?"

Tommy winces, tries to stand. "Just a way to stay in shape."

"Doesn't seem like it worked," Miranda comments.

"Been out of the league two years," Tommy says and hobbles over to sit. "Knee injury."

Miranda eyes Jae. "What do you say, big fella? Wanna try me out?"

"I need my knees," Jae says.

My eyes drift to the woman at the desk, whose attention hasn't wavered from her papers.

"Tracey goes into these trances," Jae explains. "We find it's best to just leave her alone."

Still massaging his knee, Tommy eyes Tracey. "It's sort of spooky."

"Want a hug?" Miranda asks him.

Tommy considers. "Maybe."

Miranda grins. "Not until you show me you can take a punch."

I drift toward the far corner of the room, toward the astrophysicist who's leading this group. Where she's leading them I have no idea, but as I draw closer, I make out more details. She writes with her left hand, which clinks slightly from a silver charm bracelet. There's scar tissue on the back of her right hand, which clutches the edge of the desk.

I don't want to startle her, so I clear my throat.

Without turning, she says, "John Calhoun."

I glance at the paper beside her scarred hand, which is crisscrossed with equations. "Is that for fun?"

She takes off her glasses, rises, and faces me. Large brown eyes, expressive mouth, subtle dimple in her chin.

"They tell me your daughter was taken today."

I can't answer her. My eyes tingle and my throat tightens.

Tracey seems about to say something but pauses, glancing down at her folded hands, and when her eyes climb back up to mine, her gaze is gentler. "You teach biology. Maybe you can help us."

I glance at her papers. "It's nice of you to make me feel useful, but I don't think—"

"I haven't studied biology since I was an undergrad," she interrupts. "Are you willing to help or not?"

I shrug.

"Come on," she says and brushes past me.

I follow Tracey past the others, who watch us in silence. Tracey advances toward the long room's inner door but pauses, her scarred fingers on the knob. "Are your hands clean?"

"Just showered."

She opens the door, and I follow her inside. This room is lime-green tile from floor to ceiling, and a fluorescent tube flickers in the far corner. As we move deeper inside, two features stand out—the first, a thicket of floor lamps arranged to face the same direction; the second, a door at the far end.

Standing by the door is a tall woman, bespectacled and curly haired. She looks like she's in her late twenties, and I know her already. She's been in the shop quite a bit and even buys things from time to time. Horror novels and books on UFOs.

Tracey says, "John Calhoun, Beatrice Berry. My assistant."

Beatrice smiles. "Your store is my happy place."

Tracey nods at the flickering light. "Need that replaced by tomorrow."

"Kehler said he'd do it," Beatrice answers.

"Tell Jae," Tracey says. "Then it'll actually get done."

I nod at the wooden door, its blond wood sallow in the greenish light. "That where Whitey is?" I ask.

Tracey makes a face. "I wish they'd stop calling him that. His name is Eric Pruitt."

"He's a local artist," Beatrice explains, but there's really no need. I've seen Pruitt's stuff in the downtown galleries, a few murals on campus. There's one in the alley across the street from my shop. He's talented, late thirties. He browsed the art books a lot but rarely bought anything.

"He's in there?" I ask.

Tracey folds her hands. "Eric is the linchpin of our efforts. He's the only person who's seen the ones responsible for what's happening."

I stare at her. "You mean the creatures?"

Tracey nods. I look at Beatrice, whose gaze is pale with dread. The defective fluorescent stutters and buzzes.

"Eric suffered a brain injury a decade ago," Tracey says. "You've seen the scar?"

I picture the man in my mind, his colorful shirts, his skinny jeans. I think of his wispy, malnourished mustache, his tousled hair. I touch the base of my skull. "Back here?"

Tracey nods. "Eric was in a devastating car accident. His accident enables him to see what others can't."

And at her words, I recall the mural in the alley across from my bookshop. It's surreal, the colors slightly off. It features the Purdue Memorial Mall, a green space in the middle of campus fringed with maples and hickories and stately old buildings with a clock tower and fountain. But the mural isn't realistic. The light is tinged with tangerine and purple, despite a bloodred sun. It reminds me of Lovecraft. Sometimes, when business was slow, I'd stand at the picture window and peer into the alley and study the bizarre colors, the trees and clock tower and fountain all slightly askew, slightly... runny. Like a Salvador Dalí painting.

"Invisible spectrum," I murmur.

Tracey looks at Beatrice, who's watching me glitter-eyed. "That's what we think," Beatrice says.

I consider. "Pruitt claims to have seen the creatures?"

"It's not a claim, Mr. Calhoun," Tracey answers.

Beatrice nods eagerly. "He's told us about them. When he's lucid."

"And how often is that?"

Tracey's expression goes grim. "Beatrice, you're the best with him. Will you..."

Beatrice produces a key ring from her pocket. "Eric insists that we lock him in." She fits the key in the lock, which opens on a stark-white room. The reek that wafts out on the overwarm air makes my eyes water.

Tracey says, "We've finally gotten him to use the toilet. Flushing is another matter."

Beatrice ventures inside. I follow. The brightness of the space is owing to the fluorescent tubes above us and the lack of any covering. There are multiple lamps stationed about, which account for the ten-degree heat difference. The odors of stale urine and feces force me to breathe through my mouth. In the left corner is a doorway from which more lunar-white light pours. In the far-right corner, there's a patchwork wooden box with one side missing.

"Eric?" Beatrice says. "I want you to meet someone."

The only response is a whimper.

"We're sorry to spring this on you," Tracey says, "but time is growing short."

Another whimper, this one reminding me of a maimed animal.

"We're bringing him over," Tracey says.

A voice from the box hisses, "*Shut the door.*"

"Of course." Beatrice closes the door. She whispers to me, "Go slowly."

We're nearing the box, which is roughly three feet tall and six feet long. I'm reminded uncomfortably of a casket. "Tommy and Jae pieced it together from old desks," Tracey explains.

"Eric?" Beatrice says, kneeling. She's greeted by silence.

"Eric," Tracey tries, "this man has lost three family members—"

"Man?" Eric says, as though Tracey said *tarantula* or *crocodile.*

Beatrice sinks to all fours. "Can you say hello to Mr. Calhoun?"

A pause. "Calhoun?"

"The bookstore owner," Beatrice explains. "He's a fan of your art."

I don't mind the embellishment, and anyway, I suppose I do admire his art. Or at least I find it interesting.

Beatrice crawls forward. "Eric?"

"*Stay back!*" he cries.

Beatrice glances ruefully at Tracey, who murmurs, "Must not be a good day."

Beatrice waves me closer, and I lower to my knees beside her. The odors are thicker down here, sour and tinged with spoiled meat. If there's a shower in his bathroom, Pruitt hasn't been using it. As my eyes adjust to the gloom of his nook, I make out blankets and pillows, and I'm reminded of the days when my kids and I used to make forts in the family room, draping blankets and sheets over couches and chairs to construct claustrophobic hideouts they never wanted to tear down. At the thought of my children, I find myself on the brink of tears. To stem the tide, I say, "I look at your mural a lot, Mr. Pruitt. The one in the alley." When he doesn't answer, I add, "I like your use of colors."

"That's from the accident," he murmurs. "My injury . . . it changed me."

I glance at Beatrice, who nods encouragingly.

"Well, you're a really talented artist," I manage.

No answer. The silence draws out.

Finally, Pruitt says, "You can't see it very well from your shop. You should stand in the alley to get the full effect."

I nod. "My daughter and I used to get ice cream and walk around campus. The mural's one of our favorite spots."

"Your daughter... she was taken?"

My chest burns. "Yes. Along with my son. And my wife."

The wad of blankets twitches. Then a shuddery hand slithers out. I sense Beatrice and Tracey holding their breath and am conscious of holding mine. The palsied fingers drag the blankets down, and even in the murk, I can see how white Pruitt's hair has gone. The blankets crawl down his face, revealing snow-white eyebrows, then deep-set sockets from which stare the most bloodshot eyes I've ever seen. Deep crow's-feet line the corners of his eyes.

Beatrice says, "Eric, we'd like you to—"

"I know what you want," Pruitt says, his deathly eyes never leaving mine. "You want me to give you hope. But I can't."

"What do they look like?" I ask. "The creatures."

He utters a high-pitched, keening yowl that makes my flesh squirm.

Beatrice clambers forward. "You're safe," she assures him. "The aliens can't find you."

Pruitt's face melts into an expression of unutterable horror. "What if they followed him here? What if they—*oh my God, get out! Get out now!*"

"Go," Beatrice manages, and Tracey and I need no persuading. Pruitt's gibbering chases us out of the room.

17

His screaming pursues us through the closed door.

"Why do you keep it so bright in there?" I ask.

"He doesn't like shadows," Tracey answers.

We hear Beatrice murmur something to soothe him. Pruitt's cries devolve into a choking sob.

"Is she right about the creatures?" I ask. "I mean, about classifying them as aliens?"

"They're certainly alien to *us*," Tracey allows. "Where they're from is up for debate."

"Another dimension?"

"Has to be," she says. "Interstellar travel would require too much energy. That's what I believe. Kehler, too, when he's not being obstinate."

"You two don't get along?"

She shrugs. "Better than when we were married."

I blink at her.

"What's wrong," she says, a corner of her mouth lifting, "you don't think he's my type?"

"How long were you married?"

"Long enough to drive each other insane. And to have Raven." At my look, she explains, "Our daughter."

"Ah. Is she..."

Instead of answering, Tracey drifts to the dimmest corner of the room. The green tile reflects the overhead fluorescents and makes her black hair shimmer with jade highlights.

I murmur, "I'm sorry."

She braces her palms on the counter. "And I'm sorry for what happened to your family. But it happened. And you have a decision to make." She faces me. "Beatrice was a grad assistant for me. Earth Atmospheric Planetary Science Department. I specialize in astrophysics." A smile. "She's quirky, but she knows when to get down to business.

"After Raven was taken, after Kehler had been here a couple weeks and it was clear we weren't getting closer to finding our daughter, Beatrice told me about this neighbor of hers. She'd seen him fleeing through the street one day, and she was worried about him. 'It looked like he was seeing something no one else could,' she said."

"Because of the brain injury?"

"I didn't know about it then. Beatrice had been taking care of him for several days before something she said broke through to me. I was going through the motions, telling myself I was investigating the phenomenon, but all I was doing was obsessing over Raven. I couldn't look at it objectively. I kept thinking about how terrified she must be. How she needed food and water. But Beatrice was giving me updates on her neighbor, saying he was suffering a breakdown."

"What sort of breakdown?" I finally asked.

"She told me Eric sees the world differently. That you can sense it in his brushstrokes. She told me about the crash and his scar, and I damn near knocked her down on the way through the office door. She begged me to tell her what was going on as I drove us to Eric's house, but it wasn't until we were inside that I got a good look at his paintings. Seeing them that way, it was as plain as could be. There were the Before paintings and the After. Before his accident, he'd seen the world one way. After . . ."

"His injury altered his perception," I finish.

"He not only sees the aliens, but where they come through. That's just as important."

It's more *important*, I decide. For the first time since losing Emma, my brain is functioning at full capacity. I sit up straighter. "So you believe the injury . . ."

"Allows a person to see through the veil." At my raised eyebrows, she explains, "The limitations of our eyes. They're picking us off so effortlessly because we can't see them. Can't predict where they'll strike."

"Pruitt can?"

"I believe anyone like him can. My ex-husband is a plastic surgeon in Indianapolis, but before he opted to make money off of people's insecurities—" She makes a fist and punches her hip. "Sorry, that's reductive." She shakes her head. "Kehler's a brilliant surgeon. Before he started giving boob jobs, he was training for neurosurgery."

"That's why the others are here," I guess. "He's going to do to them what was done to Pruitt."

She nods. "Though Pruitt's injuries were extensive, one of them just happened to affect his vision. Kehler needs a little more material, and then he'll be ready to perform the surgeries."

"That's why Miranda kept driving by my house. You were keeping tabs on me. You figured I'd be desperate enough to volunteer."

Tracey doesn't contradict me.

"What we need," Miranda says, "is more firepower. Can't take on a bunch of monsters with bats and shovels."

"I can do a lot of damage with a bat," Tommy says.

"If that were true," Miranda answers, "you'd still be playing baseball."

"Darlin', I led Purdue in batting average junior year. Got drafted by the Rays. Made it all the way to triple-A—"

"Where you flamed out," Miranda says.

"Damn," Tommy mutters and scratches his dog's back. "Hear the way she talks to me, Koufax?"

"Most guys never make it that far," I say .

"*Thank* you," Tommy says. "Uncle Ebb always told me, 'Don't wish it were easier. Wish you were better.'"

"But you weren't," Miranda says.

Tommy motions toward her with the beer bottle. "That's some cold shit."

"Doesn't mean it's not true." She flashes a closed-lip smile.

I indicate the scar under Tommy's right eye. "How'd you get that?"

He grunts ruefully. "Struck out in a Little League game and had my head down on the way back to the dugout. My teammate in the on-deck circle didn't see me and coldcocked me in the face with a Louisville Slugger."

Jae and I dish up and join them, our paper plates sagging with rice and noodles. Tracey and Kehler sweep inside. Kehler glances in Tommy's direction, and his face falls. "Could we not have that dog in here at dinnertime?"

Tommy lays a protective hand over Koufax. "He's not hurting anybody."

"We on for the morning?" Miranda asks.

"We're on," Kehler says, "though the chances of success are virtually nil."

Jae looks up, noodles stringing over his chin. "What do you mean?"

"I have to have it," Kehler says. A greenbottle fly lights on his noodles, and he shoos it away.

Miranda makes a face. "You're still bellyaching about that book? We got you everything you need."

Kehler dishes up. "Brain surgery is a complicated business."

"It wasn't for Pruitt," Miranda answers as Tracey eases down beside her. "Dude crashed his car, and now he sees aliens."

"A fluke," Kehler says. I scoot over so he can sit between me and Jae. On the opposite side of the table from his ex-wife, I note.

"I really think you have all you need," Tracey says.

"No," Kehler answers, "I really don't."

Tommy's shaking his head. "Then what were all those runs for? Risking our lives, going through libraries—"

"You've been to *two* libraries," Kehler says. "*Veterinary* libraries. And you had help."

"But not from you, eh?" Jae says.

"I was studying."

Miranda grins. "You mean you're scared shitless."

Kehler pauses mid-chew. "Who wouldn't be? You've seen what they can do. How abruptly they strike. If something happens to me, who's going to perform the surgeries?"

Tommy tips his bottleneck toward Tracey. "I bet the professor here could do it."

Tracey shakes her head. "I'm afraid not, Tommy. I don't have the expertise."

The fly lands on Kehler's head. "You see?" he says and bats at the fly. "You all like to bash me, but maybe you should be appreciating me instead."

"You appreciate yourself enough for all of us," Miranda says, and Jae and Tommy laugh.

I study Kehler. He's older than Tracey, well over fifty, I'd guess. He takes care of himself, but there's something haggard around the eyes. I suppose the end of the world will do that to you.

"The best brain diagram I have," Kehler says, "is not even a human brain."

At my frown, Tracey explains, "Owl monkey."

Kehler chews. "So you see why I'm hesitant to cut into you people."

"What book is it you're after?" I ask.

Kehler shakes his head. "You won't know it."

"Try me."

He gives me a wry look. "*Walsh and Hoyt's Clinical Neuro-Ophthalmology*?"

"Got it."

Kehler's face goes slack.

"Bullshit," Miranda mutters.

"We have a medical section at the shop," I explain.

Kehler seems to withdraw, but Tracey's brown eyes glitter. "Can we get it? I mean, is your store intact?"

"I don't know. I haven't been there in months."

"Probably empty by now," Kehler says.

Miranda glowers at him. "Who's gonna steal a book about neuro-ophthalmology?"

"We go after we eat," Tracey says.

"Hell yeah," Jae agrees. He shovels his rice in, most of it making it into his mouth.

"Even if it's there," Kehler says, "I'll need time to digest the information—"

"You mean read it?" Miranda asks.

"—*internalize* it." Kehler shakes his head. "I don't think any of you have the slightest inkling of what this entails. I don't have the support staff—"

"You got Beatrice," Miranda says.

"One error," Kehler says, and brandishes an index finger, "the slightest miscalculation, and you'll never talk again. Or think. Or see."

"Start with Tommy," Miranda says. "That way, you fuck something up, nobody will know the difference."

"This isn't a joke," Kehler says. "You're bullying me into this. For God's sakes, I haven't performed anything more complex than a facelift in almost ten years."

Miranda tilts her head. "You do those butt implants?"

"Why," Tommy asks, "you want one?"

Miranda slaps her thigh. "I'm good there. Could use some of them lip injections though."

Kehler says, "None of you grasp the danger you're in. We're talking about an unprecedented procedure. We're talking—"

"We're talking about our daughter," Tracey says.

The energy seems to drain out of Kehler. "It might shock you to learn I don't want to hurt any of you."

Jae says, "Whatever's happening out there . . . it's getting worse. Not a single person has come back. And each day makes it less likely we'll see them again."

Kehler shifts uneasily. "You don't know that."

"I feel it," Jae says and taps himself on the chest. "Vanessa . . . she's gotta be showing by now. Probably feels so alone . . . so scared. We've got to do this. My girlfriend . . . your daughter . . . the longer we wait, the further away they slip."

"I don't feel so good," Tommy says. His complexion is ashen.

"I'll go in Tommy's place," Tracey says. When everyone looks at her, she adds, "What? We're going to a bookstore. I want to stock up."

18

We're idling on State Street, one of Purdue's main drags, and staring at what used to be a lovely if quaint storefront. Now my picture window is shattered, the one that read THE CONSTANT READER CAFÉ. I knew there might be damage to my shop, but for some reason, I always imagined the door being assaulted, not the front window.

"I'm sorry," Tracey says.

"It's fine," I answer, though it's not fine. Peering through the jagged teeth of glass that line the bottom of the window, I realize this was my last mental haven. I've been telling myself, *No matter what they take, no matter what they do, at least I'll have this.*

But I don't. Not anymore.

"It hasn't rained much lately," Tracey says hopefully. "Maybe there won't be a lot of damage."

"Pull up to the side door," I instruct, and Miranda gets us rolling. "It's not just rain," I answer. "It's the changing temperatures. The humidity."

Miranda parks. "Ready?"

I climb out of the car, and though it's only six or seven feet to the door, I feel a chill whisper down my back. *Are they watching?* I wonder. *Do they know we're here?* My hands shake as I guide the key toward the lock. The dormant campus, the obscenely cheerful late-afternoon sun, the entire situation... it feels preordained. Like the final act of a tragedy. I get the first lock open, shuffle through the keys to find the one for the dead bolt, and as I do, I imagine cold talons closing on my wrists, imagine being yanked into oblivion. I suppose, if that happens, my new companions will proceed with the mission. But I want to be part of it, want to be there when we see our loved ones again.

I slide the key into the lock, hear the hardy *thunk*, and take a deep breath.

"You gonna make love to it or open the damned thing?" a voice asks. It's Miranda, but all three are crowding behind me.

"Sorry," I say and push the door open.

"This is *sweet*," Jae says as he steps inside.

I close the door behind us and head to the nonfiction area. Jae makes for the front of the store, Miranda branching off to the rear. Tracey follows me.

"Medicine and science are just ahead," I tell her.

"What a marvelous place," she says. "I can't believe I've never been inside."

I know the tone. The guilt of the lapsed reader.

"Take anything you want. They're going to deteriorate rapidly with the front window out. Someone might as well enjoy them."

We advance deeper, and as we do, I note the scarcity of damage. Whoever shattered the window must've done it recently. Or people are simply too frightened to loot anymore. I arrive at the medical books. In seconds, I've got it. *Walsh and Hoyt's Clinical Neuro-Ophthalmology: The Essentials.* I hold it up to Tracey, but she's drifted to the thrillers, caressing the spines with her longish fingernails. She settles on *Providence* by Caroline Kepnes and slides it out.

"That one's terrific," I say. "Take it."

She glances at me, and when her eyes lower to the book I grasp, she beams. "You found it! Kehler will be so pleased."

"You sure about that?"

"Okay, maybe not *pleased*. But it'll take away his last excuse." She makes to pull another book from the shelf but pauses. "Did you notice my scar?"

I open my mouth to reassure her, but she raises her right hand, displaying it for me, the wavy scar tissue, in some places smooth, in others the flesh gathered into uneven ridges.

She smiles. "People never ask, but I know they notice. I was cooking, not being careful enough. Raven was three, bustling around behind me. I turned away to grab a pinch of salt to drop in a pot of boiling water, and when I turned back, I saw Raven reaching up and grasping the handle."

"Oh hell," I murmur.

"I panicked," Tracey says. "I pushed Raven away with one hand and shoved the pot with the other and it sloshed over me." She peers down at her scarred hand, turning it this way and that. "Third-degree burn. They did what they could, but it'll never go away."

"At least you saved your daughter," I venture.

"But I didn't save her this time," she answers, and so choked are her words that I want to hug her. I hear Jae's heavy tread approaching; then he lumbers around the corner. At his side hangs an overladen red basket containing at least a dozen Stephen King books.

He hesitates. "I don't have to take all these."

"They're yours. Even if you hadn't saved my life, I'd give them to you."

I heft the basket onto a display table. With the hardcovers stacked in the bottom, it's damn heavy, and I'm forcibly reminded of Jae's strength.

"We gotta go," Tracey murmurs. "Miranda?" she calls out.

"Is King your favorite?" I ask Jae.

"Vanessa's," he explains. "She got me into reading. Before, I never saw the point. All the stuff I read in school put me to sleep. But when she gave me *Revival* for a gift…"

I nod.

"I can't live without her," he says. "Before I met Vanessa, I had no direction. No reason."

A new heat ignites in my upper chest. I remember the first time I saw Iris…

…but I actually heard her first. We were cast in a musical together, just a community theater production of *Cinderella*, but when I strode down the hallway toward that high school music room… when I heard that voice…

"Vanessa would do the same for me," Jae says, "if I were taken. She'd do what we're gonna do."

I start to ask a question, but I'm interrupted by Miranda, who rejoins us. She's empty-handed.

"Didn't find anything?" I ask.

"Y'all got a great kids' section. Dr. Seuss, Frog and Toad, a dead body."

I feel the smile slide off my face.

"Don't worry," she says. "It doesn't stink or nothin'. It's still fresh."

The dead man is spread-eagled on the floor, his sightless eyes fixed on the cobwebby ceiling fan. Shiny scalp. Long white hair fanning out over his shoulders. Checkered sports jacket. Rumpled beige trousers.

"How old you think he was?" Miranda asks. "A hundred?"

"Seventy-three," I answer.

Tracey looks at me. "You know him?"

"Saul Bauman. Local author."

"Never heard of him," Miranda says.

I avoid Saul's gaping eyes. "He wasn't a household name. Mostly self-published, but pretty good. He wrote historical adventures and a few British period pieces."

"Sounds boring as shit," Miranda answers.

"Hey," Jae says and gestures at the body.

"He can't hear me," Miranda says.

"Does he have family?" Tracey asks.

I shake my head. "Not that I'm aware of. He was a regular in the shop. I gave him an endcap up front."

We're quiet a moment, the atmosphere muggy.

"Well, at least he had his books," Tracey says.

"That nobody read," Miranda answers.

Tracey glowers at her. "Could you watch what you say? Just this once?"

"Your ex is cuttin' into my brain tomorrow. My family's gone. I've got a stomachache, and my period started this morning. I'm not gonna stand here and pretend this dude is Ernest Hemingway just because he killed himself." At our shocked silence, she nods at the table next to a reading chair. There's an uncapped pill bottle, empty, perched atop a stack of print-on-demand paperbacks. Saul's paperbacks. One of his novels—*The Viceroy of Sussex County*—is splayed open on the chair, as if to keep the seat warm for him.

—

Kehler isn't delighted about Walsh and Hoyt's book. After handing it off and witnessing another testy exchange between him and Tracey, I follow her upstairs to a claustrophobic office, the desk snowed under with papers.

"The only place I can get away," she explains. Charts all over the walls, bulletin boards littered with diagrams, thigh-high pillars of books, the space maybe nine-by-nine. It's windowless, which comforts me, but it's on the main floor, which doesn't. Even though we were more exposed in my shop, this feels unsafe, probably due to the fact that everyone else is in the basement.

At least there are no dead bodies here.

We sit, Tracey at her desk, me in a squeaky wooden chair across from her.

"What do you know about alternate dimensions?" she asks me.

"Only what I've read." Even though I've suspected whatever's happening involves some kind of interdimensional aberration, her question still unsettles me.

There's a knock on the door, and Beatrice steps through. She gives us an apologetic smile and pushes her glasses up her nose. "Internet's kaput," she says and sits on a table, her long blue-jeaned legs dangling.

"Dammit," Tracey answers. She fixes me with her shrewd gaze. "Let's start with the invaders."

I recall the Aldi parking lot, the shoppers yanked into the sky. "There are at least two species," I say. "One that can fly and one that can't. Some, evidently, can swim. They're powerful. Most importantly, they're surpassingly intelligent."

Tracey nods. "They're also adept at improvising. The military has attempted several times to ensnare them, but they've always evaded our traps. There's no way to predict where they'll strike. Their invisibility is our kryptonite."

"You really believe replicating Pruitt's injury will help us see the gateways?"

Beatrice grows animated. "Eric talks about glowing slashes in the air. He says the creatures spread these apart and climb through." Beatrice leans forward. *"And the gateways stay open."*

I consider this. "If the military hasn't been able to capture one of the creatures—"

"None of them had the correct vision," Tracey reminds me.

"We still have no idea where they'll..." But even as I say this, I realize I'm wrong. We do have an idea of where they'll show up. "The sound," I say.

Tracey nods. "Pruitt says the slashes take a minute or so to form. Like the creatures have to buzz saw through the barrier between our dimension and theirs. What we need from you is the *why*. You teach biology. Please tell me you have some ideas."

I hesitate. Sharing what I believe with Emma is one thing. Explaining it to near strangers is another. But I lay out my theory. It doesn't take long. When I tell them what parts of the brain I believe they're harvesting, Beatrice gapes at me. "That's perverse."

"So whatever's plaguing the creatures," Tracey says, "it's affecting entire families of them?"

I nod. "Imagine two creatures, a brother and a sister, both suffering from this condition. They're losing their memories, and their parents are desperate. They want their children to retain knowledge of who they are. When prowling for brains to harvest in our world, wouldn't it make sense to target a human brother and sister? Think about how bonded siblings are. Sure, they may hate each other, but deep down, that connection, that blood tie, makes a difference."

Tracey mulls it over. "The familial link makes the procedure more successful?"

"That's what I believe. But..." I pass a hand over my mouth. "It would only work that way for a short period."

"What do you mean?"

"You've heard of behavior-altering parasites."

Tracey nods, but Beatrice shakes her head.

"Behavior-altering parasitic relationships involve two unlike species," I explain. "One ultimately subjugates the other. The parasite affects the host's central nervous system, warps the host's thinking."

Tracey's eyes are widening.

"In our circumstance, there would be minority elements of the human brain incorporated into the host's brain. We have to assume the human components would slowly fade."

"Like dying twice," Tracey says. "When our brains are harvested . . . our bodies die. Then, those facets of us that are transferred over begin to fade . . ."

"You mean we'd be *aware* of the change?" Beatrice asks. "We'd be aware of living inside the creatures' minds?"

"Until we're not," I answer. "Eventually, we'd be absorbed, and whatever parts of us are still aware, whatever memories we retain . . . they'd be gone." I mimic blowing out a candle. "Second death."

No one says anything for a while.

"So the condition the aliens suffer from," Beatrice murmurs. "Do you think it's viral, genetic, what?"

"I don't know. In the end, it's irrelevant. Their science is superior, so I'm sure they've devoted all their resources toward solving it and failed. But there's something you're not telling me."

Tracey tilts her head.

"Say it's successful. Say the procedure doesn't kill us. What are we doing afterward? What's the plan?"

Tracey laces her fingers on the desk blotter. "We'll conduct three missions."

"After your recovery period," Beatrice cautions.

"How long?" I ask.

"Seventy-two hours minimum," Beatrice says. At my look, she reminds me, "You're having brain surgery, not getting a wart removed."

"The ablative incision will be localized," Tracey says. "There shouldn't be much recovery time."

Beatrice begins to argue, but I say, "Three missions."

"The first," Tracey says, "will be finding weapons."

"I can help there."

A small smile. "Good. The second mission will be to search for them."

I lower my chin. "By 'them,' you mean..."

"The creatures," Beatrice says. "If you find them, you find their gateways."

"That's the third mission," Tracey explains. "Going through."

Her words bring a chill.

"And after that?" I ask.

Tracey stands and moves around to grasp the chairback. "Then we'll have to improvise. We have no idea what their world is like. We don't even know if we'll survive their atmosphere."

"It could be a hundred degrees below zero," Beatrice says. "Or two hundred above."

"Regardless," Tracey continues, "we'll find a gate. And once we're through, we'll locate our loved ones."

I imagine Iris, Emma, Sam, and my heart pounds at the thought.

Beatrice steps toward the bulletin board. "Should I..."

She's standing next to a plain sheet of construction paper with a corner peeled down. I glimpse a heavily shaded sketch beneath.

Beatrice hesitates. "It's really not very good. I'm a total amateur."

"I'm not an art critic," I say. "Just rip off the Band-Aid."

She plucks out the upper tacks. The sheet of construction paper is tacked at the bottom, so instead of swooshing to the floor, the obscuring sheet peels down and hangs there. What's revealed is so ghastly I can only stare.

"It's partly artistic license," Beatrice murmurs, "but most of it's based on what Eric told me."

On the left side of the drawing, there are measurements. Though the creature is stooped over—groping hungrily toward me—it still measures thirteen feet.

I clear my throat. "Most organisms grow symmetrically—hence two arms and two legs." I move over to better examine the sketch. "As far as we know, the creatures have left every other species untouched. That suggests they targeted the one most closely aligned with their physiology."

Beatrice nods.

"You drew them with scales," I say.

"I guessed on that part," she concedes.

Tracey looks at me. "Does this jibe with your cystisoma theory?"

"It might not be precisely like that," I tell her, "but whatever exoskeleton they possess would function much the same way. It would manipulate light. Ideally suited for camouflage."

Tracey joins me at the drawing. "They'd need fingers for grasping. Or talons. I suggested four for each hand, but Beatrice drew three."

I recall the indentations on my daughter's arms as she hung there in the air. "It's four."

Beatrice and Tracey exchange a glance.

Beatrice says, "We don't know how long they can survive in our atmosphere. They might need breathing masks." She looks at me rather shyly. "What else?"

The face is a macabre fever dream. Elongated, the forehead branching up and tapering into wavy horns. There are contours all over, adding shadows and malevolence. The nose is recessed, the nostrils mere slits. The mouth is hinged wide to disclose mottled teeth. They're an inch and a half long and curved like scimitars, the flexing muscles around the jaw suggesting insatiable hunger. The cheekbones are skeletal, protuberant, but it's the eyes I focus on, the glowering white eyes that promise I'll never get my family back, will regret ever trying. Those eyes promise agony. They promise death.

Staring into this face, this towering, armored body, I can't imagine our mission succeeding. Can't imagine what sort of hellscape this phantasmagorical creature might inhabit.

Beatrice says, "I have to make a confession." She removes her glasses and begins buffing them with her shirtfront. "Tracey and I have a difference of opinion regarding Eric Pruitt. Tracey thinks..."

"He's lost it," Tracey says.

"*I* think," Beatrice says and holds her glasses near her face to inspect them, "he's basically sane. Just terrified." She resituates her glasses and looks at me. "He told me how the creatures move. How their joints bend."

I glance at the drawing and, for the first time, observe how the knees hinge the wrong way.

"They're quadrupeds?" I ask.

"Eric says they're capable of moving on two legs or four."

"And he claims they look like this?"

"Yes."

Tracey sits atop her desk. "Mr. Calhoun, you said you know where we can get weapons." A nod at the drawing. "If they look anything like that, we're sure as hell going to need them."

"The people who burned down my house," I say, "they've got this place called the Boiler Barn..."

19

When I reenter my assigned room, I can only stand and stare. I work out five times a week. I don't do enough cardio, but it's not like I do none. But when I see what Jae's doing, I feel puny. Superman push-ups, they're called, an exercise I've seen online but never in real life. Despite his prodigious size, Jae's back is flat against the wall, he's standing on his head, and he's pressing his entire body into the air. The power this must require boggles my mind. He squeezes out four more reps, moving slowly up and down, the sweat trickling over his broad torso, before swinging his legs down and standing upright.

"Ever been in a fight?" he asks.

I shake my head.

He slides on a black-and-gold Van Halen T-shirt. "First, don't ruin your hands." We start down the hallway. "You've got a shit-ton of bones in your hands, all tiny, all easy to break. You're gonna need your hands. If we end up in physical combat, use your other body parts as much as possible. Elbows. Knees. Feet."

"Got it."

"Two, fight dirty. These motherfuckers abducted the people we love. Use anything you've got to hurt them. Be ruthless."

We near our turn. I hear murmuring voices.

"Lastly," Jae says, "and I can't stress this enough: Stay off the ground. These things are a hell of a lot stronger than we are. But if you keep moving, if you don't get pinned down, you've got a chance." He eyes me. "Mind telling me how you got that limp?"

In his face, I discern no pity, no derision.

"My left leg is shorter than my right," I explain. "In elementary school, everybody made fun of me for being so slow. I remember in fourth grade, our end-of-the-year track-and-field day. My least favorite day of the year. Everybody had to be in two events. People are a little more sensitive to disabilities now, but back then..."

Jae nods.

"I signed up for the shot put, but they made me participate in a running event too. I chose the hundred-yard dash. I figured the shorter the race, the better."

I imagine it. The rubbery scent of the track and the damp smell of the grassy infield. It was totally cloudless, the sky so blue and the sun so bright that the starting line felt like some spotlighted stage. I remember seeing my mom in the stands. The faces of my classmates packing the infield, the unsmiling coaches and teachers prowling about, their eyes always on their clipboards and stopwatches.

"I knew I'd chosen the wrong event even before the starting gun went off," I tell Jae. "Most of the others in the race were fifth graders, a year older and much faster than me."

Jae waits in sympathetic silence, and somehow, this brings back that day more forcibly, the way one of my teachers, Mrs. Barker, looked at me. She wanted me to succeed so badly. Not to win, of course, but to not embarrass myself. I read that in her face and told myself I could do it, I could make a decent showing.

"I remember crouching down and putting my good leg in the starting block. I glanced at the kids on either side of me, but they were in the starting position, too, their eyes straight ahead. So I told myself I needed to have the same focus. When the shot rang out, I pushed away from the starting block but misjudged it and sprawled on my face. The friction burned my palms and my knees. I heard laughter. The other runners were almost done with the race, but I hadn't even gotten up yet. When I did, I saw all the kids on the infield pointing at me and howling, and though that was bad, what was worse was the teachers. A couple of them were trying not to laugh, but others were watching me fiercely, shouting at me that I could do it, applauding me and cheering me on.

"I hobbled ahead, my knees bleeding and my palms burning, and in my periphery, I saw teachers exhorting the students to cheer for me. As I got closer to the finish line, this roar started to build, but it was a pity roar. I saw the other runners at the finish line waiting for me. They were clapping and shouting encouragement, but a few of them wore gloating smiles, like I was some pitiable mutation. I finished and limped my way through the crowd and headed straight to the parking lot. My mom drove me home, tried to talk to me, but I wouldn't answer. Just sat there crying and wishing I was dead."

Jae murmurs, "Sorry, man. That's awful."

"Before that, I always wanted to prove I could do what the other kids could do. But afterward, I wanted to show that I could do *more*. I wanted revenge on them for the way they looked at me. For the pity ovation."

I chuckle, but it's a humorless sound. "Ever since I was little, I wanted to be Superman. So when I got home, I limped to our big maple tree. I climbed way up, probably twenty-five feet..."

"Holy shit."

"... and jumped. I fractured my left leg, the one that was already a problem, and totally wrecked my foot. They tried different things. Surgeries, special shoes, physical therapy, a corrective brace. Nothing worked."

"Is that why you lift?"

I mull it over. "I guess I've always wanted to be more than I am."

"I hear that."

We get moving again and enter the large office area, where we find Miranda and Tommy.

Tommy looks up and smiles. "There they are."

Miranda appears to be mixing a drink at the counter.

"Where's Koufax?" I ask.

Tommy gives me a rueful look. "Kehler won't let him near here. Says dogs aren't sterile or some crap like that."

"Where does Koufax go to the bathroom? I'm assuming you don't take him outside."

"Why not?" Tommy answers. "The aliens don't prey on dogs."

"Tracey around?" Jae asks.

"Last I saw," Miranda says, "she and Kehler were arguing."

"What about?" Jae asks.

"The usual," Miranda says. "The possibility we'll all die."

Kehler enters with Beatrice and Tracey close on his heels.

"Let's get this over with," Kehler mutters and wheels a hospital bed over to the group. He unbuttons his cuffs and rolls them up. "I need a volunteer."

Miranda gestures with her drink. "Tommy's the most qualified."

Tommy blinks at her. "Yeah?"

She stirs her drink. "You've got a brain like an owl monkey."

Tommy gives her the finger.

"Hop on," Kehler tells Tommy. "Face down."

Tommy turns his Dodgers cap backward and complies. His

face mashed into the toffee-colored vinyl, he says, "How'm I supposed to breathe?"

"Scoot forward, dumbass," Miranda says and smacks him on the ass.

Tommy inchworms up the bed until his chin hangs over.

"Take off your cap, please," Kehler instructs.

"Aw, man," Tommy says, removing it. "I've got hat head."

"Who you tryin' to impress?" Miranda asks.

It seems to me that Tommy's blush deepens, but maybe it's my imagination.

Kehler says, "Tomorrow we'll use the operating table. The opening at the end will support your head, so you'll be more comfortable."

"Thank God," Tommy grunts.

"Beatrice will assist with the anesthetic," Kehler says.

Beatrice offers a tight-lipped smile.

"Don't they keep patients awake during brain surgery?" I ask.

"With this procedure, it'll be better for both of us if you're asleep. Once you're under, I'll make a scalpel incision right here." He taps Tommy in the depression at the base of his skull. "It's the same incision made in a suboccipital craniotomy."

Miranda chokes on her drink. "A *what*?"

"A type of brain surgery," Tracey says.

"I was wondering," Tommy says. "Do you think the reason they haven't taken me or Miranda or Jae is because of all the drinking we've done?"

Kehler tilts his head. "The thought had occurred to me."

At my look, Jae explains, "That's how we met. Miranda broke into a campus bar. Tommy happened to drive by and see the lights on. I was out hoping to find some sign of my girlfriend, and by the time I drove up, these two were shit-faced, blasting country music and spilling their drinks all over the dance floor."

Miranda flashes me a grin.

Tracey isn't nearly as amused. "I heard the three of them from my office. When I looked out my window, I couldn't believe it. Arms around each other's shoulders in the middle of the road, stumbling and singing Garth Brooks."

"George Strait," Tommy says.

"You're lucky I dragged you idiots inside," Tracey says. She nods at Kehler. "Proceed."

"The odds of success are minimal," Kehler says. "You need to understand that this could be fatal."

"That's comforting," Miranda answers. "Before I go into surgery, I always like hearing it'll probably fail."

Kehler glowers at her. "I'm only doing this because my ex-wife believes it's our one chance to save our daughter."

"It *is* your only chance," I say.

Kehler rounds on me. "Our daughter is none of your business."

"No, but my wife and kids are," I say, and somehow we're standing toe-to-toe. "Now finish the goddamn demonstration so we can go to bed and get some sleep."

Kehler's grin is wintry. "Maybe you'll volunteer to go first?"

"Oh, for Christ's sakes," Tracey snaps.

"Can I sit up?" Tommy asks. "I'm gettin' lightheaded."

Kehler glares at me for another few seconds, then returns to Tommy. "After I breach the cranium, I'll use a targeting laser to make my way to the visual cortex."

I frown. "You can be exact enough to avoid harming us?"

"Honestly?" Kehler says. "I have no idea."

We're all silent for a beat.

Miranda burps into her hand. "Well, that's a fuckin' buzzkill."

We turn in for the night. I'm drifting off to sleep when I hear a voice, and when I open my eyes, I see Jae kneeling beside my mattress.

"What's up?" I ask, confused.

"I gotta get her," he tells me. There are tears in his eyes. "She saved me, man. I can't let her stay lost any longer. Wherever she is."

I sit up and rub my eyes. "What's her name again?"

"Vanessa," he answers, and as he does, it's as though a frosty hearth has fired to life, a warmth permeating his features. "Before I met her, I was aimless. Partying too much. Putting shit in my body. But when I met Vanessa... she was like a mirror held up to me. But you know how some mirrors make you look bad and others are flattering? Vanessa's the mirror you go to when you want to feel good about yourself."

"In the morning—" I start, but he grasps my shoulder hard enough to make me wince.

"I can't wait that long. Once we get the surgery, we've got to find a gate. Every second counts."

"You want to go for the weapons tonight?"

"Tommy and Miranda are waiting down the hall. We hoped you'd go with us."

"I'll go."

Hearing all of this from Jae, I recall how my relationship with Iris once was. But the reason it changed... maybe it was because, instead of acknowledging what I saw in her eyes and working on it, I simply stopped looking. Started looking at her flaws because that helped me avoid admitting mine. I can't say any of this, not right now, so I push to my feet, and we regard each other in the nearly dark room.

"You're sure they have weapons?" he asks.

"Relatively. But we'll have to be careful."

Jae nods. "Covert mission."

"We need flashlights," I say.

Jae holds out two black beanie caps.

I take one and spot the small square on the brim. "No way." I push the button and a silvery incandescence shines out.

"Vanessa bought them so we could jog together. We never got to use them."

We slide on the beanies and head to the hallway, where Miranda and Tommy, both of them dressed in black, await us. The four of us make it to the ground floor, where we can finally speak in regular voices.

"Can't believe the science teacher decided to tag along," Tommy says.

Jae answers, "Why wouldn't he?"

"Not sure," Tommy says. "He just seems a little, I don't know, cautious?"

I'm about to tell him to piss off when Jae shakes his head. "John will do fine. Besides," he adds, nearing the door to the loading bay, "he's the least of our issues."

"Yeah?" Tommy asks.

"What's Tracey gonna say when she finds out we took her car?"

"Who gives a shit?" Miranda says. "When she sees all the guns, she'll be too overjoyed to get pissy."

We slink through the loading area, the only light what spills in through windows set high on either side of the rolling doors.

"Spooky," Tommy says.

"When did you have your testicles removed?" Miranda asks. She opens the BMW's door and there's someone in the driver's seat. Miranda gasps and Tommy shouts, "Holy shit!"

I clutch my chest and try not to die of cardiac arrest.

Tracey regards us blandly. "How dumb do you think I am? You know, you could've just asked me."

"You might've said no," Tommy says.

Tracey reaches under the seat and comes out with the keys. "I'm not letting Miranda drive my car."

We climb in, Jae shotgun, Miranda and I in the backseat.

"Why can't I drive?" Miranda asks.

"Because you're a maniac," Tracey answers.

Tommy moseys over, presses the opener, and the door rumbles up its tracks.

"I've been behind the wheel since I was eight," Miranda says. "Daddy used to have me drive him to the liquor store."

"Heartwarming," Tracey says.

We roll through the opening, and Tommy shuts the door. Tracey gets moving the moment Tommy scrunches in beside Miranda, and we creep through the alley. The moon's out tonight, not quite full but close to it, so when we emerge from the shadows of the massive brick buildings, we feel exposed on the four-lane thoroughfare. Or at least, I feel exposed. Judging from their silence, I assume the others are scared too.

It's only five blocks to the edge of my neighborhood. The campus is so deserted that even the purr of Tracey's Beamer feels like a profanation. I'm convinced the creatures will hear us, that the buzzing hum will erupt soon, maybe inside the car. Could they do that? Rip a gash in reality within a moving vehicle? Anything seems possible. As we glide past a gas station, a McDonald's, a sushi place—I don't even spare Insomnia Cookies a glance—I realize I've come to regard the creatures with superstitious reverence. I catch Tommy looking at me. "Me too, man," he says. Jae's gnawing a thumbnail. Miranda's not speaking. Tracey's face is a drum-tight mask, and I realize we're all out of our minds with terror. We can't take courage from one another because there's no courage to take. Only a shared dread. Richard and Beatrice don't know where we've gone, so if events take a downward turn, no one will come to help. We roll past Mackey Arena, the golden roof gleaming dully in the moonlight, then snake around the practice football complex. Historic houses loom on our right, but we proceed up Northwestern Avenue, past a frat house and more residences. The turn to my home is maybe a hundred yards ahead, but I tell Tracey to turn before that, onto a dead-end road called Tuckaho.

"Slowly," Tommy reminds Tracey.

Tracey gives him a look. "Really? I'd planned on opening it up, seeing how fast the old girl can go."

"*Okay*," Tommy says. "Jeez."

"Jeez yourself," Tracey grumbles and shakes her head.

We make the turn, and the shadows from the spruces and cedars devour the car. Even though Tracey's only doing fifteen, it feels like fifty on the uneven hardpack. The grassy lane to the Boiler Barn is up ahead, but because of the crypt-like murk, I can barely make it out among the towering wall of foliage. Tracey's perched over the wheel squinting into the darkness, and for once neither Miranda nor Tommy cracks wise. Tuckaho is narrow, only three houses on the lane. Jeff Marino owns one of them, Dean Dawson another.

"There," I say and indicate a notch in the trees.

"I see it," Tracey says and steers us that way.

Tommy shakes his head. "We should've removed the bulbs in the brake lights before we left."

Tracey looks at him sharply. "Thank you for that spectacularly unhelpful advice."

Tommy shrugs. "Uncle Ebb always said, 'Failing to prepare is preparing to fail.'"

"Man, fuck Uncle Ebb," Miranda snaps. "We're sitting in the middle of the lane, engine going—"

"Then turn it off," Jae says.

Tracey compresses her lips. Looks at me in the mirror. "How far is it?"

I glance at the shadowy gash that leads to the Boiler Barn. "A hundred feet. No more than a hundred and fifty."

Miranda comes out with a black-and-silver Kahr handgun. "I'm ready."

Tommy grunts. "Easy for you to say. The rest of us are unarmed."

"Then let's get armed," Tracey answers.

No one argues with that.

20

Finally, we're out and moving, Jeff Marino's house, the only dwelling that's visible. It's just the uppermost peak of his roof, but the sight of it imbues me with dread. If he wakes up, or is on guard duty, people will die tonight. Marino wanted to kill me yesterday, was disappointed when Dean insisted on doing the job himself.

Squirrels and rabbits scatter as we approach the forest, the wildlife here thriving but still skittish. Something flitters overhead that might be a bat, but I don't have time to confirm it. We duck ahead, and the hemlocks swallow us up.

We hustle forward, single-file, with me leading the way. I'm not armed, but even if I were, I'd still be dizzy with fear. If there's a guard here, we'll have to overpower him—if there's not, we'll have to break inside. How the hell do we do that without causing a ruckus? Miranda can't just shoot the lock.

We steal deeper down the hemlock-rimmed lane, and the night sounds grow muffled. If I remember correctly, the Boiler Barn isn't far ahead. The only time I was here was a neighborhood Halloween party, Dean and his wife providing pizza and lemonade but requiring every family to chip in thirty bucks. That night, the sliding door had been all the way open so people could mill in and out, but tonight I'm sure it will be shuttered tight.

We burst from cover and are almost on top of the guard before we see him. I stumble to a halt and spread my arms to keep the others behind me. The man in the chair is Chris Burkhardt. I'm only able to distinguish him in the darkness due to his phone light. Judging by the way he's using his thumbs and concentrating on the screen, he must be playing some game. Has to be, since the internet is down, maybe permanently. He appears unaware of us. I glance at Tracey, who looks at me, but before either of us can speak, Miranda is stepping toward Burkhardt, the Kahr at her side.

"You winnin'?" she asks, and Burkhardt gasps, bobbles the phone, and loses it in the grass. He reaches for something, but smoother than the night breeze Miranda's in front of him, the Kahr pressed against his underjaw. If she squeezes the trigger, the top of his head will decorate the satin-black exterior of the Boiler Barn.

Burkhardt stares at Miranda with horror-shot eyes. "Don't!" he cries. "Please—"

"*Keep*," Tracey says, "*your voice*... *down*."

Burkhardt just gapes.

The rest of us creep closer, and it isn't until Tracey says, "Your move, John," that Burkhardt notices me.

"Calhoun?" he asks.

"Give us the guns," I say, "and we won't hurt you."

"We might hurt you a little," Miranda says.

"Get up, Chris," I say. "You owe me."

Burkhardt looks like he might weep. "All you had to do was let us in, Johnny. None of it—"

"You got two seconds," Miranda says, increasing the pressure against his wattled jaw. "One... two—"

"*Okay*," he says and makes to stand up. But he's got so little room to navigate that he tangles and falls, the chair overturning with him. I flinch at the racket and throw a glance toward Marino's house. Burkhardt lies on his side, eyes squeezed shut, as if dreading the sound of a roused cohort as much as we are. I remember what lies on the other side of this pole barn: Dean Dawson's stately two-story home. Painted white brick with a pillared portico. He's the one who'll come first. Not Marino. Not Buddy Scott.

Dean. The son of a bitch who made this mess immeasurably worse. Who burned my house down.

Burkhardt is on his side, his lips quivering, and I've had enough. I step over and haul him to his feet. I catch a whiff of ineffective deodorant and red onions. He leans against me as if for comfort, so I shove him roughly away.

"Open the door," I command.

He nods, reaches into his khaki trousers, and comes out with a key chain. His fingers tremble so wildly that it takes him forever to identify the correct one. He slides it into the slot, then turns the key and twists the knob. Nothing happens.

Burkhardt lets out a brittle laugh. "Dead bolt," he says, but when I stare coldly back at him, his smile evaporates. He unlocks the dead bolt, and then we're in. He's reaching for the switch when Jae clamps down on his wrist.

"Leave the light off," Jae tells him.

Burkhardt nods solemnly.

Tracey switches on a flashlight, and Jae and I click the brims of our jogging beanies. "Watch him," I say to Miranda, and she takes a position near the door. Burkhardt leans against the interior wall as though eager to blend in.

Tracey whistles softly.

I follow her flashlight beam and discover the barn is no longer the hobbyist's space it once was. The silver '68 Corvette is cowled in a gray tarp; a John Deere riding mower, a lathe, and a golf cart have been shoved to the side. Now, rows and rows of steel storage racks dominate. Canned goods, cases of water and soda, mammoth bags of cereal and potato chips. On the far wall are half a dozen refrigerators and freezers. How this prick hoodwinked so many people into surrendering their food I don't know, but somehow he has.

Tracey asks Burkhardt, "Where are the guns?"

His throat works for a moment. "Buddy's house."

Tommy stalks over to Burkhardt and seizes him by the lapels of his shirt. "Bullshit. Your buddies might keep stuff in their houses, but I guarantee they store some of it here too."

Miranda steps closer and presses the muzzle against Burkhardt's forehead.

"The tool cabinets," he bleats. "The ones in the loft."

I rush up the steps, Tracey and Jae behind me. We arrive at some wall-mounted cabinets with CRAFTSMAN stamped on them, gaudy steel affairs with cardinal-red fronts and jet-black sides. I attempt to open one, but the door holds fast.

Tracey leans over the railing and calls, "They're locked."

"Give us the fucking keys," Miranda snarls.

Even from up here in the loft, I can see Burkhardt's bottom lip quiver.

"Last chance," Tommy says.

"I don't have those keys," Burkhardt whines.

Tommy gets in his face. "*Bullshit.*"

Burkhardt fumbles for the key ring and extends it to Tommy. "Here. Try them all. They won't work."

I know he's telling the truth. Dean would never trust Burkhardt with the keys to the arsenal. I'm amazed he let the dull-witted oaf stand guard.

"We'll have to break them open," Tracey says.

"Won't they hear?" Jae asks.

"It's the only way," Tracey says, and I know she's right. No guns, no chance of defending ourselves against the creatures. And if we can't do that, our loved ones are already lost.

We step over to the workbench, where Tracey selects a crowbar. Jae grabs a mallet. I take a claw hammer, and I can already imagine the metallic thud it's going to make on the steel cabinet. There's no way to do this without rousing Dean. I move over to the far cabinet, leaving room for Jae to take the center one. Tracey arranges her flashlight on the workbench to shine on us.

"On three," Tracey says.

Jae and I nod.

"One."

We raise our weapons. Tracey inserts the crowbar between the door and the cabinet.

"Two," she whispers.

Jae and I focus on our targets. I can hear the scrape of Tracey's crowbar against steel.

"Three," she says, and I swing straight at the circular keyhole. The crack it makes is loud, but it's drowned out by the gonging of Jae's mallet. Somewhere buried under the reverberation, I hear steel groan and know Tracey is leaning on the crow. Only when she stops do I realize how much noise we've made.

Miranda calls up to us, "Maybe you all could let off an air horn next time."

I glance at Tracey, who's dripping with sweat. Jae's frowning at his cabinet, where the keyhole area is dented but the door no closer to being opened. On the other hand, my door is mangled enough to give me hope.

"Hey, fellas?" Burkhardt calls. "Maybe we can negotiate. Dean's not so unreasonable..."

I recollect the hair's breadth I came from a public execution and don't even bother responding. Instead, I step over, find another claw hammer, and offer it to Jae. He accepts it and chucks the mallet aside. Tracey counts to three again, and this time, my cabinet door jars open. Tracey strains, her door almost there. Jae's strike is too high, but he's so jacked that the bottom of the cabinet door bows outward. I appraise the contents of my cabinet.

Machetes. Six of them, along with their sheathes. Wicked-looking but not what we need. The plan, as far as there is a plan, is to keep our distance from the creatures, to mow them down before they attack. We're not mowing anything down with machetes.

Jae and Tracey promptly beset their cabinets. This time Tracey's squeals open—Jae's is bent wildly out of shape from his hammer blows but not yet accessible. We huddle together and peer into Tracey's cabinet.

Guns. Four handguns and extra clips. Better.

But still not the action movie stockpile for which I'd hoped. As I begin loading the guns and machetes into a canvas bag, Jae and Tracey set to work on Jae's mutilated cabinet.

"Kept the heavy artillery for themselves," Jae murmurs.

"Got to be in their houses," Tracey agrees.

I imagine the creatures' armor. The guns might pierce it. But if a herd of creatures blitzes us...

"You guys almost done?" Tommy calls up.

Jae kicks his cabinet, and finally the door jars loose.

Tracey murmurs, "Oh my."

A pair of assault rifles. On the shelf below them are extra magazines. I can't believe it.

Tracey snags a few flashlights and batteries from a shelf and loads the lot into the canvas bag. Jae zips it up, arranges the cloth straps over his shoulder, and straightens with a grunt.

He heads down the stairs, and I'm marveling at our luck when a voice says, "Put it down, darling."

We stand rigid. From our vantage point in the loft, we can see a gun, a hand, and the shoe of a man just outside the Boiler Barn. He's got Miranda covered, but she's still aiming at Burkhardt. Jae is frozen mid-step, probably trying not to let the canvas bag shift. If it does, the weaponry will clank together and alert the gunman to our presence.

"Hey," Tommy says, "we can just—"

"Wait a minute," the man says slowly. "I recognize you. You're one of the bastards who assaulted us yesterday."

Oh hell, I think. I know who this is.

Jeff Marino. I crouch and see the rest of him, his broad torso stretching a white T-shirt, his taut, bulging gut. He dwarfs Miranda and Tommy. Burkhardt's peering down at his shoes like a child caught doing something shameful. Tracey touches my shoulder, mouths *the bag*. I glance at Jae, who's stuck in that awkward half-stride, and decide there's no way we'll be able to lower the bag to the loft floor, unzip it, match the ammunition to the gun, load it, and shoot Marino. Too many steps, too little time. Besides, once the shooting starts, everyone in Dean's posse will arrive, including Dean.

"I'm gonna make this simple," Marino says. "You drop the gun, and I'll go easy on you."

"I'm not droppin' anything but your friend," Miranda says.

Tracey looks at me, wide-eyed.

Marino sounds disgusted. "One job, Burkhardt. You had one goddamn job."

"They surrounded me," Burkhardt whines, and I swear the atmosphere in the barn changes, an electricity permeating the air that wasn't there before. Jae peers back at me, his expression tight.

Marino's voice is toneless. "How many are there?"

"Don't say a word," Miranda growls at Burkhardt.

"That's fine," Marino says, edging backward. "That's just fine..."

"*Stop*," Tommy commands, and I know it's about to erupt, Marino either opening fire or going for his posse.

I call out, "Wait!"

As I crowd past Jae, he whispers, "What are you doing?"

"Calhoun?" Marino asks.

I pass between Miranda and Tommy, and when I step into the moonlight, I half expect Marino to fire. He'd been the one, I remember as I stare into the muzzle of his chunky black handgun, who goaded Dean toward murder.

"On the ground," Marino says.

I move to the side to make sure Miranda has a clean shot. I don't want her to shoot—don't want *anyone* to shoot—but Marino might not give her a choice.

"I'm not gonna say it again," Marino says. "Get on the ground. Face down. Your friends too."

I marvel at how imperious this man is, how accustomed he is to others doing his bidding. I wonder how many employees he has and how poorly he treats them. Or how demeaning he is to his wife and kids. I hear a shuffling behind me and turn to see Miranda impelling Burkhardt out of the Boiler Barn. Tommy is starting to edge toward the stairs, and Marino must notice because he calls, "Freeze, little fella."

Tommy frowns at him. "What'd you call me?"

Marino grins. "Hurt your feelings? Get your ass out here and on the ground. All of you." His gun is leveled at me now. "You want to live, John, you'll tell your friends to follow orders."

"Put your gun down," Miranda says, and Marino actually chuckles.

"Or what?" he challenges.

"I'll shoot you in the nutsack."

His grin fades.

"She'll do it," I tell him.

"You'd be smart to listen," Tommy adds, "while you still have a nutsack."

Marino's positioned fifteen feet from me, about twenty-five feet from Miranda and Tommy. I can tell he's weighing his options. If I were closer, I might be able to tackle him, tangle him up long enough to wrestle the gun away or allow my friends to join me in the scrum. But something is bleeding into his face now, and it's not good. There's no fear there, nothing but the smug superiority that makes him such a jackass.

"Last chance, sweetie," he says to Miranda. "Put the gun down."

She doesn't say a word. Just stares at him.

He favors us with a half grin. "That's what I thought. You're not gonna do jackshit. You're just a mouthy little cunt." He bellows, "*DEAN!*"

A crack rends the night. Marino jolts. He glances down at his chest, which blooms scarlet within a rosebud of torn cotton. He glances up at Miranda. Blood slops over his bottom lip, and he pitches forward.

"Holy shit," Tommy murmurs.

We all stare at Marino's corpse as it collapses onto the ground.

Dean's back porchlight floods on.

"*Move!*" a voice shouts. It's Tracey, and she's already streaking across the grass, Jae lumbering along behind her with the canvas bag. Tommy's drifting after them, as if surveying a well-struck ball on his way up the first-base line, and Miranda is detaching from Burkhardt, who stares, slack-jawed, at Marino's dead body. I hustle after them, unable to believe what just happened. Shouts from nearby, not only from Dean's house but his neighbors, and it's the image of Buddy Scott and his sleazy, glitter-eyed stare that galvanizes me, that leads me to put a hand on Miranda's back and move her toward the path. We duck inside the hemlocks and make for the car. More shouts, the bangs of house doors. It sounds as if the whole neighborhood is rousing. I expect Miranda to make some wisecrack, but she doesn't. This is the first time she appears uncertain. Almost haunted. I guess killing a man will do that to you.

I hear a car door slam and an engine rev, and an irrational worry of Tracey abandoning us flickers through my head. She'd never do that, but with the shouting voices and the barking dogs, it's difficult to remain rational.

Miranda and I burst from the trees and find the Beamer's trunk yawning open. Jae beelines toward it. I scurry to the passenger's door and climb in. Miranda slides into the backseat. The trunk slams shut, and Jae and Tommy pile in on either side of Miranda. Tracey punches it the moment the doors are closed, and I buckle my seatbelt, expecting a furious gunman to lurch through the foliage and open fire. No one has to tell Tracey to floor it. If anything, she's pushing the Beamer too hard down Tuckaho Lane. We hear a gunshot, hunch our shoulders, and hold our breath as Tracey white-knuckles us around a curve. We make Northwestern Avenue, and I'm staring at the side mirror, hoping against hope that headlights don't appear behind us. Tracey burns through campus, and unless Dean or one of his people has taken an especially sly route, it looks like we've eluded them. None of us says a word as we rumble down the alley and grind to a halt behind the Physics Building. It's Tommy who gets out to activate the rolling door, and as he ducks inside and Tracey pushes the Beamer after him, it occurs to me that I've scarcely thought of the creatures since our foray to the

Boiler Barn. The door trundles shut behind us. Tracey pops the trunk, and Jae retrieves the canvas bag. The rest of us climb out, and it isn't until we move toward the interior door that we discover Kehler standing there, arms folded. We all stop, the others maybe feeling the way I do, like a grade-schooler who's disappointed his father.

"What did you get?" he asks.

"Necessities," Tracey answers.

"Let me see."

With an uneasy glance at me, Jae lowers the bag, unzips it, and peels open the flaps. Kehler surveys the contents.

"Casualties?" he asks.

"One fuckhead who didn't give me a choice," Miranda answers.

"Fine." Kehler turns and heads for the interior door. "You idiots need some sleep. You've got surgery in the morning."

21

I eke out a few hours of fitful sleep, and after showering and donning my own unwashed clothes—sans underwear; even I have *some* standards—I join the others outside the operating room.

"Take that grubby shit off," Miranda says when I enter. She's kicked back at a desk, bare feet crossed atop the blotter. She and Tommy are in cornflower-blue gowns. Jae's is white, maybe because he's several sizes larger.

"No joke," Tommy agrees. "You're a walking bacteria factory in those clothes."

Feeling besieged, I peel off my shirt. Tommy tosses me a blue gown. I start to unbutton my cargo shorts, then remember something and start toward the door.

Miranda calls, "I've seen guys in skivvies before."

"That's the problem," I tell her. "I'm not wearing skivvies."

Tommy gives me a thumbs-up. "Living free, man."

Miranda says, "You're gonna get nice ventilation with that ass crack hanging out."

I head to the hallway. I drop my cargoes and am just sliding the too-short gown over my arms when Tracey and Beatrice swing around the corner. Beatrice blushes, but after a perfunctory glance, Tracey directs her gaze studiously ahead.

"You ought to wear a bell so people know you're coming," I tell them.

"You should keep your junk covered," Tracey answers.

Gown on and chastened, I follow them inside.

"Have you had anything to eat or drink this morning?" Tracey asks Miranda.

"Couple Long Island iced teas," Miranda answers. When Tracey gapes at her, Miranda says, "No, I haven't had anything to eat or drink. How dumb do you think I am?"

Tracey addresses all of us. "Okay then. The order. Kehler and I have debated about this, but—"

"I'll go first," I say.

Everyone looks at me.

"We had Jae going first," Tracey says.

"Please," I answer. I'm about to say God knows what—maybe deliver some crappy speech—when Kehler enters and saves me.

"There's the man," Tommy says.

Kehler ignores him. "Are the patients prepped?"

"More or less," Tracey says. "John's going first."

Kehler eyes me a moment, then looks at Beatrice. "Wash up. When we enter that room, you will do everything I say, exactly the way I say it. You will be precise, steady, and focused."

Beatrice looks pasty but she nods.

"You *are* up to it, aren't you?" Kehler asks.

"It's her first time doing this," Tommy says.

"I don't care. She has to be perfect."

"Maybe you're just nervous," Jae says.

"Of *course* he's nervous," Tracey answers, and Kehler looks at her in surprise. She holds Kehler's gaze. "He loves our daughter as much as I do. Richard is many things, but above all, he's a good father." I see real emotion on Kehler's face for the first time. "Thank you for doing this," Tracey tells him. "We're grateful."

"Yeah, man," Tommy says. "Thanks."

Jae squeezes Kehler's shoulder.

"Just don't turn our brains to mush," Miranda says.

Tommy rolls his eyes. "You had to screw it up."

Kehler approaches me. "Are you ready?"

I think of my son. My wife. I think of Emma.

And start toward the operating room.

—

My face fits snugly into the vinyl-cushioned opening. I hear the squeak of casters. "What's that?"

"Targeting system," Kehler answers. "For the ablative laser."

Beatrice's legs come into view. Her tennis shoes are close enough that I can make out several ballpoint pen slogans, things like *Galadriel for Congress* and *Han Shot First*. In another situation, I'd geek out with her, but all I can think about is undergoing an experimental brain procedure at the hands of a cosmetic surgeon.

"Okay," Kehler says, and I feel something frigid swab my forearm. "A little pinch."

I clench my teeth at the prick of the needle, which feels like a harpoon puncturing my vein. Or maybe I'm just a baby when it comes to needles, like Iris always said.

Says, I correct. *Says*.

"Beatrice?" Kehler says.

Beatrice clears her throat. "Most of what exists is not detectable to our eyes. We can only see a fraction of what's out there."

I know this is scripted, but as she settles in, I realize I don't mind. I find her voice soothing.

"Arthur Machen wrote about it in *The Great God Pan*," she continues. "Machen talked about lifting the veil. About seeing what no human eye had ever seen. That's what you're about to do."

"Feel anything?" Kehler asks.

I don't feel anything except a slight weightlessness.

"When you wake up," Beatrice says, her voice beginning to echo, "you will witness things that others cannot."

"It will take a miracle," Kehler says. I hear the creak of casters, but like Beatrice's voice, this is echoey, as if heard through the throat of an interminable corridor. On the canvas of my eyelids, I see the faces of my family, the cosmos swirling behind them. I hear their voices echoing down the endless hallway. Shadows and footsteps. Shadows and voices.

Then only shadows.

PART FOUR
VISION

22

I'm not aware of waking up. There's no sound, no smell. No sight either, and when I remember the procedure, I feel a surge of terror. Am I blind? There's the pressure of a blanket. I attempt to move but only accomplish a slight torso wiggle. I lie there, listening for a sound, anything, but wherever I am is as noiseless as a crypt.

I don't feel like a convalescing patient—I feel like something that's been stored. A cadaver, or a broken appliance. I recall the convection oven that went bad on us, the damn thing costing more than two grand and quitting after only seven months, just outside the warranty. The memory still pisses me off, the impersonal customer representative, the *Sorry, sir, there's nothing we can do* attitude. We bought a replacement (financed it, actually) and kept the old one for parts. It's still in my garage—only my garage is incinerated along with the rest of my house, our photographs, videotapes I never got digitized. My kids' childhoods, our marriage ceremony. All of it gone, Iris and Sam and Emma—

I open my eyes.

Darkness.

Ah fuck, I think. *I really am blind.*

Kehler butchered me. I was an idiot to believe he could perform a revolutionary brain procedure that would enable me to see interdimensional creatures.

But I detect light. Just a smidge of it, but enough to give me hope.

It's Charles Bonnet Syndrome, a voice whispers. *You're hallucinating. There* is *no light, and there never will be again.*

I realize the light is stronger the lower I shift my gaze. I'm staring not at some fictitious conjuration of a blind-struck brain, but at glazed-green tiles. I have no idea what room I'm in, but it must be cramped because the wall is only inches from my feet. I roll my eyes left and right; beside me, the walls are *right there* as well.

I gaze about the sludgy space but can't see much of anything. Panic seeps in, so I concentrate on my hands, my fingers, and I realize I can move them, can feel, albeit dimly, the papery rasp of the bedsheet. The Physics Building wouldn't have sheets like this. And it wouldn't have recovery beds. So what am I lying on?

My fingers encounter steel and canvas. A cot. At this epiphany, I become aware of the pressure on the back of my head, the hangover-like ache. *Of course it aches*, I think. *Kehler sawed through your skull.*

A door creaks and I brace myself for what I'll see.

Beatrice. Backlit by the pink hallway glow. She steps into the room, a tidal wave of light attending her. She must notice me blinking because she whispers, "Sorry," then draws the door almost closed. "You're the first to wake up."

"Are the surgeries done?"

She's soaked with perspiration. I wonder how long she and Kehler have been at it.

"There's still Tracey and Miranda to go," she explains.

"Was it successful?" I ask.

She hesitates. "Do you feel different?"

"My head hurts."

"Oh. I'll get you something."

She goes out, the pink blast of light buffeting me again before she draws the door shut. She's back in a hurry. She hands me pills and a cup of water, and raises me to a sitting position. I manage to gulp down the pills, and then I'm lying down again, exhausted.

"Those will help you sleep," she says. "I'll be back after we're done. It's already late afternoon."

With that, she goes.

Maybe it went better for the others, I tell myself. *By the time he gets to Tracey…*

"*Jesus Christ,*" I gasp. I push myself up on my elbows and a thunderbolt of pain blasts my skull. I'm sweating, soaked through, and though I can't recollect my dream, I know it was hideous because my heart is pounding and I'm nauseated.

I force myself to sit up. I might vomit, but sitting here won't make it better. I swing my legs over the cot edge, and my bare feet touch the icy linoleum. The room is pirouetting, and I decide, if I throw up, it's best to do it in the hall. I push through the door and totter into the sickish pink light and stand there like an old man escaped from the memory ward. I peer down the corridor and wonder if everyone died or merely left me here. I catch my breath and start down the hall.

I pause at the first door. I turn the knob, and when light spills in, I see Jae lying there, his mouth open and snoring in beatific slumber. I cross the hallway and open the door, and something swings out and thwacks me on the collarbone. I stumble back as the mop handle smacks the floor, and I stand there glowering at it. "*Damn*," I mutter and massage my shoulder. I move to the next door, but it's locked. I cross to another room and discover Miranda, who at rest looks no more capable of swearing than she looks of dunking a basketball. I shuffle across the hall, open another door, and find Tracey. Her appearance gives me a start. Her hands are folded over her stomach, reminding me of a corpse at a wake. Her skin color is normal, but the way her gown is bunched around her neck, like an old-fashioned ruff, sends a chill coursing down my spine. Shivering, I close her door and glance over at the locked door.

Tommy, I think. A certainty washes over me—*Something's wrong with Tommy*—so I knock. When no one answers, I pound the door harder.

A voice hisses, "What in God's name are you doing?"

I spin and discover Kehler, still in scrubs.

"You need to be in bed," he says.

But I barely hear him. A wave of dizziness forces my eyes shut. I throw out my arms for balance. It feels like someone is guiding a drill press into the base of my skull.

Kehler's voice is close. "Can I help?"

"Something for the pain," I manage. I'm careening toward a good vomit, and perhaps Kehler senses this because he takes my shoulders and pivots me toward my recovery room. Somehow I make it back. Lying down provides a measure of relief.

"Be right back," he says. I turn my head to surrender what meager contents still reside in my stomach. But at the last moment, I pull back, an old parental instinct braking the gag reflex: If I barf, who will clean up after me? I remember when our family went down with food poisoning, Emma perched over the toilet rim, Iris zonked out on NyQuil, Sam sprawled on the couch, too queasy to watch TV. In moments like that, you realize you're the last line of defense. You simply can't be sick, even if you are. Your kids need you. Your spouse needs you. And if you go down, all of you are done. Thinking this, I somehow rein it in. Beatrice shows up moments later. She asks me how I feel.

I glance at her.

"Other than horrible," she amends.

"What time is it?" I ask her.

"Three a.m.," she answers. "Here, take this."

The pill she gives me is gigantic. When I finally choke it down, I voice my deepest fear. "I don't think it worked."

"Maybe it takes time."

"Or maybe they'll keep abducting us until we're all gone."

She averts her eyes. "How do you think they're finding us?"

I think about it. "The gateways they create into our world... they aren't guessing. You can't predict with that kind of accuracy. They show up right where we are and pull us through. They must have a method of... windowing. Of thinning the barrier between worlds and spying on us."

"God," she whispers. "You think they're watching us now?"

I hope they are. I realize I want to hurt them. Above all, I want my family back, but if I can hurt the creatures who took them, I will.

I close my eyes. The last thing I feel before going under is Beatrice taking my hand.

23

My sleep is fitful and stitched with nightmares. When I emerge from the fog, I'm shocked at the time on my phone. It's late afternoon, nearly thirty-six hours since my surgery. I put on clothes and go check on the others.

Miranda says she doesn't feel any different. Tracey's been crying—I'm sure she's thinking about her daughter—but pretends to be okay. Tommy's door is locked, and when I pound on it, he doesn't answer.

I go to Jae's room and ease down on the edge of his bed.

He rubs the base of his skull. "Damn, it hurts." He glances at me. "Any change in your vision?"

I grunt. "It's blurry sometimes, but that's it."

Jae pushes to his feet and begins jerking on his clothes. "Vanessa needs me. She's due in a few months."

I think back to Iris's pregnancies, how grueling they were. The multitude of issues, both minor and serious, that people don't tell you about. And to endure all that after being abducted by aliens? My windpipe contracts at the thought.

What have our loved ones been eating? How could they

possibly still be alive? Are they being kept in cells? Or are they already dead, their brains harvested or their bodies exploited for some other unspeakable purpose? We don't know *anything*. It's all supposition, guesswork. What are the odds we'll ever see our daughters and sons and significant others again?

Jae frowns. "You think Tommy's surgery failed? I mean, failed worse than ours?"

That's exactly what I think. But I say, "I'll try again," and make a beeline for Tommy's room. *Was* his surgery botched? I knock on his door, and this time I hear Koufax growl in response. After a long moment, I hear the click of the lock.

I go in. Tommy's room is dim, the only illumination cast by a lamp on his nightstand.

"Shut it behind you," Tommy murmurs. He climbs into bed and tugs the blanket over his shoulders. Koufax nestles between his knees. In the cheerless lamplight, Tommy looks deeply unwell. "Is it closed?" he asks me.

I nod, but he says, "*Check it.*"

I move aside so he can see me test the knob, but the terrified cast of his eyes doesn't change. Koufax watches me sullenly. I assume Beatrice has been feeding him.

The closer I get to Tommy, the more I worry about him. The trembling of his hands, the quiver in his voice...

"Have you seen something?" I ask.

He keeps his eyes down.

I step closer. "What did you see?"

Tommy strokes the dog's sable fur. "Something happened last night. I haven't mentioned this, but my brother... my twin... he's a badass. He's the successful one."

"You played professional baseball," I point out.

"Until I blew out my knee. Since then, it's been semipro, the kind of shit nobody pays to watch unless they're bored."

I sit on the foot of his bed and give Koufax a scratch. "My son and I enjoy the local team. The Aviators."

"I tried out for them last fall," Tommy says. "Got cut. Fuckers."

"Their loss."

"I never do things right. My brother, he's a Navy SEAL. A hero. He always got better grades, had more friends. Most of the time, I just tagged along. Wouldn't even have been invited if it wasn't for him." His voice is growing hoarse. "But Matty always insisted."

"You were talking about last night."

"Oh God," he moans.

I know I should give him space, but a suspicion that this is important overrules those tenderer approaches. "Tommy, what did you see?"

He squeezes his eyes shut. When he opens them again, he doesn't look at me, and maybe that's for the best. Like some insidious germ, his fear is communicating itself to me. Koufax lays his head on Tommy's lap.

"I was gonna go upstairs," Tommy says. "I told myself, 'You can't stay in this room forever.' I thought of how Matty would be. He'd face it, whatever it is. So I got out of bed . . . It was late . . . probably one in the morning. And I walked down the hallway. Felt something looking at me. One of *them*. It . . . it saw me through the ceiling."

I hesitate. "That's not possible."

"You think I'd make this up?"

"What did you do then?"

"I don't wanna talk about it."

I go to him and force his body to square with mine. Koufax begins to growl. "Whatever you saw—"

"*My eyes were closed.*"

I stare at him.

He rushes on. "I was facing the ceiling, and I could hear . . .

wings. Flapping. Like massive tarps whipped by the wind. I thought to myself, *You can't be seeing this, there's a ceiling above you—a whole building above you*—and that's when the creature came into view, right over the Physics Building."

"Tommy—"

"The creature... it was pale. It shimmered. And its head was tilting down, and I knew it would see me, just like I could see it. I shut my eyes tighter... I even ground my palms into them so I could rub out the sight of the monster..." He grabs my arm. "They're *monsters*, John. Fucking *monsters*. I've never seen anything so terrible."

There's no saliva in my mouth. "Did it see you?"

His face begins to crumple.

"Holy shit," I mutter. "Oh my God."

"I'm sorry," Tommy moans.

I begin to backpedal. The only thing I can think of is Beatrice's drawing, those soulless, skull-faced eyes.

I've got to find Kehler.

—

But he's stalking down the hallway toward me and raving, "I told you to rest!"

"We have to go," I say, and we pull up before we crash into each other.

"Three days minimum," Kehler says. "Tracey's surgery was less than twenty-four—"

"Tommy saw one of them. They know we're here."

Kehler narrows his eyes at me. "Tommy hasn't been out of his room."

I feel a surge of frustration. I haven't had time to think through what Tommy told me.

"Well?" Kehler demands.

"Tommy claims he saw one flying over the building."

An infuriating smile. "From the basement?"

"He says his eyes were closed."

Kehler utters a breathless laugh. "The surgery might enable you to see other wavelengths. Substances previously indistinguishable—"

"They know we're here."

He gives me an incredulous scowl, but before he can start with his pedantic bullshit, I say, "I don't understand it either. But Tommy said it was scanning for prey. And when its eyes settled on him—"

"That's impossible. You're talking about seeing through solid matter... or telepathy..."

"I believe him."

"Then you'll believe anything."

I turn away.

"Listen," he says, moving with me. "What you're describing can't happen. It simply can't."

"Or you're too stubborn to believe in something you can't see."

"For Christ's sake—"

"Why would Tommy lie?"

"Because he's afraid."

"You're telling me he concocted this story to get out of the mission?"

"How could Tommy see through the ceiling? Educate me."

"What if the surgery could result in other anomalies?"

"Other anomalies?"

"Just consider it," I say.

"Fine. Let's say this 'anomaly' is possible. Wouldn't you have it, too? Wouldn't all of you?"

“What if there was a variation?”

There’s real heat in his eyes. “You’re calling me a butcher.”

“Kehler—”

“You’re saying I got in there, and like a toddler who can’t color inside the lines—”

“It was *experimental.* You said so yourself. Isn’t it possible there were variations from patient to patient? We’re talking about infinitesimal differences in a mysterious region of the brain.”

“You’re accepting the word of a frightened, irrational young man over mine… *Now* what the hell’s the matter?” he demands.

Because I’m not listening to him. I’m hardly aware of him. Beyond Kehler, far down the murky corridor, something is watching me.

Something silver white. Something with wings.

The creature steps out of the shadows.

24

“What’s wrong?” Kehler asks, but I can’t formulate a word, much less a sentence. Can’t remember how speech works, so deep is the dismay reverberating through me. Perhaps fifty yards away and shimmering as its silvery body slinks through the guttering cones of pink light, the creature is watching us.

“John?” Kehler asks. He has pivoted to follow my gaze, and for a few seconds, I imagine he’s as awestruck as I am. Then the truth slams home.

He can’t see the creature. Kehler enabled us to look beyond the veil, but he couldn’t perform the surgery on himself.

Its face a leering silver-white mask, the creature edges closer. I grasp Kehler’s arm.

“Come on,” I murmur.

The creature is monstrous, far too rangy and long limbed for the hallway. It’s bent over, creeping on all fours, but I estimate it’s fifteen feet tall. Beatrice’s sketch was ghastly, but this… this is worse. Infinitely worse.

Thirty yards away, the creature begins to move faster, its fluidity stunning, its body *flickering*. One moment I can see it;

the next it's gone. But each stroboscopic glimpse is worse than the last: It's armored in a chitinous shell. Though it's slender, I see hints of striated muscle and tendons under its translucent casing. But this doesn't prepare me for the face.

An alabaster goblin. A lengthy brow, vertically creased with wavy contours. Curving edges where the head tapers in sleek, helmetlike extrusions. Temple spikes that jut out like antennae. The recessed pit of nose. The slitted white eyes that glare with ungovernable sadism. The gaping mouth. The black tongue writhing inside a bed of champing teeth. The flexing jawbones and deeply sinewed throat, the mutant folds of tissue. A spray of muscles and a carapace radiating outward from its neck and shoulders.

As it stalks toward me, one moment visible, the next moment gone, I wish I'd never had the surgery. Some things are better left unseen.

I drag Kehler with me, away from the abomination. But there are fifteen yards to the staircase, and we'll never make it, not with the creature accelerating.

"You're deranged," he says, but he's moving with me.

The creature breaks into a lope, and I wonder if this is the same one that Tommy saw last night. We're shambling along when the creature lunges. I'm propelled into the wall, and Kehler is slammed to the floor. A sickening stench swims over me, like dead insects fermenting inside a soda bottle. I scramble around to find the creature already cinching its walking-stick fingers around Kehler's ankle and bearing him in the direction from which it came. For a moment, it's like Kehler is floating down the hallway alone—then the creature swims back into focus.

"No!" I bellow, and from far down the hall, I hear an answering voice. Kehler is dragged along behind the creature, his head thumping the concrete. I give chase but know I have no chance. The creature's too fast. I note that its wings are furled behind it like a cicada's.

At the far end of the hall, directly in the creature's path, two figures emerge from their rooms. Miranda and Jae. Miranda carries an assault rifle, Jae a pistol.

"Let go of him!" Miranda shouts, and the creature skids to a halt.

Jae is gawking at the beast, but he raises his weapon.

"I said let go of him, goddamn you!" Miranda shouts, and despite the fact that I'm behind the creature, Miranda opens up on it, her weapon spitting hellfire and battering our eardrums in the narrow tube of hallway. I hit the ground to avoid being torn in half, and she must have wounded the creature because it twists, screeching. It raises Kehler as a shield, and Jae forces Miranda's muzzle lower.

I lose sight of the creature, but when it appears again, rushing toward me now, silvery liquid sluices from its torso. As it nears, it swivels its demonic face toward me and takes Kehler by the throat.

Kehler's eyes find mine, and the helplessness in his gaze makes my stomach plummet.

"No!" Jae shouts. "Put him down!"

But there's nothing they can do as the creature's other hand grips Kehler's chin. I hear an appalling popping sound, the skin tearing, the blood jetting over the creature as Kehler's head rips free. The creature flings the head and body in different directions, lets loose with a bestial roar, and bounds past me. Its body vanishes, but the spatter of Kehler's blood on its shell allows me to track it before it disappears up the stairs.

"Follow it!" Miranda yells. I'm so horrified by Kehler's messy remains that I barely register her words.

The others have emerged from their rooms. Tracey, Tommy,

even Koufax. My friends sidestep Kehler's corpse, collect me, and we shamble up the steps together. A cacophony of shattered glass and bent steel echoes down the stairwell to us. We round the corner and hurry toward the atrium, where we discover the pulverized front doors and a meadow of shattered glass. Taking care to avoid the glittering shards, we make it to the sidewalk.

No sign of the creature. Koufax barks wildly. We pivot, casting glances about. I mutter, "It's gotta be here... It can't just have—"

"Look," Miranda says, and when we follow her pointing finger, we see it, maybe eighty yards above Northwestern Avenue: a coruscating slash that sparks and shimmers, half fire, half liquid, gold and fuchsia and chrome.

The gateway.

"We have to go," Jae says. "It'll come back. It's gonna be mad."

"Where do we go?" Tommy demands. "If they know we're here... if they're coming—"

"We find a gateway," Tracey answers.

Tommy's eyes wander to the glowing lozenge above us.

"Not that one," Tracey hastens. "One we can actually reach."

"It's not disappearing," Miranda says softly.

"I don't think they do," Tracey agrees.

"That doesn't make sense," Jae says. "You know the government's gone to the abduction sites, used different kinds of scanners..."

"Maybe they've seen them," Tracey agrees. "But they haven't figured out how to activate one."

Tommy squints up at the coruscating slash. "It's just a line. How the hell could something go through it?"

"We gotta move," Miranda says.

Jae looks at Tracey. "We go to an existing gateway?"

Tracey looks at me.

I shrug. "My house was on fire, but yeah, the gateway might still be there."

But that means…

A ruthless fist wrings my heart. If the gateway is still open, if they really linger, I could have pursued Emma. Could've saved my daughter.

The clap of footfalls approaches. I snap out of my self-torture and find Beatrice stumbling toward us with Eric Pruitt in tow, both of them out of breath. "We were going for a walk. What happened? Where's Kehler?"

"Oh man," Tommy murmurs.

But it's Tracey who says, "He's dead."

Beatrice's eyes bug out behind her thick lenses.

"We have to get you to a safe place," Tracey says. "You'll set up a new base for us."

"Where is safe?" Tommy demands.

Beatrice looks at me. "The bookstore?"

"There's a basement there," I say. "It's as good a place as any."

"Okay," Tracey says and takes Beatrice by the arms. "Get anything you think we'll need. Throw it all in the backseat of my car. No more than ten minutes—"

"We don't have that long," I say.

They all follow my gaze. Far down Northwestern Avenue, two hundred yards and closing, a pair of creatures lopes straight for us.

"Van," Tracey says, and we sprint toward the demolished entryway. Pruitt seems to fathom the danger because he's running even faster than Beatrice is. The others pull ahead of me, but not by much, my terror giving me extra speed. Even carrying the assault rifle, Miranda beats us there. We crunch over the litter of glass.

"Dammit!" Tommy shouts. He's slightly ahead of me, and he's hopping on his left foot. I realize he's the one member of our party not wearing shoes, and he's savaged his heel on the shattered glass. Koufax whines up at him, his haunches low and his coat bristling.

"Come on," Jae snaps, and scarcely breaking stride, he slings Tommy's arm around his neck. The two of them shambling together like that are even slower than I am, but I refuse to bypass them.

I make the mistake of sparing a look back and feel my intestines roil. The creatures are closing. They're wingless, their movements reminding me of a video Sam and I watched of a charging silverback gorilla, the arms giving it extra propulsion. And though these creatures are longer and lankier than gorillas, the unbridled power in their bodies is the same. Even if I hadn't seen Kehler's head torn from his body, I'd know we were no match for these things.

Even as I'm staring at them, they both disappear.

My body rippling with goose bumps, I surge ahead. As we clatter down the stairs, I hear Jae ask, "Why didn't they come through closer to us?"

"Must take time to make a gate," Tracey answers. "They passed through an existing one."

We're nearing the garage. As we shuttle through, we hear a plangent shriek from behind us.

The creatures are in the building.

Miranda holds the door for everybody. Tracey hustles through first, followed by Beatrice and Pruitt. Jae and Tommy and Koufax are next, with me on their heels. Practically dragging

Pruitt by the hand, Beatrice heads for the Beamer. I help her load Pruitt into the passenger's seat. He's curled on his side and whimpering, and he doesn't so much as look at me, but at least he's not in the basement waiting for the creatures to take him.

"Keys are on the seat," Tracey says to Beatrice. "Be safe."

Beatrice nods, but she looks miserable as she climbs inside.

"Wait," Tracey says. "Koufax can't go with us."

Tommy shakes his head faintly.

"She's right," I tell him. "He's got to go with Beatrice. He'll be safer."

Tommy looks like he might argue, then his shoulders slump, and he squats down to gather the dog in his arms. Koufax sets to licking Tommy's face as he hauls him over to the BMW. I open the passenger's door, and Tommy deposits the dog in the backseat.

"We gotta go," Tracey says.

Tommy whispers something to Koufax I don't hear. Koufax whines and licks his cheek. Tommy hugs the dog, kisses the top of his head, and closes the door. With tears in his eyes, Tommy backs away from the car. Miranda puts a hand on his back. Jae hits the garage opener, and the tall door trundles up.

Beatrice guides the Beamer outside, Koufax peering through the window at Tommy the whole way.

"Move," Tracey tells us.

We pile into the Sienna. Tracey slides behind the wheel, Jae riding shotgun. Tommy and Miranda take the middle seats, and I climb into the back. We've got to get out of the building. The creatures will be through the garage door any moment.

Tommy's head is down. He's weeping. I squeeze his shoulder.

As Tracey steers us out of the bay, she mutters, "Wish I'd collected some of their blood."

"Hell with that," Jae says.

"I got some," Miranda says, and we all glance at her. She

reaches down and rips off a swath of her heather-gray shirt. "Here you go, Little Miss Curious." She wads up the fabric and hucks it at Tracey.

Tracey catches it, lets the piece of T-shirt unfurl, and eyes the glistening patch of alien blood. Like the creatures themselves, like the gateways through which they attack, there's something almost beautiful about their blood. That shimmer, that way of catching the light and glistening like veins of precious metal.

She finishes backing out of the bay and is about to pull away when a creature bursts into the garage, skids to a stop, and shrieks at us. The sound is feral, blood-chilling.

"Go!" Miranda shouts, but Tracey has already floored it, is fishtailing us down the service alley. I glance out the back window and see the aliens explode through the doorway and lope after us. Stadium Street is coming up, and though Tracey's got four lanes to make a turn, the aliens are gaining ground. She pushes the van, decelerates when we reach the road, and then Miranda's rising out of her seat, the assault rifle in her arms. She leans out the side window, and as the van corners and she faces the creatures bearing down on us, she opens up, the thunder of her weapon deafening. I see one creature jerk, then tumble. The other one staggers, shivers its head, but never stops. The first one is recovering, too, its satanic face stretched in a snarl.

Then it blurs out of focus. I think for a second it's disappearing—then I realize *everything* is out of focus.

"My sight is messed up," I tell them.

"Join the club," Miranda says. "This morning, I couldn't see anything."

A thunderstruck silence, the only sound the growl of the van.

"Why didn't you say something?" Tracey demands.

"Kehler told me it would freak you guys out," Miranda answers.

"I *am* freaked out," Jae says.

"Dammit," Tracey mutters. My vision starts to clear as she tells Tommy, "Grab the other rifle."

Tommy wipes away his tears, rises up, perches in the window opposite Miranda, and raises the weapon. Positioned that way, the bottom of Tommy's bare foot is visible, and my vision is clear enough I can see how sliced up it is, one gash tracing the curve of his heel like an evil smile. Blood patters onto the gray van seat.

Tracey accelerates.

"*Go go go*," Jae urges.

I throw a look through the back window and see the creatures gaining on us.

How fast can they run? I wonder.

Tommy opens up, the noise earsplitting. I swivel in my seat, and though my sight wavers in and out of focus, I see a creature tumble.

"Nice shot," Jae says.

"My brother showed me how," Tommy mutters.

"What kind of gun is that?" I ask.

"CZ Bren 2," Tommy answers. "Matty had one similar to it."

Miranda's weapon roars, and the second creature somersaults. Tracey surprises me by slewing onto Northwestern, back toward the Physics Building.

I lean forward. "I thought we were going to my house."

"Want to lose these bastards first. Otherwise, they'll just follow us through the gate."

Her words make my stomach clench. The thought of entering an alien world is bone-chilling enough—odds are we'll simply perish in the hostile new atmosphere—but the notion of going through with the creatures right on our tails is even more horrifying.

We're passing the Physics Building when Miranda says, "Ah, shit."

She's peering up, and even before I lean over, I know what I'll see.

Winged creatures. Joining the hunt.

"Step on it," Miranda cries.

"I'm doing seventy," Tracey answers.

"Then do eighty."

"Here they come," Jae says.

"How many?" Tracey asks.

"Three," Jae answers.

"Wonder if one of them killed Kehler," Tommy says.

"Who gives a shit?" Miranda snaps. She's already sitting in the open window. The Bren 2 looks bigger than she is, and for the first time, I remember the rest of the guns stowed in the back.

A creature swoops out of nowhere and arrows straight at our windshield. Miranda is already firing on it, the delirious rocking of the van spoiling her aim. The winged creature only twitches once as it beelines toward us.

"Suicide bomber," Tommy moans. He fires. The beast jerks, tilts sideways, one of its wings twisted out of shape. Tracey swerves but the alien crashes into us and spiderwebs the top of the windshield. I glance back and see it tumbling in the road. The van shimmies as Tracey wrestles the wheel, then we're smoothing out and roaring away from campus. Away from my house.

"You have to go back," I say.

"I know," Tracey answers between gritted teeth. She flicks a look in the rearview. "Jae and John, keep your eyes peeled for another gateway. Miranda, Tommy, if you see—"

"Shoot the motherfuckers," Miranda says.

We motor through the frats and sororities and start across the Harrison Street Bridge. Out here we're totally exposed. My vision blurs, and an intense wave of nausea steamrolls through me. I grasp the seat until my eyes refocus.

When they do, I see Jae looking over his shoulder. "They're coming," he says.

Miranda resituates herself in the window, and Tommy calls, "Watch where you point that thing."

"You're the one who shoots like your ass is on fire," Miranda answers.

"Up here will do," Tracey murmurs. "Tommy, Miranda. Get inside a second." Tracey gooses the accelerator, and I see what she has planned.

"Aw, man," Jae mutters and begins to buckle in. The rest of us follow suit.

The flying aliens are thirty yards and closing when Tracey veers off the bridge toward Canal Road. She stomps on the brakes.

"Tracey!" Jae yells as an alien dive-bombs us.

We're shuddering toward a stop sign when Tracey cuts the wheel, our back end skidding, and for a second, I'm certain we'll overturn. But the tires seize the road, and we surge ahead, shoot beneath the overpass, the alien whooshing behind us, and Tracey never falters, corners the van toward the on-ramp leading back to Harrison Street Bridge.

"Sweet driving," Miranda says, sounding way too cheerful.

"Think I'm gonna be sick," Jae mutters. I'm woozy, too. Tracey handles the van like a goddamn Indy car.

"Shooters," Tracey says, and just like that, Tommy and Miranda take their positions.

We rumble up the ramp, and ahead of us, hovering over

the road, are two creatures, neither one deceived by Tracey's U-turn ruse.

Tommy takes aim. "Miranda, you get the one on the—"

But she's already firing, and this time, with the van moving in an undeviating line, she bull's-eyes one of them. The creature squalls and swoops to the right, where it disappears into the trees. The other creature wings straight at us. Tommy fires, but the creature doesn't react at all. It halves the distance. Miranda crouches down to reload.

"Tommy?" Tracey says.

Tommy squeezes the trigger, but the creature merely barrel-rolls and keeps coming.

"Blow the damn thing away!" Jae shouts.

"I can barely see it," Tommy moans and fires again, but the salvo is abbreviated, his ammo gone. "Fuck!" he shouts. Miranda rises and cuts loose, and pearlescent fluid hemorrhages from the creature's torso. Its wings tangle, and it spirals toward our hood.

"Oh sh—" Tracey starts to say, but she never finishes because the thing smashes our grill, the vehicle lurching, the alien tattooed against the front of the van, one wing jutting up at a broken angle, and its venomous face glaring at us over the hood. Tracey pounds the brakes, the creature's eyes widen as it loses its grip, and the next moment, we're bouncing over it, its wings and limbs crunching like sodden matchsticks.

"Nice work," I tell her.

Tracey nods at Miranda. "She's the shooter."

We pick up speed. In moments, we're over the bridge and rumbling into campus. We're feeling pretty good—at least I am—until we reach the intersection of Northwestern and Grant.

Where an aluminum light pole has been knocked over and the roadway is completely blocked.

25

"Tracey—" I start.

"I see it," she answers. She hops the curb, all of us bouncing, and slashes over the grassy lawn of a fraternity. We're nearly to Grant Street when a rending crash sounds behind us and a wingless creature charges through the entryway of the frat.

"There's only one of them," Tommy says, but in the next instant we see how wrong he is. There are two more ground dwellers, moving fast. Worse, as we careen onto Grant, a winged creature swoops over the fraternity roof and launches itself toward the van. I see Tracey's tense face in the sliver of mirror, and though she practically stands on the accelerator, the winged creature reaches us, slams against the roof, its talons scrabbling for purchase. Tracey slaloms the van to unseat the creature, but it won't go away, and worse, the ground dwellers are drawing even with us. One leaps, its wide maw unhinged, the banshee shriek deafening as it sinks its claws into the van's side.

"We're too exposed out here," Jae shouts. "Gotta find cover."

There's a thump as another creature latches onto the rear

bumper. I peer over the seatback and see it being dragged behind us.

"Grab the guns," Tracey says, but I'm already on my knees, reaching over to gather what I can. The van is swaying like a storm-tossed clipper, three creatures assaulting the vehicle. I snag the handle of the canvas bag, heft it over the seat, and bear it onto the floor. Jae joins me. I end up with a black pistol that's not much bigger than my grandpa's Ruger, but at the thought of that gun, the memory of Emma taken, I decide this is better than nothing. I'll be damned if I go without a fight.

Miranda screams.

She's being hauled through the window as effortlessly as a cheap doll from a plastic box. I grab her legs, and a whir of movement from across the van draws my eye.

It's Tommy, perching in his window and sighting the alien over the roof. The concussion of the Bren 2 reminds me of someone hammering a steel door with a calloused fist, the weapon's resonance a deep counterpoint to its tinny report. We hear a shriek as the ceiling bows downward and another thump as the creature tumbles into the road. Then I'm dragging Miranda back inside the van. Tracey wrenches the wheel. A creature squalls, the one on the side losing its grip.

Hell yes, I think.

The back window implodes. Chunks of glass pepper our shoulders. A creature climbs through. Despite its prodigious size, it contorts its swirling silver body through the aperture, its leering canines dripping with slaver. But I notice something else. The eyes, up close, are all wrong. They're overlarge, as though protected with something, and all my thoughts evaporate as it cinches its bony fingers over Jae's forearm, that godawful dead-insect stench wafting over me.

I thrust the pistol into its chest and squeeze the trigger.

Its body jerks, and if the screams these things emitted before were shrill, this sound is almost intolerable. I've knocked it halfway out the back window, but it's still grasping Jae. A steady pulse of iridescent blood squirts from its chest. A putrid stench surrounds me. I stick my gun in its face, and just as I pull the trigger, its other hand swings up to seize me by the throat and my shot goes wild. The creature recedes out the back window, but it's hauling me and Jae with it, the jostle and shimmy of the van greasing its efforts. I throw out my free hand to brace myself on the seatback, but the creature is too powerful, too heavy. Jae's eyes are huge, his resistance futile. We're sliding toward the shattered window, the wind buffeting our hair, the creature's fingers vising my larynx.

The world goes black.

I blink my eyes, but it doesn't help, my vision is gone, and beneath the immediate danger of the monster dragging me toward the window, an atavistic horror rises up and sinks its fangs into me: *You're blind, John! You're blind!*

I feel myself sliding, and I smell the creature's putrid body, but I can't see it.

"Shoot it," Jae says, his voice thin.

"I can't see!" I shout.

The creature yanks, and though I can feel the suck of the open window, the world remains black.

"I dropped my gun," Jae says, panting. "If you don't shoot it—"

I bare my teeth and swing the gun up.

"Higher," Jae says.

A jerk, and now the wind is whipping my hair. It almost has us out the back window. I should give my gun to Jae but there isn't time. We're tilting out the window.

"A little to your left," Jae grunts.

I shift the gun, feel the backseat headrest scrape over my belly.

Jae shouts, "*John!*"

I squeeze the trigger. The creature jerks, then releases us, and I hear it tumbling into the road.

Jae helps me back inside, and as he does, it's like someone switches on the light. His face swims into focus. He's lathered with sweat, his hair sticking up wildly.

"Better?" he asks.

I nod.

Jae winces. "Smelly bastards, aren't they?"

I give him a half smile, but movement draws my gaze: two more creatures swooping toward us through the trees. I assume Tracey's going to meet them head-on, but another light pole groans toward the roadway, and I discover the ground dwellers leaning on it, their shells swirling pink and yellow and mauve as they strain to bring the massive pole down.

Tracey has maybe three seconds to decide. If she veers right, she might beat the light pole before it crashes into the road. If she does that, we're no better off, but at least we're still moving. Or it could land on us, and we'll be easy prey in a wrecked van. The only other place to go is a parking garage, and while I suppose there's an exit on the other side of the building, the murky entryway fills me with dread. I think she's going to swerve away, but the light pole crashes down, the aluminum base tearing, and Tracey can only cut the wheel toward the parking garage.

Toward the darkness.

Nobody speaks as we slip inside the garage. There's no need. Either we'll make it to the exit or we'll be trapped in here.

Finally, Tommy says, "This reminds me of something Uncle Ebb used to say. Just when you think things are gonna get worse—"

"Tommy, I'm gonna tell you something," Miranda interrupts. "And I mean it from the bottom of my heart. Your Uncle Ebb was the dumbest motherfucker on the planet."

Tommy gapes at her.

She leans in and kisses him on the cheek. "Thanks for saving me."

His smile reappears.

Jae has moved to the passenger's seat. "Up there," he says.

"I know where to go," Tracey mutters, her expression grim. This parking garage might become our sepulchre, and she knows it. I catch her expression in the mirror, and that sick look of having failed the ones you care about, that crushing guilt… I feel it so much that I have to look away.

"They're in," Miranda says.

The ground dwellers race behind us. They sprint upright, then lope like silvery panthers. We're nearing the place where Tracey can curve left and proceed up the ramp, or take a slight jog, head underground for a short spell, then attempt to shoot up the exit ramp onto the road. Tracey decelerates only slightly before taking the jog. Jae is shaking his head, and a couple seconds later, I comprehend why. We've only gone halfway up the ramp when a pair of winged creatures appear in the exit opening, hovering, their membranous wings flapping.

"Drive through them," Jae says.

I'm convinced Tracey will do just that, but two more winged creatures descend behind the first pair, blotting out most of the dusky glow.

"Ram them!" Miranda shouts.

But even as she yells, a winged creature darts toward the grill. I think for a second it's going for the engine, but it disappears, we bounce over it, and the sound reminds me of the air mattress we once owned, the mattress Sam would leap onto when it was time to let the air out, a squishy hissing noise that now balls my stomach in a knot. We're juddering on a ruptured tire, grinding to the left, the van moaning like an ailing animal. Another creature swoops toward the passenger's side, its brethren arrowing in behind it.

"Dammit," Tracey growls and skids to a halt.

Just as the winged creature snatches for the tire, Tracey reverses the van hard. I'm hurled forward between Tommy and Miranda, and Tracey jounces us up the ramp, toward the second floor. The creature in the lead pursues us, snatching at the van and snarling. Behind it, I see the other winged creatures—I throw a look out the side window and spy two ground dwellers giving chase, too.

Five creatures speeding after us. Our odds of outmaneuvering them are virtually nil, especially reversing on only three good tires.

Maybe Tracey's thinking this, too, because she floors it, the van shuddering. She says, "Hang on," and pumps the brakes, spins the wheel, and somehow we make the looping one-eighty without crashing into the sparse coterie of cars still parked here. We're picking up steam when a winged creature surges toward the missing back window and reaches out. I rise up and blast the son of a bitch with my Ruger, the shots like thundercracks. As it tumbles to the pavement, I glimpse something fall away from its face.

"It was wearing some kind of goggles," I say.

"So?" Miranda demands. "How the hell does that help us?"

I don't answer, but I suspect it might help us a great deal. If we survive the parking garage.

The van is limping along, but I know this isn't sustainable. The creatures are in pursuit, and there's another curve coming up. Soon, we'll be on the third level of the garage, and if we somehow make it to the fifth, we'll be stuck up there with nowhere to go.

The van is shuddering violently now. Another ten seconds and they'll have us. We've got guns, but if we try to make a stand here, eventually we'll run out of ammo, and then what? We try to hoof it to my house? It's a mile away. Even if we kill these creatures, more will follow.

"Tracey?" Jae says.

"I see them," Tracey answers, her voice tight.

"Game time," Miranda says. She and Tommy perch in the side windows.

I brace myself on the seatback and take aim.

The nearest winged creature is maybe ten feet away when I blast it in the chest. Jae leans out the passenger window and fires his handgun. Tommy and Miranda pepper a creature with Bren 2 fire. My ears are absolutely ruined, but the creature goes down, tumbling in a tangle of limbs.

"The wings!" Tommy shouts. "Go for the wings!"

"What the hell do you think I've been doing?" Miranda demands.

They open up on the second winged creature, which rolls from side to side and shimmers in and out of my vision, but with Tommy and Miranda spitting fire and Jae and I pounding away, the creature can't evade everything. It lurches and skids face-first on the pavement. The two ground dwellers hurdle it, snarling.

We round the corner to the fourth floor, and I can't help but imagine more winged creatures spinning down from the sky and taking the van apart.

"Get us to the stairs," I say.

Tracey shoots me a questioning look, but I point to the stairwell in the far corner.

"Floor it," Miranda calls.

Tracey glares at her in the mirror. "It's floored."

We're putting distance between us and the ground dwellers, but not enough. Not nearly enough.

Then they pull up short.

Miranda fires a volley anyway; I hear a click. "I'm out," she says. She kneels on the floor and rummages through the canvas bag until she finds another magazine.

"Here," Miranda calls and flings a clip to Jae. She pops another into my hand. We're almost to the stairwell.

"They're hiding," Tommy says.

I glance back and see the ground dwellers taking refuge behind abandoned cars. The garage lights don't seem to work anymore. It's unnervingly gloomy in here.

"Take these," Miranda says and distributes the machetes and sheaths. I latch mine to my hip, the weight slightly reassuring.

Tracey nods at Tommy's foot. "You gonna be okay?"

Tommy shrugs. "It's gotta stop bleeding at some point, right?"

"So macho," Miranda says, but her eyes hold on Tommy's for a beat.

"We'll go underground," Tracey says, and I feel a combination of hope and terror.

"There's no way out of there," Jae responds.

"Yes, there is," she argues. "There's an exit at the edge of campus."

"*What*?" Tommy asks.

"She's right," I say. "It's a warren of tunnels down there, but if we follow the right ones, we'll come out eight blocks from my house."

We skid sideways, Tracey aiming the passenger's side at the stairwell.

"You first," Tracey says to Jae.

Jae pushes out the moment Tracey stops, and the rest of

us pile through the side door. Jae shoulders it open, and I can't help but notice how queasy he looks, how pale.

"You okay?" I ask him.

"Feels like I just had brain surgery."

Miranda and Tommy bustle past him and hurry down the stairs. I'm about to follow when I discover Tracey leaning into the van, rifling through the canvas bag.

"*Tracey*," Jae says in a harsh whisper.

I pad over to her. "We gotta go. Those things—"

"Here," she says and stuffs a jogging beanie into my hands. I take it and open my mouth to speak, but the words die in my mouth. Because at that moment, a chitinous arm slings over the parking garage wall.

26

My friends hustle down the stairs. I'm clattering down after them and shooting glances out the stairwell windows, knowing at any moment a coruscating gateway could appear. Or a horde of aliens. If we can reach the tunnel, maybe we'll stay below their radar.

If such a thing is even possible.

I shunt the thought away and loop around the landing, my bad leg protesting. Almost to the ground floor.

"John?" Jae calls up.

I shout back, "Go. Don't wait for me."

Below, I hear a door wheeze open and shut. I glance up the stairwell and see no sign of the creatures. Soon, I reach the ground floor, push past the swinging sign that reads PURDUE MEMORIAL UNION UNDERGROUND PASSAGE, and darkness swallows me. I reach up and click the button on my beanie.

I sigh. It's useless as an actual flashlight. Sure, it emits a glow, but its reach is only a few feet. Just enough light to mark you. This naked feeling grows as I open the door that leads to the tunnel. It runs beneath the Union and, if you follow the right branches, all the way across campus. But it's so dark down here that I've lost my bearings. I turn left and hobble through the murk. I haven't gone far before I realize I've chosen the wrong route. Gunshots erupt behind me.

"Dammit," I mutter and retrace my steps.

More gunfire. I hustle toward the sounds and see silver light splashing the tunnel walls. I round the corner and discover two creatures stalking toward my friends, who retreat rapidly, moving away from the creatures and away from me. The bastards must've followed us down here, and when I turned the wrong way, they got between us. I raise my gun, careful to aim high so I don't pick off one of my friends, and squeeze the trigger. The creature nearest me jolts, squalls, and whirls toward me.

I begin to backpedal. Beyond the creature, I see the other one gaining steam, loping toward my friends, who are dashing away. I spin and pound in the other direction, my bum leg aching. The creature, one of the ground dwellers, clatters behind me.

My light is so feeble, I nearly crash headlong into a wall. But I stumble, stiff-arm away from the smooth concrete, and make the turn. There's a door on my right, so I take it. The creature is gaining, and my foot won't let me outrun it. For the millionth time, I curse my disability. As a child, it caused me to lag behind others. As a father, it made me feel less athletic than the other dads. Now it might end my life.

This stretch of tunnel is narrower. There's no light anywhere, so I pump my arms and squint and hope I'll spot the next turn before I give myself a concussion. The door crashes open behind me. The creature shrieks. I consider turning off the beanie light but quickly discard the thought. I suspect the creature can see better in darkness than I can, its special lenses no doubt suited to such a situation. A drab gray door materializes in front of me, its base leprous with rust. I jerk the handle down, pray it opens.

It does. I step through and realize I'm in a storage room. Blind panic grips me. If there's no way out of here, I'm done. It's just me and the creature. Before it can blow through the door behind me, I lurch forward, leg throbbing, and spy another door. I stumble over something and am surprised to find shoe boxes, a thigh-high pyramid of them, the shoes spilling out old-fashioned, almost like…

I open the door and realize where I am.

The bowling alley. I peer into the broad, low-ceilinged space. I used to take Sam and Emma to these lanes when they were little; we even had Sam's sixth birthday party here.

I've got to hide. Hands trembling, I fish out my phone, power it up, and swipe the flashlight on. I shine it through the black space, and though the intense cone of light doesn't reach far, I can at least make out the glimmer of the polished lanes, the racks of marbled balls. A brief memory of Sam venturing too far up a lane strobes through my mind, me and Iris forgetting to tell him how slick the wood was, his feet flying in the air and the ball, thank God, bouncing harmlessly into the gutter rather than crushing his skull.

From the storage room comes the scrape of the creature's body.

I pocket my phone and huddle behind a rack of bowling balls. A half second later, the door creaks open. With a gasp, I remember my beanie. I tear it off, ball up the fabric to muffle its glow, and listen, certain the alien has spotted me.

The click of talons on wood. The stertorous huff of its breath. I clench the pistol handle and tell myself to breathe soundlessly, but I'm panting, my skin slimed with sweat. I hear the creature slink closer and rue my hiding place. Why didn't I advance deeper? Why didn't I simply push on, all the way to the exit?

I hear its breathing. Then it's past me, its footfalls barely audible on the carpet. I close my eyes—can't see a damn thing anyway—and try to dispel the tingling in my throat. I've always had that problem, needing to cough when it's least convenient. In church, in movie theaters. Whenever it's imperative I'm completely silent, the need to cough overwhelms me.

Steeped in gloom, I curl my toes inside my shoes and try not to make a sound. The creature's breathing circles toward me, my throat itch unbearable. I strain against it and shake my head, and after what seems an eternity, I hear something that makes my eyes swing open in dismay. The storage room door opening and closing.

Oh my God, I think. *The creature's gone.*

Almost laughing with relief, I slide the beanie on and tiptoe toward the storage room, taking time to allow the creature to move away. I throw a look over my shoulder, see nothing, and when I turn, I find myself staring directly into the creature's leering face.

"*Jesus!*" I shout and thrust the Ruger up.

It swats my hand aside, the Ruger skipping over the carpet. The creature seizes me by the shirtfront and breathes into my face. A rancid dead-crab odor washes over me. In the glow of the jogging beanie, I see its bloodthirsty eyes fix on mine, and numbly, I grasp the only object within arm's reach and slide my fingers into it. The creature opens its maw, the tombstone-like incisors dripping, and I swing the bowling ball at them and see the teeth shatter. The creature shrieks, doubles over, and I slam the ball on its head. Its carapace splits. It crumples and flops onto its back. I straddle its head, grasp the ball with both hands, and slam it onto the creature's face with all my might. Its face caves in, its scream an anguished gurgle. One of its special lenses falls away, and when I glimpse what's beneath, my body temperature seems to drop by twenty degrees. Gagging, I bring the bowling ball up, almost lose my grip on it because it's so greasy with the creature's blood, and bash its mangled face. This time, the alien goes silent, but I'm possessed now, all my fear and rage gushing out. I smash it again and again until there's nothing but a pulp of brains and shell fragments amid a puddle of iridescent fluid.

I stand there panting and riding out waves of lightheadedness. Then I remember the others. I drop the bowling ball and shuffle over to retrieve my gun. Finding it, I limp toward the exit.

27

I retrace my steps, my footfalls overloud in the crypt-like silence. I wonder how far ahead my friends are. Though the tunnels are marked, I'll only be able to read them as long as my beanie and phone light work. I have no reason to believe they'll give out, but if they do, I'll be well and truly screwed. Entombed down here. The prospect chills me so profoundly that I grasp the phone tighter and set off at a jog, the unhelpful pool of light bobbing and washing the concrete ahead with pale silver.

Not unlike the color of the aliens. As though my back has been pressing against the spill gates of a dam, the terror of what took place crashes over me, thrusts me forward, chugging wildly now, as though I might outdistance the churning waters of memory:

The creature pursuing me through the tunnels.

Being trapped in the bowling alley. The certainty I would die.

The feel of its shell cracking and the sight of it on the ground, one of its eyes revealed.

My God, that *eye*.

Nictitated like a crocodile's, green and huge, the gaze so

fraught with sadism and contempt that it bored into my brain and took root there. The alien's hatred of me was so palpable, so deep. Any hint of sympathy I might have harbored for the creatures is incinerated by the memory of that hateful eye. They relish this. The sport of it, the suffering they inflict. They revel in our fear.

I force myself to slow down. I've passed multiple doorways, likely maintenance or storage areas. I reach a branch in the tunnel and halt. There's a sign just above eye level, so I wash it with the phone light. MARSTELLAR STREET PARKING GARAGE, the left side reads. STEWART CENTER, declares the right. I go right.

Stewart Center used to have a gift shop where I'd buy the annual college basketball magazines for my grandfather. In a minute or so, I'll be directly under the shop, and something about that notion dizzies me. Would I, in a million years, have guessed as an undergrad that three decades later I'd be scurrying under the building in an attempt to reach the gateway to another dimension? That I'd have a family, that I'd *failed* that family, and all that was left was a desperate plan built on theory?

Hopeless, I think. *It's hopeless.* But I keep going, hunting for the right pace, one that'll carry me through these tunnels as fast as possible but that won't drive my overtaxed body so hard I'll puke. I know I should pause to listen for my friends, but unless they've been creeping along, they'll be much farther ahead.

Unless they're dead.

No, I think. If I can kill an alien with a bowling ball, my friends can stop one of them with their guns.

But they didn't bother to come back for you, did they?

That's bullshit. It's not their fault we were separated. It happened in a flash. In fact, they're probably looking for me.

Yeah? And what if they shoot you?

This slows me down. Sure, they'll see my phone light, but

their nerves are as keyed up as mine, and it would only take one errant bullet to end my life. I imagine Tommy whirling, spraying the tunnel with his Bren 2, and that slows me *way* down. The kid is skittish as hell. No reason to give him the chance to make a mistake.

But traveling slower allows the dread to leak in. Every sound is magnified. Beneath the clop of my footfalls and the scrape of the machete sheath, the tunnel gives off an undersea sound, a ghostly roar I can't quite pass off as imagination. And beneath that…

No. No buzz-hum. No need to conjure the monsters.

I get moving again. I've got to catch up with them. Down here, it's like time has ground to a stop, has become its own awful dimension. I charge ahead, discover a wall, and decelerate before I crash into it.

Left sign: STONE HALL

Right sign: HEAVILON HALL

I go right. Heavilon is where my literature classes used to be, the site of numberless insecure and elating afternoons studying the Romantic poets, Shakespeare, the early American scribes. Their stories opening new worlds, confounding me and revealing vistas I'd never dreamed of. But as I hustle down the lightless corridor I remember how alone I sometimes felt, how futureless. The way I felt before I met Iris.

Iris. How badly I wish she were with me now. I'd feel more hope if we were saving our kids together. I'm choking up, but who gives a shit? I'm alone down here, just as I was alone up there in Heavilon Hall as an undergrad. Rudderless. Until I met Iris in my late twenties, and she became my compass. My partner. My friend.

I should have been better. I should have listened more, opened myself. I loved her at arm's length, cosseted my heart away so she couldn't break it—and she deserved more, deserved all my love. I should have worried more about her and less about money. She drove toward South Bend not to get away from me but to keep Emma safe. She couldn't have known what would happen on that highway. I don't know what I should have done, but I know I should have done it with more consideration, with more heart.

Ahead, I spot a faint glow. I shamble forward and hear my name and nearly cry out in relief. I raise my hands to show I'm no threat, and Jae calls, "Johnny!" and then he hugs me. Behind Jae, Tracey is smiling, and a surge of warmth rolls through me.

In the phantasmal silver light, I see Miranda appraising me.

"Your hands are pretty shiny," she says. "You kill one?"

I nod.

"Holy shit," Tommy says. "What'd you use, the gun?"

"Bowling ball."

Jae claps me on the back. "You killed one by yourself? That's seriously metal."

I smile wanly. "What about the creature that was following you guys?"

Miranda pats her Bren 2. "We used these, but it took a lot of ammo. We're almost out." She frowns. "Didn't you see its body?"

I feel a twinge of unease. "I think I took a different route than you did."

There's a silence as we mull this over.

I nod at Tommy. "Your foot okay?"

"Still attached," he answers.

Tracey says, "Let's go. We're only a few minutes away from the exit. The quicker we get there, the quicker we can find our people."

"You hear that?" Tommy asks as we hurry along.

Jae holds his arms out, barring our way. All our focus is on the subterranean soundscape.

But we can only hear our breathing and the rustle of our clothes as we shine our lights slowly around.

"Move," Tracey says and starts off. We follow. We're nearing the Electrical Engineering Building when we hear it. The buzz-hum sounds distant, but there's no mistaking it. I've heard it too many times to delude myself.

"Ah, hell," Tommy mutters.

"It's in front of us," Miranda says.

Tracey shakes her head and points. "It's coming from back there."

We strain to listen.

"They're on both sides," Miranda whispers. She raises the Bren 2.

"Ah, fuck," Tommy moans.

"If we're gonna bust through them..." Jae starts.

"We might as well do it in the right direction," I finish.

We start forward. It occurs to me as we wade through the strangling darkness that the Electrical Engineering Building is right next to the Physics Building. The sound of Kehler's head being torn off echoes through my brain. The ruthless bastards. They never even tried to communicate with us. They abduct or kill.

Or they abduct then *kill.*

No!

They're gone, Johnny. Your wife and kids are gone.

"Wait," Tracey says, and we rattle to a stop. She puts a forefinger to her lips. We listen. The buzz-hum is gone. Before us, behind us, all is silent.

"They're here," Miranda says.

"You don't know that," Tommy whispers.

"She's right," I whisper. I move forward, Miranda at my side, Tracey behind me. Jae and Tommy fall back to guard the rear. I can hear Tommy's breathing, rapid and shallow, like a parched animal.

"Hallway bends," Miranda says in her not-quiet-enough voice. I follow her flashlight beam. I'm disoriented, but if I'm right, this is where the tunnel passes under Northwestern Avenue, then runs another couple blocks before terminating at the last parking garage on the east side of campus, the side closest to my house. Or what used to be my house.

From there, it would be eight blocks. Eight blocks of hoofing it in the evening sun. But first we have to make it out of this lightless tomb.

"Careful," Tracey whispers.

We reach the bend in the corridor and turn the corner. This stretch of hall is a straight shot for at least thirty yards.

"Think they're up there?" I ask.

"How the hell should I know?" Miranda answers. "They're the ones with super-vision."

My stomach clenches tighter.

"Anything?" Tracey asks.

I glance back and see Tommy poking his flashlight into the gloom behind us. He and Jae are blundering along in a graceless backpedal, Tommy limping badly. His beam quivers left-right, up-down, but I don't see anything.

"I'm scared," Tommy murmurs.

"We all are," Tracey says.

But Tommy doesn't seem to hear her. "Uncle Ebb always said my brother was the brave one."

"Uncle Ebb woulda been dead by now," Miranda says. "Dumbass would've shot himself by accident. You need to get that old fucker out of your head."

"Can't," Tommy says. "I was so nervous back when I played baseball, I had to poop every time I got up to hit. I was so sure I was gonna shart myself, sometimes I wouldn't even swing."

"Keep it together," Tracey says.

"I *can't* keep it together," Tommy moans.

Miranda halts. "Take this," she says and hands me the flashlight. I accept it and hear a flat crack, and when I turn, Tommy's holding his cheek, an astonished look on his face.

"What the hell?" he demands.

"You can do this," Miranda says.

Tommy stares at her without comprehension.

"In the van," she goes on. "When those things came after us, you sat tall in that window and shot the hell out of them."

Something new dawns in his face.

"You showed guts, Tommy." She squeezes his shoulder. "Now get your head out of your ass, and get ready to do it again."

Tommy draws in a deep breath and nods. Miranda pivots, and when she accepts her flashlight from me and shines it down the hallway, I see it, the silvery shape creeping forward, silent as a winter breeze. Even hunkered down, it's massive, its spiky shoulders nearly brushing the ceiling, and in the moment before I bring my gun up to fire, I see its lipless grin, its fearsome mandibles unhinged.

Miranda shoots first, that deep, tinny *tap-tap-tap* like a claw hammer on steel, and the alien squalls and rears up. I begin firing, and for a moment, I'm sure we're too late, it's gonna dive at us anyway, but it whirls and tries to lope away. We follow, Miranda popping holes in its chitinous back. It slumps forward, and Tracey shouts, "It's dead!"

Miranda finally stops shooting and curses under her breath. The son of a bitch is face down, its wishboned legs stretching from one wall to the other. We tightrope around it. The rancid odor burrows up my nostrils, still reminiscent of old seafood, but even worse now, with a sewery undercurrent. I keep my gun trained on the back of its head. My shoe comes down beside its face and I'm certain its gonna bite my ankle, so when Jae speaks, I almost cry out in fright.

“They’re coming,” he says.

But it isn’t until Tracey shouts, *“Go go go go!”* that I realize how much danger we’re in.

I hurry forward with goose bumps scuttering down my back, the clatter of the creatures sounding right behind us. There’s a dull throb in my skull, probably the surgery, but it could just as well be dehydration or terror.

“Look out!” Tracey shouts, and by the flickering light, I see one charging straight at us. I fire. Miranda opens up, and the creature squalls, throws up an arm to shield its face, and beyond it, I see another alien clambering fast along the ceiling, its upside-down leer ravenous. I sight it, fire, but it shifts and absorbs the bullet. I try to track the ceiling alien as it leaps, but it crashes into us, and suddenly we’re a wild tangle of arms and legs.

I’m dimly aware of screaming behind us, concussive gunfire, Jae and Tracey and Tommy holding them off back there, but this is a distant concern because the wounded alien is thrashing, and Miranda and I are on our backs, trying to scramble away. An uninjured alien is climbing over its baying comrade. I fire as it seizes my wrist and yanks me forward. My shot goes wild. It hauls me toward its gaping maw, and an ear-shattering *TAP TAP TAP* erupts from my right, Miranda firing at the creature’s chest, pocking its carapace with slugs. For just a moment, I feel its iron grip vise tighter, the bones in my wrist surely splintering, but then it releases me, dead. The injured alien squalls into our faces. I jam the gun in its mouth and squeeze the trigger. Its scream cuts off as the back of its head explodes.

I wiggle out from beneath their armored bodies and hook Miranda around the armpits. Then we’re upright, mired in the stench of the alien corpses.

“We can’t hold ’em,” Jae says.

“Gotta run for it,” I agree.

"Is the way clear?" Tommy asks, and no one bothers to answer, perhaps feeling like I do, that it doesn't matter. If they're attacking from both sides, forward is better than backward.

I climb over the twitching aliens and say, "Light," to Miranda.

She aims the flashlight down the corridor, and I wish she hadn't.

Two more on the way.

"Watch behind us," I say, and Jae and Tracey drop back a few paces.

Miranda fires as she charges ahead. I can't imagine her hitting anything that way, but a high-pitched alien squeal proves me wrong.

"I'll help," someone says, and a shape brushes past me. It's Tommy. Ahead of us, Miranda skids to a stop, fiddles with her weapon, and mutters, "Shit. I've only got one more mag."

Tommy is almost to Miranda when an alien leaps at her. He swings the weapon up and cuts loose, the flash of his muzzle strobing over the shrieking alien, its silver-white armature pulsing as it twists toward Miranda. She thrusts up a forearm, but it crashes down on her and pins her to the floor. She shoves her forearm against its throat as it presses toward her, jaws unhinging. She writhes and whimpers, and I raise my gun to fire, but nothing comes from it but a click. Miranda is about to die.

Tommy sticks the muzzle against the creature's back and fires.

It bellows, the keening sound sharp enough to blow our eardrums open. It whips its seething face around and grabs Tommy's wrist, jerks down. I hear a crack. Tommy howls and sinks to his knees, and the creature holds on, pain and rage commingling on its face. I fumble out the machete and swing as hard as I can at the creature's forearm. It slices all the way through. The creature brays, its head thrown back, and I drag Tommy to his feet.

"We gotta move," Tracey says, and behind us, I see myriad shapes capering in the murk.

"Busted it," Tommy says, his arm at waist level. "He fucking busted it."

I want to tell him he's wrong, but he's not. The wrist droops at an unnatural angle, and there are agonized tears in his eyes. All I can do is snatch a handful of his T-shirt and wrench him away from the howling alien who's so lost in the anguish of its amputated arm that it doesn't seem to notice us.

"Conserve your ammo," Jae mutters.

"I'll lead," Tracey says, and without waiting for us to respond, she barrels ahead, Miranda behind her, me half supporting Tommy, Jae in the rear. I don't even look back to see how many of them are pursuing us.

"Left or right?" Tracey calls over her shoulder.

"Left," I tell her.

She veers around the corner, gasps, and I think, *No!*

Gunshots. Flashes. Brilliance bleaches the tunnel and leaves coral afterimages in its wake. I blink and palm sweat out of my eyes. Miranda is smacking a mag into place. The Bren 2 explodes, the resonant tap like a chisel lancing my skull. Tommy and I weave around the corner, and it's only after I see Tracey and Miranda hustling past the downed creature that I remember I haven't reloaded my gun.

I reach down, try to extricate the last clip from my cargo shorts, but Tommy murmurs, "Reload it and trade me."

As we shamble along, I see how pale he is. I glance at the Bren 2 and he says, "It's easy. As long as you've got two hands."

We fall behind, and when I finally pop the clip in my gun and give it to Tommy, Jae is right on our heels.

“I’m almost out,” Jae says.

I’m surprised at how light the Bren 2 is. I suspect Tommy firing it with one arm would be more accurate than my firing it with two, but it’s too late to worry about that now.

“The exit!” Tracey calls. “I can see the red glow.”

“Hear that?” I say to Tommy. He’s lurching along, his broken wrist pressed against his stomach, but he smiles at me.

Jae cries out. I turn and see a winged creature vault at him, the corners of its mouth stretched wide with psychotic glee.

28

The creature takes out three of us—me and Jae and Tommy—and we land in a meaty heap. The light is paltry without the flashlights, but with my jogging beanie, I can see the creature writhing atop us, the alien held back by Jae's powerful arms. But it's gaining, its lethal claws inching closer to his face. I squirm out from under it, aim the Bren 2, but I don't want to hit Jae or Tommy, who are still pinned under the creature. Teeth bared, Tommy rolls away. Jae is making a gargling moan, the creature overwhelming him, pinning his hands to the concrete, unhinging its jaws.

Tommy boots it in the face. The creature snarls at him, but Tommy fires the Ruger. It smacks his hand away, and the gun skitters past me. I take a step after it, freeze, and see them coming, two more creatures loping side by side. I hear thunder ahead, Miranda and Tracey under siege, too.

They've got us trapped.

Jae's straining to push up from the floor, but the creature won't allow it. Before it can deliver its killing bite, I shove my gun against its snout and unload. Its head snaps back, but as it falls, I hear them coming, practically right on top of us, so I spin and fill the tunnel with thunder. I fall on my back as a creature hurtles over me. I track it with the rifle, opening holes in its torso, and it tumbles in a screeching heap. Jae rises, but another creature leaps at him.

It's intercepted by Tommy. He's latched onto the creature, bear-hugs it from behind with his one good arm. Before I can level the Bren 2 at the creature, it breaks free of Tommy's grip, whirls, and plunges a hand into Tommy's stomach. *Through* Tommy's stomach, the strike so powerful its claws puncture the back of his shirt.

"*No*," I whisper.

The creature leers at Tommy, who's gaping at it, sallow with shock, and then the creature's head snaps forward as if struck with a two-by-four. I grab on to Tommy as the creature crumples to the floor, Jae having shot it in the base of the skull.

But I can only gaze into Tommy's face. His bloody mouth. His pain-racked eyes. I lower him gently to the floor. His good hand clings to my shirt.

Gunshots from down the hallway.

"We've gotta go," Jae says.

I know he's right, know Tracey and Miranda need our help. Know that more of them might be marauding toward us, but it's impossible to let go of Tommy. I ease his head down, hear his shallow sips of breath. His eyes roll in my direction, seem to distinguish me for a second. I want to say something, want to comfort him. Then he's gone. *No*, I think, but the light's gone out of his eyes, and he's not breathing at all.

I lean down and press my forehead to his. I feel moisture on my knees, the concrete wet with his blood. My vision gets blurry. So many years ahead of him, so much he might have done. I run a hand through his sticky hair and know it's Sam I'm thinking about. My boy taken by those things, probably slaughtered. I feel hands grasp my shoulders, and I cling to Tommy a moment longer.

Then Jae's helping me to my feet. I glance back at Tommy's body, hoping it will move, but it doesn't. Just lies there, his bare toes pointed at the ceiling.

Footsteps shuffle toward us. Beyond the flashlight, I see Miranda.

"I'm out of ammo," Tracey says. "Miranda, too."

Jae pats his machete. "I'm down to this."

I look at the Bren 2. "I don't know how much is left. Tommy was using it."

Miranda looks around. "Where the hell is he?"

Jae hesitates. "He didn't make it. He died saving me."

He steps aside so Miranda and Tracey can see Tommy.

Miranda's face goes tight. She punches her thigh.

Tracey appears shell-shocked. Miranda kneels over Tommy and cradles his head. She leans lower and presses her lips to his, then eases him gently onto the floor.

She stands, wipes her eyes, and draws in a shuddering breath. "His brother looks like him but with a crew cut. Tommy showed me a picture. Let's get him back." She starts toward the lurid glow of the EXIT sign. Numbly, we follow. I turn back once before we round the corner, but I don't see any creatures in pursuit. I don't see Tommy either, and that makes me glad for the darkness.

We emerge into the early evening. The parking garage exit is washed with a tangerine glow, but despite the brilliant sundown light, we can't make out any threats on the ground or in the sky.

But the world has changed. Iridescent shimmers. They remind me of those slender bubble hoops we used to buy for our kids, the kind you dip in a tube and sweep through the air and the multicolored bubbles appear like magic, wobble and glimmer, then pop in a spray of droplets. These shimmers are more like ocean waves lapping through the air, only they're amorphous and constantly altering as they undulate in the August evening.

"What the hell am I seeing?" Jae whispers.

"Wavelengths," I say.

"I don't see them," Tracey says.

I remember she had the surgery after we did. Maybe that's why she can't see the indigo and orange shimmers in the air, or the scintillating rose-gold penumbra around the streetlamps. There's a lump in my throat, tears in my eyes, and I realize it's because the colors in the air are so beautiful.

Or maybe it's because we've lost Tommy.

We hustle through the McDonald's parking lot, then we're crossing Stadium Avenue, and right in front of me is Insomnia Cookies. I freeze, despite the fact I'm in the middle of the road.

"John?" Tracey says.

"This is where I lost my son," I tell her.

"Think there's a gate here?" Jae asks.

Tracey shakes her head. "That was months ago. I don't think they stay that long."

In the improved light, I catch glimpses of Miranda's arm, a wound on the inner elbow, droplets of blood flicking from her fingertips as she runs. She doesn't seem to notice.

We make it beyond the campus boundary, past whole blocks of rental houses. We cross Meridian, bypass my school, and we're in my neighborhood. I clamp down on the memories, but they slip through my defenses. Family walks together, the double stroller. The blue-and-yellow ride-behind I used to attach to my bike, the "Chariot" we called it, and not long after that, training wheels.

God, it all went so fast. I wanted my kids to stay little forever, knowing even then how selfish it was. There's nothing like the way you love your children, the joy you get from them, how happy you are to just sit and feel loved when they look at you. Like you're someone. Like you matter. Because to them, you do. Whatever mistakes you've made, no matter how unworthy you are, they love you.

"You'll be with them soon," a voice says, and I'm amazed to see Tracey smiling at me as we run.

I nod. "We'll find Raven, too."

We both have tears in our eyes, and we can't help but laugh, and though my side aches and I'm terrified, I feel in that moment it's possible. I might get my kids back. Might get Iris back.

"Look," Jae says, and we skid to a halt next to him. On the expansive front lawn of a Craftsman-style home, an entire herd of deer graze. I count fourteen of them before one sees us, then another. For a moment, several of them stare at us. We stare back, breath held.

Then they lose interest and continue to graze.

We continue onto Ravinia Road, which leads all the way to Hillcrest and my home. My breathing is ragged, the others laboring, too. My foot throbs but I'm keeping up.

We reach the arduous hill, Ravinia climbing up and up and up, and despite the fact that there are no cars, we keep to the sidewalk, maybe because we feel less conspicuous that way. We soldier ahead, the endless incline stealing our wind and flash-burning our muscles. I guess it's closing in on eight o'clock, and though there's still plenty of light, it'll fade fast.

“Turn soon?” Jae asks between gasps of air.

“Just up here,” I confirm.

“Let’s cut across,” Miranda says. The yard we scamper through belongs to a widower who cuts animal shapes in his woodshop and displays them in his backyard in a two-dimensional menagerie. My kids loved the animals when they were little, though we haven’t stopped to see them in years.

The heavy feeling returns, so to fight it off, I jog harder, my limp worse. I burst into the woodcutter’s yard, not even bothering to glance at the animals. I don’t want *memories* of my kids, I want *my kids*. And if the gateway hasn’t disappeared…

Chugging down Hillcrest, past my neighbors’ homes, my yard just beyond…

I reach my house and stop in my tracks.

The whole place is caved in, a pitiful helix of smoke rising from the heaped remains. I stand there and can’t believe this ruin was our home only a couple days ago. We bought it when Sam was an infant, our dentist’s wife telling us about it before it went up for sale. And now, faced with its destruction, I can’t escape the idea this was where it was always heading.

Miranda creeps along the edge of the ruin, kicking shingles and fragments of siding. Tracey joins me.

“There’s nothing you could’ve done,” she says.

I lower my head. Glance at her. “I’m sorry about Kehler.”

She averts her gaze.

Jae moves up between us and grasps our shoulders. “Let’s find that gate,” he says.

Together, we move around the side of the house. When we reach the fence I built, I see that it’s also been incinerated.

Everything is gone.

When we reach the back patio, I'm struck with a sense of unreality. How can this collapsed heap of shards and bricks and insulation be the place where Iris and I raised a family, the place where we were happy for fifteen years?

Or most of those years.

Miranda hauls a charred length of cement board off the mound. "You said the gateway was back here somewhere?"

I nod.

Jae drags a whole heap of shingles off the pile, which is twelve feet tall.

"A little to your right," I tell the group. "Emma got taken at the rear of the house."

"You gonna help us," Miranda says to me, "or you gonna mope?"

Jae gives her an incredulous smile. "Take it easy. He's hurting."

"She's right," I say. I begin heaving chunks of rubble. Scorched planks. A twisted skein of fiberglass window frame. Tracey goes to work beside me.

Jae gasps and sucks on a finger. "Glass."

We toil in grim silence, the evening slowly dropping into twilight. The cirrus clouds are touched with scarlet here and there, some purple showing in the west. The cicadas are chirring raucously now, and I don't like that because between them and the near-constant clamor of our digging, we can't hear anything else.

And then I see it. Sparks at the crest of the mound.

"Holy shit," Miranda says.

We're digging wildly now, everyone heaving hunks of wood and cement board, Jae and I dragging a massive section of scorched joist out of the way. The peak of the gate is visible now. Within the oval of brilliant sparks, I see the shimmering iridescence that resembles the aliens themselves.

“Hands up!” a voice shouts.

I freeze—we all freeze—and when we turn, we see people fanning out around us, their weapons drawn. Buddy Scott on one side, Chris Burkhardt on the other.

It’s Dean Dawson who steps up to me. “Hey, Johnny.” He nods at the Bren 2 lying on the patio. “I believe that belongs to me.”

29

Dean retrieves the Bren 2 and smiles. "Unless you want to get shot, I'd put down your weapons."

There are nine people in Dean's posse, all armed. We have to comply. But Miranda doesn't.

Dean glowers at her. "Put. Down. The gun."

"We give up the guns, we'll never get them back," she answers, and she seems so sure of herself, I can almost forget she's out of ammunition.

Dean taps his chest. "They're my guns."

"And you've shown you can't be trusted with them," she answers. "Just another middle-aged dipshit playing action hero."

Dean raises the Bren 2 and approaches Miranda. "I'll show you how much I'm playing."

"Miranda," I say.

"I've known men like you," Miranda says. "Insecure. Gutless. Always compensating for your two-inch dicks."

"Johnny?" Dean says. "You better talk some sense into this whore."

"Don't call her that," I answer.

I consider making a move, but there's simply no way. I'll be killed. And my wife and kids will stay lost.

"Put the gun down," I tell Miranda.

"No," she says without taking her eyes off Dean.

"*Listen to me*," I growl, and this time, she gives me her attention. "We can't do anything if we're dead."

"You think you can reason with these asswipes? They burned your house down."

"I need you to trust me."

She opens her mouth to argue but doesn't. Just holds my gaze for several beats, then hands over the gun.

Dean chucks it into the myrtle, where it lands near one of his men.

"You're making a mistake," Jae says.

Dean grins at his cronies. "This guy says I'm making a mistake." He strides up to Jae. "You're the ones who drove up in that piece-of-shit car and jumped us."

"That piece of shit was mine," Miranda says. "And I should've run your dumb ass over."

Chris Burkhardt steps forward. "She's the one who killed Marino."

Dean looks at her. "That right?"

"I'd kill him again if I could," she answers.

Dean grins a sleety grin. "Buddy, I believe we've got a winner."

Eyes glittering, Buddy approaches Miranda. Several voices begin to shout. The semicircle of posse members closes, a couple of them stumbling on the boards we've cast aside.

"Tell you what," Buddy says to us. "You four get your asses out here in the yard."

Tracey looks at me, and I know what she's thinking: That would take us away from the gate. But Buddy sticks his gun right in Miranda's face, and we have to move. I go first, Tracey and Jae behind me. Miranda holds out a few seconds longer, but when Buddy presses the muzzle against her forehead, she finally goes. Dean's people make room for us to pass, then close ranks. We stand in a line, the mob facing us, the smoldering pile of my house behind them. Over Dean's shoulder glows the apex of the gateway. At the sight of it, I get a little short of breath.

"We'll do them one at a time," Dean says.

"The girl first," Buddy agrees.

I step forward. "I'm the one who stole your guns. That's on me."

"Oh, I agree," Dean says. "That's why you're gonna be last. I want you to see your friends die." He chuckles. "It'll be just like your family. You got them all killed for your bullshit principles."

Fists clenched, I step toward him.

"Stop right there, John," Burkhardt says.

I turn to Dean. "You're a coward."

Dean snorts. "*I'm* a coward." He puts a forefinger to his lips. "Who was it that broke into my barn in the middle of the night? Who was it that put himself above the welfare of the neighborhood?"

I scan the remains of my house, hoping to find something that might help. Only thirty feet away. Agonizingly close. I should've clambered up the heap the moment it was exposed, should have never hesitated...

Dean glances at Buddy. "The girl."

Buddy aims at Miranda, and hardly knowing what I'm doing, I step toward Dean and shove him. He tumbles backward and lets out a surprised bleat. Two of his people converge on him, and the others aim their weapons at me. I brace myself for the bullets, but none come. Not yet.

A man and a woman attempt to help Dean up, but he shrugs them off. He grimaces, and when he makes it to his knees, I see why. He landed on a board with nails jutting out of it, one of which has plunged straight through his palm. Dean holds up his hand, the board grafted to it, and stares in horror at the blood streaming in runnels down his forearm.

His eyes go cold. "Shoot him."

Buddy takes aim.

Tracey gasps, and peripherally, I see it. The smoking mound of ruins is shifting, something disturbing the rubble. Buddy is about to fire when someone tackles him. It's Jae, slamming into Buddy like a defensive end blindsiding a quarterback. I draw the machete and leap at Dean. We crash to the ground, and I shove the machete under his Adam's apple. With a glance, I see Jae has wrested Buddy's gun from him and has him in a headlock, the gun against his temple.

"Put down your weapons," I tell Dean's posse.

Dean manages a laugh. "You think this changes anything?"

A board slides down the ruins and plinks on the hardscape.

Miranda creeps forward, but Burkhardt is there. "Stop," he commands. "I swear to Christ I'll shoot you."

"No, you won't," Miranda says.

"Don't move!" a man shouts, this guy younger.

"Shoot the girl," Buddy says, though his words are strained because Jae is compressing his windpipe.

The pile of rubble shifts, exposing more of the gate. Shingles tumble to the patio.

"What's happening?" a woman asks.

"It's just the mess settling," the man beside her answers. "That's what happens in a fire."

And on the word *fire*, I see it. The silver-white fingers poking through the gate. The gaunt, glistening arm. The horrible face. I can hardly breathe as the creature spreads the glimmering slash and crawls through.

"Shoot her," Buddy manages.

Miranda smiles at Burkhardt. "Sure. Shoot me, sugar. You know you want to."

"What are you doing?" Jae demands, but I know what she's doing. Everyone in Dean's party is looking at her.

But the creature... the creature is staring at the youngest posse member, the man closest to the gate. The alien bellies down the wreckage like a shimmering salamander.

"Drop your weapons right now!" the younger man shouts at us, gun up and quivering. I notice he's got a weaselly look, his eyes too close together.

Dean nods in my grip. "That's my boy."

The creature steps closer, and beyond it, I see another alien begin to climb through. Behind Dean's son, the creature rises up, at least twice his height.

Tracey is creeping forward. "We're all going to forget about this," she says.

A pair of gunmen step forward and aim at Tracey.

And for a moment, all of us are immobilized. Jae with a gun to Buddy's head. Me with a machete to Dean's throat. Burkhardt with his gun trained on Miranda. Tracey likewise covered. No one moves.

No one except the alien that's now right beside Dean's son. And the young man doesn't have a clue. The creature bends at the waist, its face less than a foot from his head. It studies him, circling slowly.

"Time's up," Dean's son says, and before he can fire, the creature seizes him by the hair and bears him toward the pile of rubble.

"*Junior!*" Dean bellows.

"Shoot at it," someone shouts, and two of the gunmen fire at the creature they can't see. They don't wound the creature dragging Junior up the heap, but they do nail the second creature, the one atop the pile. It shrieks, claps a hand to its side, then glowers down at the gunmen. It leaps, knifes through the air, and slams one of the shooters to the grass.

And for a moment—a flickering, breathless moment—I almost slide the blade over Dean's throat. But I don't. I let him go, and he scrambles after his son.

I hear a bellow of pain and turn in time to see the alien's limbs whirring at the pinned gunman. The man is nondescript, just another businessman in his early sixties, but now his neck is latticed with wine-dark grooves, his blood spraying the front of the alien. Drenched, it rises to its full height, nearly fifteen feet, and stalks after Dean.

"Dean!" someone yells. "Look out!"

Buddy has broken away from Jae and is shambling toward Dean. The creature dragging Junior by the hair is nearly to the gate. Junior blubbers in terror. Dean scrambles up the heap, but he's too late. The creature ducks down, spreads the gate, and disappears through it, Junior slipping through behind him.

Dean glances back at me. "Where'd he go, Johnny? Where'd he go?"

I can't answer. Because my eyes are riveted on the blood-lacquered creature, the one Dean and his posse can only see as a red-spattered shape.

The alien grasps Dean by the shirtfront and lifts him into the air. Dean gapes at the alien's bloody outline.

"No," he whispers. "No, please—"

The alien bites down on Dean's face. Dean's legs begin to scissor.

"Put him down!" Buddy shouts. He grabs a jagged two-by-four and swings it at the creature. It leaves off chewing and swivels its blood-slicked features toward Buddy. He recoils, overbalances, and falls and begins to crabwalk away, but the creature stalks after him, Dean's convulsing body still in one hand.

"Shoot it!" Buddy screams.

Most of the mob members have hightailed it away, but Chris Burkhardt, his jowls quivering, steps toward the creature and fires. The creature jolts. Pearlescent liquid spurts from its shoulder. Its face a rictus of fury, it squalls at Burkhardt.

Buddy grins fiercely. "Yeah! Shoot it again!"

The creature raises its free hand and plunges it through Buddy's breastbone. The only sound Buddy makes is a truncated gurgle, and then he slumps on the patio, limp and gushing blood.

Someone grasps my shoulder. I suck in breath and raise the machete.

Tracey throws her hands up. "Easy. Time to go through."

I turn and find the gate unguarded. We'll never get a better chance.

As we climb onto the heap, I realize that everyone but Burkhardt has fled. The creatures' victims lie like gore-stippled beef carcasses. Burkhardt sinks to his knees, the gun held before him. "Please," he moans. "Please don't..."

Tracey clambers up the ruins of my home, with Jae, Miranda, and me following. At the top, Tracey pauses. "My eyes... they keep swimming out of focus."

But she touches the coruscating slash. Her hand merely passes through it. My spirits plummet. Then she tenses, and I notice there are dazzling pinpricks of light at the top and bottom of the sparkling diagonal slash. Tracey spreads her arms and inserts her index fingers into the pinpricks, and the slit blazes a brilliant gold. She hesitates just a moment before sinking her hands into this brilliance and expanding the slash. I finally understand why no human has passed through a gate inadvertently.

Unless you activate it in this precise way, you can't gain passage. I watch in awe as Tracey climbs through. Without pausing, Jae follows. Miranda goes next.

I reach the gate and spare a glance back.

Burkhardt fires. The creature jerks and drops Dean's body. Before Burkhardt can shoot again, the creature seizes his forearms and squeezes. Though the evening light is failing, I see well enough the way Burkhardt's flesh splits, hear the vivid sounds of his bones crunching. He begins to wail. The last thing I see before crawling forward is the creature biting into Burkhardt's throat. Then I'm pushing into the shimmering iridescence, leaving what's left of my home—and my world—behind.

PART FIVE
THROUGH

30

For a moment, I'm convinced I'm dead. An existential dread floods through me. There's a blinding golden light that forces me to turn away, but I keep crawling and the air gets colder. I inch ahead and realize the brilliant light has ebbed. I see my friends ahead of me; they appear to be stopping.

"My God," Jae breathes. "Do you see it?"

We're in some sort of cave. In the upside-down U of light ahead, I make out violet and magenta patches of sky. The air is redolent with vegetation, though I don't see any yet.

The others are pushing to their feet, so I rise, not only so I can see but because my skin is pursed into goose bumps from the spongy, gelid composition of the cave floor. I totter to my feet and become aware of two hopeful truths. One, I can breathe. Just as importantly, there are no creatures here in the cave, no sentinels who might make our rescue mission the shortest ever.

Then, like a static shock, I hear my son's voice in my head: *I'm here, Dad.*

I freeze. The voice wasn't imagination.

I push past Miranda, who stands spellbound. I join Tracey at the cave opening and take in my first view of this surreal new world. Sam is here. I know it. And if he's here, Emma and Iris must be too. But... my God. This place. I can barely believe my eyes.

The sky is obscured by dense vegetation, but even the intermittent swatches I see are evidence that Eric Pruitt saw much more than different colors after his car accident. Somehow, he glimpsed this world. Or at least the sky in this world.

"They'll be coming," Tracey says. "We gotta go."

In the distance, I catch hints of tenebrous spires rising into the sky, but we need to move. The creatures who less than a minute ago were butchering Dean Dawson and his men must be close, one ahead of us, one behind.

"John?" a voice says, and it's so quavery that I don't recognize it as Jae's. He's staring at his hands, which are slick with blood, even if the blood is a muted mauve in this bizarre new atmosphere.

"It's from that dude's son," Miranda explains. "Junior. The one the alien dragged through."

We glance at the cave floor and see the blood trail. I have blood on my palms, too. Did the creature eat Dean's kid, or use him for whatever grotesque procedure they're performing? I take a step, but something seems off. Gravity is slightly different here. I leap into the air, and I rise maybe four or five inches higher than I would on Earth.

"Listen," Tracey commands.

At once I hear a host of noises, none of them loud, but presenting such a dense tapestry of sound that my goose bumps regather. Rustling, slithering, creaking, and... sighs.

That last one is what creeps me out the most. It sounds like a series of whispered sighs, and what the hell could be making them? All at once, I'm struck with an obvious truth, one of the many notions I should have considered already:

So many species exist on Earth. A different dimension capable of sustaining life would contain a multitude of living beings as well. I consider Earth's biodiversity—humans, microbes, blue whales, rose plants, vampire bats. How many life-forms must exist here too, as exotic and nightmarish to our eyes as we are to theirs? And the sounds I'm hearing... the rustles and slithers and sighs... those must be generated by living things.

The cave opens onto a bioluminescent forest. The foliage is dense, tall—it rises fifty feet at least—yet there are no broad trunks, no thick boughs of any kind. Instead, the supporting framework for the broad fronds is fluorescent green, bamboo-thin, and delicately filigreed.

I step forward onto... not grass, not soil... It's not moss either, but that's the closest to it I can come. It's moist and glistening and even under the soles of my sneakers, I can feel it wriggle. As I step, purls of faintly glowing light, peach and green and violet, radiate from my soles.

"John?" Jae says, and his voice is tight.

Miranda pulls ahead, so I speed up to catch her, and then, about fifteen feet from the forest, we stop, and I hear Miranda gasp.

The forest is alive but not in the way earthly forests are alive. The primary species ahead of us is the reedy lime-colored stalks with deep-green fronds the size of bedsheets, but there are myriad other types of plant life here, all emitting a neon glow. The plants range from green to carmine to periwinkle, in size from the mammoth fronds to knee-high sprays of burgundy plants that remind me of peppermint sprigs or nuclear-irradiated wheat. Higher up, larger plants are tinseled with gossamer-thin strands of platinum, which makes the air above us sparkle like a firefly-studded meadow. But what leaches the warmth from my skin is the fact that all the plants *move*, undulating in a slow, hypnotic dance.

"It's beautiful," Tracey says.

I can see why she's so enraptured. It *is* beautiful. Or would be if it weren't so goddamn spooky. It's not difficult to imagine those knee-high sprigs latching on to my leg and stripping the flesh to the bone. Or those swirling trees swarming us, enfolding us like the toothy lobes of Venus flytraps and sucking on us until blood dribbles from our pores.

"We have to go around, don't we?" Jae says.

"Let me catch my breath," Miranda answers, and I'm alarmed to note how sickly she looks. Then I realize something else. We all look slightly plum colored. The light in this world is dimmer, mellower than that on Earth, as though we're in a permanent twilight. For all I know, it *is* twilight here. Maybe it's the same time it is on Earth. Or maybe this *is* Earth, just a different version of it. My mind reels with the possibilities. So when Jae grabs my arm, it takes me a moment to haul my thoughts out of the mist.

"Don't move," he whispers.

But I do, just enough to see what's standing behind us at the cave mouth.

An alien. The ground dweller who murdered Dean and Buddy and Burkhardt. Its front is slathered in human blood, which looks almost black in the magenta atmosphere. It's panting either from exertion or from the satisfaction of glutting itself. As the cave darkness falls from its face, I discover something both logical and horrific: It's carrying the goggles it wore in our world, and its eyes are visible, and if I thought the fleeting glimpse I got earlier was disturbing, this sight is enough to pull the oxygen from my lungs. The crocodilian eyes are overlarge, viridian, and hideously bloodshot. Moreover, there don't appear to be eyelids, which makes the creature's horrid bloodshot stare all the more unsettling. It shuffles out of the cave and tilts its face heavenward, as though we aren't standing thirty feet away.

I want more than anything to flee, but the sight of it is too extraordinary. Here in its own world, the creature's iridescent body absolutely *glows*. Its exoskeleton swirls and shimmers like some freakish Christmas ornament, the fluid within dancing to an unheard symphony. The creature's face exudes beatific ecstasy, a being grateful to be back on its home turf. It touches its blood-splattered chest, glances at its fingertips, then absently tongues the blood off them.

Jae jerks his head toward the forest. Tracey shakes her head.

I realize how exposed we are. Just standing here waiting for the creature to discover us. It's shaded near the foliage, but it's not like we're invisible. As if goaded by the thought, the creature strides forward, *straight at us*, and I grapple with the urge to bolt.

"Oh shit," Miranda breathes, but she doesn't run. None of us run, and incredibly, the creature doesn't look at us, just strides forward and stops a dozen feet away. I've never been this close to one of them, not with its eyes showing, and my entire body shivers. Its viridian-red eyes strafe the forest. I'm terrified my friends will bolt, but they must be thinking what I am, that it hasn't noticed us. How that can be, I'm not sure. But we stand there, frozen. It takes another step toward us, and an odor wafts over me, an aroma so noxious and corrupt my gorge rises. I imagine it's what a mass grave would smell like. I hold my breath, and I'm sure the others are doing the same. It scrunches its nose, its eyes narrowing. For an unendurable moment, I'm sure one of us will faint.

The creature bends slightly at the waist, leans forward. My

hand is on the machete handle. The creature scrunches its nose again, its bloodshot eyes sliding toward us.

A screech from our right. The creature whips its head around and stares. Then it suddenly darts toward the sound, so swiftly that I almost stumble back.

For a full ten seconds, none of us move.

Then Jae says, "The jungle then?"

I start toward the foliage, and the others fan out on either side of me. We push into the swaying, pungent vegetation that will either shelter us or feast on our flesh.

The plants undulate around us, the noise within the caul of semidarkness louder than it was outside. The air in here is torrid and almost tropically moist. The fronds chafe my skin as I shoulder past, but the spindly, tensile reeds feel rubbery to the touch instead of prickly.

"John?" someone says. I look around and find Jae, who's knuckling one of his eyes.

"Yeah?"

"Slow down. The way you're barreling through, the plants keep whipping me after you pass."

"Sorry. Maybe we should stay closer. All of us."

"Tethered," Tracey says.

"Tell that to Miranda," Jae says, and I look up to see the plants swishing as she blazes ahead.

"*Miranda,*" Tracey says.

She either doesn't hear or decides not to respond.

"She's unhinged," Tracey says.

We start forward, but Jae puts a hand on my shoulder. "The creature back there. Could you smell it?"

I nod.

He blanches. "My brother's an undertaker. I ever mention that?"

I shake my head. Tracey is pulling ahead of us, the jungle parting and reclosing like a pulmonary valve. If we don't speed up, Jae and I could get separated from them.

"Keep moving," I tell him.

But Jae seems determined to get this out. "A couple years ago, Vanessa and I visited my brother and his wife. A three-story Victorian. The smell wormed its way into me when I entered that house."

"Chemicals," I say. "The embalming fluid."

"That wasn't it," Jae says, his tone manic. "I'm talking about something underneath."

I'm limping faster. I don't want to hear this right now.

"At first I told myself I was imagining things. But I smelled it in the dining room, at lunch. At night when Vanessa and I were in the guest room. I wouldn't make love to her. The only time that ever happened. I couldn't with that odor all around us."

God. I hurry ahead to escape his story.

"It was a rotten smell, a shitty smell. Like diarrhea and old skin. Somehow damp and dry at the same time."

We've lost track of the others, and if I have to keep listening to this, I'm going to scream.

"My brother asked if I wanted to see where they kept the bodies."

"Jae," I begin.

"He had three corpses at the time. When I walked down those stairs into the room with the refrigerating lockers and the crappy lights that left these creases of darkness in every corner—"

"*Please*, Jae."

"The smell was coming from down there. The basement was drowning in it. When my brother opened one of the fridges… the moment he slid out that drawer… the odor burrowed up my nostrils, and I knew I had to get out of there. I ran. I didn't stop until I was in the front yard hacking and wheezing."

Ahead, I see a displacement of the plants.

"*Tracey*," I rasp. "Wait!"

"Miranda won't stop," Tracey answers over her shoulder.

Jae pushes ahead of me. I'm sweating, and not just from exertion and stress. The jungle is dramatically warmer than the cave was. The deeper we venture, the more the febrile heat envelops us. And the odors. Cloyingly sweet and somehow aggressive. Like the entire jungle is a malevolent being that could at any moment seize us and suck our lifeblood until we're sacks of skin and bones.

Movement from ahead. I fumble for the machete, and the bright pulsing creepers thrash, and I'm sure it's the blood-spattered creature from the cave. I raise the weapon.

And exhale as Tracey drags Miranda through the vegetation.

"Let go of me," Miranda snarls.

Tracey does. "You gotta calm down."

"Fuck calm!" Miranda shouts.

Her raving chills my blood—Can the creatures hear us? How close are they?

But Tracey's voice is steady. "Our people have been gone for months." At my look, she amends, "*Most* of them have been gone for months. Rushing now to gain a minute or two won't make any difference."

The plants undulate around us. The feel of the burgundy wheat swishing against my shins is creepy as hell.

"We can't fight them," Tracey says. "Our only chance is to stay low and silent. To sneak in and find our people."

"You realize they could be anywhere," Miranda says. "We might be a hundred miles from where they're being held."

"We're close," I say, and everyone turns to me. "My father-in-law was right about one thing. There've been more abductions in our area than anywhere else in Indiana. That means this is where our people are being kept."

Jae says, "Are we not even going to discuss the fact that the alien back there couldn't see us?"

"Their eyes work differently than ours. That's why they wear those special glasses." I touch a deep-green frond. "Their eyes are accustomed to bioluminescence."

Jae only looks semiconvinced. "What about everything else? How do they dodge obstructions, deal with different elevations, rocks—"

"How the hell should I know? Gravity's a little different here. A fall might be more forgiving. Plus they have those exoskeletons..."

Then we hear it. A whirring sound different than anything in the jungle. A mechanized sound.

"*Get down!*" I shout.

Tracey dives toward the wall of vegetation. Miranda drops and the plants swallow her up. So it's Jae and I who are still standing when the lime-green stalks bend. Something forces its way through, something circular and black and twenty feet in the air, with an appendage protruding from its base.

A drone.

Jae and I backpedal into the plants.

A camera appendage swings toward us. Liquid spumes from either side of the camera. Jae and I plunge deeper into the jungle and dive on the spongy ground. I hold my breath and am conscious of Jae doing the same. The whirring intensifies. The drone almost on top of us. I look down. See the colors under me pulsing dully, lilac and plum, and I force myself to lie still and hope that the ground will stop pulsing.

But that's not what's triggering the lights, I realize. It's my warmth, the blood flowing through my veins. Somehow the ground is alive, or at least, it responds to life. I hope the plants enveloping us are enough to obscure the glow of the pulsing ground, the drone high enough that all it can detect are the plants themselves, not the intruders.

The whirring ceases.

The drone is directly overhead.

I realize the ground glow is pulsing with my heart. Like a pebble in a pond, the light waves ripple from my body, a gentle purple hue, and amid my disordered thoughts, I remember what this particular color is called, too light to be violet, too deep to be lavender:

Iris.

And as the iris surrounds me, the glow muted but persistent, I breathe in, breathe out, and though I'm lathered with sweat, my heartbeat begins to slow. Sensation returns to my extremities. I stare at the iris glow and think of my wife. The first time I saw her and the last time I hugged her. I feel Iris around me, her warmth, the scent of her skin.

The whir kicks in above us, then slowly drifts away. I expel a long, shuddering breath. Jae grabs my wrist and smiles at me.

"Thought I was gonna piss myself," he says.

We stifle our laughter. I help him to his feet, and Miranda and Tracey join us. The others are as sweaty as I am; the jungle's a sauna now. I start forward, but Tracey cautions, "Not too fast. You don't want to catch the drone."

Good tip, I think.

"Wait," Jae says. He moves to a chest-high frond, passes a finger over it, and I see the way his fingertip glows.

"Ah, man," Miranda says. "The drone sprays that crap so it'll get on us. Mark us."

"So we make sure we don't get marked," I answer.

I make my way forward, moving warily now, and feel the others close behind me. Within a minute or two, I become aware of a draft, the air cooler ahead. The jungle will end soon. And then...

Then *what*?

I have no idea. But whatever happens, I know we'll stick together. Or at least I'm reasonably sure of it. You can't know how you'll react when it's life or death, but you can remember the goodness of other people and hope you'll find your courage, too.

The breeze intensifies, delicious on my sweat-dappled skin. I listen for the whir, hear nothing but the rustle and swish of the plants, and when I push past a massive frond, I glimpse a patch of sky. We're almost to the end. The surreal violet magenta veins the horizon. The jungle seems to sense our impending exodus and undulates more frantically. Then, as the last of the fronds give way to that otherworldly sky, I reach the edge of the jungle and stare out.

Time seems to stand still. Faced with the unimaginable, I forget to breathe.

The valley spans at least two miles. It's not deep, perhaps forty feet or so, and in the far distance I see spires rising deliriously into the sky, the shortest of which are fifty feet, some of them so tall I can't even guess where they end. Lightning flashes sporadically, sometimes in giant heliographing swashes, others in jagged bolts. But it's what's in the valley that makes my body go limp, that makes me want to shriek in horror.

Greenish-blue platforms, slightly oblong, hover perhaps three feet off the ground, pairs of platforms that stretch on and on and on. Each pair is the same: one human being, one alien, both prostrate, none of them stirring. I stare at the humans nearest us and see that their clothed bodies are stippled with the luminous substance.

We were right, I realize. *We're being harvested.*

This sprawling field of bodies is the site of the largest medical procedure in human history. And my wife and children are down there.

We descend into the valley. The bodies stretch endlessly before us, the aliens shimmering, the humans only visible because of the luminous paint splotches and the green-blue glow of the platforms.

I think of Iris. Of Sam and Emma.

I'm coming. No matter how terrible things get, no matter how many of those creatures swarm us, I'm coming.

None of us speak as we stride down the decline. Into the valley.

Into the harvesting field.

31

"I have to tell you something," I murmur to Tracey.

She nods, but I can see she's hardly listening. I don't blame her. The sight of the harvesting field precludes almost any other thought. We make our way down the valley. The terrain is craggy, rocks woven with vegetation, but it isn't steep.

"Tommy," I start. "He saw a creature before your ex-husband was attacked."

Tracey glances at me. "Saw it where?"

"In his mind. Telepathically, I guess. It was flying over the Physics Building, scouting for us." She begins to shake her head, so I hurry on. "I don't understand it either, but he was telling the truth. A little while ago, right after we came through, I . . . heard my son's voice."

She searches my face. "Maybe you were thinking about him?"

"I think about him all the time, but it wasn't that. It was a message. I know it. He was trying to help me find him."

"How is that—*careful*," she says as my foot slips. I grab ahold of her, and she steadies me. "How is that possible?"

We proceed toward the valley. "Could be the surgery. But whatever it was, I know it was Sam. It wasn't wishful thinking."

"You think that's how they found us? Through Tommy?"

I continue down, my bum foot aching. "Maybe."

Behind me, Jae says, "Watch for those drones. There's no cover out here."

"Thanks for that," Miranda answers. "Got any suggestions for when they do come?"

"I guess we hide," Jae says.

"What're you gonna do," Miranda asks, "burrow underground?"

"I'll do anything to—" I start, but when I see the look on Tracey's face, I break off. "What's wrong?"

We all turn and see what's wrong.

A drone. Emerging from the jungle. Its camera appendage is folded down, and it's spraying the glowing yellow liquid.

It's heading straight for us.

"The valley," I say. "Now."

"What the hell's that gonna do?" Miranda shoots back. "There's nothing—"

"The platforms," Tracey says, picking up on my thought. "We can hide under the platforms."

"Holy shit," Jae murmurs.

We set off, shambling awkwardly down the slope. I'm slower than the others, but we're halfway there, and I think we might make it.

Ahead of us, another drone appears.

"*Miranda*," I call down to her.

"I see it," she answers and begins angling away from it.

The platforms nearest us are bare, about twenty pairs bereft of human-alien pairings. Miranda and Tracey have almost reached them, with Jae only a few feet behind.

I labor down the uneven terrain. It's slow going, and I can hear my shallow breathing, a phlegmy wheeze-whistle that reminds me of a parched dog. I look behind me and feel my guts shrivel.

The drone is nearly on top of me. I desperately blunder down the hill, but I have nearly thirty feet to go, and the drone is almost directly overhead.

"*John!*" Tracey calls, and I see that my friends have taken refuge under the floating platforms.

I advance down the ridge in lurching strides, but I'm too slow. And with the slightly diminished gravity here...

I suck in breath. I recall the tree out of which I jumped all those years ago, my brain full of superheroes.

Jump, I think.

I take two strides to gather steam, and I kick out into the air. The ground beneath me drops away, and I'm arching toward the glowing platforms, tilting, my arms and legs swimming in the air, and I glimpse Tracey's incredulous face and wonder how the hell I'm gonna land.

My upper body topples forward, and then my shoulders and back roll on the spongy ground, somersaulting, and when my momentum slows, I sprawl out, starfished on my back, amazed I haven't broken my neck. I scuttle under an empty platform and peer up at it, not liking its oblong shape. Too much like a coffin.

The drone hum crescendos. Lemon-yellow liquid spatters the platforms. Then it passes.

I stay like that for maybe thirty seconds. Then I crawl out from under the platform and see the others doing the same.

"You okay?" Jae asks me.

I nod.

He squeezes my shoulder. "Hell of a jump, man."

This end of the valley tapers to an oval, so the first row only contains five sets of platforms. Gradually, however, the valley spreads until there are at least forty or fifty pairs in each row. Nearly all the platforms are populated, people on the left, aliens on the right. All face down.

"Wish we had guns," Miranda says, way too loudly.

Jae cringes. "Wish you'd keep your voice down."

We're navigating the center of the field when I spot something unexpected: pairs of platforms with one side vacant. There are aliens, but where people should be there's only the mellow blue green of the hovering beds.

"For the next victims," Tracey says, and I shake my head at my own slowness. Of course. These aliens are the next recipients of the procedure. They're awaiting human counterparts.

The thought brings a shiver.

"Holy shit," Miranda says, and I look up in time to see a creature limping down the valley face.

"*Get under*," Jae says.

We huddle beneath the platforms, me and Tracey under one pair, Jae and Miranda under the other. Nearby rests a dormant alien with a barren platform beside it.

The limping alien comes into view, and I realize what's wrong with it. Its leg is slathered with bioluminescent blood, a lime-green shade in this weird otherworldly light. Also, it's dragging something. Dean Dawson's son.

The kid's in wretched shape. Whatever's been done to him, his eyes are half-open, but his head is lolling and bouncing with each step the alien takes. Unsurprisingly, the alien's taking no care to be gentle with Dean Jr., who looks closer to thirty-five than twenty-five. It's difficult to tell with the blood on his forehead and his hair sticking up in matted spikes.

The alien is dragging him directly toward us. A cursory scan of the platforms reveals why. The pair nearest us—the one with an alien but no human—is one of the first platforms in the field. These creatures are malevolent, I decide, but they're orderly.

"Don't move," Tracey whispers.

Its injured leg oozing blood, the alien shuffles to the empty platform. The goggles it wore in our world are rucked up to its forehead, disclosing its infernal eyes. It releases Dean's son, who crumples to the ground, semiconscious and moaning. As we watch, the alien limps over to the dormant alien and stands peering down at it. A new expression bleeds into the alien's face. I realize with astonishment that this might be what passes for sorrow. The alien reaches out and caresses the back of the sleeping alien's head. My God. Are these creatures related? It's possible the aliens are so close-knit that they feel emotion for any member of their species, but the longer this alien gazes at the dozing one, the more I suspect the two are partners, or perhaps parent and child.

I don't feel a damn bit of sympathy.

At the alien's feet, Dean's son shifts. One of his cheeks is badly abraded, the flesh a glistening patchwork of pink and crimson. When the young man's eyes flutter open, glazy at first but then focusing and falling on the four of us, his face twists into an expression of awareness. Of terror.

We're shaking our heads, but Dean Jr. shouts, "Help me! Please!"

The alien jolts. It reaches up to draw its goggles over its eyes, and I know in two or three seconds it will be on us, screeching and clawing and alerting every alien in the vicinity of our presence.

Before I can react, someone pushes past me, Jae scrambling toward the creature, his machete out. As the creature fits the goggles over its eyes, Jae plunges his machete into its belly. It utters a strangled cry. He shoves the machete deeper and pushes the creature back, and as it falls, Jae lands on top of it. I scramble forward to help him, but Miranda is already there. She slams her blade into the creature's throat, and the creature's limbs splay out. Miranda strikes its throat again, and the alien jitters in its death throes. Something grips my calf. I raise my machete but pause when I see Dean Jr. gazing up at me.

"Please," he implores. "Please take me back."

I open my mouth to answer, but it's Tracey who says, "We can't. Your legs are ruined, and there's no way we can carry you."

She's right. One of his legs is a slushy mess. The other is ruptured below the kneecap. Beneath his black golf shorts, the shinbone tents the skin in a compound fracture.

Dean Jr. seizes me. "*Please,*" he moans. "I didn't mean for them to torch your house. I know I should've said something, but I was too chickenshit."

I almost believe him. Then I call to mind his face from that day. Contorted with hate. Lusting for my blood. Shouting right along with the rest of the mob for his father to execute me. I reach out and remove his hand from my leg.

"*No!*" he shouts. His expression changes, his eyes blazing bitterly. "You son of a bitch. You owe it to me. You got my dad killed. It's your fault—"

"Oh shut the fuck up," Miranda says and kicks him in the face. His head snaps back, but he cries out, gibbering through his hands, and Miranda raises her shoe and stomps on his forehead. He moans. But it's clear he's fading.

“Hey, Miranda?” Jae starts, but she rears up and stomps Dean Jr. a third time. This time, his body goes limp.

Mouths agape, the rest of us stare.

“You killed him,” Tracey says.

“No, I didn’t,” Miranda answers. “Though it would be better for him if I did. The dumbass.”

Miranda strides on, and after I exchange glances with Jae and Tracey, we follow.

32

It's only been about eighty hours since Emma was abducted. I can't imagine the aliens have taken that many more people since then.

She must be nearby.

I scan the pairs of figures and wonder if I know any of these people. It's impossible to tell by the backs of their heads. Will I even recognize my daughter?

Of course I will. Her height, her long hair, her shape. *Of course I'll recognize my own daughter*, I tell myself. Still, I slow down to make sure I don't miss her.

The harvesting field has grown wider, about fifteen pairs across now. The bodies on the peripheries are harder to see because of the fading light. Yet the pervasive veins of bioluminescence on the ground give off a glow, and the platforms themselves are lucent enough to shed light on each sleeping person.

"See her anywhere?" Tracey calls to me.

I don't, and the deeper we venture into the harvesting field, the more my hopefulness wanes. The paint-spattered humans are so much smaller than the aliens. I tell myself I haven't passed Emma, but what if I have? I cast glances right and left and wonder if she's at the far edge of the field, enshadowed by the growing dark.

And what, I wonder, will I do when I find her? Lift her off the platform? Will removing her from her alien counterpart harm her? Will it kill her?

I stumble to a halt, a grotesque new possibility arising.

What if she's already dead? What if she, like Kehler, was murdered rather than assigned an alien partner? Emma's a fighter. She's never been one to quit at anything. Maybe she put up too much of a battle, and because of her resistance...

No, I tell myself. That simply can't be. She's alive. I take a steadying breath and get moving.

Think, John, think. What's the order of abduction?

Emma first. Next would be... I rummage through my memories... Miranda's father. Then Iris. After that, it would be Tracey's daughter... Jae's girlfriend. Then Miranda's mom. And Sam.

Don't forget Tommy's brother, a voice reminds me.

Dammit. I *had* forgotten. His twin brother was taken around the same time Iris was. I scan the field of bodies and realize the chances of locating any of them is small. There are so many here. So many. I hear something, and at first I believe the sound is my own beating heart. Low, a constant rhythm.

My breath congeals as I realize, too late, what's making the sound. I seize Jae by the shoulder and call, "*Hide! Everyone hide!*"

The winged creature is almost on us when we hit the ground and roll under the platforms. Under the sleeping bodies.

A spastic clenching grips my guts. Even though I've been among the bodies for several minutes, I've been spared their faces. I don't have that luxury now. Directly over me is an alien, its ghastly eyes mercifully closed. To my right and directly over Jae…

Oh my God.

It's Emma.

I stare in disbelief at my daughter's sleeping face, then glance at the gap between the platforms. I don't see any wires or tubes connecting her to her alien counterpart, no visible link at all. Are the platforms themselves making the connection? Like wireless internet, somehow transferring the necessary parts of Emma's mind to the creature's?

I become aware of a hum. Not the buzz-hum that heralds abduction—this is smoother, an almost musical sound that, in other circumstances, might be soothing. But it isn't. It's the accompaniment of their unforgivable violation.

The creature swoops toward us, the sound of its wings beating louder. I can't peel my eyes off my daughter's face.

I'll save you, Emma. I'll save you if it kills me.

I glance at Jae. He rolls his eyes up to Emma and looks at me for confirmation. I don't know how he knows this is my daughter—she does look a little like me—but when I give him a slight nod, he breaks into the warmest smile I've ever seen.

The slow beat of the alien's wings grows softer, moving away. I exhale pent-up breath. Swallow. Glance up at the creature on the platform above me.

Its eyes are open. Staring at me from less than three feet away.

It squints through the platform at me, and I realize that, from this close, it must be able to make out my shape. Its face twists into a look of utmost hatred. I slide out the machete and thrust it at its chest. For a moment, I worry the platform will repel the attack, but the blade slips easily through and skewers the creature's shell. It lets loose with an earsplitting screech, and my daughter's eyes shutter open. She only stares straight down for a couple beats, looking toward Jae but not seeing him. Then her eyes shift, her forehead pinches, and she discovers me staring up at her.

The creature's long arms snake out over the edges of the platform. Its talons find me. Still squalling, it grasps my shoulders and lifts me toward it, but that only compels the machete deeper, and all around it, the fluorescent blood spews, pooling on the platform, its body a thrashing flurry. Its shrieks are deafening. In moments, it will revive others or alert the winged creature to our whereabouts. Tracey seems to comprehend this because she clambers to her feet, and just as the creature's razor-sharp nails sink into my shoulders, she scythes down with her machete, straight into the alien's skull. It drops me, the entire platform drenched in the glowing lime blood.

I clamber to my feet. By the time I'm at Emma's side, she's rolling over and gaping at me. I gather her into my arms, squeezing her much too hard, but I can't temper my joy, can only clutch her to me and weep into her hair. Her arms slide around me, her embrace strong. I kiss the top of her head and hear her whisper, "Thanks for coming after me."

I scoop her up, and she throws her arms around my neck and rests her head on my shoulder. I'm reminded forcibly of the many times I carried her like this at the end of amusement park visits, the parks shutting down, all of us exhausted but thankful for the closeness.

"You're sweaty," she murmurs.

I hug her tighter, laughing, and through my blurred vision, I make out my friends. Jae and Tracey are smiling, tears in their eyes. Miranda's expression is different, almost sorrowful, and I want to tell her we'll find her parents, too.

But Tracey's asking Emma, "Are you hungry?"

I frown. We don't have any food. Hell, we don't have anything.

Emma shakes her head.

Tracey steps nearer, her eyes gleaming with an odd intensity. "What do you remember?"

Emma nestles into me, and I have to quell an urge to shut down this questioning. But whatever Tracey's reasons for asking these things, I'm sure they're important.

"I remember being taken," Emma says. "I remember screaming... crying... I fought the one that took me, but it didn't do any good." She shudders. "It brought me here. I saw these people. I knew what it meant to do with me..."

"You're sure it brought you here right away?" Tracey asks. "That first day?"

Emma nods.

"Why does that matter?" I ask, but even as I ask it, my brain starts to click.

"She isn't hungry even though she's been here for days," Tracey explains. "There's no feeding tube... I assume she's wearing the same clothes. They don't look soiled or wet..."

My mind is racing, scampering after Tracey's train of thought.

"They've found some way to keep people in perfect, healthy sleep," she says.

Jae's face spreads into a look of wonder. "That means Vanessa could still be alive?"

"I think it's likely," Tracey agrees. She looks around at the bodies. "It all depends on how long the procedure takes. We know it's more than three days." She peers closely at Emma. "Do you feel like yourself?"

"Yeah," Emma answers. "I remember everything. Being stuck in the house with Dad. That day on the highway..."

At the thought of Iris, I kiss the side of Emma's head. Inhale her hair, which doesn't smell unwashed. It really is as though she's the same as she was the day she was taken. I start to wipe the glowing liquid from Emma's clothes. There isn't much of it, which means it must evaporate pretty quickly.

"*Dad*," Emma says as I wipe the glow from the backs of her arms.

"Hey, John?" Tracey says.

"You're right," I reply, straightening. "We should get moving."

"It isn't that," she says, and the uncertainty in her voice makes me look at her. "Do you want to take her back?"

I feel the eyes of the others on me.

"*Back* back?" I ask.

"We're not far from the gate. The chances of finding the others—"

"Sam was abducted five blocks from here." I look at Jae. "You and your girlfriend live nearby. Tracey, your daughter was taken from—"

"Your wife," Tracey cuts in, "was abducted on a highway. What are the chances she would have been dragged—"

"She didn't have to be dragged. She could've been flown. And look around you. What are the odds all these people are from our town? There haven't been that many abductions in West Lafayette alone."

Emma burrows deeper into my shoulder. She'll probably grow heavy in my arms eventually, but for now, the sensation is pure bliss.

I nod. "I want to get my daughter somewhere safe. But we've got to find the rest of our people first."

"Fine," Miranda says. "Let's get our thumbs out of our butts and get moving."

I ask Emma, "Want me to carry you?"

She slides down to stand on her own. "I'm good."

Jae grins. "You've got a tough kid, John."

"Tougher than him, anyway," Miranda says.

I grin at that. Then, the five of us trudge on, weaving between the multitude of floating platforms.

Other than the sleeping ones, we don't see any aliens for several minutes. I scan the purple-magenta sky for winged beasts or drones, and keep Emma right behind me.

"We know how to rouse our people now," Tracey murmurs. "Eliminate the alien partner, and the human will wake up."

"Who's next?" Emma asks. I know she's hoping it will be her mom, but I appreciate her tact in not saying so.

"Miranda's father," Tracey says.

"Describe him again," I say, and Miranda does.

"Shouldn't we all describe the people we're looking for?" Jae asks.

He's right, of course, so we do. We keep our voices low, and it doesn't take long, but when we're done, we have a much better idea of who we're searching for.

We advance slowly, scanning the paint-spattered people as we go. I avoid staring at any person for too long. The sight of them next to the freakishly tall aliens with their spiderlike limbs and pale-armored bodies only reinforces how much danger we're in. We haven't been spotted yet, but once we are, I can't imagine how we'll make it through an armada of these creatures alive. What if they all wake up at once?

"Can I ask a question?" Miranda says. "Why are we walking so close together?"

We halt.

"She's right," Tracey says. "I can barely see the people on the valley edges. We could pass right by them."

"So we spread out," Jae says and moves away. Miranda

heads in the opposite direction. The valley is now thirty pairs wide. Soon it will be forty. Tracey edges off after Miranda, but when Emma starts after Jae, I seize her arm.

She flinches. "*Dad.*"

I release her. "Sorry. But you're not going anywhere without me."

"I can help."

"You can help by not getting taken."

"If it happens, it happens. Tethering didn't work, remember?"

The memory brings a wave of nausea. I take her by the hands. "Please. It's not a matter of not trusting you. You mean everything to me." I search her face. "Understand?"

She regards me in silence. Sighs. "Fine."

We set off again, Emma a few feet in front of me. I like this better, having her constantly in my sight. If anything moves on her… if I see the slightest sign of danger…

A thought occurs to me. "Can you see the creatures?"

Emma frowns. "Not with my eyes. But I saw them when I was asleep. I saw them in my head."

The notion makes me feel slightly ill.

"Drone!" Jae calls.

I whirl and spot it, this one coming faster than the others. Are they alerted to our presence? Did they find the alien we killed? Jae stashed the body under a vacant platform, but those surfaces are almost transparent. I make to seize Emma's hand, but she's already scurrying under a pair of platforms. I join her, taking care to keep her under the sleeping human rather than the alien. As the drone burrs nearer, I can't help but glance up at the alien on the platform.

Its eyes are closed.

Exhaling, I put a hand on Emma's shoulder and wait for the drone to pass.

In a hushed voice, Emma says, "He's even younger than me."

The boy above her is maybe eleven. His black hair pokes up in tufts, and his turquoise T-shirt advertises an amusement park called Beach Land. Maybe he's in the school system where I teach. Maybe I know his older brother or sister. Part of me wants to murder the alien beside him, but if I start down that road, freeing every human I find, there's no way we'll escape detection, and Sam and Iris will remain in this alien world.

Selfish, a voice condemns, but dammit, that's not fair. I take Emma's hand and lead her forward, thinking as I do that we, our little band, might be the only people who've made it this far. How slim are the odds that someone else has an Eric Pruitt, as well as a surgeon to help them replicate his injury and sight? And then to battle these creatures, to locate a gateway and pass through...

We might represent Earth's best chance at finding a way out of this mess. Of fighting back. And if we devote our first mission to saving the people who matter most to us, that's just our payment for getting this far. If we survive, if we're able to retrieve our loved ones and return to our dimension, there'll be time to architect a grander plan. One that might stop this wholesale annihilation of the human race. We've been walking several minutes when Emma says, "Dad."

I follow her gaze and realize what she's staring at. It's Miranda, who in turn is peering down at a platform.

"Her dad?" Emma whispers.

I nod. Tracey and Jae have also noticed Miranda's frozen form and are converging.

Emma and I start toward her. I make out the immobile figure of Miranda's father, black T-shirt, too-tight jeans. We're almost to them when Emma says, "What's she doing?" and I see Miranda raise the machete, her arm quivering, and think, *You're standing over the wrong body! It's the alien you want to kill, not your—*

Miranda plunges the machete into her father's back.

It sinks in deep, her father's arms shooting straight out. The alien jolts. Tracey is backing away, her hand over her mouth, but Jae is lurching forward, racing toward the alien, which is shaking its head groggily and pushing up from the platform. Miranda wrenches the blade out of her dad's back, heedless of the roused alien, and swings it again. Her dad spasms, his blood spurting.

I remember too late to turn my daughter away from the butchery. As the alien stretches a leg off the platform, Jae meets it, wielding his machete like a big-league slugger, and buries it in the alien's throat. Its blood sprays everywhere.

I know I should help him, but I can only cling to Emma and try not to hear Miranda's anguished words: "... begged you to stop. But you never did." She jerks the blade out, hammers down again. "You told me not to tell anybody." Blade out, blade in. "You acted like it was normal!" Miranda's dad is no longer twitching, his back a bloody goulash. "Goddamn you, you son of a bitch. *Goddamn you!*"

When it's done, Miranda sinks to the ground and weeps. Emma is trembling, and I realize I am, too. We've got to keep moving, but after this, I'm not sure how we can. We remain in that shocked tableau for the better part of a minute. Then Miranda rises unsteadily and drags a wrist across her nose. Eyes red and wet, she glances at my daughter, at me.

"Sorry she had to see that," Miranda mutters.

I don't answer. Can't.

Tracey approaches her. "You had brain surgery, you entered another dimension ... for revenge?"

Miranda looks at her. "You really believe that's all it was?"

"Why else?"

A slow, sad smile touches Miranda's mouth. Tracey frowns and opens her mouth to speak, but Miranda's harsh laugh cuts her off. "Jesus, you all really are dense."

I think of Miranda earlier in the evening, in the tunnels, her heartbroken sobs. "You were in love with Tommy," I murmur. I move in her direction.

"Don't," she says. She wipes her eyes. "All I wanted was to protect him. Why did the dumbass have to get himself killed? I never even told him how I felt about him... I mean, I was about to so many times, but I was scared of what he'd say... what if he didn't—"

"He loved you," Jae says.

She starts to shake her head, but Jae cuts in. "He loved you. I saw it. You were the one he cared about the most."

Miranda looks up at Jae with red-rimmed eyes. She heaves a shuddering breath. Someone touches my hand, and I discover Emma at my side, Emma with her understanding smile. I wish she could've met Tommy.

Miranda sniffs, rubs her eyes. "Who's next?"

"Tracey's daughter," Jae says, "and John's wife."

Tracey murmurs, "Maybe we should wait a couple minutes. Give her some time..."

Miranda catches us staring at her. "The hell y'all looking at?" She wipes the machete on the leg of her shorts. "Let's go find your people."

33

It isn't long before the next drone comes.

As Emma and I take refuge—this time under a broad-shouldered man and an even broader-shouldered alien—I wonder when our luck will run out.

When the drone passes, we push on, spreading out to comb the entire field, which is now fifty pairs across. What strikes me as we move deeper is how many kids we encounter. The aliens paired with these children aren't nearly as small as the humans, but relative to their adult counterparts, they're undersized. We pass a human toddler, face down and motionless, and I study its counterpart, a young alien close to five feet long, its body proportioned exactly like the fully grown aliens and similar in every way, except for a paler sheen and increased translucence. The alien children sparkle in the deepening violet atmosphere.

Whatever disease afflicts them is also ravaging their children, but I don't feel an ounce of pity. The human race has endured hardships beyond counting. Sickness, disease, viruses that culled vast swaths of the population. Yet even if we were capable of interdimensional travel, even if we discovered a means of healing our sick, we'd never stoop to this abomination.

At least that's what I tell myself.

I ask Emma, "What was your mom wearing when she was taken?"

"Black leggings," she answers. "Black tank top. Those white sneakers she just bought."

Yes, I think. I picture Iris behind the wheel of the van just before the semi rammed into it. I remember her frightened eyes and her half-open mouth.

I'm coming, Iris. I'm coming.

I no longer possess a speck of anger toward her, only a longing to get her back. And a deep, pulsing regret for everything I didn't do. The husband I failed to be.

As I follow my daughter past the rows of floating bodies, I understand that I don't merely want to bring Iris back, I want to bring her *all* the way back. To me. It's true I don't have a home, not anymore, but if I can rescue her and Sam, I don't give a shit where we go. The best place to be is together. That's all that matters, all that should have ever mattered. To hell with money. We'll live in tents if we have to.

But first I have to find them.

I'm scanning the rows when Jae calls out, "Is this your daughter?"

It's Tracey he's addressing, and she takes a few halting strides in Jae's direction, her face slack with surprise. Then she's sprinting, flying past platforms, past me and Emma, and when she nears Jae, she yells, "Raven!"

Jae moves into position, raising his machete. A split second before Tracey arrives, he hacks into the creature's neck. Its body jags, and Tracey's little girl goes ramrod straight. I have a quick, frantic thought—*Did he hurt Raven when he struck the alien?*—but as Tracey gathers her daughter into her arms, the girl's eyes blink drowsily, like she's attempted to stay up past her bedtime and is fading fast.

"*Oh my baby, I love you so much,*" Tracey whispers. Raven slips her arms listlessly over her mother's shoulders and rests her head in the crook of her mother's neck. Tracey caresses the girl's hair, kissing her and murmuring in her ear, and I sense Emma beside me, her posture expectant rather than moved.

And I understand why.

Iris.

Because of the physical distance from where she was abducted, she's the longest shot. If Emma has considered this, she hasn't said so, and I'm sure as hell not going to bring it up. The kid's had enough trauma for three lifetimes—better to let her hope for a little while, even if at the end we can't find her mother.

"Tracey," I begin, "if you want to take her—"

"We're staying with you," Tracey says, and I know she means it. But a five-year-old is different than a thirteen-year-old; Raven's not as portable as my daughter. Emma lived through months of this nightmare before being abducted. Raven was taken near the beginning and has no inkling of what's happening. The horrors around us might be too much for her.

But I can see Tracey's considered all this. "The faster we find our people, the faster we can get back. We just have to be quick. And stay out of sight when they pass by."

As though drawn by these words, the dull whir of a drone sounds in front of us, coming from the spires, which aren't nearly as distant now. In the moment before we take cover, I glimpse the nearest spire: three hundred yards ahead, its circumference perhaps fifty feet at its base. The violet light makes it tough to be sure, but I'm guessing there are notches in the side of the spire, indentations up which these creatures might climb. As I sink under the platform, my daughter's hand in mine, I glimpse taller spires, and beyond those, ones that soar to delirious heights.

Thunder rumbles in the distance.

"Mommy?" Raven asks. Tracey shakes her head and makes a hushing sound. Raven is still groggy, but she must get the message because she doesn't speak as the drone burrs closer, its camera appendage down, and I think, *Movement? Is that all it's trawling for? Because if that's all it is, we might just make it out of here.* If it's hunting for anything else… barren platforms, signs of violence… if the camera has infrared capability… we're absolutely cooked.

The drone overhead stops.

Jae and Miranda are huddled together catty-cornered from me. Jae's eyes are wide, but Miranda doesn't even look at the drone, her mind perhaps drifting toward her father. I fight down a shiver.

Tracey peers at the drone through the narrow gap between the platforms. Raven is gazing up in awe at the sleeping human directly overhead—a girl not much older than her. A chill breeze soughs over my arms at the sight of Raven's face, which grows less and less foggy by the second. *Don't freak out, kid. Don't freak out.*

Then my guts clench. We forgot to drag Raven's butchered counterpart under the platform. It's right there, legs spraddled and head half-removed by Jae's machete blows.

And the drone is slowly rotating in that direction.

I wave my arms to get Jae's attention. He's nearest the alien corpse. If he sees me, maybe we—

The drone begins to float toward it.

I have to risk it. "*Jae.*"

Everyone whips their heads around to gape at me. I point at the alien and mouth, *The body.*

Jae gives me an anguished look. Then he begins to crawl toward the corpse.

"*Stop*," Tracey hisses.

Jae freezes, half-under the platform, half-exposed. On all fours, he gawks at Tracey, who jerks a thumb sideways. Jae does as he's told, disappearing just as the drone reaches him. For a moment, I'm certain I've doomed us all. The drone over Jae doesn't move, the camera appendage like the tensed hood of a cobra. Then the drone floats directly over the alien corpse.

Keeps going.

As its burr slowly abates, I allow myself to exhale. Emma sinks into my side, her body trembling. When the drone is a good distance away, Tracey says to me in a low voice, "They're just motion detectors. Otherwise, we'd be dead by now."

I start to nod, but movement catches my eye. Something on the ground, a mere twenty feet from Miranda.

"Dad," Emma whispers.

I open my mouth to say something reassuring, but nothing comes. A creature the shape of a salamander is approaching us, but it's the size of a Komodo dragon.

Gooseflesh covers my arms. I tell myself to chill out. Of *course* there are other species. This is just one of many. But does it have to be so hideous?

Not counting the thick, slimy tail, the creature is four feet long, its flesh dusky and mottled with light-brown splotches. Nothing bioluminescent about this thing. It advances on all fours, its bullet-shaped head tapering into crocodilian jaws. A slimy black tongue lolls from the side of its mouth, but it's the eyes I can't stop staring at, which are small and pink and filmed over with milky membranes.

The creature crawls over to the dead alien, sniffs it, then runs its tongue over the alien's ruined face. It opens its jaws, and just when I'm sure it will bite the dead alien's head off, it freezes and sniffs the air. It swivels its head toward Miranda and begins to crawl in her direction.

It was drawn by the smell of alien blood, I think, *but why didn't it feast on the corpse?*

An unwelcome voice answers, *Maybe it wants fresher prey.*

Emma burrows into me as the creature creeps closer, only ten feet from Miranda now. She's leaned back on her elbows, but she's got her machete out, and I'm afraid she's going to attack it. The creature isn't as large as the aliens, but those teeth, the hooked claws protruding from its feet… I don't know how long she'll last against it. I'm also not sure if I could reach her in time to fend it off.

Miranda's raising the machete when the creature pauses, samples the air, then rears up on its hind legs. It makes a wet clicking sound in the back of its throat and grasps a platform with its forepaws. Miranda bares her teeth, and for a swollen second, I'm sure she'll plunge the machete into the creature's glistening belly. Then the creature hoists itself onto the platform, where one of the aliens lies hibernating.

From behind us comes the hum of a drone.

"That thing's gonna get us killed," Jae hisses.

Miranda spares him a glance, but she doesn't move. None of us move as the hum burrs closer. Raven buries herself in Tracey's arms. Emma's head is pressed against my shoulder, but by shifting my body slightly, I can see between the platforms. The creature is crawling over the alien's body, its loathsome jaws oozing slaver onto its back. It pauses on top of the alien's shoulder blades. The creature's jaws hinge wide, and what looks likes like a bloodred earthworm slithers out of its gullet. My stomach roils at the sight of it.

The appendage is two feet long, and as we watch, appalled and fascinated, the bloodred tip shivers and sprouts comblike teeth. With no hesitation, the creature plunges these teeth into a spot at the base of the alien's skull and begins to suck.

Great, I think. *An interdimensional vampire.*

As it slurps, the appendage expands and contracts, and the creature's long body undulates.

The drone is almost on top of the creature before I notice it. It sprays its yellow phosphorescence and spatters the dusky creature. The creature inclines its head and screeches at the drone. Its sucking appendage retracts, and it tenses to run, but a lightning flash fills the night, and the creature explodes in a thousand pieces. A scrap of its guts lands on the back of my hand, and though I know Emma sees it, I don't dare move. We all remain frozen.

The drone makes a brief *snick* as its firing mechanism retracts, and it floats away.

"Jesus," Miranda breathes.

In a subdued voice, Jae asks, "Who's next?"

"My wife," I answer.

"Tommy's twin was abducted only a mile from Miranda's mom," Tracey says as she indicates to Miranda. "We'll go that way."

I glance at Miranda's blood-stippled face, at Tracey. "Maybe it's better if you and Raven come with us."

As if she's read my thoughts, Miranda says, "I'm good now."

I hesitate. "Your mom. Are you gonna..."

Miranda regards me, her eyebrows raised. "Wanna know how young I was when he started abusing me? Mom should've stopped it."

I shake my head. "I'm sorry."

Tracey takes my hand. "Meet us in the center of the field about a hundred yards up?"

That seems about right to me. Or as accurate as this inexact science allows.

Tracey surprises me by wrapping me in an embrace. "Please be careful, John."

I hug her back, noticing the way Raven watches me. Miranda has already set off. Jae and I nod at each other, and we part ways. Emma and I move toward the periphery of the field. She takes my hand as we walk.

"What if she's not here?" Emma asks, and as she utters the words, paradoxically, I find my tension easing. Emma's the most positive person I know, but that constant positivity has to come at a price. No one feels hopeful all the time, which suggests many of her smiles and rosy predictions are feigned.

I give her shoulder a squeeze. "This field is far too populated for just our town, which means it must be the harvesting ground for the surrounding areas."

She looks at me, her face pinched. "*Harvesting* ground?"

"Sorry."

She considers. "How broad an area does it cover?"

"No way to be sure."

"Do you think they know we're here?"

"No. Otherwise, they'd be converging on us."

A look of terror flits across her face. "But Jae killed that one. And you stabbed the one that was..." She swallows. "...paired up with me."

"The drones are programmed to spot movement. Tracey's right about that. Equipping drones with motion sensors is probably cheaper than the technology behind the goggles that the creatures wear."

"So the drones won't notice the empty platforms?"

I smile bitterly. "I don't even think the drones are for us.

They're for those blood-sucking salamanders. And as a safeguard, the drones spray the salamanders with bioluminescent liquid, so the aliens can see them and kill them."

"How can you be sure?"

"This whole time, I've been wondering why we haven't been caught. But when we saw the drone blast that thing to pieces, I realized the truth: The aliens are so sure of themselves, so certain of their superiority, that they haven't considered an incursion like this. It's the ultimate insult. They don't think humans are smart enough to find the portals. If they were really concerned about us busting up their plan, they'd have sentries posted, a more sophisticated means of surveillance. I mean, they've mastered interdimensional travel and complex brain transplants. Why would they worry about a lesser species like us?"

Emma stops, her forehead furrowed.

"Hey," I say, going to her. "What's wrong?"

"You said 'brain transplants.'"

"It's just a theory."

"It's true," she says. Her arms hang limply at her sides, her haunted gaze downcast. "I was asleep, but it was like I was dreaming the whole time. And it felt like evil hands were pushing things around in my head. Shoving things aside it didn't care about and snatching up things it did. And turning over those things. Studying them. Figuring me out. Learning everything about me and... *taking* it. Running away with it. Running away and laughing at me."

I'm acutely aware of how exposed we are, how with every passing moment the odds of discovery rise. But not only does Emma seem to need this unburdening, I suspect in some fundamental way, we can use her knowledge—if not now, then later.

If there is a later.

"What else?" I ask her.

She gazes up at me. "I saw its thoughts, too. I saw into its mind."

I'm aware of a dull beat in my throat.

"They *hate* us," she says. "They hate us, but it's not the kind of hate you feel for an enemy. For a rival. It's the kind of hate..." She licks her lips. "It's the way I feel when I see a maggot. Grossed out. There's also some of the attitude we have for cows and pigs. Like we can use them, but we never really think about what we're doing to them. Imprisoning them and raising them for slaughter."

Her words strike me like club blows: *maggots and pigs.*

"You're right about them thinking we're stupid," Emma says. "And there's something else."

I'm anxious to get moving, not only because we're pushing our luck, but honestly, I don't know how much more insight about the alien psyche I can take.

"They've done this before, Dad."

I stare at her.

"Remember how there were only a few abductions at first, then they accelerated?"

I nod. "Maybe they were testing their technology, seeing if—"

"Not their technology," she interrupts. "They were testing *us.*"

My thoughts spin at her words.

"They sent a small number through the portals first because they had to see if they could survive our atmosphere, if there was anything... toxic or contagious. They also had to learn if our brains could... could..."

"Meet their needs?"

She nods. "The alien I was connected to, he was just a... I don't know. Just a commoner? But he knew what they were doing because they've done it before. To other planets. After those first few abductions, they ran tests to make sure it would work. Then…"

"The day of the highway?"

"Yes. That's when they really came for us. All the tests had come back. Everything checked out." Her eyes widen. "Dad?"

I follow her gaze and see the body on the platform, the black leggings and tank top. The white sneakers.

Iris.

We sprint toward her, Emma pulling away from me, and before I can stop her, she begins shaking my wife, rousing her. I hustle the last few paces and tell Emma not to wake her mother yet, but Iris's eyes are open, she's rolling onto her back and staring at us, not recognizing us yet, and I have time to think, *She's gone. They've stolen her mind, her memories. You're too late—*

"Emma?" Iris breathes.

Emma nods, the tears streaking down her face. Iris reaches up and touches Emma's chin, and I grasp Iris's hand. She looks at me. "John?"

I smile.

Her look is wondering. "You came for me?"

My eyes blur with tears and I don't give a damn. In Iris's face, I see none of the accusation, none of the anger or hurt or baggage I once saw. I lean down and kiss her cheek. "I'm so sorry."

"You came for me," she murmurs. "You came."

And the three of us are clinging to each other. We're better together. Stronger. And I'll never—

A hand clamps over my forearm. I scarcely have time to swing my head around before the alien beside Iris jerks me into the air and heaves me. I land on my side and roll, but the alien isn't concerned with me anymore; it's grasping my wife and daughter in each of its hands and lifting them…

I unsheathe the machete, but there's no time. The alien

is leering into the faces of my loved ones, is opening its maw wide. I'm several feet away, and it's going for Emma first, her legs scissoring and her eyes huge.

I lunge toward the nearest sleeping alien. "Hey!" I shout.

The alien grasping my wife and daughter swivels its head and discovers my machete pressed against the base of a sleeping creature's neck.

The alien drops Emma and Iris. Its face twists into a mask of rage. Its horns are longer and curvier than many of the monsters I've seen, like a blackbuck antelope. As it stalks over to me, I can't help but notice the glances it shoots at the alien under my blade, and I wonder briefly if they're related. I raise the machete, and the curvy-horned alien lunges at me. I spin and thrust the machete at it. The blade sinks into one of its fog-lamp eyes, and its body is already spasming as it crashes into me. I push up and stare at its head, where the machete handle is jutting straight up and jigging with the creature's death throes. I wipe my hands and step on the twitching creature's forehead. I jerk the machete, which slides out with a chill-inducing scrape, and feel a hand on my back.

It's Iris. She keeps hold of Emma's hand, but with the other arm pulls me into an embrace. Emma clutches us both, and a wave of euphoric dizziness sweeps through me. We stay like that for a moment, until I hear a voice say, "You found her."

Four people are standing near us: Jae, Miranda, and two newcomers. The woman beside Jae must be Vanessa. Her shirt is black, her pants purple and white, her eyebrow, nose, and ears pierced. She's lovely, and just as lovely is Jae's smile, and I think of what he said about her: *Vanessa's the mirror you go to when you want to feel good about yourself.*

My gaze shifts to Miranda, who nods at the short, muscular guy at her side. "Crazy, isn't it? Looks like Tommy with a buzz cut."

She's right. Tommy's twin has militaristically short hair,

slightly more muscle tone, and no scar under his right eye, but other than that, this could be Tommy standing in front of us. I feel a hollowness spreading inside me and fight against it.

"Two more to go," someone says, and I see Tracey and her daughter approaching.

Iris looks up at me. "Sam?"

I nod. "I'll find him."

She smiles, her eyes shimmering, then reaches up and touches my face. "I like the beard."

I savor her touch for a moment. Then I tell her, "You need to get Emma somewhere safe." I look at Tracey. "You and your daughter should go too."

"We stay together," Tracey says. "That was the agreement."

Jae and the others are nodding, but I shake my head. "There're too many of us. The larger our group, the more likely we'll be discovered. It's a miracle we haven't been yet. Jae, you and Tracey have found your people. You know the way back to the cave. Take Iris and Emma with you and—"

"We don't split up," Emma says, and when I shake my head, she grasps my shoulder. "Dad. This is not the time to prove your toughness. We stick together until we have everybody."

"Your dad's right," Miranda tells her. "The rest of you need to get back. John and I'll go on."

Iris's forehead crinkles, but I can tell she's thinking. Getting Emma to safety, getting the others to safety, makes sense.

I say to Miranda, "You could help lead everybody back."

She shrugs. "I need to find my mama."

Tommy's brother steps forward. I mentally flail for his name. Then I remember it. Matty.

"You all saved my life," he says. "I'm not abandoning anybody."

"Damn straight," Vanessa agrees.

A gasp makes us all turn. It's Raven, and she's pointing to something, her brown eyes wide.

"Oh shit," Jae mutters.

For a moment, I don't know what everyone's so freaked out about, but then I see it approaching in a gap between platforms, maybe sixty yards away.

A drone with wheels. Rolling under the platforms. Heading straight toward us.

"Get on top of them," Tracey says.

We all stare at her. She hefts Raven onto a platform beside a sleeping woman, and Matty begins to follow suit. No one climbs up beside a sleeping alien. I glance back and see the rolling drone is forty yards and closing.

I'm starting to help Iris and Emma onto one of the sleeping people's platforms when Jae's girlfriend shouts, "Another one!"

I whip my head in that direction and scour the ground for the other rolling drone, but she's pointing into the air. My stomach, already sour with dread, gives another lurch.

A flying drone, spraying the glowing liquid.

"Fuck me," Miranda mutters.

"Under," I whisper.

"*Under?*" Iris demands and jabs a finger at the rolling drone. As it closes, I can see it's almost identical in size and shape to the flying drones. Its two wheels have a deep tread and a balloon-like girth, reminding me absurdly of my son's adolescent RC car obsession.

"He's right," Tracey says. "We have to cling."

Vanessa gapes at her. "What do you mean, we have to..."

But Jae's already hurrying toward Raven. "I'll keep her safe."

Tracey nods and ducks under a pair of platforms with Raven and Jae. Shaking her head, Vanessa follows. I see Matty lowering to a crouch.

I take my daughter and wife by the hand and lower to the

spongy ground. The drones burr louder. The aliens have synchronized them, I realize. Of course they have.

Crouched down, I see Jae grasp the edges of a platform with his strong hands and swing his legs up to hook his heels over the slender base. He nods to Tracey, who whispers something to Raven, then helps her climb into the narrow gap between Jae's chest and the underside of the glowing platform.

"This is insane," Matty mutters.

Miranda is already hoisting herself up. "Afraid you're not strong enough?"

Matty seems to notice Miranda for the first time, and the look he gives her is so much like Tommy's good-natured smirk that my heart hurts.

"I don't know if I can do this," Iris says. "I'm so weak."

"You can do it," I say with a confidence I don't feel. She and the others have been in hibernation. Will they be able to support themselves? Yes, gravity is diminished here, but enough to allow for this miracle?

"Come on," I say and help Iris up. The platform she's chosen is occupied by a square-jawed young man just about Sam's age. I hope she doesn't notice.

"Over here," I say to Emma, and as we scuttle over to a pair of floating bodies, I cast a backward glance and see the drones are only fifteen yards away.

"What if I fall?" Emma asks. Tears glisten in her eyes.

"You won't," I say and help her up. She slips trying to get one of her sneakers hooked over the platform, but I steady her until she's situated.

"Dad?" she says, and her tone is so panicked that I look down and see the rolling drone is almost upon us. I reach up, grasp the edges of the platform beside Emma, and push off the ground. It isn't until I'm dangling there, my body feeling suddenly leaden, that I realize I've selected an alien platform. Reluctantly, I swivel my head to stare into the alien's face.

The eyes are closed.

But they could open at any moment now. And worse... are the drones slowing down? They're nearly to our platforms, and I can see the appendage poking out the top of the rolling drone—it casts an alabaster column of light maybe two feet high, starting on the ground and ending just about where our butts hang down from our desperate perches. My muscles are burning, and I cast a glance over at Emma. She's looking at me, her tears flowing freely now, and I can see she's about to lose her grip. Her teeth are bared, her chest is hitching, and as I watch, horrified, her body performs a downward lurch. Her right hand, the one nearest to me, is clinging to the platform edge by her fingertips. On instinct, I shoot out a hand, grasp hers, and pin it to the platform. Above us, I glimpse the spatter of the glowing yellow liquid on the sleeping bodies. Which means...

I chance a look down, and there, even with our feet, is the rolling drone.

Its pallid searchlight strafes the area beneath the platforms, and I realize it's going to pass directly under me. With what reserve strength I have, I thrust my midsection toward the platform, and now the drone *is* right under me, its insectile burr somehow scornful.

I hear a little whimper and peer beyond Emma to where Raven is lying on Jae's chest, face-to-face with a man she's just met. He's shaking his head vigorously, but her little face is crumpling, and though I can't blame her, I pray the kid will hold it together just a few moments more.

Then I hear something I can't quite credit.

Someone's singing.

It's Tracey, clinging to the platform beside Raven and Jae's.

Her voice is just loud enough I'm able to make out the song: "Lovely Day" by Bill Withers.

Raven's face is no longer squinched up. She's staring at her mom with something akin to wonder.

Tracey gets to the chorus, and now Jae joins her in a surprisingly tuneful voice.

"Shhh," Vanessa admonishes, but she's smiling. So is Raven.

I glance back at Emma, who's laughing a little through her tears.

I crane my head to spot the drone, but I can see it's a good distance away now. Still, we cling to our precarious perches a few seconds longer.

Iris is the first to lose her hold, Matty second. I release Emma's hand, and she tumbles to the ground with a relieved moan.

"Sing more," Raven says as she and Jae and Tracey lower themselves.

We emerge from the shadows of the platforms, a few of my companions wiping their hands on the ground to rid them of the yellow liquid. Matty is wiping off the toe of one shoe.

I look from Iris to Tracey. "See why you have to go?"

Tracey plants a hand on her hip, but Iris nods. I can see how shaken she is from the drones.

"You all go," Miranda says. "It's dumb luck they didn't catch us just now. There's no way we'll make it out of here if you all stay."

"She's right," Matty says. When we all look at him, he flushes and hangs his head. "It feels gutless. But I'm so goddamned weak. I could barely hang on. And if I can't . . ." He glances at Emma and shrugs.

"Go now," I say.

Tracey looks at me. "This feels wrong."

"No guilt," I tell her. "If you get my wife and daughter back to our world, it will all have been worth it."

Iris moves between me and Tracey. "I hate it, but… John's right. We have to go."

Vanessa is frowning at Iris. "What about your son?"

Iris takes my hand. "John will find him."

I swallow back the thickness in my throat.

Iris leans toward me. "But you've got to hurry," she says. "Listen. About the… procedure. Whatever they did to me… I could feel everything. I was aware at least part of the time. But there was… seepage. Some of its consciousness bled into mine."

I begin to shake my head, but she overrides me. "You're not getting it." She taps her temple. "Some of its memories are *still in here*. I could feel myself pouring out, my thoughts and memories… so much of me. But that transfer went both ways, and now it's swirling around in my brain."

"Anything that can help us?" Tracey asks.

Matty steps forward. "They're not stopping. This…" He nods at the harvesting field. "This is just the start. They've got preservation areas set up. Underground."

The words are too ghastly to process. I shake my head. "We've got to get you all out of here."

Then Iris's arms are around my neck, and she's crushing herself against my body, and it fills me, edifies me. She pulls away only enough to press her lips to mine. Taken aback, I breathe her in, savoring it, and then my daughter moves forward, and I hug her so hard I'm afraid I'll hurt her. But her embrace is just as fierce.

"I loved being shut in with you, Dad. The last few months were the best."

I can't help but smile.

"I love you," I tell them. "Now, seriously… go."

Tracey nods, her hands on her daughter's shoulders. "We'll get them home, John. I promise."

A distant screech reaches our ears. I give Iris and Emma one more hug, and then the group is moving away.

Miranda and I watch them go. Jae's holding Vanessa's hand, Tracey holding Raven's. Emma is right behind Matty, and Iris is trailing Emma.

But Emma still watches me over her shoulder. Watches me with an expression so grown-up I can imagine the woman she'll one day be. It's as though she's memorizing me for when I'm gone. I realize I'm doing the same thing to her, channeling all my mental energy into imprinting her on my mind.

Stay safe, I think. *Stay safe, my amazing girl.*

34

For once, Miranda's got nothing to say. We set off toward the spires, the platforms widely spaced enough for us to walk side by side. We've been moving that way for a couple minutes when she says, "You shouldn't beat yourself up."

I don't answer.

"The best thing a dad can do is give a damn," she says. "You do."

I glance at her. "Thanks."

We soldier on and hear nothing but the susurrus of the breeze, the almost-undetectable hum of the platforms. I scan the prostrate bodies.

"Get down," Miranda says.

I drop and follow her under the platforms just before a flock of birdlike creatures swoops over us, eight or ten of them, their bodies glowing amber, their eyes a spectral silver. Other than the vampiric salamander, we've yet to discover a species that isn't bioluminescent, and that gives me hope. If that's how vision works for most life in this dimension, we still might find my son and escape without dying.

The breeze kicks up, the chill settling into my bones. I've always despised frigid weather, and with the wind whispering over my bare arms and the certainty growing in me that I'm too late to save Sam, I begin to shiver. I glance at Miranda, but her expression is unreadable. If she's experiencing the same disquiet, she's good at hiding it. She's scanning the rows of platforms, intent on finding her mother, intent on—

Go back.

It's just the breeze, I tell myself, just the weird noise of an alien landscape. No one is speaking.

Go back.

I stop. Not only were the words clearer this time, the voice was familiar. I rotate slowly, scanning the bodies.

You're too late, a voice that can't be Sam's tells me. *You have to go back before they get you.*

"No," I whisper. If I'm hearing my son's voice, he must be close. Just as importantly, he's aware of my presence.

I hurry ahead, concentrating all my mental energy on tuning into Sam's psychic frequency. I have no idea if I'm hearing him because of the surgery or because of this bizarre environment, but it comes to the same thing. He's communicating with me, and that means he's alive. My son is alive.

I'm rushing between platforms, my strides surer than they were on Earth. Sam is alive, he's *alive* dammit, and when I see him, I'm going to crush him to me and kiss his beautiful stubborn head and tell him how sorry I am for failing him, how much I love him, and how I'll never fail him again. *Where are you? Where are you, Sam?*

I'm racing between the platforms when I hear the unmistakable sound of a machete blade cleaving an alien's carapace.

Miranda.

I skid to a halt, scan the platforms, and there she is at the edge of the harvesting field, hacking away at an alien, the one no doubt connected to her mother. As I start toward her, she drops the machete and starts to shake her mom awake.

I need to get to Sam, but Miranda is clutching her mom's shoulders, and I notice something as I race closer, something I try to ignore, despite the nameless fear it evokes: While the platforms here glow, their luster isn't as brilliant as the ones in the rest of the field. Miranda's voice comes to me, choked with sobs, and though she's shaking her vigorously, her mom remains unresponsive. Is she in a coma?

On the heels of this, a monstrous thought arises:

Miranda's mother was taken the same night Sam was.

I shake my head against the implications, but that cruel, wheedling voice won't be silenced: *If her mom is catatonic, Sam will be too.*

No.

I run harder.

Look at the platforms, John. They're almost dark. That means the brains are nearly harvested, or the harvest is complete.

Miranda is slapping her mom's face, but she's a rag doll in her grip.

You're too late, John. Too late.

Miranda's wailing, her body tremoring with sobs. As I draw near, I see something that freezes my bones. The aliens near her are stirring. Some of them resemble sleepers in the throes of nightmares, but one is pushing onto its hands and swiveling its head toward her.

I make for this alien and extract my machete. Its movements are sluggish, but it could easily kill Miranda, who's crumpling, her sobs heartbroken. The alien's feet touch ground, it begins to rise, and I leap, plant a foot on an unmoving human, and leap again, and maybe sensing danger, the alien turns and spots me. Its eyes widen just as I plunge my blade into its throat and crash into it, my momentum sweeping us under platforms, where I tumble, roll, and spring to my feet.

Miranda is within arm's reach of me, but she's slumped on the ground, and no fewer than three aliens in the vicinity are rousing. I note with dismal horror how none of their human counterparts so much as twitch, the bodies dead or as good as dead.

"Miranda," I murmur. She punches the ground, which pulses with each blow of her fist. "*Miranda*," I say, louder now. The aliens are rising, they're . . .

. . . *still unable to see you*, a voice reminds me. *Without those special lenses, you're difficult for them to see.*

But they're not hard of hearing.

I gather Miranda to me, both of us on our knees. "Shhhh," I soothe, but she continues to sob. "*Miranda*," I snap. "You've got to stop. They're coming."

I cut off as a pair of alien feet steps into view. They stride closer. I clap my hand over Miranda's mouth. She bucks in my grip, and her eyes batten on mine, and my terror must shatter the dome of pain that surrounds her because she shifts her gaze to the alien towering over us.

The alien reaching toward us.

I roll with her under the platform, and the alien snatches at us. Another alien steps around the platform containing Miranda's mother, and I see how her body droops over the side, her upper half dangling, her unseeing eyes staring past us as though peering into a fathomless void. The alien squalls, and I see it grasping the alien Miranda slaughtered. But Miranda is staring at her mother's lifeless face, and whether or not her physical body is dead, it's clear to me she's gone, her essential life force removed.

Miranda lurches toward her mom's upside-down body, and

I'm just able to catch her, to say into her ear, "She's already gone." She's struggling in my grip, but I whisper, "She was absorbed by the one you stabbed."

She looks at me. I nod at the dead creature, the one being mourned by two aliens.

"I'm sorry," I tell her.

Miranda turns to look at her mom's as-good-as-dead face, and I think I've broken through. These aliens will bear their dead loved one away, and then we can escape—

My thoughts cut off as movement draws my gaze. An alien crouching to peer under the platform. Its eyes slide away from us, and I have time to hope we'll be safe. Then its gaze fastens on something, and Miranda's body tenses.

"John," she whispers. "My arm."

And I see it. Her arm is rimed with yellow-green alien blood. Bioluminescent, glowing horribly bright, it dribbles from her shoulder to her fingertips. We look up just as the alien's eyes widen, and it's throwing back its head and screeching, and this isn't sorrow. It's a signal.

The other two aliens erupt with earsplitting screams.

"I'm marked," Miranda says. "You gotta go."

Without waiting for an answer, she clambers forward and swings her machete two-handed at one of the screeching aliens' knees. The blade chunks in, the screech devolves into a wail, and the creature crumples sideways. I spring forward, my machete out, and hammer down at the creature's neck. The machete cleaves the shell, and glowing blood sprays my shirt. The creature jags wildly. I push to my feet and face the other two aliens, who leave off their warning shrieks to stare at us, or rather at the parts of us that are glowing with blood. My shirt is spattered. Miranda's arm glows. The aliens separate and stride around the platforms. Miranda and I fan out to face them.

The one moving toward me isn't as tall as the one menacing Miranda, but its body is brawnier, its green, bloodshot eyes alight with fury. I hear cries in the distance and know other aliens will be here soon.

As if to confirm this, a towering shape shambles toward Miranda, approaching from behind, and she's so focused on the alien hulking over her that she doesn't register this new threat. I make a move toward her, but something smashes me in the head, and I'm down, my vision carouseling, and I realize the brawny alien managed to hit me while I was distracted. It reaches for me, but it stops short, its talons scrabbling on the spongy ground. The glowing blood on my shirtfront is what drew this alien, what allowed it to strike. Because I'm on my belly now, the blood is obscured, and the alien is going by feel. If I lie still, maybe its talons won't find me, but I have to help Miranda, who's hemmed in between creatures. She's swiping at the one before her, but she's backing right into the other.

I scramble under the platforms, and behind me, I hear the alien's claws whicker through the space I just vacated. I'm only ten feet away, but Miranda's body is mere inches from the alien at her back, and she has no idea.

"Miranda! Behind you!"

She begins to turn, but the creature is too fast. Its talons seize her under the chin, and it lifts her. The other alien, the tall one, reaches for her back. She's borne into the air, eye level with the aliens, her feet dangling. The tall alien behind her grabs her around the waist.

A vision of Richard Kehler being torn in half flickers through my mind.

"*No!*" I cry.

From behind, I hear the brawny alien clambering after me. I'm nearly to Miranda when she raises her machete, her eyes twitching toward mine. "*Go*," she whispers, and she embeds her blade in the alien's face. It lets go and reels away, but Miranda remains suspended in the air, the tallest alien still gripping her from behind. I pull my machete back, aiming for its leg, but in the split second before I strike, it plunges a clawed hand into Miranda's back, puncturing her flesh and splaying her arms and legs. My blade sinks in just below the hinge of its knee, but the damage to Miranda is done, its glistening claws having punched all the way through her sternum, and as the alien squeals, Miranda hangs from its arm, already dead.

I stifle a cry. *She's gone*, I tell myself. *Find Sam*.

I unseat my machete and make to turn, but something vises over my ankle—the brawny alien—and when it tugs me, I slide backward three feet, the creature's other hand scrabbling over my leg for purchase. I roll onto my back as I'm dragged, and the monster's eyes widen at the sight of my glow-spattered shirtfront. Its leer of triumph is unmistakable, noxious slaver drooling onto my throat. I raise the machete to strike, but it's still hauling me under its body, and when I swing, the blade barely pierces its shoulder. I haul back on the blade, but before I can remove it, the alien catches my wrist and squeezes. I feel my tendons compress, the pain a white-hot blaze, and I lose my grip on the handle. I think the alien will snap my wrist in half, but instead, it leans over and sinks its incisors into the meat of my forearm. I bellow, and dimly I hear the other aliens in the vicinity clatter toward us. Desperate, I reach up and plunge a thumb into its eye. It squeals, and though I try to crawl away, its weight is too great. Its sewery smell envelops me. My forearm is drizzling, so I strain my other arm over and grip the machete handle. The alien seizes my neck and slams me back down. Its face lowers toward mine; its maw opens wide, its daggerlike teeth dripping with my blood. I shove the machete against its throat and drag it sideways, the blade slicing deep. Its blood sprays over me, and it jackknifes onto its back, its talons scrabbling to unseat the blade. I glance down at myself, see my entire shirt is soaked with bioluminescent blood, and the alien who murdered Miranda is crawling under the platform toward me, its eyes battened onto my glow-soaked chest. I reach down, and though my bitten forearm is howling, I manage to drag off my shirt. I wipe my face with it and cast the shirt aside. The alien lunges for it, squalls in frustration. I scuttle out from under the platforms, and then I'm up and moving, my injured forearm pressed to my belly.

Behind me, I hear the creatures' enraged roars. There are answering shrieks in the distance.

They're coming for me. Maybe all of them.

I shamble forward and scan the barely glowing platforms for my son.

35

"Sam," I whisper, "can you hear me?"

If that faint voice in my head answers, I can't discern it above my labored breathing and the warbling alien cries. Something small and rabbitlike darts away, but I don't have time to study this new species. The platforms are growing dimmer the deeper into the field I go. A glance ahead makes my stomach drop—the spires are looming very near now. I'm almost to the edge of the field.

Still no Sam.

A perverse thought grips me: What if Sam was never brought here at all? He was one of the first humans taken. What if the test subjects were transported to a different area, an alien hospital maybe, replete with a surgical theater where these vicious fuckers could witness the procedure?

I think of the storage area Matty alluded to. My God, what if Sam was taken underground?

He's gone. He's been gone since the night you lost him.

No.

And maybe he was gone before that. Had you loved him

the way you should have and found a way to reach him rather than digging in like you always do—

No no no no no

—Sam would still be alive. But you failed. You failed because you refused to change.

My chest feels like it's on fire, the alien cries drawing nearer. I think I hear the drones whirring closer, but I can't be sure. This is how it ends.

Dad?

I skid to a stop. "Sam?"

You have to go, he says. The voice is echoey and faint, but the words are clear enough. I'm not imagining it.

"Sam, where are you?"

If I can home in on his voice, if I can find the right pair of platforms, I can murder the creature siphoning his mind and bring my boy back.

Sam's voice: *They're coming.*

I stand there agonizing. I'm pretty sure the source is somewhere ahead, but if I get this wrong, we're both going to die.

I take a deep breath and close my eyes. "Talk to me, Sam. Help me find you."

A shriek from my left. A drone whirs behind me. They're closing in.

"Please, Sam," I whisper. "*Please* help me find you."

His voice is softer now, and I have to strain to make it out: *. . . back. You have to go back.*

I bare my teeth, drag a hand through my sweat-soaked hair. I start forward. But not only are the alien and drone sounds drawing nearer, the platforms' glow is failing. Several pairs barely glow at all. I lean forward and stride out, but that sense of fruitlessness, of desolation, is swelling. I hear a hum, and for a moment, I expect a gate to open ahead of me. Then I realize the hum is behind me, so I hit the ground and roll under a platform a split second before the drone cruises overhead. I hardly spare the human above me a glance, some guy in his early thirties with a goatee and a Chicago Bears jersey.

I think: *Sam. Where are you?*

No answer.

Something draws my eye. Not movement, not another drone or even an alien. In a way, those would be more reassuring.

What draws my gaze is the vacant platform beside the Bears fan.

The drone is a safe distance from me now, but I can't move. There's no alien here. The Bears fan's platform is nearly dark. Only the faintest blue-green tinge shows against the deepening violet sky, and...

...that means the procedure is complete. This man, whoever he is, has been absorbed by the alien. Whether he's dead or not, he'll never inhabit his body again. I don't want this to be true, but what else could it be? If he's part of the alien now, if he's harvested, too much of his mind is gone for him to ever be normal. No memories, no motor skills—

You don't know that!

I climb out from under the platform and reach for the man's neck, and while it isn't deathly cold, the flesh is cooler than it should be. There's a pulse but I'm guessing not for much longer. I scan the platforms around me, and where there should be aliens, I only find barren ovals, each person companionless on a darkening dais.

"No," I whisper. "Please, God, no."

I'm only thirty yards from the field's edge. Beyond that is a modest rise, then the first spire. I rush ahead, noting as I do how some of the platforms don't glow at all.

Dead. Just like—

NO! I clamp down on the thought. Sam isn't gone. My boy is here somewhere, I only have to—

I see it. Ahead, on the very edge of the harvesting field. Two platforms, one empty. The other... the other...

The face down body is a teenage boy. Royal-blue shirt, black shorts, white sneakers.

Sam.

I stagger to him, already weeping, and when I gather him in my arms, he lolls, cool and lifeless. I bury my face in his shoulder and support his head like I did the day he was born. My baby boy. The child who made me a father. The most sacred responsibility of my life, the one I botched so miserably. I want to scream but I can't, can only sob into Sam's shoulder. *I'm sorry for failing you. You deserved so much better, someone who would bring out the best in you, instead of trying to change the worst.*

I pull away and kiss his cheek, and sitting on the platform, I cradle him and bathe his smooth forehead with my tears. If I'd only gotten here sooner. A day might have done it, maybe two. I might have saved him, might still have my son.

I know the drones are drawing nearer, know the aliens will be here soon, but none of that matters. All that matters is how Sam will never draw breath again, never wallop another fastball. Never grow up and start a life of his own, never find his profession or meet his soulmate, never be the amazing father I know he would have been.

It's this thought that undoes me, that forces me to lay Sam's body down, to rest my head on his chest and sob. Sam would have been an extraordinary dad. He had that nurturing, encouraging side. He had that enthusiasm, that smile, that energy. I push up, my face hovering over his, and I think...

The day we had you, I was afraid of losing you. That moment

in the hospital when they handed you to me, I experienced a love like nothing I'd ever felt, like nothing I knew could exist. Even then, from the very beginning, I knew the moment you moved out of the house would be the most painful of my life. I knew how selfish it was, but I couldn't escape it. I wanted to hold you forever. And the thought of you growing up, the possibility of not being with you anymore... I began dreading it that first day, when you were just a newborn. Your sweet, beautiful face. I looked at you and I wanted to stop time. I wanted it to last forever. I breathed in your goodness and thought, *This is why I'm here. This is my purpose.* And all those years we spent together passed in the blink of an eye, and all through it, I wanted to stop time. To freeze every moment. You toddling around the house. Me scooping you up and dancing you through the living room, you laughing and gripping me as tightly as I held you. A little boy in pale-blue pajamas with green turtles on them. A little boy who never let me stop at three bedtime stories. The boy who'd hike in the woods with me, who took night walks with me through the graveyard. The boy who never seemed to be afraid and made me feel brave too, braver than I ever was on my own. I was selfish, always yearning for more time. Coaching you in Little League. Watching all those movies through the years. Cubs games every summer and sledding every winter. And all the time we spent together, I was haunted by that specter. The specter of goodbye. The one thing I feared most, the one thing I knew I couldn't avoid.

I love you, Sam. I love you more than you'll ever know. I wanted to be the dad you deserved. I wanted to be so much more. You were better than I dreamed a son could be. You were so much more. You're my miracle. My boy...

I'm sobbing, and maybe that's why I don't hear the creature stepping closer. It's only a few feet away when I finally turn and see it, one of the winged aliens with its shelled body and slender frame. The curved horns gleam with iridescence, and the rest of the face is very much like the others.

But not the eyes. The eyes glow green, but they're not bloodshot. There's no malice in them. They're full of warmth. Full of love.

They're the eyes of my child.

The eyes of my son.

I push to standing but keep one hand on Sam's shoulder. I peer at the alien gazing down at me and hear Sam's voice in my head:

You made it through, he says.

My lips tremble, but I force out the words: "Not fast enough. I'm so sorry."

You came, he answers. *That's what matters.*

"Can it be reversed?"

A sadness in the alien's eyes. *I don't think so.*

I start to approach, but the alien takes a step back. *Don't, Dad. It's not safe.*

I shake my head.

I have to fight it, Sam says. *Every moment. Even now, I…*

The alien puts its talons to its forehead, its internal struggle plain, but the knowledge that my boy is in there, or at least part of my boy… I can't help it. I throw myself against the shelled body and embrace it. My face doesn't even reach the creature's chest. I feel its body tense against me, knowing if that other intelligence takes over, I'll be dead in an instant, but I can sense Sam in here, his goodness. His love. And after several seconds, I feel the arms close around me.

"Sam," I whisper.

He squeezes me back, and I sense his teen embarrassment, even here, in this other body.

Hey, Dad.

"I love you so much," I tell him.

Are Mom and Em safe?

"Yes," I answer.

The arms relax slightly.

"If I'd known what would happen that night," I say, "I never would have let you out of my sight."

You couldn't have known.

"I should have been better. So you didn't walk so far ahead of me."

We all walk ahead, he answers. *That's what kids do.*

And so adult-sounding are his words, so ancient and wise, that I can't respond. Can only hold him tight.

They'll be here soon, Dad. Any moment.

"I'm not leaving you. I can't."

You have to.

"Sam—"

You have to let me go, Dad.

I begin to shudder, the tears streaming down my face.

You have to let me go.

"I can't," I tell him.

I can buy you time. But if you don't leave now, they'll kill you.

I become aware of the drone hum, of the shrieks and wing-beats of the creatures. I glance to my left and see the ground dwellers pouring over the valley rim, a score of them at least. I turn to the right and discover a fleet of winged creatures arrowing closer.

He forces me away, his arms so strong that my hold is broken.

It's time, he tells me. I watch in awe as his wings unfurl.

"Sam," I start, but he's pushing off the ground, his immense wings beating the air. I reach for him, but it's too late.

I can scarcely breathe. The sight of him rising into the sky, floating toward the spires, rends my soul. I watch him go, a creature that looks nothing like my son but carries my heart wherever it goes.

The alien in which my son resides spreads its great arms and lets loose with a high-pitched bellow. The winged creatures and ground dwellers change course and veer toward it. The drones scud in that direction. I assume Sam will flap away into the night, but he peers over his shoulder at me instead.

Dad? he says.

I look up at him.

I love you, too.

And with that, he wings away. Lightning jags in the distance, and in its brilliance, I see dozens of winged creatures following my son toward the spires.

36

I watch Sam until he's out of sight, his graceful form swooping and disappearing into the plum-colored night. Beyond him, a few miles distant, heat lightning strobes the churning clouds, and I wonder what an alien storm might be like. Gentle, like a summer shower, or apocalyptic, with lightning bolts blasting the spongy ground and acid rain pummeling the field of bodies behind me?

The vision brings my gaze down to Sam's body. I'm about to lift him in a fireman's carry—I'll be damned if I'm leaving him here—but as I touch the back of his hand, I feel, not a spark, but a psychic vibration against my fingertips. It could be imagination, but I don't think so. I realize the platform supporting him isn't completely dark. Faint, yes, but there *is* a glow. A green-blue ember under his light-brown hair.

If I remove his body from the platform, that glow will die. I know it. And if the glow dies, Sam's body will too. His skin is cool to the touch, but it's not as frigid as the air.

Is he being preserved? And if so, for what purpose?

I stand there agonizing.

The squall of a creature makes me jump. I crane my head around and spot it, a ground dweller loping in my direction. Whether it's aware of me or not, I don't know, but if it finds me here—if it's wearing special lenses—I'm dead.

I glance down at my son. If there's the slightest chance of restoring him to his body and funneling all that was taken back into his brain, I have to cling to that chance. Don't I?

The ground dweller races closer. Sixty yards. Forty.

"I love you, Sammy," I say and kiss his forehead. I caress his face one last time before hurrying away.

I cast a glance over my shoulder in time to see the ground dweller pull up beside Sam's body. It glowers down at him, and I think to myself, *Don't touch him, you bastard!*

But the creature does touch him. It grasps Sam by the shoulders and lifts him. I put a knuckle to my mouth to stifle my scream, and just when I'm sure the alien will do to Sam what was done to Miranda, to Tommy, to Kehler, the creature rolls him onto his chest and arranges his arms and legs as they'd been before.

Then the alien faces me.

I sink to my knees and scuttle under a platform. I hold my breath but can't hear anything. I see the ground dweller's feet, still planted beside my son, and a revelation, maybe wishful thinking, dawns on me:

The ground dweller isn't just hunting for the one who moved Sam's body. He's *guarding* Sam's body. And if he's guarding Sam, doesn't that lend credence to the possibility that Sam's body is more than just a useless husk? The alien wouldn't guard something without value, and that means they might still need Sam. For what, I can't be sure. Further harvesting? Periodic mining of his brain? As hideous as these suppositions are, they represent a vestige of hope. Sam might be kept alive.

The bodies on the platforms are in perfect stasis. Perfect

preservation? I don't know. But if I remove him from that platform, whatever's keeping him alive will cease to work, and my son truly will be gone forever.

The ground dweller tosses back its head and shrills out a scream, the scream I recognize as their summoning signal. In a few moments, the area will be teeming with aliens. Whatever rescue plan I devise for Sam will have to wait.

With a plummeting heart, I crawl away.

I crawl for nearly a minute before I risk a backward glance, but now I'm far enough I can't make out much of anything. I know the creatures are congregating near Sam's body and wonder if I've doomed him. If they suspect the truth, will they decide Sam—or the alien he's been paired with—isn't worth the trouble? I've seen how little they care about human life. The evidence is all around me. Why keep this teenage boy alive after they've slaughtered so many?

The answer comes to me: *Look at the lengths to which they've gone to save their species. If the human bodies are in some way useful or necessary, wouldn't they do all they can to preserve them?*

I climb out from under the platform and look at the cluster near my son. I take quick stock of my body. Tiny droplets of bioluminescent blood speckle my arms, so I rub these briskly into my skin. When I look up, the aliens appear to be gesturing at one another, their cadaverous arms flailing.

I get moving. There's so much to sort out, so much to consider, and as much as I want to bring my son back, now isn't the time. Chances are there will never be a time, but if I let myself believe this, I won't be able to go on.

My leg is throbbing, but the thought of my wife and daughter galvanizes me. God, I hope they've made it back. If, after all this, they get captured, if the only thing I have left is a burned-down house and a bookstore with a broken window...

I'm almost upon the drone before I spot it, this one floating fast, its appendage in constant revolution. There's a ground drone directly below it, rolling faster than any I've encountered. I dive for the safety of a platform, hoist myself up, and hold my breath as the drones burr over and below me. How long will Sam be able to keep the aliens occupied? How long before they cease following him and double back to capture me? I'm so absorbed by my thoughts that I don't even spare the person above me a glance. Maybe I should be waking up more people, beheading their alien counterparts and leading the abducted back to the gate. But the more of us there are, the more attention we'll attract, and the less likely I'll be able to reunite with Emma and Iris. I recognize this as the sort of attitude I despise, the fuck-everyone-else worldview that's gotten humankind into so many messes, but I've got to make it back, got to hold my daughter and wife again.

The drones pass.

I forge ahead, the faces of my daughter and wife in my mind. But under their smiling faces, the memory of my son remains.

I reach the jungle.

My overtaxed body has gone numb, so the sensations of the fronds and burgundy sprigs scraping my flesh don't even faze me. What consumes me is thirst. I've been so focused on completing my journey that I've ignored the arid itch in my throat. But now it descends on me with an urgency that teeters on panic.

Blindly, I plunge through the jungle. I stumble and fall, but I get up and keep charging. Once they realize what happened, once they discover the alien corpses we've left behind, they'll converge on me with all the wrath of their species. They'll close the gate and trap me here.

A stitch pierces my side, and my hamstrings threaten to cramp. But I bare my teeth and bull forward through the stifling heat, and after I don't know how long, I burst through the far edge of the jungle. I scramble up the short hillside, enter the cave mouth, and rush through the darkness. Just when I convince myself that the gateway has closed, I spot it, a slash of amber ahead. I stagger forward, hoping they don't follow me through, hoping I won't doom Iris and Emma and everyone else by leading the aliens to them.

As I near the gateway, I wonder if my loved ones even made it. Our party was so large it might have been discovered. But I refuse to believe that, refuse to believe my wife and daughter were captured.

I reach the gateway, insert my fingers into the correct spots, spread the portal apart, and push through.

37

The pitch-blackness melts into a deep, velvety blue.

I crawl forward, the air warmer, and my hand falls not on a spongy cave floor but something scabrous and sharp. Smoke fills my nostrils. Before I realize what's happening, the ground beneath me lurches and I'm tumbling. I realize I've crawled onto the rubble of my house; despite the shards of glass that bite my flesh, I understand I've made it back to my world. And if I've made it back…

I look up to find Emma rushing toward me. She's smiling and there are tears in her eyes. I rise and she crashes against me. I throw my arms around my daughter, and she's sobbing into my chest. I close my eyes and sway with Emma, and soon there are other arms around me. It's Iris and she's crying, too.

"I couldn't get Sam," I tell her, "but he's alive. I'll explain everything."

Iris squeezes me. "The others are at the neighbors'. I told Emma it didn't make any sense to wait out here, but she wouldn't listen. So I figured, if she was going to…"

I hug them closer and kiss the top of Emma's head. "Your birthday's next week," I whisper.

"I'm glad you came back for it," she answers.

"Oh," Iris says, and she goes away for a moment. "You probably want this."

She hands me a water bottle, and I guzzle it down, my body teeming with warm chills.

As I lower the bottle, I remember we're outside, exposed, the gate less than twenty feet away. The corpse of Buddy Scott lies glistening in the starlight, but it's far enough away that I can't see the damage inflicted on him clearly. I know our neighbors' house isn't safe, but it beats standing out here in the open. We head that way.

I ask, "We staying here tonight or going to the bookstore?"

We climb onto the front porch. Iris says, "The Everetts have a van. Jae was looking for the keys, but I don't know if he found them."

We're nearing the door when it opens and Tracey steps out. She beams when she sees me. I return her smile and follow Emma and Iris inside.

Raven and Vanessa are on the couch, snacking on Cheez-Its. Jae and Matty enter. When Jae sees me, his face lights up. "Johnny!" He bear-hugs me, and my back actually pops. When he pulls away, he scans the room, and his smile slips a little. "Is Miranda..."

I shake my head, and he lowers his eyes. We stand in silence a moment, but he doesn't ask about Sam, and for that I'm grateful.

Matty says, "Found the keys," and jingles them. At some point during this nightmare, the Everetts went away. Somehow, I don't think they'll need their Honda Odyssey anymore.

Before the reality of our situation—we're in as much peril as ever—can plunge me into a frantic emotional state, I turn to Tracey and ask, "Heard from Beatrice?"

She shakes her head. "I think the cell towers are down for good, but it's only a three-minute drive."

Iris asks, "Are we sure the shop is safe?"

"Safer than being next door to that gate," Jae answers.

No one disagrees.

I take Iris's hand and lead her to the Everetts' pantry, which is steeped in shadow. "I need to tell you something."

I tell her about her parents as gently as I can. She puts a hand over her mouth, and tears stream down her cheeks, but she allows me to hold her, and after a time, she asks, "Does Emma know?"

I shake my head.

"Don't tell her yet," Iris says. "Let's let her enjoy tonight." She takes a breath. "What about Sam?"

I tell her what happened with our son, as well as my belief that his body is still alive. The hope in Iris's face restores some of mine.

"John?" she says. "I underestimated how much you… That day on the highway. The day I was taken?"

I nod.

"When I saw you looking through my window, when I realized you'd followed me and Emma… I understood how stubborn I'd been. How unfair."

"Iris—"

"Just listen, Johnny." She touches my face. "We were good together. But we lost sight of what matters. We let money and life…"

I draw her closer, and she rests her cheek against my chest.

"Thanks for not giving up on me," she whispers.

I kiss her hair and squeeze her. We hold each other in the dark for another minute. Then we rejoin our daughter.

Not long after, we load into the van. It's snug with eight of us inside, six of us full-grown adults, but I'm delighted to find the storage area in the backseat crammed with food and sleeping bags.

With Tracey driving, Matty riding shotgun, Raven on the floor between Jae and Vanessa in the middle, and Iris, Emma, and me tucked in the backseat, we back out of the garage and start up Hillcrest. The moon is radiant enough to reveal the silent houses, and for a moment, I wish we'd stayed at the Everetts', where there were beds and enough space for everyone. But there's also a gate nearby, and if they were able to abduct Emma from inside my house, who's to say they couldn't do the same thing in the house next door?

Who's to say they can't do the same thing anywhere? What makes the bookshop any safer?

The front window of the store is shattered. Not only could the aliens waltz right inside, so could jackals like Dean Dawson. Though Dean is dead, I'm sure he and his crew weren't the only vigilantes roaming the town.

The Odyssey's clock reads 12:26. I can't believe it was less than an hour ago that I was journeying through an alien world. Saying goodbye to my son.

Iris threads her fingers through mine and gives me a hopeful smile. I smile back, despite the indelible images replaying in my head: Sam's motionless body, the alien that absorbed Sam rising into the air. Sam growing smaller and smaller as he flew away. My boy. My son. Gone.

"I love you, Dad," Emma says, and I tell her I love her, too. Iris turns to look out her window. I pray we reach the bookshop so we can figure out what to do next. I hope Beatrice and Pruitt are there. I hope Koufax is, too.

We reach The Constant Reader Café at 12:29. The first thing we see, other than the shattered front window, is Beatrice pushing through the side door. She doesn't bother with hugs or greetings, instead ushers the kids inside, Emma leading Raven by the hand. After a brief debate, Matty, Tracey, and Iris consent to let the rest of us carry the supplies, and as they disappear into the shop, I decide Matty doesn't look so good. Pale. The hollows of his eyes bruisy.

Beatrice joins us in collecting the sleeping bags and food.

"Miranda and Tommy," she murmurs as we're leaning into the back of the van. "They didn't make it?"

I shake my head, choke down the lump in my throat, and snag a rolled-up memory-foam mattress. Even though the van is parked right next to the door, I'm sure this is the moment our luck will run out and the aliens will find us. Jae must sense it, too, because he moves too hastily, fumbling several cans of food on the way into the shop and having to scramble to scoop them up. Finally, we're all inside and congregated in the basement. This is the used-book area of the shop, six long aisles spanning all genres and eras. We lug everything down the steps and bear it to the rear of the basement where my office and storage areas are. It's cramped back here, but there's room for the sleeping bags and the totes full of food we scrounged from the Everetts'. Pruitt, I discover, has taken up residence under my desk, but at least he's not whimpering anymore. He visited my shop a lot before the nightmare began—maybe he feels safer here.

Jae moves up beside me and murmurs, "How are your eyes?"

I realize I haven't thought of the surgery for several hours. "It's strange," I answer. "Mostly, my vision's the same, but lights, they put off these coronas…"

Jae is nodding.

"...And people... even Koufax... they broadcast a glow. It's subtle, but it's there."

Vanessa wanders up, gives Jae an inquisitive smile, and he takes her hand. I watch them go, my mind racing.

Just what did the surgery do to us? I wonder. It's not exactly infrared or ultraviolet light we can see. So what the hell is it? I think of Tommy, of his story of seeing the creature with his eyes closed, and I go cold all over. What sort of abilities did the procedure unleash?

I pace the aisles of used books and scan the faces of my friends. Emma and Raven are on the floor scratching Koufax. Iris is talking to Tracey.

I have to keep them safe. I have to figure out how the aliens have been finding us.

I troop back to the van to collect the few spare cans we couldn't haul in the first round. I open the back of the van and feel my stomach muscles contract at the brightness of the interior light. Hands shaking, I gather the remaining cans—five of them—and use the bottom of my shirt to carry them. I close the van door too gently the first time, the interior light remaining on, so I slam it and cringe at the bang it makes. Heart thumping, I hurry inside and close the door and damn near run into someone inside the shop. The cans go twirling across the floor, and Matty is apologizing, and I have to grab the wall to keep from fainting.

"Sorry," he mutters. "I had to talk to you where the others couldn't hear."

His tone resurrects my dread.

"I can tell you how they do it."

I frown at him.

His voice quavers. "Once the process has begun... you know, the pairing? They exploit what's in our brains. That's why they take family members."

I shake my head, not getting it.

Matty steps closer. "When they took your son, they could see where you live. That's how they were able to make a gate inside your house."

Oh my God, I think. *How could I not have figured this out?*

"But Iris," I say, "they got her on the highway."

Matty shrugs. "Dumb luck. Was she the only person taken that day?"

"There were tons."

He nods. "I think I can explain that too."

The ramifications of what he's just told me spread ice-cold tendrils through my brain. "They absorb what we know and use it?" I ask.

"That's right."

"Oh Jesus," I mutter, and then I'm racing toward the stairs, and he's calling my name, but I have to get us out of here, have to get us to a place none of us know. Matty is shouting, and I'm halfway down the steps when his hand falls on my shoulder. I tell him Sam knows about the bookshop, and even though he'd never willingly divulge our location, it's not his decision; the aliens will figure it out, especially once they discover the others we've rescued.

"They've mostly been sticking to houses," Matty says. "I think we're safe for a little while."

I want to believe this, want to believe it with all of my soul, but Matty's declaration is too fresh, its implications too head-spinning. Once they abduct someone, they can mine the person's memories. They know where you live. That's how they found Emma. Through Sam. Or Iris. If they know about our house, they know about my shop. Because Sam knows about it.

"There's more," he says heavily. "It's my fault."

"What is?"

"Them finding you."

I frown.

"I always suspected it," Matty goes on, "but that stuff about twins sharing a special link—a . . . I don't know what you'd call it . . . a psychic link? It's true."

I don't have time for this. I start to go, but he seizes my arm, and the strength in his grip gets my full attention.

"When I was asleep . . . I could feel that fucker probing my mind, feeling around in there for something he could use. He learned early on I had a twin. He told their leaders. The ones spearheading the effort. It's like . . ." He slides his fingers over his scalp. "Like *live look-ins*. If they capture a twin, they try to zero in on that wavelength. The one they share with their sibling."

Matty backs against the stairwell. "It took a while. Once I realized what they were trying to do, I fought it. I fought it so hard. I tried to think of anything but Tommy. A few years ago, I was stationed in Iraq, so I tried to stay there, mentally. I tried to live there in my mind and bury everything else. Pretend it never existed. That I never had parents. Never had a twin."

I imagine how nightmarish it must have been for him. Body dormant, at the mercy of that horrifying alien intelligence. Waging a fruitless battle against its merciless mental warfare.

"You know the rest," he says. "They dug deep enough. Or I wore down. But they learned about Tommy. They sent a scout to fly over the building where he was staying. They found him. And the rest of you."

"You couldn't have stopped it."

"I should have been stronger," he says, his teeth showing. "I should've kept you guys safe. Tommy's death . . . it's my fault."

I know I should comfort him, but I say, "You mentioned something about the highway. About Iris . . ."

"There must've been a twin there somewhere. You said there were a lot of people?"

I nod.

"I'd wager anything they had a live feed of it. Some twin being used as a homing beacon. That's how they knew what was happening there. All those people."

I recall the video Emma and I watched of Dale Lake in Tennessee, of the hundreds, maybe thousands of partygoers celebrating their freedom before they were hauled away. What are the odds one of those people had a twin? Pretty high, I decide.

I put a hand on Matty's shoulder. "You fought harder than most would. It's not your fault."

He looks away.

"How much are they able to see in our minds?" I ask.

"Everything," he answers. "It might take more time with some people. If they're really stubborn. But like you said... no one can hold out forever."

38

Matty tells them everything. Tracey wants to leave right away, and I don't blame her. She's just gotten her daughter back and is in no mood to expose Raven to more danger. The question is—if we leave, where do we go?

"A farmhouse?" Beatrice says, and I'm forcefully reminded of Emma pleading with me about this very thing. At the time, I believed our home to be safe, but I was wrong. Catastrophically wrong.

Then again, if we *had* left, Tracey and her people would've never found me, and Iris would be stuck in that other world.

Sam still is, a voice whispers.

I can't think about that. Not now. I haven't lost all hope for my son, but right now I have to protect the people who are here, and the next several minutes might determine our success or failure.

"Getting off the grid makes sense," Iris says.

"Especially considering there might not be a grid much longer," Beatrice agrees.

I give the overhead fluorescents an involuntary glance.

"Beatrice is right," Tracey says. "Internet's gone. Electricity is spotty. It's only a matter of time before conditions become primitive."

"All the more reason to get away from people," Vanessa says. She sweeps her orange hair off her forehead. "Once it all breaks down, you know people are gonna get vicious."

"They already have," Jae says.

"But where?" Matty asks. "The places you're talking about, houses with acreage... they're in families for generations. People are protective of them. Hell, I would be."

Iris looks around. "Does anyone know a place?"

No one answers. The silence thickens, the others perhaps considering how ill-suited the shop is for long-term living. One bathroom, no shower. Sleeping bags for beds. Food enough for a few days, a week if we stretch it. And then we become scavengers?

"I know a place," a voice says. We turn around and discover Eric Pruitt standing between the sci-fi books and the children's section. His stark-white hair juts in greasy spikes. His expression is still frightened, his voice soft and croaky, but he doesn't wilt under our collective stare, and that, I decide, is progress.

"Where?" Vanessa asks.

"My parents were older," Pruitt answers. "My mother died several years ago, but my father only passed this January. They left me their farm."

"How big is it?" Emma asks. She steps into view from behind a bookcase. She's holding Raven's hand. Koufax stands protectively beside them.

"Five hundred acres," Pruitt says, "including several orchards."

Tracey asks, "Is the house big enough to accommodate everyone?"

"It's huge," he says. "They'd planned on filling it with kids, but since they weren't able to… they adopted me." He frowns. "I was a disappointment."

"You're sure no one lives there now," Jae says.

"As far as I know," he answers. "I was there in May… just before…" A panicked look flits across his face. "Unless someone broke in, no. It should be empty."

Emma rushes over to me. "Can we go?"

I glance at Iris. "There's still the matter of food."

Matty says, "Be nice to have some protection too. In case the aliens find us."

Tracey and Jae look at me, and they're smiling even before I say, "Boiler Barn."

Then the group is talking excitedly and uttering giddy sounds at Pruitt's description of the farm, which runs on propane, is equipped with two wells, and has its own septic system. His father, Pruitt explains, was a "Puritanical twat," but he was also a believer in preparation. There's enough propane in the pole barn to last us through the winter.

Emma and Raven celebrate. Jae and Vanessa kiss. Iris hugs me, and I hug her back.

Koufax only barks a little.

We leave in a few minutes. The food is in the van. We've resolved to drive to Pruitt's homestead first. Then, once everyone is situated, we'll get as much sleep as we can before a smaller party heads back to town and the Boiler Barn. Pruitt says his father also owned a full-sized pickup truck and a pull-behind Airstream camper with ample space for supplies. There could be resistance from the remaining members of Dean's posse, but somehow I doubt it. The survivors scattered when the aliens attacked in my backyard, and the most violent of them—Dean, Buddy, and Marino—are dead.

I don't believe we'll have any trouble taking what we need. I know how that sounds, and I know someone might argue we're as bad as Dean. But I don't think so. I think after all he and his people put me through, we're entitled to a little recompense. Emma and Raven deserve stability. So do the rest of us.

No one else knows about the farmhouse. Pruitt had a partner, but they broke up almost a year ago, well before Pruitt inherited the property, and because he and his parents were estranged, he never talked about them with his ex or his modest circle of friends.

On the farm, Koufax will be able to roam. He's already bonding with Matty. Maybe they need each other as much as I need my family.

Tracey just informed me we're ready to leave. She's going to drive the Odyssey, and I feel safe with her behind the wheel. Or as safe as I can feel in this bleak new world.

It's time to go. I can't stop thinking about my son, and I haven't given up on getting him back. But for tonight and for the next few days, I have to focus on my wife and daughter.

Iris hasn't said anything about us getting back together. There hasn't been time. All I know is how it feels—that this is right. Iris and I together with Emma. I might not be a completely different man than I was before all this started, but I'm better. I have to be. Emma and Iris deserve the best version of me, and every moment I have left, I'll devote to that end.

So I leave my bookshop, maybe for the last time. I'm taking a few grocery sacks stuffed with paperbacks, ones I know Iris will enjoy, and books I hope Emma will read. I brought along some for myself as well.

I won't bother locking up. If people want to pilfer books, that's fine. Whatever helps distract them. Whatever keeps them sane.

My wife and daughter keep me afloat. But I'm haunted by Sam. I can't stop picturing the platform, how the faint bluish-green light shone as long as his body remained there. How the moment I lifted him, the glow disappeared.

If there's a way, Sam, I'll return to you. I'll bring you home. You saved my life, and if I can, I'll save yours. I'm not ready for you to fly away. Even though you're in another world, in a body so different than the one I cradled when you were born. Even though it doesn't seem possible, I'm going to get you back. Because with love, there's no such thing as too far.

No such thing as impossible.

ACKNOWLEDGMENTS

Thank you to my wife and my three children. Monica, Jack, Juliet, and Evana, you four are my world. I'm thankful for every moment with you, and I love you more than I can express.

Thanks to my mom for always cheering me on. Thank you to Grandma, Grandpa, and Aunt Letha. I miss you every day.

Special thanks to my friend Andi Smith for answering all my science questions. This was a research-heavy book, but Andi was the one I leaned on the most. Please attribute anything right to her and lay anything wrong on my doorstep. Thanks also to my ophthalmologist sister-in-law Esther Penn, who helped me enormously with the subject of vision.

Thanks to Stephen King, Steven Spielberg, John Williams, George Lucas, Christopher Reeve, Mark Hamill, Carrie Fisher, and Harrison Ford. You inspired a little kid to dream, and your fingerprints are all over this book. Thank you for being my heroes.

Thanks to my prereaders Tod Clark and Tim Slauter, who remained patient while I asked them a thousand questions. Thanks to Brendan Deneen, Priya Doraswamy, Windy Goodloe, Candice Edwards, Rebecca Malzahn, Francie Crawford, and Blackstone

Publishing for championing this story. Evergreen thanks to my big brother Brian Keene. Thanks to Ryan Lewis for showing so much enthusiasm for this book. Thanks to Patrick White for his friendship and collaboration. Thank you to Adam Kolbrenner for his support. And a massive thank you to Josh Malerman for his friendship and his invaluable support of this novel.

Finally, thanks to all of you who made it this far. I hope you enjoyed this story, and I hope you'll join me again soon.